Also by Thomas Holland

One Drop of Blood

KIA

A DR. KEL MCKELVEY NOVEL

Thomas Holland

SIMON & SCHUSTER
New York London Toronto Sydney

SIMON & SCHUSTER
Rockefeller Center
1230 Avenue of the Americas
New York, NY 10020

First Simon & Schuster hardcover edition January 2008

SIMON & SCHUSTER and colophon are registered trademarks of Simon & Schuster, Inc.

For information about special discounts for bulk purchases, please contact Simon & Schuster Special Sales at 1-800-456-6798 or business@simonandschuster.com.

Designed by Jaime Putorti

Manufactured in the United States of America

10 9 8 7 6 5 4 3 2 1

Library of Congress Cataloging-in-Publication Data

Holland, Thomas D.
  KIA / by Thomas Holland.
    p. cm.
  1. Vietnam War, 1961–1975—Missing in action—Fiction. I. Title.

PS3608.O48454K53 2008
813'.6—dc22   2007025434

ISBN-13: 978-0-7432-8001-3
ISBN-10:   0-7432-8001-6

For JSH
It was a Wonderful Life

Why suffer'st thou thy sons, unburied yet,
To hover on the dreadful shore of Styx?
Make way to lay them by their brethren.
There greet in silence, as the dead are wont,
And sleep in peace, slain in your country's wars!

—*Titus Andronicus,* Act 1, Scene 1
(William Shakespeare)

KIA

PROLOGUE

He didn't have the stomach for it.

The man who'd seen death and had touched and smelled human wreckage; the man who'd stared into the bloody maw as it devoured the youthful promise of his generation; that man didn't have the stomach for what he had to do now.

There was nothing in the General Order about where the Status Review Board had to meet, or where, or how long its deliberation should be—only who would sit on it: three military officers at the rank of full colonel or higher. There was nothing in the General Order that stipulated what outcome was to be reached—but they knew.

Colonel Paul Fick, the ranking member, had secured a small meeting room off one of the long, featureless corridors in the C-ring of the Pentagon. Windowless and austere but sufficient for what had to be done. He hoped this wouldn't take long. He didn't have the stomach for it.

They'd all read the file. At least they were supposed to have.

More important, they'd all been given marching orders. The fire was lit; letters from a couple of highly energized congressmen eager to snip off the nagging national hangnail that the Vietnam War represented had seen to that, and now it was time for the board to meet and do its duty. Tie up a loose end.

Make it happen.

Yes, sir, yes, sir. Three bags full.

Colonel Fick was reading through the thin file for the third time this morning when Colonels Temple and Joyner bumped in, carrying Styrofoam cups of coffee and laughing loudly. The humor of the story that dragged in with them was directed at a certain secretary whose career skills were measured more accurately by her anatomy than by the number of words per minute she could type. Both men were well junior to Fick in date of rank, and certainly in experience, and they dampened down appropriately when they saw him already seated at the conference table. He had a reputation for being totally humorless when he had work to do, especially work that he found unpleasant or that chafed the skin of his character, and it was clear that the pressure he was under now hadn't done much to improve his frame of mind.

Paul Fick was approaching the crest of middle age but could not yet see the horizon of his life. Physically, he was unchanged from his youth—he was still tall and spare and tempered so hard that he might as well have been constructed from lengths of welded steel rebar—but mentally his patience had been pared to a sliver. Three long tours in Vietnam had seen to that. The last had been on special assignment for the Criminal Investigative Division, but the first two had been as a dirt-eater with the Twenty-fifth Infantry. *Tropic Lightning.* As a platoon leader, he'd written his share of letters to stunned widows and grieving mothers and bitter fathers. He'd come home in the spring of '69 hoping to never deal with that aspect of the military again.

And now this.

Of all the good men he saw die, even the not-so-good ones, now he had to deal with this. It was the price he paid for being the senior-most full colonel in the United States Army. The price for not retiring a year earlier.

The price for not dying in Vietnam like he should have.

By all the accounts he'd read, Master Sergeant Jimmy Lee Tenkiller was a deserter. He'd run. By all the accounts he'd read, Tenkiller had turned rabbit, and that was all there was to it. He'd run and hadn't returned. For whatever reason, he'd done what a thousand other young men might have wanted to do, been tempted to do, what Fick himself might have thought about doing, but the difference was that they hadn't, Fick hadn't, and Tenkiller had. It was that simple. But now, because the country was in feel-good mode, and because there were congressmen and senators so cashed out of character and resolve that they were willing to write letters and twist the knob on the burner, and because the postwar military was so desperate to curry favor and please everyone and forget the past as if it were an unpleasant social gaffe at a cocktail party, Colonel Fick was under orders to revise history.

Make it happen, Colonel.

Yes, sir, General, three bags full.

There were two types of senior officers in the army now. Those who were really, really good—men like Paul Fick—men tempered in crucibles like Cu Chi and Kontum and Pleiku, men who loved the army while hating the job it had to do, men who also understood better than anyone else that there were sometimes no alternatives. Men who valued duty and character above breath and dreams. Men who would do what they were told to do because they were told to do it. And then there were those men, and now women—men like Joyner and Temple—who opportunistically filled the vacancies left by all the good ones who hadn't come through it, either physically or emotionally.

Hole pluggers.

Human caulk.

Welcome to the *New Army*.

Neither of the two junior members of the Review Board had served in Vietnam. One had made it as close as South Korea—if that could be considered close to Vietnam. The other had advanced stateside, with a couple of thick-cushioned, short postings in Germany and Italy. Both were AGs—Adjutant General Corps. Administrators.

REMFs. Fick thought. *That's what we called them back then— Rear Echelon Mother Fuckers*. Paperclip Soldiers.

Fick didn't even look up as his two fellow board members pulled up seats at the table and unclicked their briefcases, loudly removing their copies of the case file and slapping them down on the scratched-glass sheet covering the tabletop. Their coffee was hot and they made loud, obscene slurping sounds as they drank. It annoyed Fick beyond all possible words.

"Gentlemen," Fick began, struggling to curtain his disdain. Only the top of his thinning gray crewcut was visible to the other two as he spoke. That and his hands. Thin, wiry, brown hands etched with a complex mesh of hard-earned pale, cream-colored scars. And the knobs. The shiny, hardened knobs on his misshapened right hand. "I trust you have reviewed the case file on Master Sergeant Tenkiller, Jimmy L., 4219878. Discussion?"

John Joyner shifted in his seat and shot a prodding glance at Bob Temple. It was clear that Temple wasn't going to engage until he had to; he had no desire to "get Ficked," as they said in the rings of the Pentagon, an extremely accurate way of describing Fick's ability to melt junior, and occasionally senior, officers into pools of butter. Joyner slurped some more coffee, as much to stall as to clear the syrupy thickness in his throat before responding. "Not much to discuss. You know . . . Paul, my view from the foxhole is that this case is pretty straightforward." He began reading from the scrub sheet clipped to the front of his copy of the file, verbally highlighting the bullets. "Let's look at the facts. Tenkiller was a master sergeant—an E-8—with over fifteen years in, fairly cushy assignment in the supply depot near Saigon, no action other than what he could probably score with some chocolate bars . . ." He paused and glanced around to see who was smiling but quickly dropped his head and pushed on when he realized no one was. "Ahhh . . . where was I? Yeah, so, good job in Saigon, finishing up his second tour in Injun country, and on his way back to good ol' Fortress Hood in less than two months. Signs out of his unit on the morning of 28 September for a couple of days of leave and is never seen or heard from again. Listed first as AWOL and then a month later dropped from the morning report as a deserter. Not seen since 1970. Had no reason to run . . ." He concluded, but began flipping through the pages of the full document, keeping his head down so that his eyes wouldn't make contact with Fick's should he decide to look up. "Ya gotta admit . . . pretty straightforward. Not the profile of your average deserter."

"Your average deserter?"

"Yeah, well, you know, Paul . . . doesn't seem like a deserter to me anyhow."

"You think not?" Fick asked. He still hadn't raised his head.

"Yeah, I think not. How about you, Bob?" Joyner responded, looking over to Temple, trying to prompt him for some support, even a sound. Had he been close enough, he'd have kicked him under the table.

Temple didn't look at all happy about being involved in the discussion. He wanted nothing more than to sign the paperwork and take the rest of the afternoon off. Eighteen holes were probably unreasonable, but nine were a solid possibility. "Yeah . . . well . . . ahhh . . . I guess I got to . . . ahhh . . . to agree with John. You know . . . ahhhh . . . it doesn't make a lot of sense for someone about to punch a one-way ticket out of Vietnam to piss his life away with a desertion rap. I mean, he could be pulling a good pension right now. I mean, it just doesn't make much sense."

There was no immediate response.

"So tell me, Colonel, what do you think happened to Master Sergeant Tenkiller?" Fick asked quietly after a pause. There was a coiled spring in there, restrained by the thinnest of tethers.

Temple didn't answer. He puffed his cheeks like a blowfish and dropped his focus to the scratches and fingerprints on the tabletop.

Joyner took another quick, noisy slurp of coffee to wet his tongue and bolster his courage, and then he responded. "Got whacked, would be my educated guess. Does it really matter how? He didn't come home; we know that. Bottom line, Colonel Fick, whether the VC got him or his mama-san rolled him for his loose pocket change—he's dead. BNR, as they say—Body Not Friggin' Recovered."

In the silence that followed, Joyner and Temple could hear the constant throng of people scurrying by in the corridor. A human buzz, like a humming clothesline. Everyone always in a hurry. As the pause lengthened, they both wished they could join the scurry.

"And so we amend his status?" Fick said at last. Quietly. "He didn't desert. We sign the paper, and he gets added to the list of Killed In Action. Simple enough. One of the three hundred Spartans."

"*Hooah*," John Joyner replied. He meant it lightheartedly but it came out sounding particularly ridiculous in the building tension of the small room. His smile faded quickly. "Well . . . why not? I mean, goddamn, what difference does it make at this point? For Christ's sake, the war's over, Paul. Over. Make the family happy. Give 'em a Purple Heart and make his mama smile; most important, make all the friggin' congressmen go away—right? That's what it's all about." He started to smile again.

Fick slowly raised his head, and Joyner saw his eyes. A flat mottled gray, like a galvanized washtub. They matched the color of his hair. John Joyner briefly wondered if they had always matched his hair. Then his own eyes caught sight of the gnarled hand and the hardware above Fick's left pocket—the purple ribbon with an oak leaf cluster that signified being wounded twice in action. Had he really just told this man, *Give 'em a Purple Heart and make his mama smile?* Joyner couldn't maintain eye contact even if he'd wanted to, and he dropped his eyes to the folder in front of him. He hunkered his shoulders as if to brace for a physical blow.

"Colonel Joyner . . ." Fick's voice was edged and shivered with thin control. "This country is getting ready to put fifty-eight thousand names on a black granite memorial at the Mall. Fifty-eight thousand young men Killed In Action. Fifty-eight thousand KIAs. Fifty-eight thousand men who didn't run away, and you're telling me it doesn't matter?"

Neither of the two junior colonels answered. They felt a heavy stickiness in the air like a storm about to break overhead. Even the sounds from the corridor seemed to momentarily cease.

"Maybe it doesn't," Fick said. He closed his eyes slowly as if the effort of keeping them open was more than he could manage any longer, and just that quickly the storm passed. That simply. That quickly. He sighed in a manner that exhausted them all. "Maybe it doesn't, Colonel Joyner. Maybe it doesn't at all. Not in this country.

Not in this building. Not in your army." He slowly pushed the change of status form across the table, his fingers barely touching the edge of the paper.

Both Joyner and Temple signed it quickly.

Fick didn't have the stomach for it.

By a two-to-one vote, Jimmy Lee Tenkiller became KIA.

CHAPTER 1

Baghdad, Iraq
THURSDAY, OCTOBER 18, 2007

"Clear your weapon, sir."

Robert McKelvey shook loose from his heat-dulled thoughts and looked up. He saw a young staff sergeant in desert camo, his Kevlar helmet cocked at an angle in an effort to impart some style to the baggy uniform. The eye contact, even shielded as it was behind dark sunglasses, made it clear that McKelvey had missed something. "What's that, Sergeant?" McKelvey asked. His voice broke from dry heat and disuse.

The staff sergeant nodded at the nine-millimeter holstered on McKelvey's hip. "Check your weapon, sir."

McKelvey was following the sergeant's look to his own hip when someone slapped him on the back of his head, knocking his ball cap over his eyes. "C'mon, Doc. You been out in the desert too long." It was Lieutenant Colonel Dennis Perkins, head of one of the ISG's mobile task forces. "This ain't Dodge City. You're back in civilization now, son—if you get my meaning. Check your weapon, and let's get us some chow. I've been eating goddamn MREs for the last two months." Perkins stepped in front of McKelvey, worked the bolt on his M-16, and dry-fired into a fifty-five-gallon drum half-filled with sand.

"Hey, bubba," McKelvey recovered from his surprise and replied as he pushed his cap up and began fumbling with his holster flap. "Heard you were up north somewhere." The two men had first met six months earlier when McKelvey was searching for a helicopter crash near the Kuwaiti border and the Iraq Support Group had been tapped for support. Perkins and his Mobil Task Force Sixteen had been pulled off their search for WMDs to augment the recovery team.

"Was. Got back this morning. How 'bout you? Word was that you were out west. Any success?" He watched McKelvey struggle with his holster as long as he could before reaching out and jerking the restraining flap up. "Let me help you there, Sergeant Rock."

"Thanks. Velcro can be tricky."

"Not to a trained professional. C'mon, I hear little Styrofoam bowls of Jell-O calling my name."

"Shit," McKelvey said as he removed the pistol from his holster. As the guard watched, he cocked and dry-fired it into the sand barrel, verifying that it was unloaded. It was always unloaded. They nodded in mutual affirmation, and McKelvey secured his weapon before returning his attention to Perkins. "They got Jell-O here?"

"You bet. Cool little squares of quivering paradise. I'm partial to the ones with banana slices in 'em. I like to suck 'em down in one gulp—kinda like oysters." He was holding several long strips of plastic that hung in front of the door aside with his forearm, suggesting that McKelvey should go first. The cool of the air-conditioned interior filtered past the plastic strips that hung over the mess trailer's doorway. "Unfortunately, they're the first to go—as in you need to get there early—if you get my meaning."

"In that case, you best leave me behind. Every man for himself under the circumstances."

"Negative. Ranger rules. I will not leave a comrade behind even when the Jell-O is in sight. Nothing in the book that says I can't kick you in the ass, though, if you don't hurry up."

"Ranger rules?"

"Ranger rules."

McKelvey smiled and ducked through the doorway. Actually, they were early and the dinner crowd was light. They worked their way through the food line quickly, filling their trays with slabs of grilled steak and dollops of mashed potatoes and colorful mixed vegetables, all served by somber-browed local hires that McKelvey felt sure had been asked to leave their vials of ricin at home.

Perkins detoured past the dessert bar and arrived at the seat next to McKelvey with a tray overloaded with bowls of Jell-O. As McKelvey watched, he slurped down four lime-colored squares as if he were a finalist in a gelatin-eating contest. With a loud satisfied sigh, he looked up. "Man oh man, if that doesn't clean out the dust. I gotta buy stock in Jell-O. Gotta."

"You and me both. And to think they bothered flavoring it."

"They flavor it?"

McKelvey laughed and shifted gears. "So tell me, still lookin' for WMDs?"

Perkins smiled broadly and bobbed his head at McKelvey's waist. "Doc Kel with a sidearm. Shit if that isn't the closest thing to a weapon of mass destruction that I can think of."

"That's why they don't give me bullets. But, hey, if y'all aren't still lookin' for WMDs, then what's the Iraq Support Group up to nowadays, anyhow? In case you haven't heard, Saddam's history."

"Other duties as assigned." Perkins shrugged as he stacked his Jell-O bowls. "Nothing I can talk about—if you get my meaning." He said that a great deal, whether you got his meaning or not.

"Hmmm," McKelvey acknowledged. He said that a great deal, especially when he didn't get the meaning. "Hmmm," he repeated as he forked some peas and carrots into his mouth.

"How about you?" Perkins asked as he began organizing the remaining food on his tray. "You involved in that war crimes shit?"

"I believe I'm innocent until proven guilty."

"Too bad. I was going to ask for your autograph. No, what I meant was that shit up north. Isn't someone digging up some of those mass graves north of here? I'd heard it was some guys from the Park Service or the Forest Service."

"Try Ringling Brothers. Nope, not us. Our folks are giving a wide berth to that tar baby." McKelvey took another bite of peas and carrots.

Perkins readjusted the empty Styrofoam bowls on his tray and squinted at McKelvey. "So what then? Secret squirrel type shit?"

"Not really. Three guys in a Humvee. No radio contact. No visual. Just disappeared."

"Shit to be them—if you know what I mean. Any luck?"

"Let's just say we found the Humvee. More than that, I can't talk about."

"Roger that," Perkins said. "Understood. But tell me, Doc, why the hell you here? You did your time here six months ago. I don't know the details about this case you're working, but if it's not that sensitive, couldn't you have sent someone else? Things can't possibly be so bad at work that you'd volunteer for another trip to this shit show."

McKelvey took a bite of steak and chewed. "You have no idea."

CHAPTER 2

Fort Knox, Kentucky
SATURDAY, OCTOBER 20, 2007

Sisal Johnson's brief, rampant moment of fame had come sixty-two years earlier. For an eye blink of a day and a half, young Tech Sergeant Sisal Johnson had been the fill-in driver for General George Patton, Jr., during the hell-bent gallop across Western Europe. At the time it had been a case of being in the right place at a most opportune time, but over a thousand renditions, over sixty Memorial Days and Veterans' Days of telling and retelling, that day and a half had grown in meaning and duration to a point where Sisal now remembered himself as a friend and close confidant of the general; as a man whose vision and judgment Patton valued and solicited. He had been a cog in the most magnificent machinery in history.

He could be found almost any day somewhere in the mnemonic cocoon of the George Patton Museum near Keyes Park at Fort Knox—always ready with a story or an explanation for any available or sympathetic ear. As a retired sergeant major he had ready access to the post, and his continued and regular presence had finally resulted in the staff at the museum acknowledging him as a fixture not unlike the tanks and armored cars planted out on the lawn. An unofficial docent.

He didn't get to see his family much anymore. His wife was gone six years this coming August, and his two daughters were married with busy lives of their own to manage. One lived in Cincinnati, and he saw her occasionally but not with any particular regularity; the other lived in Dayton, which might as well have been somewhere in the upper Ukraine. As hard as that was, it was his two grandsons that he missed the most—they so loved his stories, and he so loved telling them.

Which was why when they came to visit, as they had now, he made the most of it.

The sun was out, stretching broadly across a clear sky, but the day had the sharp-edged snap of a hurried autumn. The air was clean. Sisal Johnson had his two young grandsons at the Patton Museum. It was time to show them the tanks, and the cars, and the jeeps that he and the general used to drive around in; the ones that they'd planned the invasion of Europe from; the ones that they'd used to bust through the brittle Siegfried Line. He'd come to rap on the armor and slap the tracks, to once again have an existence and an identity and a magnetic center on which to home his life.

They had arrived too early, and Sisal was anxious. It was only eight-thirty and a Saturday, so the museum wouldn't be open for another hour and a half. So much the better. More time. More memories. In the meantime there were the static displays outside, including one of his favorites, the Soviet T34 medium tank, a monster of thick steel plating and even thicker Slavic functionalism. You could feel the thunder and clank of the treads just looking at it.

As they stood in front of the tank, Sisal Johnson animatedly explained to his two grandsons how the turret revolved and how the gun fired, and how the concussion would ring your ears for hours and make beads of sweat form on your brow. He explained how the tank turned by stopping one track and allowing the other to continue, and how he'd once seen a good friend crushed beneath the churning cleats of one of their own monsters. He rapped on the cold metal and pointed and gestured and relived. As he was explaining how the ammunition was taken aboard through a loading hatch he led the two boys to the rear of the tank. The gravel underfoot scrunched and talked under their feet, and it was only then that he noticed a smell—

an odor like rusty nails and old copper pennies and damp packets of Sweet 'N Low—and something else. It was a familiar smell. Familiar and strange at the same time.

He couldn't quite recognize it.

Until they reached the rear of the tank.

And then their lives were changed forever.

CHAPTER 3

McKelvey saw the lips moving but all he heard was a buzz. Like a fat, brown summer cicada. In fact, it was so loud he couldn't concentrate; he could only watch the lips move.

"I'm not sure I like your attitude, Kel," Colonel Peter Boschet buzzed. The CILHI commander's face was screwed into the same knot that always formed when he was forcing his brain to work. It looked like a colorful ball of rubber bands and was discomforting to witness. He was short and pear-shaped and possessed of a solid vein of the pure stupids that they still talked about at the Academy in awed whispers. Colonel Boschet—known behind his back as Colonel *Botch-It* for his ability to screw up even the simplest task—was, in fact, only marginally smarter than a coffee can full of pea gravel. "Your little time off running around in the desert playing Indiana · Jones doesn't seem to have helped your attitude."

"Call me Dr. McKelvey," Robert McKelvey roused his interest long enough to say. It had just popped into his head as he listened to the buzz. In truth, McKelvey was called Kel by most people, had been since shortly after he was born. In what was perhaps the first mystery of his life, his parents had given him the name Robert, but then never used it. His father had the ownership rights to both Robert and Bob sewn up, at least up until he died of lung cancer at too early an age, and Kel's mother wouldn't tolerate the use of "Little Bob" or "Junior" in her presence. As a result, in the world of dwindling options, their youngest son became Kel. It was an awkward name—people usually assumed that his name was Cal—but it had avoided confusion growing up at the supper table, and for better or worse he was stuck with it now. In fact, even though his father was now gone, Robert and Bob were seldom used except in formal situations and by strangers and those trying to piss him off. Occasionally, his wife would begin sentences with "Oh, Robert," but in those cases the inflection was the same as that with which she might say "Oh, Lord," after hearing that her twin sons were in the principal's office again—sort of a resigned expression of utter and complete exhaustion.

Kel had been asked to come down to the Botch-It's office to discuss some special assignment. Whatever the assignment was, as absolutely mindless as Kel knew it would be, he also knew that the worst part was having to sit quietly while two minutes of information was strung out over sixty minutes like a long tug of administrative taffy. There was a time when he'd had the patience for it, when one of his strong points was suffering fools lightly, but those times had long ago faded in the rearview mirror. He'd eaten too many sand-flavored MREs; spent too many nights away from his wife and children; reinvented the wheel with too many come-and-go commanders. This one had put him over the edge. Botch-It had a hard-earned reputation for staffing everything to death and then being totally incapable of making a decision or acting on common sense, and on the rare occasion when he accidentally did make a decision, the odds were well worth betting it would be a bad one. It was leadership at the peak of incompetence. In fact, Kel had resigned three times in the last year only to be talked down off the ledge by the deputy commander, Leslie Neep. He'd even sent himself to Iraq twice in order to keep his hands as far away from Botch-It's throat as possible and still justify earning a paycheck. Fortunately for all, Botch-It was on the downward slope of a three-year assignment with sixteen months to go, and every member of the staff could rattle off the time remaining—down to the day—481 as of yesterday.

Boschet tightened the knot he'd made of his face and cut a quick look at Les Neep sitting in the chair next to Kel. He tended to use Neep as a translator when he couldn't understand his scientific director—which recently had become always. He looked back at Kel. "Say again."

"Call me *Doctor* McKelvey."

There was a pause while the response percolated through to his brain. "See? See? That's the sort of thing I'm talking about," Boschet erupted. His voice was too loud for his office and there was a scurrying sound from the outer room as people either found other things to do, or, as Kel suspected, positioned themselves to eavesdrop better. "I hear you tell everyone in this entire building—even the goddamn janitors—everyone in this building to call you *Kel,* but you tell me to call you *Doctor.* Me. The commander. I don't get it. Check that. I do get it and what I get, I don't like. Are you trying to piss me off?"

"Why, is it workin'?"

"You pompous prima donna. I don't have to—"

"Whoa, whoa. Time out." Les Neep sat forward in his chair and inserted himself into the rapidly closing space between Kel and Boschet. "Sir, I don't think Kel, ahhh, Dr. McKelvey meant that as it came out. Right, Dr. McKelvey?" He continued before Kel had a chance to respond. "My read on it is that the Doc—see, I call him Doctor too—he just wants to keep things professional between the two of you. You're the commander and he's the lab director. You all need to maintain a sense of, a kind of . . . help me out here, Kel. A kind of . . ."

"Professional detachment."

"Bingo." Les snapped his fingers. "Detachment. It's a professional thing. That's all that it is. Right, Kel—Doc? A professional kinda thing."

"Les, do you take me for a moron?" Boschet's face remained screwed into a knot of rubber bands. "Do you? And how about you, *Doctor* McKelvey? Do I look like a moron to you?"

Les tried to stop Kel but reacted too slowly. He barely had time to mutter, "Oh, crap."

Kel leaned forward to better peer around Neep's intervening

shoulder. "No, sir, Colonel. I think by definition, morons have to have an IQ over forty-nine. I suspect you're more in the imbecile range."

Boschet exploded. "Get the fuck out of my office. You goddamn overeducated prick bastard. Les, get this son of a bitch out of my sight before I forget that I'm a professional in the United States Army."

Les Neep had already grabbed Kel and was shoving him toward the door.

CHAPTER 4

U.S. Army Central Identification Laboratory, Hawaii
THURSDAY, NOVEMBER 8, 2007

Les Neep closed his office door and shook his head. He could feel each of his sixty-three years in his bones. "Are you out of your damn mind?" He moved around Kel, sat down, leaned forward with his elbows on his desk and his head in his hands, and spoke into a pile of papers in front of him. "Why do you do that? Why?"

Kel dropped into the chair in front of Les's desk as if he had bricks in his pants pockets. He let his head fall back on his neck and closed his eyes. He didn't respond.

"Dammit to hell, what gets into you? All you had to do was come down here, sit quietly, and nod," Les said to the papers. "Just nod."

"Easier said than done," Kel finally responded.

"Like hell. I do it all day long. Sit and nod. Sit and nod. Shit, son, sometimes I even smile. Smile and nod." He looked up. "But no. *Doctor McKelvey,* he can't just nod; no, sir, he's got to go poke a stick in the colonel's eye. A big, long stick that he spends his time sharpening on a dull rock."

"Yeah, well maybe there's only enough room for one noddin' dog in the back of this car."

Les Neep leaned back in his chair and stared at Kel for a moment before responding. "Like I deserved that. Like I really deserve a rash of shit from you. Who just defended you in the Old Man's office? This nodding dog, that's who."

Kel stood up and walked to the window. He crossed his arms and squared his stance. "Don't need you to defend me, Les. Not from the likes of Botch-It anyhow."

Les snorted. "Right. You're handling it so well. How many times you volunteered for Iraq? Twice? Tell you what, when your parts come back in a damn box next time, I'll remember to nod at your funeral. How 'bout that? I'll sit on a wide pew in the back and nod."

The two men went quiet.

Kel broke the silence. "Sound like my wife," he said softly.

"And you act like mine," Les responded. "About as reasonable."

Kel turned away from the window and smiled. He shrugged to break the growing tightness. "Hey, got me out of whatever numbskull assignment Botch-It had in mind."

Les looked down at the papers on his desk and sucked in a deep lungful of tension. "I wish it were that easy, buddy. It ain't."

"Oh, yeah, it is," Kel answered. "Can be anyhow. You just keep sittin' there, and I'll go back to my office and try to figure out what I was doin' when Colonel Numb-Nut called me down here."

"Afraid not," Les sighed. He took up the papers on his desk. It wasn't a loose pile but rather a bound report the thickness of a small phone book, a plastic spiral corkscrewing along one edge. "The Old Man's got some concerns."

"The Old Man's got shit for brains. On a good day."

"Maybe so," Les conceded. "Maybe so, but he still has some concerns, and he's looking for someone to share them with."

"That right?" Kel's voice regained an edge.

Les flipped the report at Kel. He waited for him to look at the title page. "That's the army's guidelines for developing a Diversity Awareness Plan in the workforce."

"Forget it, Les." Kel laughed as he tossed the report back in the other man's lap.

"Don't make me order you."

"Order me? Try. Last time I checked, I didn't work for you. I work for the little pear-shaped man with the IQ to match."

Les put the report back on his desk and stood up. He drummed his fingers momentarily. "You're shooting the messenger here, my friend. Maybe you don't work for me, but dammit, Kel, he's dead serious about you doing this."

"Doin' what? A Diversity Awareness Plan? I'm so goddamn tired of other people tellin' me how to do my job."

"No one's telling you how to do your job."

"No? How about that memo last week? As I recall, I was instructed to make sure that half of the scientific staff is female."

"That's just a target—"

"Is that right? A target? And is someone goin' to tell the North Koreans? Last time I checked, our friends in the workers' paradise wouldn't let us send any women in with the teams. That changed? 'Cause if it hasn't, then who'll pull all those fun-filled missions? Do the math, Les. If only half the staff can deploy to North Korea, then the same folks are goin' to keep gettin' their tickets punched to that shithole. Not that that causes any morale problems or anythin'."

"I've been in North Korea. I know—"

"Like hell you do. You know what two, three days in a North Korean hotel is like. I'm talkin' about thirty, forty days in a base camp with eighteen-year-old American-hatin' guards pointin' guns at you the whole time and calculatin' how many extra bowls of rice they'll get for shootin' your ass. You know, the fastest way to get the staff balanced might be to piss all the men off to the point where half of them resign. That'll at least take care of sex, though race, creed, and astrological sign may still need some equalizin'." Kel started for the door. "Diversity Awareness Plan my ass."

"Kel, look. As a man of color—"

"Man of color?" Kel stopped and turned back to face Les. "And what color would that be, Les? Feelin' blue today? And since when? You've been a Texan the whole time I've known you. Don't pull this man-of-color shit on me."

Les smiled. "Texan-American, actually. Look—no one's telling you how to do your job or how to assemble your staff or who to hire—"

"Like hell you aren't. You and Botch-It, both. I can only pull so many rabbits out of the hat. Every year it's 'do more, do more,' and every year I get less and less. You know how many qualified applicants we had for the last vacancy?"

"Kel—"

"One. One. That doesn't give me much opportunity to diversify the staff when I have one applicant to choose from, does it?"

"Kel—"

"Don't 'Kel' me. How can I recruit anyone—of any friggin' color—when I'm so fed up dealin' with Botch-It that even I don't want to work here myself? As you pointed out, between Iraq and North Korea I almost have my Axis of Evil club card filled up. If I can figure out how to send myself to Iran I'll win a free pound of anthrax. I'm the closest thing to a postal employee that you'll ever meet, and I'm supposed to talk people into comin' to work here?"

Les sighed and picked up the report from his desk. He slowly held it out for Kel. "He's got you on this one. Don't be stupid. Diversity Awareness—it's a PC thing and that means he has your nuts in a vise—which is just what he wants. Take this. Assign it to someone on your staff, and stall like hell. Haven't I taught you anything over these years? Smile, nod, and wait the sonofabitch out."

CHAPTER 5

Kel swung his old Volkswagen Jetta into his driveway and killed the engine. As he opened the door and stepped out, he made sure to tuck the seat belt back inside. That had become a habit ever since one of his sons had slammed the rear door shut, with the belt hanging out. Normally that wouldn't have been a problem except that he'd slammed it shut so hard that the lock broke, forever trapping the belt on the outside. Now the buckle dragged along on the asphalt, sparking and pinging. Kel kept intending to cut it off but never got around to it.

The other habit that had developed as of late was casting a glare in the direction of his neighbor across the street, or if the neighbor was not outside, a glare at the house served as a satisfying proxy. Mililani, Hawaii, was a small bedroom community of mostly two-income families that had sprouted from a smudge of red dirt in the central highlands of Oahu. Thirty years earlier it had been a sea of prickly green-and-gold pineapples. It was the sort of town that focused on its children, and husbands received calls to remember to stop off on the way home from work to coach the Little League team (and to stop off at the grocery store and pick up a twenty-pound sack of rice for dinner). Kel's neighbor was a small Japanese man who always seemed to be wearing a muscle shirt and flip-flops and who never seemed to work outside the confines of his property. He could usually be spotted, on his hands and knees, cutting his grass with a pair of scissors—a feat made possible by the fact that his front lawn was only slightly larger than an AAA roadmap. When he wasn't snipping his grass, he was tracking down errant leaves that blew into his space as if they were illegal immigrants flooding his border. It was, in fact, the leaves that were at the root of the glaring. Ever since the neighbor had pounded on Kel's door early one Saturday morning to demand that Kel keep his mango leaves on his side of the street, Kel had been glaring at every opportunity that presented itself; glaring and hoping that his neighbor would honorably deal with his frustration by committing hara-kiri with a leaf rake.

Mary Louise McKelvey looked up from the stack of papers she was grading. "Robert McKelvey, you haven't been home this early since," she paused, she looked at her watch, it was midafternoon. "Well, since I don't know when. Are you okay? See your neighbor anywhere?"

Kel had walked in the front door of his house and dropped his backpack in the entryway as if it were an anchor chain. The slope of his shoulders had the soft curve of an eroded hillside, and he had all the appearance of the elements wasting him away. He stood in place momentarily before summoning up the energy to bend at the waist and jerk the knots in his shoes free. He didn't respond.

"Bless your heart, if you don't look like somethin's been chewin' on you. A big dog, maybe. You okay?" Mary Louise would bless the devil's heart.

Kel walked slowly into the living room and sat heavily on the sofa next to his wife. After a moment he lay down with his head in her lap and closed his eyes. He didn't speak.

Mary Louise eased a stack of papers out from under his head and set them aside. She stroked his hair momentarily, gauging his silence. "You're goin' back to Iraq, aren't you?"

Kel sighed through his nose but didn't answer.

"Kel?"

"No." He sighed again.

"North Korea?"

"No. I promised."

Mary Louise nodded slowly as she looked for a loophole in the answers. "So tell me."

Kel adjusted his position slightly. "Remember the movie *Harvey*?"

"Remind me. Glenn Ford?"

"Jimmy Stewart."

"Was that the one about that big rabbit?"

"Umm. A very big rabbit that only Jimmy Stewart and his psychiatrist could see."

"Oh, Lord, don't tell me you've started seeing big rabbits. That's all we need."

"I wish. No, it's the psychiatrist. Remember there's this scene where he's describing how he'd like Harvey to stop time? Harvey could do that, stop time, and the psychiatrist said that he wanted to go off to Canton, Ohio, and have a kind woman pat him on the head and say somethin' like, 'you poor, poor, man; you poor, poor, man.'"

"And that's what you want?"

"That's what I want."

"Too bad you don't know any giant rabbits," Mary Louise replied.

"Too bad I don't know any kind women."

"Keep lookin'. I'm sure a rabbit will turn up." She paused. "What happened today, Kel?"

Kel shrugged. He kept his eyes closed and took several slow breaths. "The usual. Botch-It. Reinventing the wheel. Scaling Mount Paperwork. I used to think that the myth of Sisyphus best described the lab. You know, always rollin' the same rock up the same hill, only to have it roll back every night." He took another slow breath. She smelled of flowers and soap and stability.

"And now?"

Kel smiled and turned his head, working it deeper into his wife's lap. "And now I think Prometheus is my role model. You know, you try and try to bring light to the darkness and as a reward you get to have your liver eaten out every day, only to have it grow back every night. God, I can't take this much longer."

"So maybe it's time to leave. You always said that we'd leave when you didn't enjoy the work anymore. Sounds like you're there. We're there."

"Almost. I still believe in the mission. And the people. It's just—" The thought snuffed out.

They sat quietly for a moment and then Mary Louise patted his head. "You poor, poor, man," she said.

CHAPTER 6

The old Russian-made MI-17 helicopter slowly throbbed in low, angling in from the northeast, shuddering and whipping dry thatch from the bamboo and wood huts. The crowd gathered in the swirl below like rice chaff concentrated by the downdraft. As it neared the ground, one of the Vietnamese crew chiefs jumped out, stumbling momentarily onto his knees, and began moving the curious villagers back, away from the spinning tail rotor.

A half minute later, the massive craft wobbled to a heavy landing and slowly began its long, complaining shutdown.

Senior Colonel Nguyen Van Dich was the second man off the aircraft after the crew chief. He stretched and popped his joints. He smoothed his shirt and pinched the crease on his pants as he looked around. Nguyen Dich was aging. The man who'd once been able to subsist on a ball of rice every two days and who could curl up under a palm frond and sleep during a monsoon rain now found that he didn't handle these long flights as he once had. It hurt his back and his hips to spend time on the canvas cargo seating, feet propped up uncomfortably on bags of rice and dried fish and plastic jerry cans of fresh water—resupplies for the Vietnamese workers—and he found himself wondering more and more about why he did it. Why did he spend his days helping the Americans search for their two thousand war dead? He didn't have an answer. His own country had plenty of dead. Maybe two million, maybe more, and who was looking for them? The Americans had killed his parents and two brothers. Who was looking for them? His pretty, young fiancée was missing and would never be found. Who was looking for her? He too had almost died. Many times. Instead the Americans had merely blown out his eardrums. In 1969 he'd been a young sapper with the Fatherland Brigade in Quang Tri Province when he'd been caught by a surprise B-52 strike. He was far enough away that he hadn't been killed, but he also hadn't had time to open his mouth to equalize the pressure, and the concussion had blown out both eardrums. One had never grown back properly, and now, at sixty-two, the other ear was starting to fade rapidly. Soon he would be stone deaf, hearing nothing but distant memories.

The flight had been a short one. They'd overnighted in Da Nang after leaving Hanoi the previous afternoon. Nguyen Dich had had personal business to attend to last night, and his loins still tingled when he thought of her. Even at his age, even with other faculties fading, he was enormously vital. Perhaps it was the extracurricular aspects of the job that made it worthwhile.

The helicopter blades finally stopped turning and the ends bobbed slowly, as if nodding in satisfied agreement at the decision to stop. Several small, brown, curly-tailed dogs had overcome their initial shyness and were circling underfoot, occasionally yelping when they were kicked, but otherwise glad for another day out of the stewpot. The curious villagers formed a tight ring around the aircraft and its strangers, having turned out for what promised to be the day's—if not the year's—entertainment. Nguyen Dich cast a disapproving look at them—he didn't think much of southerners, who had been less than reliable partners during the War of Liberation—then he looked back at the doorway to the MI-17 where the Americans were only now awkwardly crawling out of the helicopter. He didn't think much of them either. They always took a long time, these Americans, and they were much too concerned about their physical comforts. They had to collect their sweatscarves and hats and expensive, mirrored sunglasses and colorful backpacks. And MP3 players. And water bottles. Always many water bottles. Always a delay.

He wanted them to hurry up. His bowels were getting restless, turning over and over with something he'd eaten last night, and he wanted to get this interview over with and make the short flight into Ho Chi Minh City and get to the newly constructed Norfolk Hotel and its flush toilets and cool marble floor tiles.

Always many water bottles.

There was a stink here that burned his nose. This village was not unlike the one he'd come from—sixty some years ago—but he'd put the fetid, sour smells of the country behind him. The garbage and the rot and the fecund smell of Mekong silt as it worked its way slowly south. *This better be worth it,* he thought. *The American better be buried here.* A Red Indian, the report from the provincial office had said. Nguyen Dich had seen movies of Red Indians, painted and feathered and whooping like wild animals. *Had this Indian been whooping when he died?*

Than Chu stepped forward from the crowd. He was a small wire-framed man, with dark brown skin that betrayed the bloodline of a mountain tribe, who smoked anything that he could keep lit. He looked as if he'd been up most of the previous night. His thin white cotton shirt and dark trousers were always stained and wrinkled, and Chu never failed to remind Nguyen Dich of a sheet of crumpled newspaper. But he was good at his job. And as the provincial representative of the Vietnamese Office for Seeking Missing Persons he was responsible for his boss's coming here now. It was Than Chu who'd reported the information about the dead American—the *Red Indian*—to VNOSMP headquarters, and now he could only hope that it met with his supervisor's expectations. The senior colonel didn't look pleased to be here.

Staff Sergeant Ed Milligan had dozed off during the flight, the throbbing rap turned up so loud on his MP3 player that everyone else on the bird could hear it leaking past his headphones above the noise of the MI-17's massive rotor. He awoke to find himself alone in the cabin, the flight crew and the rest of the joint team having already filed out. He paused his music, collected his rucksack and Camelback and extra water bottle, and hurried down the steps. He adjusted his dark sunglasses against the pulsing throb of the Vietnamese sun and took in the situation before him. There were naked children and slack-ribbed dogs everywhere, and bone-thin brown men in green pith helmets and loose sandals and even thinner women in conical straw hats were surrounding the aircraft—simply staring in moon-faced interest. Over to the side, Milligan saw that Swinging Dich and the team's interpreter were talking to someone that he could only presume was the local VNOSMP contact. They seemed to have everything well in hand, and Milligan briefly thought about stretching out again on the cargo seat and resuming his dream before it melted forever away into the gritty creases of his brain. He didn't. Instead, the American team leader pulled his headphones down around his neck, adjusted the sweat rag at his throat, and walked over to where Dich and the other men were talking. He stood and listened to the conversation—not understanding a goddamn word.

Just like chickens clucking, he thought. *Cock-a-doodle-doo.*

Sergeant Thomas Stephenson was also listening. He understood every word—almost as well as the Vietnamese themselves—except for when they lapsed heavily into local dialects. But even in that area he was improving. Now he listened and nodded to himself and, from time to time, made a small notation in his yellow hardback field book.

Then, abruptly, or so it seemed to Milligan, Nguyen Dich and Than Chu reached some sort of understanding, and together they began walking toward a concrete building on the nearby northern edge of the hamlet. It was the only building of any substance in the village, and Milligan recognized it as the hamlet's Communist Party meetinghouse.

Stephenson and Milligan followed. The other members of the team—Vietnamese and American—stayed near the helicopter, keeping the villagers away from the helo and swatting at flies. They were using the same motions for both.

The building was roughly made of hand-mixed concrete thinly buttered over sun-dried clay blocks and was remarkably uncomfortable in appearance. Its brick tile roof was patched in places with irregular sheets of flattened metal—remnants of a downed U.S. helicopter or aircraft. It was built French-style, narrow and long, and had a cement floor, polished by the horny calluses of countless bare feet, which had been covered with a woven fiber mat. It was cool and dark, like a tunnel, and there was no door and no glass covering the small windows. A blackboard stood in one corner, and the walls were hung with posters and calendars of smiling, pretty young Vietnamese women with dark oval eyes and colorful *ao dai* dresses and conical straw hats. There were words on the posters that Milligan didn't understand—but the women were pretty, and he kept staring at them, animating them in his mind.

To the side, two skinny brown men—wound as tightly as clock springs—sat in wooden chairs, looking nervous. Had there been loaded pistols pressed against their temples, they wouldn't have looked any more uncomfortable. They stood when the two Vietnamese governmental officials entered, but otherwise didn't move or volunteer a sound. Both held tiny stubs of smoldering, hand-rolled cigarettes between thumb and middle finger. The smell of the smoke suggested that they were made of something more than common tobacco.

Than Chu talked to his boss, directing his attention to Nguyen Dich's better ear, and he motioned repeatedly to the two skinny men as he did so. Sergeant Stephenson had been listening intently and during a pause moved closer to Milligan and translated. "Pretty interesting. Those two are what pass for village elders here. Mr. Than says that they claim to have information on the burial location of an American soldier."

Milligan shook his head. "Yeah, yeah. That's what every one of these shittin' little pencil stubs tells us. Just once I wish it'd pan out. Instead, these two will stand around smoking joints and laughing at the gringos while Swingin' Dich has us spend the next two hours digging up banana trees at two hundred dollars a pop."

"No. That's what's really interesting. The Dickster there, really—and I mean really—wants to get the interview over with. He says he has official business in Saigon and that we need to be wheels-up in fifteen—buried American or no buried American."

Milligan looked at Stephenson and then at Nguyen Dich. "Fifteen? Shit, bro, we just got here."

"Fifteen." Stephenson shrugged. "Like you say, it's not at all like Swingin' Dich."

"Fifteen. Well, then let's get on with it," Milligan said.

The two of them took up wobbly chairs near the two village elders. Than Chu joined them and motioned for the two elderly men to sit down as well. Nguyen Dich remained standing, looking out the doorway at the MI-17, his body language betraying his obvious impatience with the procedure.

Sergeant Stephenson didn't need direction. He'd done a hundred investigations over the last two years, and he could conduct an investigation like this one in his sleep. He offered the two men cigarettes. He himself didn't smoke, but he always carried a couple of packs of Marlboros to help smooth out the introductions. As the men tucked the cigarettes into their shirt pockets for later use, Stephenson turned to a fresh page in his field book and triple-clicked his pen. Than Chu quietly provided the two elderly men with some additional explanation of what was going on, and what the ground rules were, and then Stephenson began. He started at the beginning: names, ages, occupations, years living in the area . . .

Chickens clucking. Milligan listened momentarily and then returned his singular imagination to the young women on the posters.

"Ed . . . Ed . . . Staff Sergeant Milligan . . ." Stephenson slapped Milligan's arm with the back of his hand. "Ed."

"Yeah," Milligan responded. He took a lingering look at one of the posters and then turned his attention to Stephenson. He suddenly realized that he'd been daydreaming and that the interview must be nearly completed.

"Anything else you want to ask?"

"Huh? What you got?"

"These guys say they know where an American soldier is buried."

"Of course they do. They always say that. And how do they know it's an American?" Milligan asked.

"Well, they aren't sure that it is; they admit that. They say this whole village was relocated during the latter part of the war . . . moved east a couple of klicks to a strategic hamlet . . . at least until sometime in early 1971 when they began filtering back. So nobody lived here for a couple of years, but some of the older men continued to work the rice paddies near here and they would make occasional short visits to the old homestead. Checking up on things, you know?"

"And? The body could still be a Vietmanese." Like a lot of the soldiers on his team, he transposed the m and the n in the word.

"Doesn't sound like it . . . Mr. Slim and Mr. Jim here say that they used to see several ARVN officers and an American soldier meeting here frequently. They don't know what for, or who they were, but they were here regularly."

"And?"

"And so, when the folks moved back home in '71, there was a new grave in the village cemetery." He turned back to the two men and quietly clucked something completely unintelligible to Milligan.

The older-looking of the two men responded in kind. The other man and Than Chu nodded like cork bobbers in the middle of a pond.

Stephenson also nodded his understanding and looked back at Milligan. "Yeah. Ahh . . . well, there was no name on the grave marker—not even a marker really—but it definitely was a grave, and it definitely had been dug between late June of '70 when they made their last check-up on the place and February 1971 when the village all began moving back."

"Okay. But what makes them think it's an American? Hell, it's not like there was a shortage of Viets getting killed around here in 1970 and 1971. Could be anybody."

"True, but they say the only ones around the village, besides the occasional VC patrol, were those South Vietnamese officers and that American soldier that they saw here frequently. They met regularly. They also say that neither the People's Army nor the VC would bury their dead in the village cemetery, and the ARVN probably wouldn't either and if they did, they'd put a name on the marker. So, if you eliminate all the other suspects, they figure it must be an American. Either way, they can take us to the spot if we want."

Milligan squinted, then pulled a blue folder from his rucksack. He began speaking as he thumbed into the folder. "Time frame's about right. Tenkiller disappeared in mid-September 1970—but it doesn't make any sense. Who buried him? Why here? If it were South Vietmanese Army—ARVN—they were on our side, they should have reported it to someone. Right? And if it was bad guys—VC or PAVN—they wouldn't have put him in a cemetery . . . would they? I can see hiding the body in a ditch or hole somewhere—I mean, there's like shittin' bomb craters out the wazoo—but I can't see advertising an American body by putting it in a cemetery . . ."

"Your call." Stephenson shrugged. "You're the team leader. They say it's a short walk from here . . . less than five minutes or so."

"Shit, we're here, ain't we?" he said as he tucked the folder back in his rucksack and picked up his water bottle. "Nothing to lose but some inches off the ol' gut. Short walk? Might as well check it out. Let's see what Swingin' Dich says." Milligan looked up at the senior colonel, expecting to receive a nod of approval.

Instead, the senior colonel was standing in the doorway, motioning to the helicopter pilots to get the rotor spun up.

Milligan and Stephenson looked at each other in dismay. It was a short walk, and they'd come all this way.

Sixty seconds later the big motor began to whine.

CHAPTER 7

Leslie Neep, the CILHI deputy commander, walked into Kel's office with purpose. He always walked that way, whether he really had a purpose or not. It was an unfortunate side effect of being raised in the heart of Texas. He looked around at the scientific director's cluttered office with an admixture of humor and disbelief. It never failed to remind him of a bird's nest, everything being interwoven the way it was. How Kel could find anything always amazed him. But he could—almost always—or so he always claimed.

There was an unfortunate resemblance between the man and his office. Robert Dean McKelvey was approaching middle age with more speed than planning, and lately, the cumulative effect of too little sleep and even less exercise was starting to show—not to mention the strain of having to work around a dysfunctional and incompetent commander. Kel increasingly was arriving at work looking as if he'd fallen off a box of Dixie firecrackers.

Davis Smart, the deputy lab manager, was also in the office when Les Neep walked in. He and Kel had their feet propped up on the corner of Kel's desk and were discussing something that they both found enormously funny. Davis was one of the things that kept Kel coming to work. A year earlier, Kel had been offered a professorship at a small university on the Mainland. It was an attractive offer; good money, very good money for a teaching job; plenty of freedom; great location. Kel had been sorely tempted to accept it until he had the sobering realization as he looked around the room at the faculty assembled for a party in his honor that there wasn't a single one of them that he wanted to have lunch with. For all the spirit-busting aspects of the CILHI job—and Colonel Botch-It—Kel still enjoyed being around his staff. Still wanted to have lunch with them.

"Well, glad to see the two of you so hard at work this morning," Neep groused before he could check himself. It was the first that he'd seen Kel laughing in over a month, and despite being on the verge of his own bad mood, he didn't intend to dampen Kel's spirit. "What's the occasion for all the levity?"

"Hey, haven't you heard?" Kel responded. His voice had an almost giddy quality to it. "Leilani told me that Botch-It is supposed to get a call from Branch this mornin' to talk about his next assignment. Know what that means? Only one thing. It means he's leavin' early. Early. He's about to be history."

Les Neep's bad mood quickly returned. "The commander's secretary shouldn't be discussing his phone calls with anyone." His voice took on a serious tone that he made no attempt to check. "And you need to learn to show him some respect."

There was a pause while the air returned to the room.

"Respect? Botch-It? Are you out of your ten-gallon mind?"

"No, Dr. McKelvey, I'm not. I'm a professional, and he's the commander. Whether either one of us likes it or not. And the sooner—"

"Botch-It? Commander? Have you got a fever or somethin'?" Kel looked at D.S. "This is one of those pod people, isn't it? He hatched out of some giant pea pod in the janitor's closet over the weekend. This isn't our Les."

"I'm thinking Roswell," D.S. responded.

"Crop Circle, Texas."

"Cut the crap, will you?" Les snapped. "Yeah, the guy's a friggin' disaster in uniform, but we're stuck with him, and you two don't make it any easier. Always calling him Colonel Botch-It. Hell, to his face even. I'm awful damn tired of getting jammed up between you and him, you know that? Why don't you try thinking about the rest of us? I've got three years until retirement. Can't you try to get along with him?"

"Ah, c'mon, Les. What's this Rodney King shit? Just get along? Jesus Christ, we're about to emerge from the goddamn dark ages here. This guy's been like the Black Death, and now he's gettin' early orders out of here. Lighten up and enjoy the Renaissance."

Les looked at Kel momentarily and bit back his response. He took a breath and then made a show of looking at his watch. It was eight-ten. "Taking a break already?" He forced a lighthearted tone to freshen the air. "Must be the life."

"Break? Naw, gotta actually start work in order to take a break," Kel said. He acknowledged Neep's attempt to lighten the mood and change the subject.

Neep looked at his watch again.

Kel answered his look. He also made a show of looking at his own watch. So did D.S. "Actually we were just scratchin' our nuts. Kinda like zoo monkeys."

"I'm so proud to know the two of you, I really am."

"The honor's all ours, Les. Now, what can we do you for?"

Neep shook a paper he was holding. "What you can do is tell me if either of you have read this."

"Havin' absolutely no idea what it is that you're referrin' to, I'll err on the safe side and say, no. How 'bout you, D.S.?"

"Nope. Never learned to read."

"That's true, you know," Kel replied. "Or write either. He still signs stuff with a big, sloppy X. The man sure can scratch though. Show him, D.S."

"That's all right," Neep replied quickly. He took a deep breath and nodded. "Did I say how proud I was to know you two?"

"Yes, sir, I think you did. Feelin's mutual."

"Good. Now, as soon as you two get to a stopping point with what you're doing, could you take a look at this?" He waved the piece of paper at them again as if he were fanning a fire—which, in fact, given the content, he might have been.

Kel reached up and caught the paper. "What is it?" His Arkansas accent was light this morning. When he was tired or mad, particularly when he was both, his voice took on a soft slur common to the hills of western Arkansas. But it was early and there was little discernible accent.

"Daily SITREP from I-T-One in Vietnam," Neep responded. Each investigation team in the field filed a Situation Report on its activities over the previous twenty-four hours. The recovery teams did the same. Usually the SITREPs were filled with logistical humdrum such as how many bottles of water were consumed, team morale, number of witnesses interviewed, number of blade hours put on the helicopters, or the number of archaeological grid squares excavated. Kel didn't normally read them unless there was a compelling reason to do so. In this case, Neep asking him to do so seemed to correctly spell out the word "compelling."

"I-T-One? Which case are they investigating?" D.S. asked.

"Tenkiller," Kel responded out loud as he quickly read the report. "Remember that one?"

"Tenkiller? The Indian?" D.S. asked.

"Yup."

"I believe we call them Native Americans," Neep corrected.

Kel looked up from the paper. "Yeah, like that's what you said growin' up in Rock Salt, Texas. Hey, you heard about the Indian that went to visit the whorehouse in Texas?"

"Making progress on your Diversity Awareness Plan, I guess."

"Diversity Plan?" D.S. perked up. "That sounds like fun."

"Didn't the good doctor tell you?" Neep smiled. "Shame on you, *Doctor McKelvey.*"

"Yeah, lucky me," Kel replied. "Botch-It tasked me with puttin' together a Diversity Awareness Plan."

"A what?"

"You heard me. He wants the scientific staff to be more aware of diversity."

"The staff is made up of anthropologists," D.S. replied. "Does he know what an anthropologist is? What we do?"

Kel's expression answered the question.

"Right. Right," D.S. said as he shook his head. "Haven't had my coffee yet. But you? *Perversity* maybe, but a *diversity* plan? He out of his mind?"

"Don't look so smug or I may put you on the committee I'm formin'." Kel turned back to Neep. "But as I was sayin', this Indian goes to this Texas whorehouse—"

Les sighed again. "Gentlemen, as much as I really do enjoy your company, can we get back to the Tenkiller case?"

"You bet," Kel answered. He smiled. "Did I mention that Botch-It will be leavin' soon?"

"Tenkiller. Do you mind?"

Kel turned his attention back to the paper he was holding. He looked over at D.S. "Sure. Anyhow, D.S., as I was tellin' you before Mr. Grumpy interrupted, Tenkiller's a strange case. Real strange. Master sergeant gettin' ready to leave Vietnam on his way back to the States takes some leave and then disappears. Army says he deserted; family says he didn't . . ."

"Family writes congressman, is what the family does," Neep continued the narration, glad to be back on track. He pushed a stack of file folders aside and sat down on the couch, leaning back against the cushion and putting his hands behind his head. He often sat like that, and it always made Kel think that he looked like a hostage in a liquor store hold-up. "The army finally had to back down and change his official status in the mid-eighties. A review board met and examined the file. He's presumed Killed In Action now. KIA, Body Not Recovered, to be specific."

"So what's to investigate? We have a location for him?" D.S. asked. D.S. had been with the laboratory for over fifteen years and knew the complex mechanics of fieldwork better than anyone. To his disappointment, he had the salty gray hairs in his head and beard to prove it.

"Yeah, maybe. Accordin' to this, the VNOSMP scared up a couple of witnesses who say they know where an American was buried at about the same time Tenkiller went missin' . . . But . . ." Kel looked up from his reading and directed his attention to Les Neep, "is this serious? This can't be right . . ."

"Thought the same thing," Neep answered in his flat, West Texas prairie tones.

Kel looked over at D.S. to lock his attention and then returned his eyes to the report, reclaiming the line where he'd left off. "Seems that the team interviewed two Vietnamese village elders . . . so on, so on . . . ahhh . . . village relocated durin' the war . . . ahh, here it is . . . they told the team they could lead them to the burial site—all of five minutes away—in a marked cemetery, no less. But instead of surveyin' the site, the team up and left and flew on into Saigon."

Kel looked back at Neep.

"What I'm hearing is that you can thank your good buddy Nguyen Dich for that," Neep responded.

"Swingin' Dich?"

"The same. By your reaction, can I assume that we're in agreement, Dr. McKelvey?" Neep asked. He stood up and stretched his legs.

"If you mean that we ought to get a team right back in there, we are. But I tell you what, we might think about sendin' a recovery team in next time rather than another investigation team. That way, if there's somethin' there, they can excavate it and save havin' to send another team in later on to do a recovery. No point pissin' away any more time than we already have."

"I thought you'd say that. I just checked with operations. Last word from R-T-Two is that they wrapped up their site today and are packing up to redeploy home; we can turn them around and have them to the cemetery by Friday—Vietnam time. You comfortable with that?"

"Who's on Recovery Team Two?" Kel looked at D.S. One of his deputy's primary duties was assigning anthropologists to the recovery teams. Not all anthropologists were created equal. Some were better at excavating crash sites; some were better at burial sites—D.S. had a talent for making the right matches.

D.S. closed his eyes and thought. "Ahh, that'd be Caroline," D.S. said.

"I can live with that. Should be a quick recovery. She supposed to go anywhere else after this that'll domino the whole schedule?"

"Nope. We were going to let her sit out the next two missions to get caught up on some reports and make some repairs to her personal life."

"Good. This'll be short. She can catch up on the paperwork later."

"And her personal life?"

Kel sighed. "Occupational hazard. We'll make it up to her. Somehow. Other than that, you good with it?"

D.S. nodded. "I'm good."

Kel looked back up at Neep and held out the SITREP for him to take back. He arched his eyebrows as if to say, "It's okay by us."

"Doctor Thompson it is, then. Operations needs to start the prep work to make it happen. Don't wrap them around the axle any more than they already are. You want to tell them, or you want me to do it?"

"We got it. Don't you, D.S.?"

"That's the singular form of we, isn't it? Yeah, I got it."

"Good," Les Neep responded as he began walking to the door.

"Hey, Les," Kel called after him. He waited for Neep to turn. He paused and shrugged apologetically. "Hey, ahh, I'm sorry about jammin' you up between me and Botch-It. Okay?"

Les nodded. "I know. Listen, Kel—about Botch-It and his new assignment . . ." He paused again. "I wouldn't get your hopes up is all."

CHAPTER 8

Doctor Caroline Thompson was glad for the promise of a diversion—even if it looked to be a short one. She had finally wrapped up her excavation in Song Be Province, north of Ho Chi Minh City, at the 1965 crash site of an F-105D Thunderchief—a *Thud*—that had impacted a dry rice field doing somewhere in the vicinity of 550 knots. The wreckage, at least all that hadn't been carted away during the war by the local villagers, was buried deep in the oily red clay, and it had taken three recovery efforts—almost ninety days' total digging time over a five-month period—to finish. They'd finally had to stop at almost twenty-two feet deep when the pumps were unable to keep the muddy ground water out and the walls were sloughing off faster than they could excavate. It was probably deep enough; they hadn't encountered any human remains or pilot-related artifacts since about fifteen feet in depth.

The team was glad to get out of the field and into Ho Chi Minh City—what most of the locals still called Saigon despite the central government's efforts to mandate the contrary. HCMC had languished in the long postwar stagnation of the trade embargo, but now, with all of the restrictions lifted, life in the city was booming. It might not have the buzz of Bangkok, yet anyhow, but Saigon was definitely a live wire, and after thirty-plus days in the field, clean beds, showers, flush toilets, restaurants, female company, and bars were welcome. The latter two didn't particularly interest Caroline, but many of the otherwise all-male team had a demonstrably different opinion on the matter. Caroline Thompson was from western Kansas and had grown up—if being five foot two qualified as growing up—hearing the colorful lore of the cattle drive. She occasionally wondered how closely her male team members resembled the cowboys at the end of the long trail.

Just like *Rawhide*.

She caught herself humming softly.

> All the things I'm missin',
> good vittles, love, and kissin',
> are waitin' at the end of my ride.

Good thing her team wasn't issued six-shooters, she often said, they'd kill each other by accident for sure.

The orders from Hawaii to conduct a recovery of an isolated burial promised to be an answer to her prayers for a constructive diversion. She was instructed to handpick the personnel from the several teams that were assembling in Saigon in preparation for redeployment to Thailand and then Hawaii. It was to be a small team, and a small site, which meant fewer headaches, and it was close enough that they could drive to it rather than helo in and out. That was a good thing. None of the team particularly relished flying in the old Russian MI-17s that the Vietnamese insisted they use—especially since one had gone down in the mountains a few years back, killing seven U.S. team members. The subsequent investigation showed the crash to be weather-related, but it still had managed to dampen the early bragging rights value of being able to say that you'd ridden on a taped-together Russian aircraft. This recovery site was drivable, and even if the exhumation did stretch out into two or three days—which she doubted given the little she knew about it—they could still spend their nights in a Saigon hotel.

The team was reduced to essentials: the medic, in case someone got snake-bit or chopped a foot off with a pick; a linguist, to handle the interview with the witnesses; and two army mortuary affairs specialists to work the screens and heft the equipment. She'd handle her own photos, and there didn't seem to be any need for an explosive ordnance disposal tech—not in a marked cemetery. The VNOSMP sent two representatives, Mr. Than Chu, the local provincial headbuster, and his assistant, a little man who never said anything but picked at his walnut-brown teeth with a sliver of bamboo constantly. And, of course, three Vietnamese drivers for the Mitsubishi SUVs that they were riding in. Americans weren't allowed to drive the vehicles—presumably because they couldn't honk the horns frequently enough.

The team left the hotel before seven, but even with the early start it took about an hour and a half to clear Ho Chi Minh City's creeping sprawl and another hour to reach Thanh Lay Hamlet in Dong Nai Province. They lost another hour and a half drinking scalding green tea and warm Coca Cola with various provincial and local officials. Bobbing heads and shaking hands and bobbing heads some more. By eleven-thirty they finally reached the cemetery.

It was small—the area enclosed by a whitewashed cement wall measured less than thirty yards in diameter—and generally well kept in spite of the occasional burst of plantain grass. It looked to be a Catholic cemetery, a vestigial reminder of the colonial French, like so many of the older ones in the south. Most of the stone markers were chipped and pitted—some by age, more by anger. More than one displayed a rosette pattern of damage indicative of mortar or rocket shrapnel.

The provincial VNOSMP representative, Than Chu, introduced Caroline Thompson to two little stick figures. They were wiry and brown and looked as if they'd been constructed from a couple of used pipe cleaners. When they smiled their teeth looked like little stumps of creosote fence posts. They were chronic betel nut chewers. She didn't catch their names but Tech Sergeant Michael O'Brien, her linguist, did, as always, and he'd written them down, along with the other required information. When he'd finished, he looked at her and nodded. It was her show now. She was the scientist.

"Okay. Well, why don't we start at the beginning, shall we? Start by thanking them for coming and agreeing to talk to us. Stress that this is a humanitarian mission. Ask them to be patient with us as we try to get a better understanding of what happened here. Tell them that we know they've answered some of these questions before, but we're going to repeat a few of them. Ask them, who's buried in this cemetery? People from this village? Several villages? Just this one? Only one person in the grave? How deep? Is he in a container or simply in the ground? Is this a primary interment or were the remains moved here from somewhere else? You know the drill, Mike. You don't need my direction."

She then took a half step back and watched O'Brien as he translated. She'd been trying to learn some Vietnamese on the weekends back in Hawaii and in the evenings in her tent in the field, but her flat Kansas accent seemed completely unsuited for mastering the rise and fall of the required tones. Her attempts always brought quick smiles and slow comprehension on the part of the locals. Now she was the one smiling at how perfectly at home O'Brien seemed with such a strange and interesting language.

Like music, she thought, *just like music.*

O'Brien bobbed his head like a quail as he listened to the men recite their answers. He made little bleating sounds of affirmation as he took down just enough notes to jog his memory. Then he turned to Caroline and paraphrased quickly, hitting only the highlights that he knew she wanted. "This is a local cemetery. Old. Been here a long time. Only people from this village are buried here. Oldest ones date to about 1952 or so. There was another cemetery located on the western edge of the village but it hasn't been used in anyone's recent memory. That one's Buddhist. This one's Catholic. Left over from the French days."

Other questions followed. More translations occurred. Back and forth. When the issue of where an American soldier might be buried was posed, the two elderly men grew animated for the first time and walked over to a burial plot near the southern lip of the cemetery. It was marked only by being unmarked. The plots in the cemetery were organized chronologically rather than by family affiliation, and started in one corner and snaked back and forth to the opposite corner. There were graves on either side of the unmarked one. The one to the left had a faded photograph of a young woman affixed to it behind a fogged glass plate. Information on the stone suggested it was that of an eighteen-year-old girl who had died on July 3, 1968. The grave on the right was that of an elderly man who had died sometime in April 1971. Between them, reasonably well tended but unmarked, was the unknown grave plot.

"Now, Mr. Loc, he's the older of the two gentlemen," O'Brien continued his translation, "he says that everyone here was relocated during the war and when they all came back to this village in early 1971, this unmarked grave was here." He nodded at the ground. "Said it had been recently dug when they got here—or so they all decided."

"Any sort of marker at the time? Anything?"

"No. They say that it was never marked. He also says . . . well, they both say, actually . . . that they personally know everyone in the village and that none of them dug this one. They've always assumed it was the grave of an American soldier."

Caroline Thompson screwed up her face. "Why's that?"

"Long story, but basically there was this soldier that was always hanging around here—after the village was abandoned, that is. People saw him meeting some ARVNs here on a regular basis. Always this same GI. But then he stopped coming and shortly after that, they found this unmarked grave. Figured it was him, that's why it's so well tended. Some of the older folks remember us kindly and feel like it's the thing to do—even if it's not . . ."

"Politically correct," Caroline completed the thought.

"You got it, Doc. That's not how they said it, but that's the idea, anyhow. They feel like it's kinda like . . . almost sorta like their duty, ya know?"

Caroline Thompson listened and nodded and then looked at Than Chu from the VNOSMP office. His spoken English was broken and often awkward, but he understood it with surprising clarity—a talent that he exploited with great effect. He'd been listening to both the witnesses and to O'Brien's translation. She smiled at him. "Yeah, I know. And if it is an American, then it's our duty to dig him up," she said.

Translations completed, the team went to work. The excavation proceeded quickly. They had brought several small hand-held screens with them, but there was little need for them. The soil was dry and sandy and dug easily. Twenty minutes of shovel work was all that was required to remove the overburden, revealing a U.S.-issued poncho liner that shredded and frayed into fibers upon being touched. Another fifteen minutes of trowel work had the poncho liner fully exposed. Wrapped up inside it were the articulated skeletal remains of a large adult male.

As she carefully lifted the skull from the grave, Caroline Thompson could see the spidery fractures of an entrance gunshot wound in the middle of the forehead.

CHAPTER 9

Over the last several years the U.S.—Socialist Republic of Vietnam Joint Forensic Reviews had become something of a formality, an exercise in the First Principle of Bureaucratic Inertia: that a procedure put in place will remain in place long after anyone involved can remember why. In the late eighties when they were started, the JFRs, as they came to be called, served a real purpose. Recovery missions for unaccounted-for U.S. servicemen back then were largely unilateral efforts by the Vietnamese, with untrained and unsupervised personnel doing the work and no U.S. eyes on the process. The result was entirely predictable; the recoveries were successful in digging up a great many things besides U.S. soldiers. Even worse, bone trading was rampant throughout the country. Bone traders duped poor Vietnamese peasants and disenfranchised middle-class southerners desperate to flee the country into buying fragments of bone under the pretext that they were the remains of missing Americans. *The Americans will give you a big home in California if you turn in some remains. You don't have any? Lucky man, you, I have some remains to sell for a modest price.* Some of the fragments were indeed those of missing Americans, especially early on in the game, but most weren't. Most were the remains of elderly Vietnamese men and women who had resided peacefully in their hamlet cemeteries until their bones became, literally, more valuable than gold. Some were the remains of dogs or pigs, and occasionally a water buffalo made a cameo appearance, still showing the cuts of a butcher's knife. It was these latter cases that gave rise to the Joint Forensic Reviews—the need to cull out the dog and the pig and the elderly Vietnamese man before they were shipped to the United States and accessioned into the Central Identification Laboratory, Hawaii. Once they had been accessioned, the thick bolus of paperwork necessary to administratively eliminate these cases from the system overwhelmed the lab's resources.

In the early days, the JFRs had seen a great deal of give-and-take. Forensic anthropologists and odontologists from the CILHI met with Vietnamese counterparts in Hanoi's Institute for Forensic Medicine several times a year to examine the suspected remains that had been confiscated by the local authorities. Each side would derive a conclusion independently about the age, race, sex—or species—and then strive to reach consensus, each side careful not to appear to be a rubber stamp for the other. Often there was negotiation, but in the end there was always consensus.

Over the years, though, the reviews had become boilerplate. Remains trading had subsided, having been driven deep underground by a Vietnamese government anxious to curry favor with the West, and the unilateral recovery efforts had given way to incredibly choreographed joint endeavors, with CILHI anthropologists leading each excavation. The result was that fewer and fewer animal remains, and very few indigenous Vietnamese skeletons, reached Hanoi for examination. But following the First Principle of Bureaucratic Inertia, the American and Vietnamese scientists still met, still drank liters of lukewarm Coca Cola and boiling-hot green tea, still smoked cloudy blue roomfuls of Marlboro cigarettes, and still nodded in mutual agreement which each other's findings. It was a bureaucratic terminal patient for which no one had been able to find the plug to pull.

Which was why this review stood out. Davis Smart had been doing these for years. He and Kel and the other lab managers usually rotated the duty and had seen the evolution; lived the evolution. The script said: drink warm Coke, blink hard to clear the sting of smoke from your eyes, nod when spoken to and smile a lot, drink green tea, sign documents. It had been the same for a decade, but today Dr. Dang Minh wasn't reading his scripted lines—at least not on the last case.

Dang Hoang Minh had been a battalion surgeon during the War of Liberation. His operating room had been almost forty feet underground amid the massive earthen tunnel complex of Cu Chi. He sometimes still smiled at the irony. His operating room had been a dirt-floored oval cavern hollowed out one wicker basket of delta clay at a time. The sides were perpetually slick with condensed breath and sweat and blood. It had been the size of a small garage and by the quivering light of fuel-oil lamps he had removed limbs and sutured wounds and even delivered babies, while forty feet overhead—almost directly overhead—American GIs sat in an air-conditioned infirmary. He'd heard that they drank cold milkshakes and had pretty blue-eyed nurses apply ointments to their jock itch. Now, at sixty-three, Senior Colonel Dang Hoang Minh—Dr. Dang whenever he had his starched white lab coat on—was the head of the Socialist Republic of Vietnam's Institute for Forensic Medicine in Hanoi.

"Well, Dr. Dang, we seem to be in agreement with everything except Case C-E-oh-three," D.S. said. He shuffled the notes in front of him so that case CE03 was on top of the stack. They'd broached a snag on it earlier and had agreed to put it at the bottom of the pile while they dealt with the other six cases. "Shall we talk about that now, or do you want to take another break?" The reality was that they hadn't been working all that long, but the Vietnamese savored their breaks like rock candy, sucking them slowly and wooling them around on the tongue until the edges softened. A break at this juncture would not be out of order if they followed the usual script.

"No, Dr. Smart, I believe we should press forward on it." Dang Minh no longer required a translator. He had been trained in Moscow and East Berlin and spoke—or so he claimed—quite passable Russian and German. And French, of course. All educated Vietnamese of his generation spoke colonial French with lazy fluency. But over the years he had slowly acquired a heavily accented English as well. The translator who accompanied the Americans was a formal diplomatic appendage whose main function was to review the typed versions of the final diplomatic transfer documents—what the Vietnamese still insisted on labeling the *Procés Verbal,* as if they carried some diplomatic import—before the joint signing.

"Very well then. Case C-E-oh-three involves a relatively complete skeleton recovered by a joint U.S. and Vietnamese team from a cemetery in Thanh Lay Hamlet, Dong Nai Province." D.S. nervously cleared his throat, paused, and glanced up at Dang Minh. The senior colonel was not looking at his papers, but staring directly at D.S. He didn't blink, but D.S. did. Several times. He cleared his throat again, a nervous habit that he'd been working unsuccessfully for the last twenty years to break. "My examination . . . ahh, our examination," he bobbed his head at Ken Shiroma, the CILHI dentist who had made the trip with him, "ahh, it shows it to be a moderately large adult male with a probable gunshot wound to the forehead."

Dang Minh nodded—though almost imperceptibly—and kept staring.

"His body was found wrapped in what appears to be a U.S.-style poncho liner. Corroded U.S. belt buckle . . ." D.S. read off his notes. ". . . jungle-boot fragments, U.S.-style pocket knife, keychain with a P-38 . . . ah . . . that's a U.S.-issued can opener . . ." He cleared his throat and again looked across the table at Dr. Dang. He looked as if he was preparing to say something, so D.S. paused.

"And yet I think he is Vietnamese and of interest not to your country, Dr. Smart. We will retain this remain here."

"Ahhh, well," he cleared his throat once more, this time intentionally, to give himself a moment more to think, then he pulled his chair closer to the table and straightened his back. "Ahhh, hmmm, I think we are in agreement that the skull shows some mongoloid characteristics. Yes, you're right about that. High, flat cheekbones, round vault, shovel-shaped central incisors—but, having said that, as you're aware, we believe this may be associated with the loss of a U.S. soldier of what we call American Indian ancestry. He'd show many of the same skeletal traits—as I'm sure you are aware."

"You refer to Master Sergeant Tenkiller. He was a Native American."

"Yes, that's right. A Native American." D.S. was a little surprised by Dang Minh's use of Tenkiller's name. Usually he knew very few background details about the cases. But then this had been one that Senior Colonel Nguyen Dich of the VNOSMP had gotten personally interested in, and Swingin' Dich had a way of making his interest everyone's interest. And yet, Senior Colonel Dang Minh was no political welterweight and was not usually influenced by others— especially Dich, whom he considered a political hack rather than a real soldier. D.S. cleared his throat once again and lowered his head slightly as if he was preparing for a collision. "That's right. Based on what the local witnesses tell us, this skeleton was found in a grave that dates to about the time of Sergeant Tenkiller's loss . . . unmarked, but the location's right—at least from what we know . . . Saigon area . . ."

"I believe this is a Vietnamese body and is of concern not to your country, no," Dang Minh repeated. If there had been any good humor in his tone the first time, there was none now.

D.S. smiled. He bounced a quick glance at Ken Shiroma, who flexed the muscles of his shoulder in a discreet shrug, as if to say, "I have no idea what's going on here." D.S. returned his attention to his Vietnamese counterpart. He spent several seconds clearing his voice this time, all the while trying to understand the dynamics of the apparent power play that he found himself in the midst of.

"Doctor Dang, with all due respect, sir, I think that this is a case that I'm going to have to insist upon. You may be correct, but the available evidence shows that this may be associated with the loss of Master Sergeant Jimmy Tenkiller, and . . . well . . . we formally request to repatriate these remains to the CILHI for analysis. This is the official U.S. position on this case. We have to err on the side of caution in a situation like this. You appreciate that."

"This is of concern not to your country."

Davis Smart looked again at Ken Shiroma for help.

"You more afraid of Kel or Dang?" Ken whispered.

"Who signs my time sheet?" D.S. whispered back. He turned back to Dang Minh. "Perhaps, sir. Still, the U.S. position is repate."

Dang Hoang Minh looked at D.S. His eyes were dark and reflected no highlights. The gristle in his jaw worked and flexed. There was a look in his features that D.S. had not seen in their decade-long working relationship. A glimpse of unscabbed hostility. Dang Minh had lost a wife, two young daughters, and a brother during the war, he himself still carried an almond-sized piece of shrapnel near his spine—or so the story was told—but he had always dealt professionally with the Americans. But now there was a look. And there was something else as well. Usually when there had been disagreement about whether remains would be returned to the United States, Dang Minh had chided the American team for wanting to burden their lab with what he thought were pig bones or the remains of old Vietnamese men and women—but he'd never shown any real opposition, never tried to stop it from happening. The look had always been more like amused resignation—like that of a teacher who has failed to lead a student to the right answer and smiles knowing that he must ultimately learn from his own mistakes. But this was different. Dang Minh clearly didn't want the remains repatriated to the United States. But he also had no choice—not when the U.S. representative made it an official request. To deny the request would be to suggest that the Vietnamese government was not being cooperative.

With a quick, definitive motion he stood up, his wooden chair screeching back on the ceramic tile floor. He rapped his paper notes on the tabletop twice to align the edges and then abruptly turned and walked from the room. "Prepare the documents," he said to the translator in Vietnamese as he disappeared through the door.

CHAPTER 10

Thanh Lay Hamlet, East of Saigon, Republic of Vietnam
SATURDAY, SEPTEMBER 12, 1970

Jimmy Lee Tenkiller was a man of modest proportions. His father had been tall and big-boned, as Choctaw men often are, but Jimmy Lee more closely reflected the physical image of his mother, a small, quiet, full-blood Cherokee whose great-great-grandfather had walked the Trail of Tears from his boyhood home in Alabama. What features Jimmy Lee did take from his father were a broad forehead covered with the thick brown leather of a childhood spent under an unclouded yellow Oklahoma sun and sharp cheekbones that arched and strained at his skin as if they'd push their way through any minute. The effect was to set his dark, blue-black eyes deeply into his face as if he was in a perpetual glower against the sun, a look that was accentuated by his mouth. His lips were meaty and well defined, and they curled unconsciously into a self-satisfied smile that the Methodist spinsters and dried-up husks of old men who'd run the Indian Boys School outside Broken Arrow, Oklahoma, had never seemed to be able to correct no matter how long the switch or how regular the application.

He was also a born runner. As a child he would sneak away from school to run the baked-clay fields of eastern Oklahoma. He would run, fast and long. He would run all day long. He would run until they caught him and made him return. And the next day, the welts still burning from the caning, he'd sneak away and run again.

When he was seventeen he ran, and they didn't catch him.

He checked his watch again. It was late. They were late again. Rolling the dice. He hated these people. Even more, he hated what he'd allowed himself to become.

He was looking forward to breaking clean. For the last fourteen months he'd been sending his brother money, buying a working share of a bait-and-tackle business near Checotah. *Couple more weeks, couple more weeks,* he thought over and over, a couple more days and he'd never have to see these sonsofbitches ever again. He looked at his watch and then at the tree line.

They were late. They usually were, and Jimmy Lee Tenkiller found himself scotching the ground like a corralled horse; resisting the urge to run. It was all bad, everywhere was bad, but meeting here in this abandoned village month after month was plain asking for trouble. The area had never been made safe, and it was getting worse by the day. If the VC didn't sniff them out, a U.S. patrol would eventually stumble onto them—and he didn't know which would be worse.

Rolling the dice.

Jimmy Lee hugged the inner rim of the village. It was abandoned, its inhabitants having been relocated to a more-secure location twenty klicks down the road. Even so, Jimmy Lee felt eyes on him. He stayed near the sagging bamboo and thatch huts, staying out of easy sight but keeping an unsettled eye on the exposed dirt common in the center. As he waited, his skin filmed over with a sticky layer of sweat that refused to evaporate in the hundred-degree heat, and he swatted constantly at the ever-present mosquitoes and biting flies. The heat he was comfortable with—it had been the same, or worse, growing up in the skillet pan of eastern Oklahoma—but he would never adjust to the mosquitoes and the flies.

He looked at his watch again and had decided to clear out when he heard the fluttery whine of the jeep. He stepped quietly behind the edge of one of the huts and peered around a support pole at the dirt road that snaked into the village.

It was them—only three of them by his count. That was common now. As the area had heated up in recent months, with more and more enemy raids, and more and more U.S. retaliations, these meetings had become considerably more hazardous to everyone's health. He seldom saw them all in one place anymore. Not all five, just two or three at a time. The minimum needed to conduct business.

The Brothers.

Jimmy Lee Tenkiller moved out from behind the hut, showing himself as the jeep rolled to a stop. General Ngo Van Thu of the Army of the Republic of Vietnam said something to the other two in clipped, efficient-sounding Vietnamese, and then he stepped out from the passenger side. Always very efficient. The driver, ARVN Colonel Pham Van Minh, remained seated, staring straight ahead, both hands gripping the wheel. He was a wide-built muscular man, too big for a common Vietnamese. He looked to be ethnically Chinese. The third man was a small, muscular Vietnamese air force major with weak eyes and an even weaker chin, Doan Minh Tuyen.

It had all started simply enough. The Brothers had wanted some specific items and didn't want bureaucracy. That's what they'd said. Jimmy Lee was the man in a position at the depot to accommodate. That's what they'd said. In the beginning it had been a case or two of cigarettes, a case or two of American hard liquor, a few electronic items such as cameras or transistor radios or stainless-steel Seiko watches shipped in from Tokyo. They always said it was gifts for loyal supporters; for hardworking, unsung enlisted Vietnamese step-ons like him. Jimmy Lee Tenkiller could sympathize with that—he'd been a step-on his whole life. He kept telling himself it was all for a good cause. It was for the hardworking drones who made the machinery turn. That it was all right. And if he made some money in the process—money to send to his brother—well, he was owed.

But then the requests began to escalate. The General Electric radios and Leica cameras gave way to weapons. A few small arms and automatics in the beginning. Some .45s and M-16s. And ammunition, of course. They said that the weapons were for protection. They said that as high-ranking South Vietnamese military officers, they needed well-armed bodyguards. Praetorian Guards.

That's what they'd said.

It was too easy back then to hunker his head into a hole, to believe them even while he didn't believe them. To go along to get along. Hell, ammunition and weapons were so plentiful in the Republic of Vietnam that they were like door prizes. But then the requests became demands—demands enforced through hinted blackmail and implied threats. And the demands got greedier, too. Medical supplies—lots of medical supplies. And more armament. Grenades gave way to rockets; rockets to small mortars.

It was after some Joes from the Twenty-fifth Infantry Division had been shredded by a bank of antipersonnel mines that he'd really begun to wonder. He'd delivered a crate of claymores to *the Brothers* a week or so earlier. He'd known their story didn't wash at the time. Bodyguards didn't need antipersonnel mines—not a whole case of them anyway. It didn't make sense. But he hunkered. He went along. And then the guys from the Twenty-fifth ID walked into a sausage grinder. It didn't wash. He'd heard they were still picking body parts out of the trees a week and a half later. All the intelligence guys said it was a fluke for the VC to capture that many claymores. An unfortunate fluke, but a fluke nonetheless.

But Jimmy Lee Tenkiller was beginning to wonder.

He was still wondering as General Ngo Thu began removing his soft calf-leather gloves as he walked around the nose of the jeep. He was a small man, even for a Vietnamese, and his hands were even smaller. They looked feminine. His shirts were always tailored and hugged his torso like a wetsuit.

"Master Sergeant Tenkiller, good day," Ngo Thu smiled. He pronounced Jimmy Lee's name as if it were Teen-KHEE-la. "I trust that you are fine this morning. I hope you have not been waiting long for us this day."

Jimmy Lee hated the general the most. The others were flunkies, but the general always left Jimmy Lee feeling as if he'd been covered with a film of motor oil. "Been waiting long enough, General. For all of us, I hope not too long. Did you see anyone on the road as you came in?" He looked past the general to the road. They were rolling the dice. His legs hummed. He wanted to run.

"No, my friend," Ngo Thu said. The dark-green lenses of his

aviator-style glasses hid his eyes, but the flicker of his thin mustache betrayed a shadow of his persistent disdain. He made a show of looking around the abandoned village. "You are always so . . . tense. You act like a gentleman with something to conceal." He looked back at Tenkiller. "Do you have something to hide, my friend?"

"You would do well to be tense, General. I believe we all have something to hide—I hope we all understand that. All of us have something to be tense about—you should remember that. I hope all of you remember that."

Ngo Van Thu continued smiling as he placed his gloves on the hood of the jeep. There was an irregular ticking sound as the engine cooled, and out of the corner of his vision, Jimmy Lee could see ripples of heat rise from the green metal. Both men paused as they took each other's meaning. Ngo Thu spoke first. "Master Sergeant Tenkiller, I believe you have some items for me. Supplies. Am I correct on this matter?"

Jimmy Lee was not entirely sure how to answer. His plan had been to bury his head once more and deliver the goods one last time. Soon he'd be long gone and far away. All he had to do was buy a couple of weeks. But as he looked at the general, he noticed something for the first time. Always before he'd concentrated on trying to see beyond the dark lenses of Ngo Thu's sunglasses, to see where his eyes were focused, what they revealed. This time he didn't look beyond the glass. This time he noticed the reflection in the lenses, and he didn't like what he saw.

He saw himself.

It was a galvanizing moment in his life, and he suddenly realized that he had his answer.

"I'm afraid there's a problem, General," he said. "I don't have the items, and I'm not sure when I can get them . . . if ever. I think we've pushed the system about as far as we dare."

The general stiffened visibly. He said nothing for what seemed a long time. "I see," he finally replied. "And what, Sergeant Tenkiller, would this problem be?"

Jimmy Lee Tenkiller adjusted his stance so that his weight was balanced over both feet. He crossed his arms. "Maybe a number of things, General. Does it really matter?"

"Yes, my sergeant. I believe to me this does matter. My . . . colleagues . . . my comrades . . . are quite in need of these items. They are expecting them. If it is a matter of money, perhaps we may negotiate these things."

"It's not a matter of money. I think you understand. You and your associates won't be getting any more items from me. Not from me or anyone else at my depot."

Ngo Thu had taken Jimmy Lee's measure long before. He hadn't risen through the Byzantine world of South Vietnamese politics without acquiring the ability to probe a man's mind and feel for the softest spot. "Ahh," he said as he reached out and began pulling on his gloves, "I see. That is too unfortunate, I believe. Do you not agree?" He slowly walked over to the driver's side of the jeep. "Do you not? Master sergeant?"

Jimmy Lee Tenkiller didn't answer.

"Yes . . . I think so. I think it is too unfortunate." Ngo Thu held a gloved hand palm up in front of Colonel Pham Minh, still sitting quietly behind the wheel. "Colonel—the pistol, please," he said in English.

Pham Minh looked up at the general for the first time. He seemed to hesitate momentarily before withdrawing a U.S.-issued Colt .45 from between the seats and placing it into the general's hand.

Ngo Thu fisted the automatic, adjusting his grip, squeezing and relaxing. Feeling its weight and balance and power. With his left hand he worked the slide, chambering one of the fat, brass rounds, and clicking off the safety. "Recognize this pistol, Master Sergeant Tenkiller? No? I believe it is an item you obtained for us . . . is it not? Ahh, but you have obtained so many of these things that I think you may not remember."

Jimmy Lee's eyes briefly went to the pistol and then back to Ngo Thu's face. It had been one of the first items he'd supplied to the general.

"It is a curious fact about Americans, Master Sergeant, a most curious fact, that you are a most talkative people. Americans talk like many chickens. Yes. You cluck like so many chickens, yet you do not have an answer for me now when I am asking you a question. Do you not find this curious?"

It happened so quickly it hardly registered in Jimmy Lee Tenkiller's mind. The general's hand rose in one smooth, fluid movement. Jimmy Lee reached for the general's arm. His mouth opened to scream but produced no sound. The cold muzzle of the Colt .45 made contact with skin.

Jimmy Lee Tenkiller closed his eyes involuntarily.

The general fired a single round. And then he smiled.

CHAPTER 11

Hickam Air Force Base, Hawaii
THURSDAY, FEBRUARY 28, 2008

It had rained overnight and the dark tarmac was puddled irregularly. The trade winds had gusted up since sunrise and dried up most of the water, but in the shallow dips and swales of the taxiway apron, water was still standing, reflecting the soft clear blue of the midmorning Hawaiian sky. Robert Dean McKelvey stood on the grass yard to the side of the Hickam Air Force Base Operations building, shifting from one foot to another, listening to the flags snap in the breeze, anxious to get on with the day. It was already ten-fifteen, and the ceremony hadn't begun. There was a lot yet to get done, and the day wasn't waiting for him.

He wasn't alone. There was a good turnout for the repatriation ceremony. There usually was, but for some reason today's attendance was beter than most. The usual representatives from the Central Identification Laboratory were there; the military in a vague, organic formation yet to be called into order; the civilians clumped into two or three clusters depending on which section of the organization they worked in. There were the old vets there as well, in their salted beards and ripe bellies and worn leather motorcycle jackets with numerous unit and POW/MIA patches. The press was milling about, not as many as had once shown up, as repatriations and identifications were too frequent these days to warrant more than filler status on the local news, but some were there with their cameras and microphones and spiral-topped notebooks. Fortunately, Botch-It was nowhere in sight, but Les Neep was standing near the corner of the Operations building talking with a tall, angular vice admiral whom Kel didn't recognize but knew he should. Les had a nose for seeking out rank.

At ten-twenty-five someone, somewhere out of Kel's sight, gave the appropriate signal, and the droop-winged Air Mobility Command C-17 taxied to its assigned spot seventy-five yards from the front of the Base Operations building. The engines throttled down as the plane braked to a stop and began its long, whining shutdown. There was a brief pause, and then an army major in blue dress uniform and white gloves called the honor guard and the spectators to attention, and three dark-blue buses slowly filed out onto the apron. Each would carry remains to the lab.

Davis Smart quietly took up a place at Kel's right elbow as the ramp of the huge sky-gray plane began to hum and lower. The repat bird had actually landed two hours earlier and had parked discreetly at the margin of the black tarmac out of sight from Base Ops. D.S. and the other passengers—Ken Shiroma, the dentist, and members of the Joint Forensic Review team and the military escort that had flown over to Hanoi to receive the remains—had been able to unload their luggage and clear immigration and customs. Often they would go straight home to begin unraveling their jet lag. It was a two-day flight from Hanoi, if you counted the short overnight stay at Anderson Air Force Base in Guam that was required for crew rest, and that amount of time in the red, webbed cargo seating of the C-17 could seriously interfere with your beauty rest—not to mention REM sleep. For that reason alone, Kel was surprised to see D.S. fall in for the ceremony. Ordinarily he'd be home sleeping by this point.

The first of four honor guards—one navy, one marine, and two army—were slowly lock-stepping up the ramp at the rear of the aircraft. Kel, locked at attention, glanced out of the corner of his eye, acknowledging the arrival of his deputy.

"Just in time," Kel whispered. "Welcome back."

"Thanks. How's it here?"

"Haven't killed myself or anyone else. Yet. Though I'm startin' to see the wisdom of makin' people wait a week to buy a handgun."

"Glad to hear it. I assume that the commander's being his usual thick-brained self."

"Too nice a day to get me talkin' about that prick—so don't."

"Bad?"

"Bad. It's official. Not only is Colonel Botch-It not leavin' early, the sonofabitch is extendin' for another year."

"Crap."

"Crap is right. I said don't get me started."

"You got it. Crap."

"We get Tenkiller?" Kel asked after a pause.

"Maybe," D.S. whispered. "Won't know until we get it into the lab."

They watched in silence as the honor guard slowly emerged from the back of the plane carrying a flag-draped aluminum transfer case. It took precisely one minute and fifteen seconds to traverse the distance from the plane ramp to the rear door of the waiting blue bus. Another forty-five seconds to secure the door and salute the bus. The Joint Forensic Review had resulted in three cases' being repatriated. They watched the procedure repeated three times in silence.

When the last of the transfer cases was loaded, the buses departed and the honor guard stood down. The crowd dispersed slowly, knots of people talking and shaking hands.

"You don't sound so sure. About it bein' Tenkiller." Kel resumed the conversation as they walked across the headquarters' lawn to his car.

"I dunno. I'm optimistic, but I've just got that feeling. You know when you get that feeling? Guess it doesn't look quite right. It certainly isn't textbook Vietnamese, that's for sure, but I can't say that it really looks American Indian either. Plus, teeth are in poor shape."

"Accordin' to the records, Tenkiller had a pretty hard childhood.

Indian boarding school, runaway . . . I doubt he had the best dental care."

"Until he got into the army, anyhow."

"Even then," Kel said as he pulled out of the parking lot. "Goin' to the lab or do you want to go home? I can give you a lift and we can talk on the way."

"Lab first," D.S. replied. "At least for a little while. I want to hear your opinion when you see the case."

Kel turned left past the Pacific Air Force headquarters building. The CILHI is located almost at the southern edge of the base in an area known historically as Fort Kamehameha—Fort Kam—and it required driving almost the length and breadth of the base. He glanced over at D.S. "About the dentition. What I was sayin' is that Tenkiller didn't make master sergeant at age thirty-somethin' by not knowin' how to work the system, and he wouldn't be the first kid from the country who managed to elude dental call." He paused. "So, explain this 'feeling' of yours."

"Just a feeling," D.S. replied. "Everything says it should be Tenkiller, right?"

"Right."

"Right. But you know what's weird? I mean as in just plain friggin' weird? Your good buddy, Doctor Dang, really didn't want these remains—Tenkiller's, I mean—or not-Tenkiller's—to get repated. I mean, he did not want to let them go."

"How do you know?"

"Oh, hints here and there. When you know him as well as I do, you can pick up on subtlety. Subliminal clues and all."

"Like?"

"Like—'I don't want you to repate these remains, Running Pig Dog—things like that," D.S. answered.

"You're right. Subtlety like that would sail clean over my head. I haven't heard Pig Dog in a while."

"Yeah, he kept saying they were Vietnamese remains and that we didn't want them."

"D'you and Ken explain that Tenkiller was Indian?"

"Of course, but he didn't want to hear it. I can't remember him ever being so adamant about a case before."

"I don't recall him ever tryin' to stop somethin' from comin' back before, " Kel agreed. They waited silently a few minutes until the slow-moving bus caravan carrying the remains arrived in the CILHI's rear parking lot, and then Kel killed the engine and looked hard at D.S. "Any idea why?"

"Not a clue, Kel, not a goddamn clue."

CHAPTER 12

Arlington National Cemetery, Washington, D.C.
SUNDAY, JUNE 28, 1970

It was cool for so late in June. Not uncomfortably so, but noticeably so, at least if you were familiar with District weather in the early summer. Noticeably so if your mind was free to wander down loosely worn memories and focus on the pleasantries of the day.

Penny Kendrick's mind wasn't. There was nothing pleasant about the day.

The walk from the Fort Myer Old Post Chapel was short but interminable, made more so by the practiced formality of the Old Guard's measured lockstep; the synchronized metallic clicks of polished shoes sharp against the quiet grumble of the hushed procession following behind. The six dark horses snorted quietly, and the wheels of the glossy black, flag-draped caisson creaked and eased like an old rocking chair devoid of comfort. It had rained earlier and the asphalt was still moist and puddled, and the drying rays of the morning sun brought out the pleasant smell of the clipped, bright-green grass and new growth. In the trees banking the road the birds were chattering and tweaking their enthusiastic curiosity. In the distance, high school students and other cemetery visitors could be seen walking in little clots or running along happily, oblivious to the parade of raw sorrow slowing making its way to an open plot of earth. It was a scene played out all too frequently of late.

First Lieutenant Patrick Kendrick had left his parents' home in Lexington, South Carolina, in November, 233 days earlier, bound for the Republic of Vietnam. It had been early on a cloudy morning and although Penny had been awake to see him off, they had decided not to rouse the children. They were too young to really understand, and Lieutenant Kendrick had instead quietly stood by their bedsides and stroked their fine wheat-blond hair and looked carefully at their sleeping profiles, intent upon memorizing their features against the inevitable fading that he knew would come, and then he had left. One year's tour of duty. One year with the Twenty-fifth Infantry Division. One year to get his ticket punched and then home to his family and his promising career.

He'd arrived at Cu Chi in South Vietnam eight days later. His assignment was to take command of a rifle platoon whose lieutenant had been injured and returned stateside. It had been a tough assignment; the men were well-tempered and weathered with the cynical grit of months of combat, and he was so very fresh. To make matters harder, he'd found himself stepping into the sizable boots of a man who had been not only admired but also loved by the men; they trusted their former leader with their lives in a way that Lieutenant Kendrick doubted that he could ever realize.

But he'd been wrong. The men had come to respect him over the short months that he'd led them and to trust him. They respected his honesty; they respected his awareness of his limitations and his unabashed willingness to listen to them. He was a natural leader who knew when and how to follow, and in turn, they trusted him and followed him.

As it turned out, they'd followed him to their deaths.

Sixteen men dead. Lieutenant Kendrick one of the first to fall.

Penny Kendrick didn't know all the details. Some nice men in starched khaki uniforms and gold-braided saucer caps had visited her on a clear Sunday morning and said some nice things about duty and honor and courage and how proud she should be and how grateful the country was. They probably had provided some of the details of his death as well, but she hadn't heard them. She'd tuned them to a low murmur, and all the while that they'd talked, she'd focused her attention on a photograph of Patrick that she kept in the living room, trying to memorize his features against the inevitable fading that she knew would occur.

She was thinking again of the photograph when she felt something brush against her hip, tugging at her hand, pulling her back to the here and now; it was her oldest, three-year-old Michael, looking about in great wonder at the men in their crisp blue uniforms and the magnificent chestnut-brown horses that pawed and snorted and rattled their harnesses. She reached out and cupped her hand on the nape of his neck and pulled his small body tightly in against her leg. Two-year-old Meredith, thumb in mouth, blue blanket draped over her shoulder, was firmly tethered by her free hand to Penny's skirt, going nowhere.

The ceremony was short and punctual, honed fine by what had become daily repetition—the horses impatiently scotching the asphalt, the honor guard carrying the casket with precise efficiency, Taps echoing off the thousands of otherwise mute white markers, the sharp crack of rifles, the folding of the flag, the soul-rending words *On behalf of a grateful nation and the United States Army* . . . Even Penny Kendrick moved mechanically—this was her third funeral in two days.

Sergeant First Class Tommy Amaker and Specialist-Five Leslie Scott had been buried the day before, one hour and six minutes apart. Tommy had been first. Penny hadn't known either man, though she'd come to feel as if she had. Patrick had credited Tommy with saving his life on more than one occasion. Leslie, Patrick had discovered, had played against him in the South Carolina state high school basketball semifinals eight years earlier, and Patrick mentioned him often enough in his letters that she felt connected. Now, all three men were dead, along with thirteen others. Sixteen men in all, scythed down like sun-dried millet.

As the ceremony drew to a close, Penny's eyes began to work the faces of the assembled well-wishers. There was family present, both Patrick's and hers, and a good show of friends, some old and some more recently minted, and there were various military officers in flat dress caps and loops of braid and colorful bands of ribbons, some attending out of respect, others out of official perfunctoriness. She thought again of the photograph in her living room, the one of Patrick smiling, almost beaming, holding one-month-old Michael. She thought of Tommy Amaker's young wife, whom she'd met the day before. Six months pregnant. She thought of her children's wide-eyed wonder at the guns and bugles and magnificent horses and deliberate, synchronized commotion. But mostly she thought of fate and happenstance and why it had been her Patrick who had drawn the short straw. She thought of another officer whom she'd never met; the one Patrick had told her about; the one he'd replaced; the one who'd been careless and gotten himself injured; the one who'd gotten a trip back home to his family while her Patrick had returned home in an aluminum box. She thought of the sealed casket that they wouldn't even allow her to open; she thought of how they told her it was best to not remember him that way. The hate began to build and throb, and she felt her face flush and had to swallow the knot in her throat—to force it down.

Well-wishers began filing past her, squeezing her hand gently and mumbling something and patting her children on their heads. She searched each set of eyes for an answer, for something that would make sense of it all, for something that would make her whole again, but found nothing. Finally she gave up and stared at the one thing that she did understand—the yawning maw of a newly excavated grave—and that's when she saw him, out of the corner of her eye, a thin, copper-headed soldier, cap in hand, standing alone, a few feet from the coffin, staring intently at something only he could see.

She had never met him, but she recognized him somehow. It was him, she knew it; somehow she knew it; he was the one who'd been careless, the one who'd come home, the one who'd grow old watching his children, while her Patrick would slowly fade from memory and thought, his image growing fainter with each broken breath that she took.

It's better that you don't remember him that way.

She felt her face flush again but was unable to swallow away the knot in her throat.

CHAPTER 13

U.S. Army Central Identification Laboratory, Hawaii
THURSDAY, FEBRUARY 28, 2008

Kel stood at the far end of the lab, arms crossed, watching through the thick glass that separated the offices from the analysis tables. His lab coat was soiled and wrinkled and resembled a cheap motel sheet. His hair had a perpetual messiness that had once looked boyish but now bespoke exhaustion. Still, his eyes were keen as he watched the cases containing the skeletal remains being off-loaded from the buses and brought into the lab. Usually the double rear doors that opened into the lab's receiving area were kept closed for security reasons. There were two occasions when they were opened: repatriations and departures. There had been a time, Kel could recall, that repatriations from Vietnam numbered ten, twelve, fourteen transfer cases at a time. It was an ironic testament to the lab's success that the numbers were dwindling; with fewer men still unaccounted for, fewer were left to be found.

Most of the scientific staff knew to stay clear. The evidence-receiving area in the main examination room wasn't very large, not much more than an open space amid the twenty or so work tables, and even the few individuals who were required to be there to accession-in the remains filled it to the point of near inefficiency. The evidence manager was there, along with a photographer, a couple of people to help open the transfer cases, and someone to fill out the arrival paperwork, but the rest of the staff either went about their normal work on the fringe or clotted together at the far end of the lab floor to watch the remains being accessioned.

The first transfer case was slowly lifted down from the rear of the bus by three army sergeants and a Marine Corps gunnery sergeant. All were dressed in their Class-B uniforms, and they wore white gloves. An American flag, its corners discreetly taped to hold the fold against any disrespectful breeze that might have an occasion to disrupt the solemnity, covered the long, rectangular aluminum case. The honor guard slowly rotated the transfer case so that the foot end crossed the threshold first. It was the time-honored tradition of the military that the foot should always enter first—whether it was the C-17, the bus, or the back of the lab.

Once inside the main exam room, the case was settled onto two low stands that stood twelve inches off the floor. They were made of lengths of two-inch metal pipe welded together and painted silver to match the color of the aluminum transfer cases. Two of the sergeants flipped up the ends of the flag, freeing the folds from the tape, and removed it. They then stepped back outside while the next bus exchanged places with the first.

Gretchen Lee, the lab's evidence manager, had been standing to the side, impatiently thumbing a sheaf of brown folders containing the accessioning documents. With the military escorts out of the way, she moved to the end of the transfer case and inspected the numbered aluminum car seal fastened to one of the butterfly compression latches. She checked the embossed numbers against the ones written on the copy of the chain of custody document that D.S. had hand-carried back from Hanoi. Satisfied that they matched, she motioned for the photographer to document the condition of the seal before she broke it.

"Can you see the number?" D.S. asked as he walked up beside Kel. Jet lag was about to catch up with him, and he was running on fumes.

Kel raised slightly on his toes, trying to get a better angle on what was happening at the far end of the lab. Gretchen and another member of the staff were raising the lid from the transfer case and a light-brown wooden box was visible, lashed tightly in the center of the base with strips of white nylon webbing. The end of the box bore a rectangular piece of paper on which the Vietnamese had written a number with a large-tipped felt pen. The number bore no relationship to the case but merely assisted their customs officials in the departure ceremony at Noi Bai airport in Hanoi.

"Looks like box number two," Kel finally said.

"That's the one," D.S. answered.

"Now if we can just prove it's Tenkiller."

"Might be easier said than done." D.S. spoke over his shoulder as he pressed his lab ID against the door sensor. The sensor beeped, and a soft metallic click indicated that the door had unlocked. He walked through while Kel scanned his badge across the sensor and followed.

"I was lookin' at Tenkiller's file last night," Kel retrieved the conversation on the other side of the glass. "Not much in it. Like I said earlier, it seems he didn't like visitin' the dentist."

"That may be a problem. This guy's got a fair amount of dental work, pretty poor dental work, maybe, but a fair amount of it. If that's your guy Tenkiller, then he'd have had to have had a lot of undocumented treatment. A whole lot. Still . . ."

"Still . . . he could. I just read the search-and-recovery report. Caroline seemed to think that the circumstantial evidence for its being our guy was good. Is good."

"Maybe," D.S. said. Gretchen Lee had opened the wooden box and photographed the contents before moving on to another table and another case, and the two men were able to examine the remains. They both snapped on latex gloves to guard against contaminating the remains with their DNA. "Here, take a look at this," D.S. enthused. "What do you think of that? Gorgeous, isn't it?" He picked the cranium up gently from the examination table and turned it so the gunshot wound was facing Kel. D.S. was the sort whose pure enthusiasm for his work sometimes bordered on the childlike, and he could routinely use words like *gorgeous* and *beautiful* when describing gunshot wounds and compound fractures with absolutely no sense of incongruity.

"That is nice—for a gunshot wound. How about an exit? Or was it a one-way ticket?"

D.S. rotated the skull slowly. Toward the back there was an irregular hole the size of a small fist with spidery radial cracks running in all directions.

"Ouch," Kel said. He reached for the skull.

"Careful. It's not all that stable."

"Neither am I."

"Yeah, but you're replaceable."

"Jet lag's showin'."

"Just be careful, will you?" D.S. gingerly handed over the skull.

"Got it. Single shot. Am I right? Anythin' postcranial?"

"Not that I saw. Nothing that shows up under a quick analysis anyhow."

Kel held the skull at arm's length to better take in its overall shape. It was large and round, with a high vault. The forehead was wide and high and the cheekbones were sharp and projected forward. The muscle markings were prominent. "Actually . . ." he said slowly, drawing the word out as he continued formulating his thought.

"Please don't say anything about 'poor Yorick.'"

"I won't."

"Yes you will. You always do."

Kel ignored him. "Don't know about you, but . . . in some respects this looks very Indian. I saw a fair number of skulls very similar to this when I was doin' archaeology in Missouri and Arkansas. Not exactly the same, but . . ."

"Yeah, I know," D.S. agreed. "But look at the teeth and palate."

Kel placed his outspread hand on top of the skull and slowly inverted it so that the base and palate were visible.

"That doesn't look American Indian to me," D.S. said. "Do you think?"

"Naw. I think you're right about that. Too narrow to be Indian. I think Tenkiller was full-blooded. I know he was Cherokee on his mother's side . . . I don't think the record says what his father was. Maybe he wasn't full Indian, although with a last name like Tenkiller . . ."

"Maybe," D.S. agreed. "But whatever he was, I doubt he was Vietnamese either."

Kel smiled in agreement. He slowly set the skull down on a cork flask ring on the table. The ring would provide some cushion and also discourage the skull from rolling off when no one was watching. He stripped off his gloves and dusted his hands on his lab coat. "We'll have to wait and see what the dentists say. Tenkiller has one set of bitewing x-rays in his folder. They're dated almost ten years before his death, but they should still be able to work with them. In the meantime, tell me more about Dr. Dang. Why do you think he didn't want this skeleton comin' back?"

"I don't know. I really don't know. But I'm serious as a heart attack—he did not want this guy repatriated."

"That just isn't like him. Doesn't figure to me."

"Me either. But he didn't want this one coming back."

"So what d'you think? Should we look into it? I mean, does it matter to us?"

"Who knows?" D.S. shrugged. "How would you look into it anyway? Dang's sure not talking, and I don't know who else would know."

"Hmmmm." Kel made a sound of agreement as he looked down again at the skull. "What I do know, though, is that sure is some hole in his head."

"Yeah, isn't it?" D.S. grinned. "Absolutely gorgeous."

CHAPTER 14

Fort Campbell, Kentucky
SATURDAY, APRIL 5, 2008

Sergeant Roscoe Charles was off duty and bored. He knew he was bucking the stereotype; young, unmarried soldiers were supposed to live for lost, drunken weekends filled with galloping carnality and requited want, but as a twenty-six-year-old bachelor who'd enlisted in the blood-pumping frenzy that followed 9/11, he was finding the weekends harder and harder to take. Certainly in college and even early on in his military career he had been known to have lost more than a few weekends to cheap beer and overly expensive women, but not lately. At least the weather today was conducive to getting outside and breathing. He'd watched every last video on post, and most of the ones off post as well, and was desperate to do something else.

It had been a hard winter up until a few days ago when it had moderated and hinted at an emergent spring, but last night's *Doppler-Five-Week-Ahead* forecast didn't look promising, and this was maybe the last real get-the-hell-outside weekend for a while. A cookout seemed like the ticket. There were at least a good dozen or so other single guys—not to mention a few geographical bachelors who he knew would come. Plus there were a few of the younger married guys who would be game. All totaled up, that meant girlfriends and young wives—all anxious to wear shorts and tank tops for the first time since well before Thanksgiving. Anxious to show their stuff despite the weather. Combine that with enough beer and barbecue and that added up to a better time than cable television promised.

Charles was pulling this together on such short notice that an on-post location would be an easier sell. Less driving also minimized the chance of a DUI.

Sergeant Charles pulled his Acura into the parking lot at one of the small recreational areas on post. It was an acceptable spot. There was no one at the picnic tables, but then it was also only nine-thirty in the morning. Even so, so far, so good.

The only other car was a bronze-colored Buick Park Avenue sitting at the edge of the lot; the passenger-side wheels off the gravel and into the dormant brown grass. No one appeared to be in it, and Charles figured that the occupants probably were out jogging or something. Besides, one car a crowd did not make—unless they hung around. The problem was that a car like that smelled of an officer—a senior officer at that, since a junior officer would have something more sporty— and senior officer smelled of no fun. Watch the language, watch the drinking, watch the hitting on women. Watch the fun.

Charles was about to put the car back into gear and recon another area on down the road when he thought again. The trouble was that it was already getting late in the morning and if he was going to make this happen, he needed to get on his cell and get the ball rolling. The days were still short and the drinks needed a lot of ice. He sat and thought.

He looked again at the Park Avenue.

"Easy enough to find out if it's an officer," he said out loud as he turned off his ignition and opened his car door. No one was in the Park Avenue, and no one was at the picnic tables, or jogging in sight. An officer would have a blue post-access sticker on the center of the windshield. If it were a colonel or general he'd have a rank insignia on there as well, and if that were the case, he'd definitely move on down the road.

He stretched, yawned, and then walked over to the other car.

It was a nice-looking vehicle. Waxed and nicely detailed. He peered in the front window.

That's when he saw the blood.

A large pool of thickened, ropey blood.

But it was the body that he'd recall for the rest of his life. It was that of a small man, curled up on his side on the front seat. All the skin from the top of his head was missing, and Roscoe Charles saw shiny, glistening, brown bone where the man's hair should have been.

CHAPTER 15

Fort Campbell, Kentucky
SATURDAY, APRIL 5, 2008

Chief Warrant Officer Shuck Deveroux had just removed his card from the credit union ATM when his cell phone rang. He had the day off and had made up his mind to spend some time with his two young boys. With all the traveling he'd been doing recently, and the overtime he'd been spending in the office to make up for it, he'd missed a lot when it came to his family—birthdays, soccer games, science fairs—too much, really, and starting today he was going to make it up to them. The Op-order called for a fast breakfast of powdered doughnuts and twenty-ounce Coca Colas, an hour or so drive to downtown Memphis, and a long, pleasant, starry-skied evening with his boys at AutoZone Field watching the Memphis Redbirds play the Albuquerque Isotopes. The boys were in the truck waiting, patiently if not quietly. One quick stop at the ATM and then on into the city for some minor league ball.

And then the phone rang. His sons had obviously been playing with it again, changing the settings, because it didn't really ring, instead it loudly played the first stanza of "Yankee Doodle Dandy." Last week it had been "Pomp and Circumstance," the week before, "Jingle Bells."

Shuck Deveroux was forty-six years old. He'd been born Thomas

Edward Lafayette Deveroux on a rainy February Monday morning in the map-speck of Eudora, Arkansas. The name Shuck had been a tail pinned on the donkey when he got to Mississippi State at Starkville. Highly touted All-American candidates for halfback needed names like Crash or Crunch or Boomer, and the university public affairs office had tried potting several names early on, usually with some alliterative satanic theme—Devil-Ray being the one they pushed the hardest—but none had taken serious root. As with many life-altering events, the solution happened in the blink of the eye. In the last home game of his sophomore year, a 320-pound sack of charging wet cement from Athens, Georgia, by the name of Cecil Eudus Dupree met Devil-Ray head-on in the seam. The collision had snapped both of Deveroux's collarbones in two. As they were carrying him off the field on a stretcher, the coach was purported to have told him that he was going to miss the rest of the game, to which, so the story had it, Deveroux had gritted his teeth and replied, "Aw shucks, Coach." The unlacquered truth was that Deveroux had always seriously doubted that that was what he'd really said. It just didn't ring true. Methodist upbringing or not, it had hurt like screaming hell—he remembered that much—and "Aw Shucks" simply didn't seem as if it would have done the situation fair and adequate justice. But it printed well in the newspapers, and the story of the gentleman giant had stuck.

Now at forty-six years of age, "Aw Shucks" Deveroux was listening intently to the lure of retirement. The "New" Army had way too much "New" and way too little "Army" for him. Quotas and sensitivity sessions and an Army of One. Lord God. Better to get out while he could, that was the operational plan for the day. He figured he was still marketable. He was tall and still able to shrug off the accumulating kinks and stand up straight—at least for most of the day; he was still a solid pick-handle wide at the shoulders and capable of casting an imposing shadow. He was healthy, despite knees that barked their concerns at him in the mornings, but more important, there remained enough kin at home in Chicot County to make a serious run at the sheriff's job.

The phone rang again.

Deveroux had thought twice about leaving the phone at home,

buried under some socks in a dresser drawer. He could always claim he'd forgotten it. After all, he'd cleared this leave two weeks earlier. But in the end, his bone bred sense of duty and guilt had held sway, and he'd clipped it on his belt, knowing full well the consequences. He muttered out loud as he unsnapped it from the holder on his right hip and flipped it open.

"Yup, Deveroux," he said. The tiny color LCD screen showed it was the office number.

"Shuck . . . hey, buddy, sorry to bother you on your day off, but something's kinda come up." Mark Abbott, another one of the CID agents, was covering the office today. His tone suggested that he probably did in fact feel sorry for the call.

"Well now, Mark, what part of that 'kinda' has come up? The kinda as in y'all can kinda handle it without me, or the kinda as in it can really, really kinda wait for Monday mornin'? Or maybe the kinda . . ."

"The kinda as in you'd better get your ass over to the park—the one just past the commissary. PDQ."

"Aw, Jesus, bubba . . . now just how serious could it be? You *kinda* got the desk today, remember?" He shot a quick look at his boys wrestling in the cab of his pickup. The whole truck was rocking, and he could hear their laughter through the glass as one of them went down in a headlock.

"Serious enough, Shuck. I ain't shittin' you, man, get your hillbilly ass over there. And get it over there quick. You read me, buddy?"

"I hear ya," Deveroux replied. He was still looking at his truck parked twenty feet away, at the flurry of feet and elbows. His boys would understand. They always did. They'd understand a lot better than their mother would. He sighed and started walking toward his vehicle. "Be there in fifteen—got to drop the boys off at home—I'm assumin' from your tone I shouldn't take 'em with me."

"Affirmative. It's some big-time ugly, I hear. That's all I can say."

"Who pulled my dance card on this one?"

"The top. The provost marshal called. Says General Anderson passed on the word to assign you by name, and you know he don't usually meddle in CID business."

"Lucky me," Deveroux said as he opened the driver's door of his pickup. "On my way, Mark. Out here." He closed his cell phone as he climbed into the front seat and keyed the ignition. Only then did he turn to look at his sons. They'd settled themselves and were sitting quietly; their expressions conveyed more of an understanding of duty and service and sacrifice than most of the New Army soldiers he knew. He reached over and pulled the bill down on his youngest's cap until it covered his eyes, and then waited for his son to right it before speaking.

"Gentlemen . . . it seems somethin' has done come up."

CHAPTER 16

Fort Campbell, Kentucky
SATURDAY, APRIL 5, 2008

The park resembled a college tailgate party without the organization. There were cars and trucks parked at every available angle, and where there weren't vehicles there were little clots of MPs and onlookers who seemed intent upon making sure the grass was well trampled down.

Shuck Deveroux parked a couple of hundred meters away from the largest group, which seemed to be clustered around a late-model Buick. Whatever was there, it was attracting quite a knot of active attention.

A young MP wearing sunglasses and an attitude directed Deveroux to halt as he crossed the parched grass on his way to the Buick. The inverted teardrop on his collar indicated that he was a specialist—a spec-four. Being challenged was actually a good sign, Deveroux realized; at least there was some access control being exercised, though obviously not much. Deveroux was in washed-out jeans, a white cotton shirt, and paint-stained Chuck Taylor high-tops, and he certainly didn't look as if he had any business there other than feeding his curiosity as everyone else seemed to be doing. He pushed the faded-maroon Mississippi State Bulldogs hat up on his forehead to expose more of his face as he worked his badge out of his hip pocket. He also took off his sunglasses as he flipped open the badge and held it up for the young soldier to see.

"Chief Deveroux, CID—who's got control of this scene?" he asked the boy as he walked by, not slackening his stride.

"Sorry, Chief . . . ahh . . . I guess you do, sir."

"Good answer, son, but I meant, before I got here."

"That would be Lieutenant Walters."

"And where might I find the good lieutenant?"

"Ahh, I think he's over by the car up there. The one with everyone around it," the MP answered.

"Carry on, son," Deveroux tossed the response back over his left shoulder. *Stupid question. Why shouldn't he be over by the Buick—it looks like the rest of the post is,* he said to himself.

Deveroux knew who First Lieutenant Walters was, though he could never remember his first name. *Numb-nuts* was all that came to mind when he thought of him. He was an ugly little northerner possessed of more of a potbelly and more of a concept of self-importance than was becoming in a man of such extremely limited potential. They'd first crossed attitudes when Walters was still a butter-bar second lieutenant, and they'd met unpleasantly on several occasions since then. He was the sort of person that you found yourself wanting to whack on the side of the head with a rolled-up newspaper whenever you looked at him, and Deveroux was not in a particularly patient mood this morning. Especially as he neared the front of the Buick, and saw that the lieutenant was addressing a large group of spectators as if he were holding a come-to-Jesus revival. His arms were waving grandly and his voice was a bellow. Deveroux shouldered his way through and came up beside the red-faced Walters.

"Good day for a garage sale, ain't that right, Lieutenant?" he stated it rather than asked it; his voice had a staged good humor, but his eyes were intent upon the faces of the assembled crowd, assessing their eyes, and not on Walters. He was coming in behind the curve on this one and needed to size up the situation quickly.

"Say again . . . ahh . . . oh yes, why I believe it's Warrant Officer . . ." Lieutenant Walters turned to face Deveroux; his piggy little eyes creased partway shut and perspiration began to bead up on his nose as if on a glass of iced tea. The recognition apparently was mutual, but he dragged out the last syllable dramatically as if he were struggling with the lapsed recognition of something unimportant to him.

"Deveroux . . . Chief Warrant Officer Five Deveroux . . . CID. And I said—*sir*—that it looks to be a good day for a garage sale. I can only assume that's what you got goin' on, given this here big crowd and all—either that or a charity fish fry."

"Chief Deveroux," Walters said, making an obvious show of inspecting his less-than-formal dress. "I assume you're not on duty—you seem best attired to wash cars this afternoon."

"Yes, sir, I reckon you're about right on that—would be a good day for that, but then what can you do when the commandin' general calls you up on your cell phone and all. Seems like he wants me to sort of mop up here. And I have to admit, my job should be easy now that you've managed to assemble every possible suspect in a five-county area." Deveroux would have paid money for a rolled-up newspaper right at this moment.

"Now listen here, Warrant Officer . . ."

Deveroux bristled so quickly that Walters was forced back a half step. "No, *you* listen here—Lieutenant—sir," he said quietly but directly, turning so that his back was to the crowd. "First of all, it's chief warrant officer, and second, this is my scene now—compromised all to livin' Jesus though it may be. Got it? When I said mop up, I meant it; mop up as in clean up a mess." He paused and turned and rose on the balls of his feet to better see over the crowd. "And here's what I need from you—Lieutenant. See that intersection over there?" He paused to give the lieutenant a chance to respond. When he didn't, Deveroux continued. "Good. I think we need some traffic control—now, I recommend that you get directin' that traffic before I forget the Universal Code of Military Justice and do somethin' we'll both regret when the swellin' goes down. I'll let you know when to quit, or when I need you to do somethin' more productive. Until then, if you got questions, I got a cell phone, and we can call the provost marshal—even better, I've got the general's private line—we can call him directly and he can answer all your questions. We clear?"

Walters quailed but hesitated long enough to save face. He wondered briefly if Deveroux was running a bluff. Unsure, he turned to comply. A pissed-off chief warrant officer on a personal assignment from the CG was not a stray cat that he wanted to grab by the tail; even Walters was smart enough to know that.

"And, lieutenant . . . *yew* can send that young specialist on over here as you go by, I can use some quality hep cleanin' this here mess up," Deveroux added, putting an extra spoonful of molasses in his accent. He smiled. "Thank you, sir."

Walters didn't look back or break stride. He'd look into taking some action against Deveroux later, but for now he wanted to distance himself from the CID agent as expeditiously as possible. He barked an order to the young soldier as he walked by on his way to the intersection, putting enough edge in his voice so that at least one person knew he was important.

Deveroux slowly made his way over to the side of the Buick, looking at the ground closely as he did. The car was partially off the gravel with one wheel in the grass, which was brittle and spare after a dry winter. In the packed dust around the passenger's side and rear of the car, he could see at least six different shoe treads—all appeared fresh. He was still looking when the specialist reported.

"Sir, Specialist Scotty Law—you wanted to see me, sir?"

"Slow down there, bubba, yes, I did. First of all, Chief or Mr. Deveroux will work just fine—I like to think I work for a livin'; second, you got any bullets in that M-16 or do you carry it around just to attract the pretty girls?"

"Sir? I mean, Chief?"

"Your rifle, son. Your gun. Your best friend. Is it by any chance loaded?"

"Ahh, well . . ."

"Okay. Got it. I tell you what, I won't tell anyone if you won't . . . deal?"

"*Hooah,* sir." His looked conveyed utter confusion.

Deveroux sighed. "Here's what I need for you to do for me now. All these folks are engaged in what's known in the textbooks as contaminatin' a crime scene. Now, you can either find yourself some bullets and shoot all them folks with that gun of yours, just mow 'em down, or, alternatively, you can move 'em on back about a hundred meters—I don't rightly care which—but get 'em off this crime scene. Now. Understood?"

Scotty Law didn't quite snap to attention, but his body language implied that he didn't need to be told a second time. He simply nodded and immediately set about pushing and directing the noisy crowd back.

Deveroux took a moment and finished scanning the ground. The unique imprint from his own worn Chuck Taylor's, worn flat on the outside of each heel, stood in sharp contrast to the other footprints in the dust and minimized the risk of his contributing to the scene contamination. Nevertheless, he stepped carefully as he walked to the front of the driver's side of the car. He glanced up at Specialist Law pushing the crowd back with newly found authority.

He could smell clotted blood now, and he heard the faint buzz of a dozen green-bottle flies. A second call from the office as he was leaving home had told him that he had either a suicide or a probable homicide on his hands. He looked through the windshield, cupping his hand near the glass to shade the glare while being careful not to touch the car. Covering what appeared to be a body on the front seat was a camouflaged army-issued poncho liner; its quilted, rip-stop material humped up in the center almost in the shape of a question mark. Another young MP—a buck sergeant this time—stood nearby, hands on his hips. He was watching Deveroux carefully and from a distance.

"You the first officer on the scene?" Deveroux asked, not looking up. He intentionally put a smile in his voice. Nothing can make an average Joe Soldier zip up faster than his thinking he's stepped on his dick somehow.

"That's right, Chief." He'd obviously heard the exchange with Lieutenant Walters and didn't need to be presented with any further credentials. "Got the call at approximately oh-nine-forty-five. About thirty, thirty-five minutes ago. Arrived to find a Sergeant Roscoe Charles here, pretty shaken up. He's the one who actually found the body. I got a statement from him and his address—then I let him go on to his quarters before he puked all over everything. He lives here on post if you need to talk to him some more."

Deveroux frowned and mumbled as he pulled two latex gloves from his rear pocket. He kept a box in his truck for situations like this and had grabbed a couple as he parked. He snapped them on and then opened the car door. "What's that?" He nodded at the poncho liner as he looked at the sergeant.

"Poncho liner."

Deveroux's expression clearly indicated that he knew what a military poncho liner looked like. It also indicated that he might be inclined to share that information with the young MP.

"Sorry, Chief," the sergeant quickly corrected, seeing the warrant officer's face. "All sorts of people been here."

Deveroux looked over at the crowd, now assembled a football field away. "So I see."

"Yes, sir, Chief. Lot of people. I figured they didn't need to be around this . . ." He made a look with his face to convey the unpleasantness of the situation. "You know."

"'Course that's the problem, ain't it? All these people around; they shouldn't have been here in the first place."

"Chief, I'm just Sergeant Joe Snuffy. Lieutenant Walters, he—"

Deveroux put his hand up to indicate that no explanation was needed. With the car door wide open he shifted his position a foot or two to take in the scene from a slightly different angle. He bent at the waist and dipped his head. "Tell me, Sarge, would that be your poncho liner?"

"Like I told you, Chief, I figured people didn't need to see all the . . . blood and all."

"Roger that. Cover it up. Of course, like I said, another approach might have been to keep all them people away and leave the body here untouched." He stepped forward to look more closely into the front seat of the car, careful where he placed his foot so as to not disturb any evidence. "So tell me, Sergeant, you have any reason to kill this here fella? He owe you some poker money maybe? Romancin' your wife?"

The sergeant looked as if he'd been jolted with a car battery.

"What? You mean me, personally? Why? No . . . I mean . . . no, sir. Why would you say that? I don't know this man. I mean—"

Deveroux interrupted. "I only say that because we're gonna send this evidence down to the lab in Georgia, and my guess is that they're gonna find your hairs on this here liner. Probably some trunk fibers from your car and maybe some of your dog's dandruff—you got a dog?"

"Sir, I—"

"A man needs a dog. Yessir, who knows what all they'll find when they start goin' over this here body with their little tweezers and cotton swabs. Amazin' what those crime scene folks can do with some tweezers. Best forensic lab in the world, they say. I believe 'em too. I just wanted to know if you had a good alibi is all."

"Ah shit, Chief. Yeah, I mean they might find my hairs on the body and all, but that's because it's my poncho liner . . . but listen here, that don't mean I . . ."

"Calm down, cowboy. Calm down." Deveroux smiled as he snugged up his gloves, snapping the latex against his wrist. "You can bleed off some of that steam. Just makin' a point, which I reckon you get by now. The point is, this scene is way too dirty."

The sergeant took a deep breath and relaxed. Class time was over.

"So, let's take a look see, shall we?" Deveroux's knees popped as he knelt. He gently lifted the corner of the poncho liner.

All the wind left his lungs.

"That's why I covered him," the sergeant remarked quietly, seeing the look on Deveroux's face.

"Holy Jesus," Deveroux said. "The man's been scalped."

CHAPTER 17

Fort Campbell, Kentucky
SUNDAY, APRIL 6, 2008

It was Sunday morning and Chief Warrant Officer Shuck Deveroux was at his office, humped over his desk, rather than at home. In fact, he hadn't been home since depositing his children the day before, as the stubble on his face and the stuporous red in his eyes testified. The investigation initiated the previous morning had rapidly spiraled out of control despite Deveroux's best efforts to keep the lid screwed down tight. The problem was that he was stationed at Fort Campbell, not Fort Apache, and it was 2008 not 1876, and middle-aged men being found scalped in the park tended to be an unusual occurrence, and unusual events have the ability to bring out the earthly stupids in people. To start with, the deputy commander had ordered the post locked down, apparently in fear that Crazy Horse and his painted warriors might try to escape capture, and on an early spring Saturday that was about the best recipe for what the military called a *cluster fuck* that anyone could order up. Even after more logical heads prevailed and got the gates opened and the vehicles flowing again, traffic remained snarled well into the evening. Of course, with no leads, no suspects, no description of a vehicle, closing the post down two or three hours after the crime had probably occurred had served no purpose. None whatsoever.

The victim was presumptively identified as a civilian from Nashville. The medical examiner announced that he wouldn't have a dental ID before Monday noon, but a wallet found in the victim's pocket suggested that he was a sixty-seven-year-old Asian male named Trinh Han, and that he owned a chain of dry-cleaning and laundry shops in downtown Nashville and the surrounding area. What he was doing on post was unclear, but a PX card found among his things offered some explanation, that and the fact that he had a lucrative dry-cleaning contract with the military. A check with the front gate revealed that a Mr. Trinh Han had obtained a visitor's pass for his '99 Buick Park Avenue shortly before 6:00 A.M. What happened next was precisely the question that Shuck Deveroux had been working on for the last twenty-some sleepless hours.

In fact, Deveroux had spent most of the remaining morning and afternoon, while the evidence techs worked over the car with their little vacuum cleaners and tweezers and cotton swabs, trying to locate anyone who knew something or had seen something. Anything. On an installation the size of Campbell—home of the 101st Airborne— with soldiers jogging at all times of the night and day, it was hard to believe that no one had seen anything. Deveroux had never personally scalped anyone, but he had gutted his share of deer over the years and that particular activity had led him to figure that taking the top of someone's head off had to involve some commotion—but no one seemed to have seen or heard a thing. The scene itself offered little more promise. The lab results would take a while, but a cursory examination revealed little physical evidence. There were fingerprints all over the car, of course, but then what car wasn't covered with fingerprints? His own truck had "Wash Me" and "Dirt Devil" and a dozen smiley faces—written and drawn in the dust on the hood and fender—none by his finger. Mr. Trinh Han's car, while perhaps cleaner, had no reason to be different. A bloody partial palm print on the back of the seat looked promising at first, but the consensus was that it wouldn't be readable. There were no usable tire tracks and way too many shoe prints—most of them seeming to match Lieutenant Walters's size-seven boot soles—to offer any real leads. There was no bloody tomahawk, no coup stick, no witnesses, no nothing.

Just an elderly dead Vietnamese dry cleaner now shy of some hair.

The afternoon saw all official attempts to contact Trinh Han's family, assuming he had some, coming up unsuccessful. One of Deveroux's NCOs had accompanied a couple of Nashville detectives to Han's house, but found no one at home. Nashville PD unenthusiastically agreed to work that scene if necessary. In the meantime, Deveroux had put a call through to INS to run immigration records to see what could be turned up. He doubted that many sixty-seven-year-old men named Trinh Han were native-born in the Volunteer State, and that meant there might be some record of his entry into the United States, but it was Saturday, and even with calling in some markers, it probably was going to take a while.

His evening was spent on the phone with the Armed Forces medical examiner in Washington, the FBI, and the Nashville police trying to work out who was going to get stuck to the jurisdictional flypaper. No one seemed eager to draw the short straw on this one, and it was resolved finally with no clear resolution. The AFME, overworked from the bodies coming home from Iraq and Afghanistan, had happily found a jurisdictional rabbit hole to dive into. The Nashville medical examiner's office was equally unenthusiastic, but finally agreed to take the body for safekeeping, but he also made it clear that he would assume no jurisdictional interest, nor even perform an autopsy, until someone officially established the body to be a Nashville native— and even then he was leaving room to look the other way. The FBI considered getting involved until Deveroux described the contaminated crime scene and pointed out that there didn't seem to be a single shred of promising evidence. Then they remembered how thinly they were stretched at the moment. The temptation to assume responsibility for a case that someone else has cocked up, and for which another agency can be made to look utterly foolish if the floor gives way, is hard to resist, but only if you can solve it. In the end, the FBI resisted the temptation, and in the end, Chief Warrant Officer Shuck Deveroux was left with his tongue frozen to the flagpole.

The cork in the bottle was a midnight briefing with Fort Campbell's commanding general in which Deveroux had gotten to say at least a dozen times that he didn't have the slightest lead in the case, and in which the general had gotten to say—just once—that he'd better find one quickly or confess to the murder himself. One way or the other, this was to be put to bed, and soon.

So Sunday morning broke with Deveroux humped over his desk, the wrinkles in his shirt matching the pattern of lines under his eyes.

"Hey, Chief. Why am I not surprised?" Special Agent Dave Pagano said as he walked into the office. He was a toe-walker whose heels rarely touched the floor, and he seemed to bounce with each step. "When I heard about it last night, I figured you'd get the call. Man, if it ain't shit to be you."

Deveroux looked up from the stack of papers on his desk. His eyes had glazed over an hour or so earlier, and he was searching the recesses of his skull for an angle on the case and finding none. "Nice of you to show up. Called you a dozen times yesterday."

"Yeah. Damn cell phone of mine won't hold a charge for more than an hour. Crapped out midway over to Knox the other day," Pagano said over his shoulder as he poured some coffee into a stained ceramic mug that read *NYSP Williams Homicide Seminar.* He'd returned the night before from a three-day trip to Fort Knox where he'd gone to pick up a young soldier who seemed to have forgotten that he was stationed at Fort Campbell.

"That's why God made rechargers," Deveroux answered.

"Maybe." Pagano slurped loudly as he took a seat in front of Deveroux's desk. "But at my age, the number of things I can remember is limited. It was either fresh underwear or my phone charger. Don't have enough brain cells left for both." He slurped again. "But enough about me. The TV said you shut the base down. That right?"

"Whole garrison locked down for three hours yesterday mornin'."

"Jesus, I'll bet that made for pleasant driving. Gimme details."

Deveroux took a deep breath and held it as he leaned back in his chair. He exhaled slowly through his nose as he searched for the loose end that would best unravel the story. "Homicide. Bad one. Some young sergeant scoutin' out a place for a barbecue yesterday mornin'.

Early. What does he find for his trouble but a dead body. And not only a dead body, mind you, but a civilian body. On base."

"You get the initial call?"

"I wish. Lieutenant Walters was already there when I got there. You know him? Fat little chucklehead MP whose gut covers his belt buckle?"

"Yeah, yeah. Had the pleasure. Don't laugh, though, I hear he's on the list for promotion. Screw up, move up. Good news is that he's also transferring in a couple of weeks. He gets to go be an instructor at the MP school."

"Great. That's just what the New Army needs. What was it Genghis Khan said?"

"Hmm. Can't say that I remember Genghis Khan being known for his speeches."

"Shows the limits of your schoolin'. He said somethin' about every man havin' a purpose in life, even if it's just to serve as a bad example."

"I like that. At least Walters'll be a bad example somewhere else."

"That's some consolation. Anyway, he gets to the scene first and instead of doin' anythin' constructive—like secure the area—he commences to walk all over everythin' that's not vertical. Next thing I know, the CG calls me in—by name, mind you—and tells me to get it fixed."

"Like I said, my friend, sure is shit to be you." Pagano smiled broadly and propped his feet on the corner of Deveroux's desk. "By the looks of you, I'm guessing that the old man's in for some disappointing news when you brief him. Need help?"

"Of course. I don't have lead one."

"Like I say, shit to be you. But, damn, Shuck, I swear to God, lately it's like we're living in the Wild West around this place. First Knox and now here."

It took a minute to register. Deveroux was still filtering information through the thick wad of moist cotton that no sleep had packed into his head. "Say again? What you mean? First Knox?" He leaned forward and knocked Pagano's feet off his desk.

Pagano's boots hit the deck loudly, and his coffee sloshed out onto his lap. "Shit, Deveroux. What the fuck, over?" He brushed at the wet drops with the back of his hand.

"What does 'first Knox' mean?"

"I meeeeean, first Knox. I was talking to Chief Sallot and his bunch over there yesterday, and they were telling me about a case they had a few months back. Before Thanksgiving; October, maybe. Some old vet and his grandkids taking in the exhibits at the Patton Museum. Finds some real-life action by one of the old tanks outside—you know that big Russian one? They say it looked like someone had taken a machete to the guy's head. Blood and shit allllll over."

Deveroux was now very much awake. "They ever hear of email? Why didn't we get a sheet? They solve it? I never heard mention of it at all. Did you? Who's workin' it?"

"Nope. Still open. We got something on it—like you ever read any of that shit anyhow. I think some big nut-busters out of Bragg caught the hook-end of the chain on that one. However, unlike you, my grits-eating friend, they were smart enough to pawn it off on the local cops P-D-fuckin'-Q—at least as much of it as they can. It's still a CID case, obviously, but they're letting the local Gomers do all the legwork for them. It was some civilian yokel from off post, Louisville maybe. They think he came on to use the commissary or something and got whacked for his pocket change. Wrong place, wrong time, that's for damn sure. They're still carrying it as an open case, but they don't have any leads. I think they're hoping it will solve itself or go away, one or the other. To hear them talk, they aren't pursuing it very hard . . . I mean, where'd you go with it? Kinda like your case here. No witnesses, no real physical evidence. You can't polygraph the whole First Armor Training Brigade—and even if you could, how many other people are on and off that post every day? But what's the big deal?"

"The big deal is this," Schuck replied as he frisbeed a stack of photographs across the desk into Pagano's lap. "Take a look. That's yesterday's victim. A middle-aged Vietnamese man from Nashville who's somehow gone and gotten hisself detached from his scalp. The whole top of this fella's head's plum gone—as in scalped. Blood every which where."

"Shit," Pagano said as he leafed through the photos. "Man oh man." He looked up and shook his head. "Where's General Custer when you need him?"

"You said it. Look, Dave, this guy at Knox." Deveroux spoke very slowly. "The victim—the local guy—what was he? White? Black? What?"

Dave Pagano creased his brow again and looked down at the photos as he thought. It hadn't been a major topic of discussion, and now he was trying to retrieve the threads of the conversation he'd had with the MPs at Fort Knox. Finally he looked up and cocked his head. "Come to think of it . . . I think they said he was Vietnamese."

CHAPTER 18

Saigon, Republic of Vietnam
SATURDAY, SEPTEMBER 12, 1970

Captain Paul Fick had already served two back-to-back tours in Vietnam. As a young lieutenant with the Twenty-fifth Infantry Division, he had already bested the odds and survived. Now he was back for a third spin of the revolver's chamber, and he wondered if the bullet would be under the hammer this time.

But this time was different. This time he wasn't a ground-pounder. He was a special agent for the Criminal Investigation Division. Special orders.

He'd gotten to Fort Benning in the gray winter of 1969, after spending almost two months rehabilitating in the hospital, and was assigned as an instructor in advance infantry tactics. Life there had been miserable, but religiously predictable. His battle injury didn't leave many options open to him and at least teaching allowed him to stay in the military and maybe save some lives. Atone. When not in the classroom he was kept busy, which was what he needed to keep the angry ghosts at bay. Well-connected majors and light colonels, whose combat experience in Vietnam—the few who had any at all— consisted of time spent in strip clubs and poorly lit bars, had him fetching coffee and sharpening pencils. Not what he'd signed up for; not what he'd done a back-to-back in the Republic of Shitland for;

certainly not what he'd stayed in for. But predictability was what he needed after the previous year and a half of living on the cusp. Order. Structure. Stability. Predictability.

And then unpredictability called.

It came in the form of a late-night phone call from a gravel-voiced full bird colonel at the Pentagon. A problem—what the voice on the phone was careful to call a "situation"—was developing in Vietnam. Check that—had developed. The always-robust South Vietnamese black market had gone malignant. Large amounts of medical supplies and armament were finding their way into the hands of Viet Cong and even North Vietnamese Regulars. A small trickle had always done so, the collateral cost of running tens of thousands of tons of supplies through a country grounded in colonial crumble and corruption, but recently the spigot had been opened full, and people were dying as a result. The wrong people. And what was worse, the evidence suggested that the organizational structure was centered on a small cabal of ARVN and VNAF officers—trusted allies—the army and air force of the Republic of Vietnam. But what was really concerning to the late-night voices in the Pentagon was the unprecedented volume of matériel that was finding its way into enemy hands. It was too much, and that quantity could only have been supplied by an American contact—a U.S. soldier whose loyalty alone was insufficient to fill his pockets.

CID needed Fick, the voice said. They needed someone undaunted and untempted by the chaos and slack-jawed opportunitism that was the Republic of South Vietnam in 1970. The barbarians were not only at the gate; they were inside the wall as well, and men with backbone were getting harder and harder to find. Fick's record was unsoiled, the voice said. He'd been tested in the crucible and emerged tempered and hardened by the experience, with character and honor intact and unwithered. He was their man, the voice said. A man beyond temptation, the voice said. A man whose moral fiber had not frayed, the voice said.

The country needed him.

The voice told him it was to be a short assignment. Temporary duty. Couple months. Not anticipated to exceed ninety days. He would be loosely detailed to the CID on special assignment and sent to South Vietnam with a blank check and a free hand. A *special* agent in the truest sense of the word. Get the problem fixed—no questions asked. Get it fixed quietly—no questions asked. Get if fixed permanently— no questions asked. But be expeditious—no one would look over his shoulder; no one would second-guess.

That had been almost eight months ago, and he'd accomplished little since then. Whoever was behind the operation was good, real good, or ruthless—real ruthless. Or both. There were no footprints in the sand. The few leads that Fick had tried to run to ground had faded when his informants disappeared, one after another, never to be seen by their families and coworkers again.

What he had determined was that the voice in Washington was likely correct in its assessment; the core of the organization appeared to be made up of South Vietnamese officers—ARVN or VNAF or both—maybe even high-ranking ones. Maybe even some government officials stewed in the same pot; the line between military and civilian officials in South Vietnam had never been drawn with too dark an ink. But that was all he'd been able to sniff out, and he'd known that much before he left Benning. What he really needed to sniff out was the source—the American on the inside. Graft and corruption in the South Vietnamese government and military were requisite traits for promotion. It reminded Fick of the fable of the crocodile and the rabbit. The crocodile smiles and convinces the rabbit to ride across the stream on the crocodile's back. He promises no harm, but midway across, the crocodile eats the rabbit, but not before saying, "What did you expect, I'm a crocodile." The South Vietnamese were crocodiles, even if U.S. policy makers couldn't always see the rows of sharp teeth lining their mouths. You accepted the corruption and worked around it as best you could. It was the cost of conducting a political war. But for an American, a fellow soldier, to be a crocodile—that was harder to comprehend, or to tolerate.

The bachelor officers' quarters at the Rex Hotel were a short distance from the American embassy. For more reasons than one, the *Powers* at the Pentagon were anxious to keep the profile on this case as close to the ground as possible, and they'd instructed Fick to work as independently of the embassy staff as possible and to keep his footprint small. That was what they'd instructed him to do, but then they'd gone and booked him into the Rex where every western reporter in the city gathered for the Five o'clock Follies.

It was two-oh-seven in the afternoon. Fick had set up the appointment for one-thirty. He'd walked the short four blocks to the Caravel Hotel in less than ten minutes. The cyclo drivers had hawked him the entire way, as had the feral children begging for handouts. They were crowded around the windows watching him, their fingers and noses pressed to the cool glass. He'd now been waiting in the bar for almost three-quarters of an hour and had started a mental egg-timer ticking. He was giving this meeting another two minutes. He was down to thirty seconds when a shadow slid across his table.

"Cigarette?" A bony man with a poor excuse for facial hair sat down opposite Fick. He was dressed in soiled tropical white—flat-tailed cotton shirt, loose pleated pants, and open-toed woven-leather sandals—and despite his thinness he sat down heavily and dramatically. He smelled of cigarette smoke and smug perspiration and soured clothing that hadn't properly dried in the tropical heat. He held a package of unfiltered Pall Malls in his right hand and a sweating bottle of 33 beer in the left. He tossed his heavy, moist hair back from his forehead with a jerk of his head.

"No thanks," Fick replied to the offer. He'd been raised by his Mennonite aunt and uncle in northern Ohio and retained a deep-bred aversion to self-indulgence.

The thin man smiled, shrugged, and then shook the cigarette package twice until one worked itself free of the rest. He took it with his lips, American style, and tossed the package onto the table should Fick change his mind. As he felt in his pants pocket for a lighter, he said, "You are Captain Fick, are you not?"

Fick narrowed his eyes to better focus on the man's face. It was angular and soft at the same time and it radiated self-absorption and moral bankruptcy. They had communicated several times through intermediate sources over the last month but had never directly met. All Fick knew about him was that he was a freelance journalist who wrote frequently for one of the leftist newspapers in France—*Le*

Rouge something-or-other—and that he was rumored to have high-level contacts within the National Liberation Army. Fick nodded just enough to convey an answer.

"Fick. It is an interesting name in English. Very . . . colorful. I suspect, Captain, that you were made a joke of frequently when you were a child . . . No?" He dipped his head as he lit his cigarette and tilted back to exhale upward. His eyes never broke contact with Fick's. "I suspect I am correct about this."

"And I suspect, Monsieur, that you had the snot beat out of you frequently as a child . . . Yes? I suspect I am right about this."

A small, dismissive smile broke across the man's face and then melted away. He took another drag of smoke deep into his lungs and let it dribble out of his nose like blue-gray water. Finally he introduced himself. "Martin Bullet," he said as he bobbed his head in a quick movement. Only he pronounced it *Mar-TEEN BOO-Lay.*

Fick checked his watch again. Two-ten. "Nice of you to make our one-thirty meeting, Mr. Bullet." He pronounced it *BULL-It.*

Bullet smiled dismissively again. It was an expression that seemed to come easily. He waved his hand, the one with the cigarette, in a sweeping motion meant to encompass the room—if not the entire city. "Colonial time, *Capitaine,* you must learn to adapt. I am afraid that it is a weakness with you Americans. I believe this is so, yes."

"So I've been told, Monsieur, so I've been told." He took a steadying breath. He didn't break eye contact with Bullet. "I was led to believe that you may have some information for me. Am I correct or is this simply going to be a lesson in Old World metaphysics?"

Bullet nodded slowly. "Ahh, yes. Business. May I buy you a beer?"

"No, you can give me information. Do you have some? It is really very simple."

"I may. Indeed, yes. I have . . . ahh . . . let us say, I have contacts . . . that perhaps you do not have access to."

"Yes, no doubt you do. And these contacts, they have names?"

Bullet smiled in a way that confirmed in Fick's mind that he had gotten the snot beaten out of him regularly as a child. In fact, Fick was about ready to kick his ass right now. "Names? But of course they have names, Captain Fick, do not all people? Indeed, yes, names. But these individuals, they wish for you to not learn their identities."

"I see." Fick took another deep, steadying breath before continuing. "Mr. Bullet, maybe the crowd that you run in appreciates your continental charm, but I find it tiresome. Your dick is longer than mine, okay? That what you wish to hear? You win, no contest, so you can reel it back in. Now, if you have information for me, please let's get on with it. Otherwise I have much more entertaining dead ends than you to talk to."

Martin Bullet had been called a great many things in his fifty-four years, but never tiresome. It stung his Gallic pride. "As you wish, *Capitaine* Fick. My contacts say that the gentlemen you seek are well-placed within the Vietnamese army—the *South* Vietnamese army." He paused and smiled, but there was no humor in his eyes. "Trustworthy allies, no?"

"Unfortunately, not all of our allies can be as honorable as the French, Mr. Bullet," Fick said in a flat voice. So far he had heard nothing he hadn't already known.

"Indeed," Bullet replied. "And there is an American too." He paused and canted his head to the side as he evaluated Fick's response. When he saw none, he continued, "Ahh, yes. But you are not surprised? No? I see. And the matériel, these they come from a depot in Long Binh. But this too, you know?"

That was news. Finally. Fick had known that an American was involved, that was precisely why he was back in Vietnam in the first place, and he'd known that the Vietnamese were well connected within their own military—they had to be for the organization to work on the scale that it seemingly was operating on—but it was the origin of the supplies that had been eluding him for months. Was it Long Binh? Or Cam Ranh Bay? Given the types and amounts of supplies, it had to be either one of the big depots or several people operating in several smaller supply companies. Fick was hoping it was the former. One person, one depot. The problem was that every time he felt like he was closing in on that piece of the puzzle, his informant would disappear, and after a while, the truncated life expectancy of his sources had had a dampening effect on new volunteers. But if

Bullet was correct, if it were the army's Long Binh supply depot, that was progress at last.

"Names, Mr. Bullet. Do you have names?" Fick asked again.

Bullet pursed his lips and paused as if the information were sour on his tongue. "Indeed. They are known only by a . . . what is the word? . . . by a . . . ahhh . . . it is like a code word, you see."

"What code word?"

"*Les Cinq Fréres*," Bullet smiled again. "The Five Brothers."

CHAPTER 19

U.S. Army Central Identification Laboratory, Hawaii
WEDNESDAY, APRIL 9, 2008

"CILHI," Kel answered his phone. He hated answering telephones with a degree of passion that bordered on the absolutely pathological. Sometimes his staff would huddle around the phone on the lab floor and call him just to hear the profanity that would erupt from his office. At this stage of his career, the telephone ringing was like the flash of lights that foretells a skull-cracking migraine. Best thing to do when it happened was to go lie down in a dark room and hope it passed. All too frequently calls meant problems to be solved. He looked at his watch. Not even 9:00 A.M.—still mid-afternoon in Washington, D.C.—plenty of time for the professional problem-mongers to gin up a crisis. Increasingly the job was becoming a burn-out waltz: one step forward two steps back.

There was a hiss of static and then two sharp metallic clicks as the long-distance connection was made.

"Well, don't I feel honored. Doctor Robert McKelvey actually answered his phone, and without any cuss words. I was sure I'd be talking to your voicemail." It was the unruffled, smooth-edged Midwest accent of Andy Baker.

Kel recognized the voice immediately and breathed a sigh. A few days earlier, his curiosity had finally gotten the better of him, and he'd called Andy to look into Dr. Dang's unusual behavior at the last Joint Forensic Review.

Colonel Andrew Baker was a tall man with large knobby joints that gave people the impression that he had been constructed out of a sack of mixed plumbing parts. People halfway expected him to clank when he moved. Before his posting as the U.S. military defense attaché in Hanoi, he'd been assigned to the Pacific Command staff in Hawaii for three years as a junior policy officer. It had been a good tour. Admittedly, the job left something to be desired at times, but the location was good. His children were active in sports and school activities, as were he and his wife, Judy. They'd intentionally opted for off-post housing, the better to fully take in the experience of living in Hawaii, and had chosen the same little bedroom community as the McKelveys. Andy and Kel had found themselves frequently on opposite sides of their children's soccer field, and over the three years had become good friends. Good enough anyway that they'd been able to maintain an easy friendship through emails and Kel's occasional visits to Hanoi on CILHI business.

Kel knew that although Andy didn't have any direct dealings with Dr. Dang, he did have some close ties to junior members of the Vietnamese Office for Seeking Missing Persons. And when you want answers, hungry junior bureaucrats looking for ladder rungs to grasp hold of are the ones to ask.

"If I'd known it was the likes of you, I wouldn't have answered. I was sure it was one of those publisher's sweepstakes fellers. Felt my time is ripe. What can I do for you, partner? What the hell time is it in Hanoi anyhow? Must be . . ." He looked at his watch again and started adding. There was a bank of clocks on the wall of the lab with the current time in every major hellhole on earth, but his eyes had reached a point where it was easier to look at his watch and calculate.

"A little after midnight, no . . . let me take that back, a lot after midnight. Almost two o'clock, actually. Tomorrow morning for you, that is."

"You're up late, bubba . . . or early. Hope you don't need bail money."

"Nah, I'm good for that. You don't need much in the way of money over here; it's all in knowing whom to bribe. Speaking of which, I've got some intel on our man Dr. Dang and that whole Tenkiller situation. Don't know how useful it'll be, but it's all yours."

"Man, you're fast. I'm impressed."

"Don't be. Like we talked about earlier, your buddy Senior Colonel Dang is very much Old School, and while he still carries a lot of clout with that generation, he has royally pissed off whole echelons of his younger comrades working in the VNOSMP. The respect for the old vets here is starting to wear a bit thin in certain circles. Doesn't take much to convince them to open their vents."

"Oh, really? I guess I didn't realize that."

"Sure. Just a matter of figuring out how to get them started. After that it was like a house on fire."

"Feedin' time?"

"You got it, and these guys can be some serious sharks when they put their mind to it."

"Who assisted you? Would that be Major Jack Daniels or Colonel Johnnie Walker?"

"Colonel Johnnie. Red, of course—this is a socialist republic, you know. Anyhow, he was enough to get them started, but then, like I said, after that, getting them to stop was more of a problem. Just managed to get free of them a few minutes ago. Some interesting shit."

"Yeah? Can you believe them, though?"

"Well . . . that's the real question, isn't it? How much is fact and how much is plain trash talk. I suspect it's mostly good, I do, I really do . . . though I'm sure they exaggerated some. You know, if you're going to stab someone in the back, it's best to use a really big knife."

"Who'd you talk to?"

"Couple of guys in the VNO. The main one, though . . . well, I'm not sure you know him. Young guy—name's Nguyen Van Loc—used to be with the Ministry of Foreign Affairs."

"Yeah, yeah," Kel said. There was an echo on the line, and he heard his answer repeated faintly twice more. "I know him . . . or at least I've met him. We had some guys from the MFA visit the lab a couple of years ago. Pretty sure Nguyen Loc was with them. Real baby-faced fella, if it's the one I recall; looks all of about fourteen or so."

"That's him. Pie-shaped face, hair sticking out in all directions, and you're right, looks about as old as my son. About as tall too. Now he's one of the up-and-comers in the Vietnamese Office for Seeking Missing Persons. And more important—at least as far as you're concerned—one of the young Turks who thinks that old-timers like Senior Colonel Dang need to be put out to permanent stud so that the country can catch up to the twentieth century."

"Twenty-first."

"We're talking Vietnam here, Kel. One century at a time."

"Roger. My mistake. So what's the story?"

"Well . . . now that's very interesting, actually," Baker's voice echoed across the phone line. "And, by the way, Mr. Nguyen has probably sobered up some since our talk, and while I doubt he remembers everything he said, I am reasonably certain that he remembers enough. Enough that he'd appreciate some discretion on our part. So would I, remember, I have to live here."

"'Course."

"Okay, where to start? Ahhh . . . I don't know how well you know your old friend Colonel Dang."

"Not much better than you do, I'd guess. I've known him longer. I've had to deal with him durin' Joint Forensic Reviews, but that's about the extent of it. If it isn't somethin' that can be discussed over warm Coke Colas or scaldin' hot green tea, then I probably don't know about it."

"I hear you. He's an interesting man. He studied medicine in East Germany and Russia before the war, maybe even a little while in France. But during the war, he was like a battalion surgeon for the North Vietnamese Army."

"Yeah. The NVA was organized differently; actually he was more like a division surgeon, as I understand it. In fact, he once told me that he worked out of the Cu Chi complex for several years. Amputatin' limbs and pluggin' up bullet holes forty feet underground by candlelight. Amazin' stuff, really. He once told me about doin' a damn C-section while Bob Hope and Dusty Springfield were performin' overhead."

"Precisely," Baker said. "And that's where it gets interesting. Not the Bob Hope business—I hadn't heard that one—but with all the other stuff. I mean, when you think about it, it's incredible that someone could do all that surgery and shit while under the damn ground."

"I won't argue that."

"Well, not to take away from that at all, but it seems he had some help."

"Really? How so?"

"That's why I'm calling, isn't it? Nguyen's story is that there was a massive black market ring operating out of Saigon—everybody knew about it, okay? Our side, their side, everybody. There were several actually, but this one was like the mother of them all. I mean, loads of supplies. Most of it was the usual stuff, you know, liquor, smokes, small electronics, pretty things for expensive women. Same shit that every war has, right?"

"Right."

"But in this case it seems that a goodly amount of material was being channeled directly into the hands of the Viet Cong and the NVA, and we're not talking a few chocolate bars and nylons either. Nguyen says major amounts of weapons were being pumped down that pipeline as well."

"No shit."

"No shit," Baker replied.

"How much of this did we know? The Americans, I mean."

"Not much. Army CID investigated it but could never crack that nut."

"But how is Dr. Dang involved? Make that, how *was* he involved? You said he was gettin' help."

"Right. Well, if Nguyen is telling me true, a lot of medical supplies were flowing through the pipe as well. And take a guess where to . . ."

"The good Dr. Dang's underground operatin' room."

"And therapeutic health spa. Yup, you got it, brother. Seems Uncle

Sam was a major—if unknowing—contributor to Dang's success as a battlefield surgeon."

"I'll be damned. But . . . okay, that's interestin' enough . . . but I still don't see the connection to the skeleton we just looked at in Hanoi."

"I'm getting there. I'm getting to that. Hold on. Supposedly, this black market ring operated out of Dong Nai Province, which is east of Saigon."

"And?"

"And. And. Aw, c'mon, Doc . . . where was your skeleton found? The one that you said Senior Colonel Dang was acting so strange about?"

"Ahhh . . . I think . . . it was Thanh Lay Hamlet."

"Which is in . . ."

"Cut me some slack, Andy. You live there; I pass through occasionally."

"How about Dong Nai Province."

Kel was silent as the pieces settled. He was hoping that a picture would emerge. When it didn't completely come into focus, he continued. "Help me out here, Andrew. You sayin' that the skeleton we excavated in Thanh Lay is connected to some wartime black market?"

"I'm not saying it, but Nguyen Loc sure is. He says the VNOSMP thinks they're connected. You see, the story he tells is that the market was run by . . . ahh . . . by what he called 'The Brotherhood of Five,' at least that's what I think he called it. I have to admit that a bottle and a half of sour mash wasn't doing much more for his English than it was for my Vietnamese."

"Been there," Kel answered. "You best be glad it wasn't the local stuff; hell, you'd be strugglin' with English if it had been. The Brotherhood of Five?"

"Yeah, pretty sure that's what he meant. How's your French?"

"*Muy bueno.* Why?"

"Because I asked him in French just to make sure. *La Fraternité de Cinq.*"

"Hmm. The Brotherhood of Five. So what the hell is that? Sounds like a bad nightclub act."

"Yeah. Well, I'm figuring that it's a group of five men—no surprise there, I guess, given the name. All were officers with our loyal and trusted ally, the army of South Vietnam. All except one, that is. You ready for this? One of *La Fraternité* was an American GI . . . one of ours."

"Tenkiller?"

"Roger that. At least that's the way I figure it anyhow—given what you've told me about the case. Mr. Nguyen didn't know the name of the American, but he knew the names of a couple of the ARVN officers that supposedly were involved. One was a, ahhh . . ." Baker paused as he looked at some notes. Kel could hear pages softly crinkling. "I scribbled it down when he wasn't looking; if I can only get my eyes to focus—which is no small accomplishment right this minute. Ummm, the big honcho was an ARVN general—General Ngo Van Thu. There were also two other officers, Linh Nhu Ngon and a Doan Minh Tuyen—something like that anyway."

"Better spell those."

"Sure. First is N-G-O, Van Thu. Next is L-I-N-H, Nhu Ngon, N-G-O-N. Last one is Doan, D-O-A-N, Doan Minh Tuyen. T-U-Y-E-N. At least that's my best guess at how they're spelled, but if I'm off, I'm not too far off."

Kel wrote down the names as he listened. "Got it. But you say our buddy Nguyen Loc didn't know the name of the American."

"Right. But he indicated that the VNOSMP was fairly confident that that body your guys dug up was one of the Brotherhood, and they figured it was the American, and the only American you have missing in that area is Tenkiller—isn't that right?"

"Right. But I'm still not clear on why Dr. Dang would give a shit one way or the other. Tenkiller or no Tenkiller."

"Well, who knows, but he's pretty old-fashioned. Whoever you dug up, they were helping him obtain his supplies. Maybe he doesn't want that whole episode exposed. Maybe he's being loyal . . . hell, I don't know. And I'm not too likely to figure it out in the condition I'm in right now. I'm doing good to feel my toes."

Kel sighed. "Hmmm. Yeah, maybe so. I doubt we'll ever find out from him, though—Dr. Dang, that is."

"You want me to try and locate this General Ngo Van Thu—if he's still alive? And those other two? Colonel Linh and . . ."

"Sure, my wife would love to see you."

"I'm not tracking."

"Well, if you're goin' to track 'em down then I assume you're plannin' on flyin' back to the States?"

"How so?"

"You said they were ARVN officers, and high-rankin' ones at that. You honestly reckon that they stayed on in the workers' paradise of the Socialist Republic of Vietnam after the war? The current government isn't too fond of former ARVN officers, from what I gather."

"True. You think they're in the United States now?"

"If they're alive, I do," Kel said. "If they're alive."

CHAPTER 20

Fort Campbell, Kentucky
WEDNESDAY, APRIL 9, 2008

It had taken a couple of days to connect the varied dots, but even then the picture wasn't all that clear. Dave Pagano had been correct in his recollection; there had been a similar killing at Fort Knox the previous October, and he'd been able to run down the information on it without too much difficulty. A couple of phone calls, a couple of faxes, a couple of emails. It was pretty much as Pagano had told Deveroux the first day: local Louisville native, owner of a string of Vietnamese grocery stores, enters the post early in the morning; by midmorning he's minus the top of his head. No fingerprints of any use, no witnesses, no readily apparent trace evidence. Nothing but a dead, middle-aged Asian man curled up behind an old Russian tank, awash with blood. Gruesome, messy, frightening. Not at all what the post commander wanted to wake up to. Other than that, nothing.

Pagano had also been correct when he said that the Fort Knox authorities had been willing to let the local police run the leads to ground. As much as the Knox Command wanted to clean its laundry in private, it soon became clear that this case wasn't going to be solved any time too soon or too easily. All the better to let someone else spin his wheels.

Not so Fort Campbell.

The installation commander at Campbell was a take-charge, no-shit, grab-your-balls-and-hold-on-for-the-ride type of guy; what the military called high-speed, low-drag, and Teflon-coated. Real *Hooah-*type. From the beginning he'd indicated that he wanted a daily "hot wash" of the investigation's results. He wanted it handled in-house, and he also made it clear that he didn't expect the investigation to stretch much past the next forty-eight hours.

It had. And it was still stretching.

At first, Deveroux's immediate boss, Lieutenant Colonel Riggins, had made the daily trip to the CG's office. It was a good opportunity for spending face time with *the general*—though he made an extremely good show of sighing and cussing and otherwise loudly protesting his having to do it. Protesting much too much, however, which was a good indicator that he wasn't about to let anyone else do it. But that was in the beginning. It hadn't taken someone as politically savvy as Riggins long to have a blinding flash of the obvious. When the answer to every one of the general's questions is either "No, sir" or "I don't know, sir," it's best to not have it be your face that's getting the time.

The realization that there were now two murders didn't help smooth matters. One murder, any murder, is bad, especially when it is so violent, but two murders—two murders is a recipe for someone's early retirement, and Lieutenant Colonel Riggins had two kids in private school and a wife who wasn't about to have him retire.

The outcome could be forecast. By Day Three, Chief Warrant Officer Shuck Deveroux was getting the face time with the general, and Lieutenant Colonel Riggins was playing afternoon golf and asking Deveroux if he knew what "BOHICA" meant. "Can you say, 'BOW-Hee-Kah'?" he'd ask slowly. *Bend Over, Here It Comes Again.* Every time he said it, Riggins would double over in laughter.

Should have never answered my phone, Deveroux was thinking. *Should have just driven to Louisville to watch the game.*

"All set, Chief? The commander's ready," the aide repeated. Deveroux was sufficiently lost in thought and hadn't heard the first summons. Now he looked up. The efficient young major didn't even rise from his desk; instead he simply pointed with his precisely sharpened pencil at the CG's door. He flicked his head once as if to convey that Deveroux had better hop to, and then he sniffed, as if to punctuate the instruction.

Deveroux remained lost in some cavernous part of his mind, walking in endless circles without the aid of a flashlight. He'd never had a case like this. There was nothing. No witnesses, no usable physical evidence, just a gruesome murder that had everyone in garrison feeling edgy. Where now? What next? Hop to. Make it happen.

BOHICA.

"Mr. Deveroux," the major was now tapping his pencil on his desk calendar and applying his most authoritative face to the matter. He flared his nostrils and formed his mouth precisely. "I suggest that you move out smartly and draw fire. The general is quite busy. Please keep it brief."

Deveroux caught the sound but not the words. He looked up and saw the pencil tapping and guessed the content of the message. He had developed a firm conviction over his years in the military that young field-grade officers like this major could be greatly improved with a good ass-whuppin'. It was tempting, but wholly against his upbringing. Instead, he stood, ran his thumbs around the inside of his waistband to smooth the tuck of his shirt, and walked directly to the commander's door, not giving the major the satisfaction of even an acknowledging look. He knocked twice on the doorframe and waited.

"Come." General Anderson stood up from his desk and smiled broadly. He was older than his face suggested, and people often focused on his smooth, almost poreless, skin at the expense of noticing his eyes. His eyes were old, and they were mottled with dark flecks of will and character and hard-purchased history. He liked Deveroux, and Deveroux sensed it, though neither man could have explained why if he'd been pressed for a reason. They'd only met a few times. "Come on in here, Chief. Have a seat. Sit down, sit down." He directed Deveroux to a pair of padded chairs in front of his desk. He looked up and caught his aide hovering in the doorway. With an almost imperceptible nod, he dismissed him.

Deveroux took up a position next to the one farthest from the door and waited for the general to begin setting down before he did so himself.

General Anderson smiled again before he spoke. He leaned back and crossed his legs. He was wearing camouflage BDUs—the new digital pattern that worked best if you were trying to hide amid enlarged computer images—and the older Vietnam-era green jungle boots. The leather was cracked and had been puttied with years of black polish. He crossed his arms across his chest and arched his back until something popped—either the chair frame or a segment of spine. "Let me take a guess, Chief. You have nothing to report on your investigation. That about sum it up?"

"Yes, sir," Deveroux said. "That'd be . . . that'd be pretty much correct, sir. Finally got confirmed names on both of the victims—a Mr. Ngon and a Mr. Trinh—both Vietnamese, but other than that, nothin' to report."

General Anderson watched Deveroux's face closely, narrowing his eyes to snake slits as if to improve the focus. "I don't have to tell you, Chief Deveroux, that the troops in this garrison are very uneasy with the prospect of a Jack the Ripper stalking the goddamn place. You read me? I need some answers and all this business of 'Nothing to Report' isn't doing much to help me out here. You understand that, don't you, Chief? You understand that we need some resolution, and we need it now? The PA folks are holding off the local press the best they can, but with twenty thousand troops coming and going daily, it's a pretty leaky sieve. We need answers. Are we on the same page of music here?"

"Yes, sir. I think so, sir."

"Think soes don't cut it, Chief. And now we got us some sort of damn serial killer. Is that what we've got here at Campbell?" He sighed loudly and pinched the bridge of his nose. His body language suggested that he wasn't finished speaking. "You think that incident over at Fort Knox is related?"

Deveroux flicked a quick look at the floor and then brought his eyes up to face the general. "I have no physical evidence to connect the two, sir, but at the same time . . . at the same time, we got us two middle-aged Vietnamese men who both manage to get themselves a serious high-and-tight haircut. You ask me, I'd say, yes, sir, they're connected. Surely are. Exactly how I can't say, but they're connected. Yes, sir."

"And your killer . . . is he on this installation? Is he one of ours?"

"No way of knowin', General, but my gut says, no. I don't think he's billeted here or on Knox either."

"Your gut?"

"Yes, sir. That's all I've got at this point."

General Anderson nodded slowly as he thought. "You say billeted . . . so you think he's a green-suiter? Or was that a slip of the tongue?" he asked after a pause.

"Slip, sir. No, sir, I have no reason to think he's one of us. Not necessarily. Could be, certainly. Could just as soon not be."

"Why does your gut say he isn't here?"

Deveroux blew air into his cheeks, inflating them before slowly venting. "The distance mostly. We haven't found anythin' that links the two victims other than nationality. Neither had any family, and they don't appear to have any business connections with each other. I'm still waitin' on some word from the immigration folks about when they came to this country, from where . . ."

"Chief, you're aware that I asked for you to be assigned to this case personally."

"Yes, sir."

"Personally."

"Yes, sir."

"Do you know why?"

Deveroux didn't answer. No answer was expected. He waited.

"You're the man that brought down General Needley, that right?"

"Sir," Deveroux started to answer. "I . . ."

Anderson held up a palm. "Tom Needley was a friend of mine. You aware of that?"

Shuck Deveroux took a breath and held it, waiting for Anderson to continue. When he didn't, Deveroux spoke. "General Needley hired and promoted his mistress to a high-rankin' position in the government and defrauded the taxpayers of this country with bogus travel and expenses. He degraded the readiness of his command and wreaked havoc on the morale of his men."

"In your opinion."

"In fact, sir, and as bad as that may be, he showed a lack of integrity and character."

"And you have a zero tolerance for that, do you, Chief?"

"I do, sir. Commanders are supposed to command, not their girlfriends."

Jim Anderson nodded slowly, his eyes on Deveroux. "Sounds like a job better suited to the inspector general's office than CID."

"If it were as simple as a misuse of resources, yes, sir, you'd be correct, but General Needley's actions endangered the lives of his men in Iraq. There're two young men dead today. Kids that wanted nothin' more than to be soldiers."

"You're on record as saying that Tom Needley was responsible for their deaths."

"Yes, sir. I think you can blame General Needley—at least indirectly."

"But you couldn't prove it."

Shuck Deveroux took another long breath. "I could."

"Say again."

"I could."

"But you didn't."

"The army didn't."

The general leaned back in his chair and studied the CID agent. After a moment he smiled. "Taking down a well-connected general officer is not the best way to advance your career, Chief Deveroux."

Now Shuck smiled. The tension lifted. "You're right about that, sir. Wife has made the same point on more than one occasion."

"But you did it anyway."

"Yes, sir. Didn't have a choice. Look, sir, no disrespect, but I pulled two hardship tours without my family because of that case. I'm not much inclined to apologize."

"No one has asked you to, Chief." Anderson paused. "Not me, anyhow. Must have been hard to leave your wife and kids. Boys, that right?"

"Two, sir. Still fairly young. And yes, sir, it was hard."

Anderson nodded again. "Tom Needley put getting his oil changed above his duty to this country. If it's any consolation, Chief, friend or no friend, he got off lighter than he deserved. My opinion."

"Thank you, sir. That's the way I see it."

"But I believe I asked you a question. You know why I requested you?"

"No, sir."

"I asked for you because they say you're the best we have. Are you, Chief Deveroux? Are you the best we have?"

"Sir, I . . ."

"Tell me, Chief, are you up to this or aren't you?" There was a tempered edge to his voice that hadn't been there when the conversation started, not malice as much as control.

"To be honest, sir, I don't know. This is big; bigger than anythin' I've ever come by. Maybe too big. Maybe it's time to call in some help here. The FBI maybe. I . . . I don't really know."

General Anderson looked at Deveroux for several minutes without speaking, then he stood up and began walking behind his desk. Back and forth. He stopped and looked again at Deveroux. "I'll answer my own question, Chief—if you won't. I do know. I asked for you. You're the horse I'm riding. We don't need anybody to wash our laundry. Am I clear? Not the FBI. Not the fricking local police. Am I clear?"

"Roger that."

"I hope I am. I better be. Now, I talked to General Proctor at Fort Knox this morning. He and I are in agreement. I also contacted your boss at Belvoir. We were at the Academy together. Called in some markers. We're all on the same page of music. The two cases need one effort. One focus. Everyone's comfortable with you—except for perhaps you, that is. Still . . ." He sat down and propped his elbows on his desk, interlacing his fingers under his chin. He paused again as he focused his thought before pressing on. His edge had softened. "I'm going to instruct Lieutenant Colonel Riggins to form a task force that will assume the responsibility for the investigations of both murders— the one at Fort Knox and the one here. It'll be headquartered here. Belvoir's blessed it. Full authority. Blank check. You're to head up that task force, Chief Deveroux. You're to get this monkey skinned, breaded, and pan-fried, and you're to do it quickly. Whatever you need, you ask. Understood?"

"Yes, sir, but . . ."

"You will find the person who did this, and when you do, you will hold him still while I chainsaw his goddamn nuts off and serve them up on a salt cracker. We clear? I hope we're clear on this. Nobody shits in my garden. Nobody."

"Roger that, sir. Sir?"

"Yes, Chief."

"Any guidance on who else will be on the task force?"

The general smiled for the first time since the conversation had really started. "That's your problem, Chief Deveroux. Dismissed."

CHAPTER 21

Fort Campbell, Kentucky
FRIDAY, APRIL 11, 2008

Shuck Deveroux was still completely lost. As best he could figure, the task force title was simply a way to formally acknowledge that he had jurisdiction for not one, but two murders, on not one, but two army installations. It was ironic that one of the biggest cases to drop in the CID's lap since Jeffrey MacDonald, the biggest case in twenty years, certainly the biggest case in Deveroux's career, came at a time when the office was understaffed and undermanned. Iraq and the War on Terror had siphoned off manning and resources like an open vein. The best that could be scrambled together on short notice were Dave Pagano, another agent named Jim Colvin, and a half dozen enlisted soldiers. More agents were on request, but with the current priorities, the request was nothing more than a paper drill. In fact, Shuck knew that as important as this case was, if some leads didn't start producing results soon, he was going to have a hard time holding on to the few men that he had.

He looked at his watch. It was a little past sixteen hundred hours, and he was due in the general's office again in less than an hour for what would be another encore performance of the "No, sir, General, I don't have clue one, sir" show. At least he could now dilute the burden and say, "No, sir, General, the *task force* doesn't have clue one." There were two sides to every play on words.

The task force had been active, even if it hadn't produced much for the effort. Dave Pagano was kept busy shuttling back and forth to Fort Knox to coordinate the efforts there, while Colvin had shouldered through over three hundred interviews—somewhere in the vicinity of four hundred men were on the initial interview list—though none had proven the least bit useful. The enlisted men were gainfully occupied with the mounting administrative matters.

Shuck's desk was layered with large color photographs and scaled diagrams, all interleafed with one another. He'd been comparing the scene photos from the Patton Museum that had been sent over from Knox with those taken of the Buick down the road. There was an obvious connection between the two events; that was clear even before his contact at the INS had called. Deveroux didn't remember a great deal from his junior class in basic statistics and probability, but he did know that if you put two middle-aged Vietnamese marbles, missing the tops of their heads, into a paper sack containing a couple of thousand black and white marbles, the odds of drawing just those two Vietnamese marbles back out of the bag were somewhere in the vicinity of one out of not-very-likely.

And then there was the immigration and naturalization evidence.

His INS contact had faxed him yesterday evening after work. It had taken several days and even more favors to search back that far, but it proved worth the wait. According to the immigration records, Mr. Ngon and Mr. Han had entered the United States on the same day, December 11, 1974, and through the same port of entry—Travis Air Force Base near Oakland.

CHAPTER 22

Thanh Lay Hamlet, East of Saigon, Republic of Vietnam
SATURDAY, SEPTEMBER 12, 1970

The large, muscular body of ARVN Colonel Pham Van Minh spasmed twice, like a bluegill pulled onto a sunny dock; then he went absolutely still. The thumb-sized, copper-jacketed .45 slug had effectively removed the back of his head, and its sticky contents were now sprayed across the rear of the jeep like clumps of pinkish cottage cheese. Major Doan Minh Tuyen continued to sit, rock-still, in the rear seat, his eyes closed, the bright glistening clumps of Colonel Pham's brain glued to his face and chest.

The echo of the blast died away, but the ringing in Jimmy Lee Tenkiller's ears didn't. General Ngo Van Thu's eyes had not left Tenkiller's face. He didn't even glance at the body of the man whose head he'd just remodeled, and he was still smiling as he eased the hammer down on the pistol. "Master Sergeant Tenkiller, now I will repeat myself. I believe you may have some items for me."

Tenkiller looked at the general and then at Major Doan Tuyen and then at the general. "You crazy sonofabitch," was all that Jimmy Lee could think to say, and even then it came out as a broken whisper.

"Perhaps this is so, Master Sergeant, I have heard this expression before, but also I am a man of limited patience. And I am now at my limit." He took his eyes away from Tenkiller long enough to say something quickly and quietly in Vietnamese to the major. He then took hold of Tenkiller's upper right arm, pinching it tightly and surprisingly hard for a man so slight, and led him away from the side of the jeep. "It is most unfortunate, the colonel's sudden death. Yes, I think this is so. War, yes? And now I must give also the news to my sister."

The general saw the confusion on Tenkiller's face. "You did not know, I see. Yes, Master Sergeant, Colonel Pham was my brother-in-law. We know each other since we were young schoolboys. Yes, it is sad. My youngest sister is now a widow, and I must tell her the bad information. Yes, this war is most unfortunate." The general still held the pistol in one hand and Tenkiller's arm in the other.

"You crazy sonofabitch." It was louder this time, more angry than awed.

General Ngo Van Thu didn't respond immediately. He had turned slightly and was watching Major Doan pull the body out of the jeep onto the ground. The major obviously was trying to touch the body as little as possible, but the late colonel's uncooperative legs had wedged under the steering column in their death spasm, and the body was awkwardly cascading onto the ground, head down, like an enormous Slinky. Blood was everywhere. The general turned his attention back to Tenkiller.

"It is unfortunate, and now you must decide what you are going to do."

Tenkiller pulled his arm free. "What, General? Are you going to shoot me too? Is that your plan, you bastard?"

Ngo Thu smiled broadly as he removed his sunglasses. He looked down at the gun in his hand, his expression suggesting that he was surprised to find it still there. "You are my friend, Master Sergeant Tenkiller, my . . . good associate. Why would I wish to harm you . . . shoot you?"

"Because you're crazy . . . because I know too much. Because I just saw you murder your own goddamn brother-in-law, you crazy sonofabitch."

"Ahh." General Ngo nodded slowly while he formulated his response. "You believe you have seen that?"

"Of course I saw it." Jimmy Lee Tenkiller sounded as wild as Ngo Thu was calm.

"I am afraid you are mistaken, Master Sergeant. The heat, perhaps. No, my friend, that is not what happened. No. Major Doan and myself, so sadly, we saw you, Master Sergeant Tenkiller, kill Colonel Pham. We were without the power to stop you; you are a most violent man. And fast. You have yourself told me stories of your violence, have you not? And your speed, this is well known. So sad." The general again turned his head slightly and looked at the progress Doan Tuyen was making with the body. "Yes. It was most unfortunate."

"Me? You're out of your goddamn mind, General. No one is going to believe that."

"No? I think you are mistaken. They cannot but believe the evidence. There are witnesses," he said, motioning to the major with a nod of his head. "And many other witnesses I can produce. Much evidence. And the gun is from your depot, is it not? Traceable? No, Sergeant Tenkiller, they will believe."

"Nobody's gonna buy that. Why would I kill the colonel?"

The general smiled again. "You are a wild Red Man, are you not? You have told me many stories of killing men and cutting their hairs off with your warrior's tomahawk—have you not? You are a most violent man, I think, or do you boast too loudly?"

"Those were just stories."

The general smiled.

"Motive," Tenkiller said. "Do you understand? Motive? I had no reason to. Without motive, nobody in the U.S. will believe . . ."

"Look around, Master Sergeant." Ngo Thu gestured to the abandoned huts. His voice took on the tone of a schoolmaster whose patience with a troublesome student was beginning to chafe. "I think perhaps you are not in the United States. No, you and my unfortunate brother-in-law were," he started to answer quickly, but then paused while he searched for the English word that he wanted, "you were, I think, involved in an illegal activity. Gentlemen involved in these things sometimes argue and disagree. Sometimes violent things happen."

Tenkiller paused while he thought through what he was hearing. "And you, General, what about you? We're all in this one together.

Don't forget that. I go down, and you go down with me. Don't forget that. Maybe they will think I did it, but I can take you down too. Don't forget that."

"Ahh, but it is you who forgets, Master Sergeant. You are who you are, but I am a general and a most trusted ally to your government. It would be most embarrassing for such a trusted ally to do such a thing as you say. Very embarrassing for your government. No, for you this is most unfortunate."

Tenkiller didn't respond. He looked over to see Major Doan Tuyen disappear around the side of one of the huts, pulling Colonel Pham's large body behind him. He was headed in the direction of the village cemetery.

"Master Sergeant Tenkiller, I am of little patience. Now, I believe you may have some items for me."

"Yes," Tenkiller said. He struggled to keep his voice free of resignation. "But . . . I'll need some more time . . . another week, maybe two, maybe longer. It won't be easy."

Ngo Thu put his sunglasses back on and smiled.

Jimmy Lee Tenkiller looked back into the general's eyes. In the shiny teardrop-shaped green lenses he once again saw his own reflection.

CHAPTER 23

Columbia, South Carolina
FRIDAY, APRIL 11, 2008

Penny Kegin had been thinking about it for some time, ever since that strange phone call almost seven months ago, but she hadn't found the courage to act; hadn't even found the courage to put the box away after the strange man had rummaged through it and taken some items. It had sat in the corner of Michael's old room like a lump of brown undigested food. Her husband, Richard, had urged her to go through it, had said he'd leave her alone or go through it with her—whichever she wanted. He'd said it'd be cathartic.

She'd been thinking about it.

Why today was different from yesterday or the day before or the weeks and months before, she didn't realize at first. Why today, after all the years, did she decide to look through it? Only later did she connect the dots of her subconscious. It was *The Day*. The date. Patrick had proposed to her on the eleventh of April his freshman year at the Citadel, on a clear bright morning on the steps of the Summerall Chapel. It had all seemed so absolutely magical then, he was so handsome and full of dash and life and promise, and now she couldn't even conjure up his face without the help of a photo album.

The box had arrived two weeks after the funeral. The scab that had started slowly to knit over was abraded raw by the forms and releases that she'd been forced to sign; abraded so raw that she hadn't even cut the tape seal on the box. Instead she'd placed it in the attic with old suitcases full of his clothes and the footlocker with his cadet uniform and his saber—unopened—an emotional time capsule to be cracked at some future date when her children found the need to plumb their roots. She'd dutifully moved it from house to house, and had more than once toyed with the idea of giving it to Patrick's parents after Richard and she had decided to marry, but by then the Kendricks were so feeble that it would have served no useful purpose but to awaken confusion and sorrow. In the end she had once again stowed the box away in the recesses of the attic as well as her mind.

Until he called.

The strange man.

Thinking back on it, Penny wondered why she hadn't been surprised. It was as if she knew he'd call, or knew he'd come. She'd had that feeling before. Somehow she knew it was the red-haired soldier; the one at Patrick's funeral; the one she'd hated for getting injured and coming home.

Saturday afternoon. Her son, Michael, and his boys were visiting from New York, and Richard had taken them to a South Carolina Gamecocks football game. Penny had wanted to go with them, not so much for the football as for time with her grandsons, but she also knew they'd have more fun without her. Instead she'd occupied herself with baking a couple of Karo nut pies for the boys. She'd just taken the first one out of the oven when the phone rang.

"Hello, Kegin residence," she'd answered.

"Hello, Mrs. Kegin," the voice had replied. "I'm trying to reach the former Mrs. Patrick Kendrick. First Lieutenant Patrick Kendrick. I realize this is awkward, but am I calling the right address?"

Penny had felt her face flush. She *knew*. "I'm sorry. I think you have the wrong—"

"Mrs. Kendrick, please, give me just a moment of your time."

"It's Mrs. Kegin now, and I don't understand what you could possibly want with me. I haven't been Mrs. Kendrick since . . ."

"Since June 22, 1970 . . . yes, ma'am, I know," the voice quietly said.

"You do? Did you know Patrick?

There was a hesitation on the other end of the phone. "Not really. No, ma'am."

"Then I don't understand." Her heart began to race. "If you'll excuse me, I have—"

"I attended his funeral," the man said quickly. Quietly. "In a way, I knew your husband quite well. And his men. All of them."

Now it was Penny Kegin's turn to hesitate. "That's right. You were at the funeral, weren't you?" Penny didn't know how she knew, but the image flashed back with a brightness undimmed by thirty-eight years. She could picture him clearly, standing by the casket, hat held strangely in his hand, looking down into the gaping hole in the ground. His red hair and gray eyes. She could picture him more clearly than she could Patrick. She shuddered at the realization.

"Yes, ma'am."

Penny sat down on a bar stool in her kitchen. She was quiet for a long time. "Why? Why? Why were you there? I've always wondered."

The voice on the phone hesitated again. When he responded it was quiet and dry and very far away. "Because it could have been me; it should have been me."

"You were the one who'd gotten himself injured; the careless one; the one Patrick had to replace," Penny stated it as much as asked it. She swallowed hard at the knot that had reappeared in her throat. "You're Paul Fick, aren't you?"

"Yes, ma'am."

"You know, Lieutenant Fick, Patrick wasn't supposed to go to Vietnam. We were going to Germany. Heidelberg. Did you know that? They say it's beautiful there, especially in the spring. Patrick had promised me we'd both learn to ski. Did you know that?"

"Mrs. Kegin . . ."

"I've spent the last thirty-eight years hating you, Lieutenant Fick. Do you know that? I don't even know you, and yet I hate you with every cord and fiber of my being. Do you know that, Lieutenant?"

Fick didn't respond, and for a moment Penny thought that he'd hung up. Then she heard him sigh and swallow awkwardly and loudly.

"What can I possibly do for you, Lieutenant?" she asked. "Please don't tell me you're calling for forgiveness. Is that what you want? Is it? Tell me, Lieutenant, what can I possibly help you with?"

"I . . . I was . . . I'm not sure you can."

Penny was sitting very straight, her body rigid. She closed her eyes and steadied her breath.

"Mrs. Kend . . . Mrs. Kegin, you've probably got good reason to hate me, and if it's any consolation, there isn't anything that you could think about me that I haven't thought about myself already. Those were my men who were ambushed and killed. I knew them. I could tell you the names of the wives and girlfriends, the type of cars they drove, the names of their dogs. I knew their dreams and hopes for the future. I trained them. There hasn't been a day gone by since that June morning that I haven't thought about what might have been. About how things might have been different. About how maybe I could have changed things, seen things in time, reacted."

Penny sat quietly, her eyes remaining closed. Finally she spoke. "What can I do for you Mr. Fick?"

"Do you still have your husband's things? Lieutenant Kendrick's things? The effects returned from Vietnam?"

She hesitated. In her mind she pictured the box, its sides now broken down from a dozen moves. "Yes."

"Mrs. Kegin, I know you've got every reason in the world to say no, but . . . would you . . . can I look through them?" he asked.

A piercing staccato beep had made Penny Kegin jump. It was the smoke detector. She'd burned her second pie.

CHAPTER 24

U.S. Army Central Identification Laboratory, Hawaii
TUESDAY, APRIL 15, 2008

Kel sat at his desk looking at his telephone, steeling himself as if he was preparing to walk on a bed of hot coals. It was bordering on something clinical. Phobia? Dysfunction? Whatever it was, he approached making telephone calls with the same degree of reflexive dread that he reserved for answering them. His palms had actually started to moisten.

At seven o'clock in the morning, the office was still quiet. The sharp rumble and throb of the day's events were still at least a half hour away. A few early arrivals were filtering in to their desks, still busy checking emails and messages and slurping coffee, but the critical mass necessary to set off the chain reaction of the morning's first crisis hadn't been reached. Kel knew that if he was to get this phone call made before someone set his hair on fire, he needed to get after it quickly. He rubbed his palms on his thighs, picked up the receiver, and dialed the number. The phone rang twice.

"Sergeant Gonzalez, CID. How may I help you, sir or madam?" answered the voice on the other end. It was officious but neutral in tone, and rattled its words off so quickly as to be almost unintelligible.

"Good mornin', Sergeant. This is Dr. McKelvey at the U.S. Army Central ID Lab in Hawaii. How you doin' this mornin'?"

"Fine, sir."

"Good, good. Hey, Sergeant, I'm tryin' to reach a Chief Deveroux. Any chance this might be the right number?"

"Yes, sir. May I ask the nature of your call?"

"Great. Ahh, well, you sure can, but it's a bit round-about really. How 'bout just connectin' me up with Chief Deveroux, if he's available. Can you do that?"

"Sir. Hold on."

There was a faint hiss on the phone and Kel knew he was being transferred. He listened patiently to a soft background hiss for almost two minutes before the phone clicked loudly.

"Chief Warrant Deveroux here. What can I do for you, sir?"

"Hey, Chief. This is Kel McKelvey from CILHI."

"Hey yourself," Deveroux replied, recognizing the voice on the other end. "Sorry. Sergeant Gonzalez musta not gotten your name. He told me it was some doc from the CID lab at Fort Gilliam. I'm waitin' on some test results from them."

"My fault. Shouldn't have said the Central ID Lab—it always confuses folks." In the acronymic world of the military, the U.S. Army Central Identification Laboratory, Hawaii—the USACILHI— was always being confused with the U.S. Army Central Investigation Laboratory, the USACIL.

"Not a problem, Kel. Long time," Deveroux said. "What's shakin' with you these days?" Five years earlier, Deveroux had been leading an investigation of a particularly gruesome murder that had occurred at Fort Bliss, Texas. The dismembered head and torso of a young female soldier had been buried on one of the isolated firing ranges, and it was only after a CILHI recovery team had spent two weeks at the site that it had been found. Kel and Deveroux, discovering that they both hailed from Arkansas, had gotten to know each other, though they'd had no contact since the resulting trial a year later.

"What isn't? How 'bout on your end of the rope?"

Deveroux laughed. "Nothin' you got time to hear, Doc. Real mess is what's on my plate. Anyhow, what can I do for the Central ID Lab—or is this purely social?"

Now it was Kel's turn to laugh. "I wish it were social, but doesn't sound like either one of us has time for that anymore. Actually, Shuck, this is kinda . . . umm . . . well, sir, you're gonna think this is kinda strange. Probably the last thing you got time to mess with, but I didn't know who else to contact. I figured you could point me in the right direction."

"Shoot."

"Well, I'm workin' a case right now. Vietnam-era case. We're tryin' to identify a young guy that we're carryin' as KIA—name of Tenkiller. Master Sergeant Jimmy Tenkiller. We had a team over there recently, in Vietnam that is. Actually it was Caroline Thompson—remember her from that case at Bliss?"

"Yeah, sure do. Tell her hey for me."

"Will do. Anyhow, she excavated a grave, recovered a skeleton, nice job, we bring it back, analyze it, so on, so on. We're still waiting on the DNA results, but the bottom line is that it may not be the guy we're lookin' for. There are some dental inconsistencies. Okay, that happens, not a problem. But where it gets interestin' is the fact that the Vietnamese were actin' all funny 'bout it. I mean seriously funny. So I had the defense attaché in Vietnam ask around, and well, like I say, that's when it gets interestin'."

"How so?" Deveroux looked at his watch. He wanted to be cordial but felt he needed to be pursuing his own case, and the sand was draining out of his hourglass.

"Turns out this KIA we're lookin' for may have been involved in a big black market ring that was operatin' durin' the war. Late sixties, early seventies. Our government—and by that I mean you boys at the CID—could never prove it, but apparently they investigated it pretty vigorously at the time. What's more, this soldier, this KIA, was part of a group of five local shitbags, including an ARVN general, that ran the show. They called themselves the Brotherhood of the Five—or some such damn name."

"Back up. We talkin' Vietnam War, right? As in thirty-some years ago."

"Yup. Closer to forty, actually."

"Hmm. And this guy's black market activities, they have anythin' to do with his gettin' hisself killed?"

"The KIA fella, you mean? Yeah, maybe, probably. Who knows? Truth is, we don't know anythin' for sure. Actually, that's where I need the assistance."

"The Brotherhood of Five, huh? So how can I help?" Deveroux asked. His interest was starting to pique despite his own problems.

"Don't know that you can, but it'd be very useful to us if we could track down his former Vietnamese partners in crime—the Brotherhood, that is. I'm hopin' they might have some information that we don't, like, you know, like maybe what happened to Sergeant Tenkiller? Where was he last seen? That sort of thing. I'm afraid the U.S. records don't help us much, and I'm admittedly graspin' at straws."

"You really think they'd talk? Assumin' you can find them, that is."

"Who knows? Certainly, I'm not expectin' them to admit to anythin' illegal. But maybe they can shed some light into where we might look for this guy. At this point, any information would be better than what we're workin' off of—which is zero."

"Okay. But you still haven't told me how can I help."

"Well, like I said, I'm not so sure you can, but I thought you might know who could. Name. Telephone number. Point me in the right direction if nothin' else. What I need is someone who can track these Five Bubbas down."

"You mean the Vietnamese? You think they're here in the U.S., or are you lookin' for them elsewhere?"

"Here or Canada, I'd guess. Maybe France, but I'm bettin' here. Most high-rankin' Vietnamese officers didn't stay on to see how the new regime was goin' to treat them. Go figure, right? So most came here; at least a lot of 'em did. Especially the more senior ones. One of these guys we're lookin' for was a general; the others probably carried his nuts around on a pillow—colonels or majors, I'd suspect."

"Hmm. You checked with INS?"

"Nope. No connections with them. I was thinkin' CID since y'all have files on these guys."

Deveroux laughed. "Had. Past tense. If we ever did."

Kel laughed. "Shit, son, I work for Uncle Sam as well. If you had a file, you have a file. How 'bout it?"

"I'd like to help, Kel." Deveroux sighed loudly into the phone.

"Just how hot is this tater? I'm really under the gun with a double killin' that I somehow got myself assigned to—check that—I mean that I've been given the opportunity of a career to pursue; I doubt I could shake a leg free for—oh, I don't know . . . maybe sixty or seventy years at the rate I'm goin'."

"Sounds like the career opportunities I usually draw. Does your job come with a parkin' space?"

Deveroux laughed. "Realistically, it'll probably be two, three months before I can tend to it. And I'm not promisin' anythin'."

"Understood."

"In that case, gimme the names of your Vietnamese, and I'll get to it as soon as I can. If I can't, I'll hunt up someone in the business who can. Good enough?"

"Good enough. Thanks."

"Don't sweat it. I still owe all y'all for Bliss."

"You don't owe us anythin', but thanks nonetheless. You got a pencil?"

"Go."

"Well, I don't know how accurate some of this is, but this is what I've got. There's three of 'em, countin' the ARVN general I mentioned. The big dog is General Ngo Van Thu; the other two were field grades, from what I can gather. Don't know if both of them were ARVN or if they might have been Vietnamese air force. All I know is that they were South Vietnamese military."

"Names?"

"Yeah. Okay, one was . . . let's see," Kel held the phone receiver against his shoulder with his chin as he searched his desk for the piece of paper he'd written the names on. "Ready? Here we go, I mentioned the general, the other two were a Mr. Linh and a Mr. Doan."

"You want to spell any of those out for me? I am, after all, a product of the Arkansas state school system."

"Tell me about it. Sure. Let's start with the general. Name is N-G-O, as in Bingo-was-his-name-o, space, then V-A-N, another space, then T-H-U."

"Whoa. Back the car up. I got the N-G-O, then Vee? Or d'you say Bee?"

"Vee as in Vinegar. Victor, Alpha, November, then a space, then Tango, Hotel, Uniform."

". . . Hotel, Uniform. Got it. Next?"

"Next is Mr. Linh—spelled Lima, India, November, Hotel. Surnames, Nhu—November, Hotel, Uniform—space, then N-G-O-N. I'm not even goin' to guess at the accent marks."

"Thank you."

"Don't mention it. Okay, the last one is a Mr. Doan, spelled D-O-A-N. Minh Tuyen, spelled M-I-N-H then a space, and then T-U-Y-E-N."

"Okay, got it. So, as soon as I get some time, you'd like me to try and track down this . . . Mr. Ngo, Mr. Linh, and Mr. Doan? Is that right?"

"Almost. Actually, I don't know if they'd be usin' the Vietnamese form of their names or whether they've Americanized them, but yeah, I'd like you to locate them if possible."

"What do you mean usin' their American names? They got other names?"

"No. You know, same names, just different order. Kinda like three-card-monte. In Vietnamese, the first name is actually the family name. So, the one you called Mr. Ngo—the general—he may be going by either Ngo or Thu; Linh Ngon may be callin' himself either Mr. Linh or Mr. Ngon, and Mr. Doan might be Mr. Tuyen. But whether they're usin' the traditional order or not is anybody's guess . . ."

"Wait a second," Deveroux said. He placed the receiver down on his desk and began shuffling the files about hurriedly. Hearing the names rearranged had set a bell to ringing in his head. He finally found the folder on the Fort Knox murder. The ME's report was near the top. He looked at the top line.

Decedent: Ngon, Linh Nhu.

He picked up the phone. "Doc? You still there?"

"Yeah. Catch a sudden itch?"

"Sort of. Say that again."

"Catch a . . ."

"Yeah, funny, no, I mean that part about the names. You sayin' last names are first and firsts are lasts?"

"Sometimes. Depends on what they did when they arrived here. You know, it's like when all the Polish and Russians landed at Ellis Island and came away with Smith and Jones instead of Smithovich and Jonesivich. Same thing, sort of. Names get changed around. In this case, might be last to first, first to last."

"So Linh Nhu Ngon wouldn't be Mr. Ngon? He'd really be Mr. Linh?" Deveroux's thick Arkansas tongue had a hard time striking the right pronunciation, and it came out closer to *EN-goon,* but Kel understood the intent.

"Traditionally, in Vietnam anyhow, he'd be Mr. Linh, but he might be known to his American neighbors as Ngon. Depends on how much he wanted to assimilate. Why, does it make a difference?"

"I . . . I don't know. I doubt it . . . How d'you suppose these guys would've gotten into the U.S.?"

"Who knows? My guess is a U.S. aircraft. C-141 or a C-5, maybe. High-rankin' Vietnamese got to use Uncle Sam's taxi service. They probably came through San Francisco. Travis Air Force Base, most likely."

Shuck Deveroux was quiet for a long time; finally, he spoke. "Doc. I think I know where to find your Mr. Linh."

"Yeah. Right."

"No. Really."

"No shit? You are good, Deveroux. Where?"

"Try the Louisville coroner's office."

CHAPTER 25

Saigon, Republic of Vietnam
MONDAY, SEPTEMBER 14, 1970

"Not an option, Sergeant." John Bergeron's voice resembled a marble lazily rolling around in a tin pie plate. Its south Louisiana modulation and volume were erratic, and he was hard to listen to and generally even harder to look at, given his tendency to seek the familiar comfort of the shadows. Today was no different. The rolling voice seemed to be coming from somewhere near the shuttered window, but in the waning daylight Jimmy Lee Tenkiller's eyes couldn't find the focus. "Not at all an option, you," the voice repeated.

"I don't think you understand, Mr. Bergeron," Tenkiller replied. He beamed his voice in the direction where the shadows seemed the darkest. "This isn't what I signed up for. It's gone too far. You don't understand."

"Oh, but I do. It's you who don't quite understand, Cochise. We've got way too much invested in this, way too much for anyone to suddenly get a touch of the cold shivers. And that's what I'm sensing here, a malignant case of no balls."

"It's not that . . ."

"No? Then what is it, Chief? You tell me, 'cause from where I sit it looks like some damn zip-head general waves a gun 'round and Tonto here suddenly can't find his dick to piss with."

"Screw you. You weren't there. He's crazy, that man." Jimmy Lee Tenkiller balled his fists at his side and tried to pattern Bergeron's shadowy form in the remaining light. He steadied his breathing. Bergeron's type pushed buttons. Jimmy Lee Tenkiller had had his buttons pushed his whole life. He exhaled completely and then slowly drew in a new lungful.

"Look 'round, Chief. This is French-Indo-Frickin'-China, my friend. Find me one person over here who isn't goddamn crazy. Jus one, you."

"That isn't all."

"No? Then tell me, Chief. Who pissed in your war bonnet?"

"You've seen the reports. Those men from the twenty-fifth ID— you seen someone shredded by a claymore, Mr. Bergeron?"

"Question is . . . have you, Chief?" Bergeron waited momentarily for a reply, and when none came he pressed forward. "Didn't think so. Quartermaster. Look, Sergeant Tenkiller, when I selected you for this operation, I did so because of your access to certain resources. I never assumed that you'd go and start thinking for yourself. Bad habit to get started, my red friend."

"Maybe. But maybe it's better than letting a suit like you do the thinking. Men like you, their thinking gets other men killed."

"Perhaps, Cochise, but my thinking will also save men in the end. And that's what this little dance is all about, isn't it? Saving men. Saving a whole friggin' country. Saving a whole friggin' way of life. Now listen carefully, Chief, pulling pitch right now is a no-go. You read me? A no-go. You back out now and the souls of all those dead men that you seem so concerned about, they gonna be on your head. They'll hang around your neck for the rest of your life. Let's remember the facts, here; you supplied that crate of claymores, and you've got nothing to show for it but some money in what must be rather a fat bank account by now. That how we end it? You just count your money and leave the dirty dishes for someone else to wash."

Bergeron waited for a response but when none came, he continued. "No, I don't think so; I think we gonna play this out—comprende? Now, if that's it, if it's about money, more wampum, well, anything's negotiable, but not by ultimatum. You want to shake me down for some more glass beads, hey, that's a book I can read, but not in midoperation. No, sir, Chief. We play this out. We clear?

Jimmy Lee Tenkiller blinked hard. The room was close and smelled of mildew and vinegar from soured clothing that never completely dried in the humid air of South Vietnam. There was the almost fecund smell of the river, and dried cuttlefish, and wood smoke. Sweat worked its way into the corners of his eyes and stung. He closed his eyes again and thought about the spinsters at the Indian Boys School. He thought about what had almost been. He thought about getting rattled and not keeping his toe pointed.

He wanted nothing more than to run, fast and long, across a treeless, red soil plain.

CHAPTER 26

Kel was late for a staff meeting with the CILHI's commander, Colonel Boschet. Time once again for a weekly dose of the commander's numb-nutted, adolescent humor and overt posturing about the burdens of being a "steward" of the taxpayers' money, all the while flushing efficiency down the toilet and wasting countless man hours in the countless meetings that were required for the staff to educate him in the basics of his job. He was sure the first ten minutes would be spent re-educating the commander about how to do something complex, like open his window or use his stapler without drawing blood, but he also knew that he couldn't just refuse to show up. He'd promised Les Neep that he'd make an effort to get along, and the commander's brittle ego would preclude adjourning the meeting until all of his courtesans had been properly assembled and provided with the highlights of how well he had performed on his last assignment in the Pentagon, which, as best Kel could reconstruct, involved driving a whole office of hardworking government employees to take early retirement. The problem, of course, was that the rest of the assembled senior staff was being held hostage until Kel arrived, by a man whose idea of humor, at its wittiest, involved rhyming things with the word "Nantucket." Accordingly, when D.S. had asked Kel if he had a minute to talk about the problem of getting a DNA sample from Tenkiller's reluctant brother, Kel had asked him to talk as he headed down the hall to the commander's office. As they drew near, they could see that his door was closed, which suggested that Kel was probably the last to arrive.

"If the brother won't cooperate, let's see about goin' around him. How's the genealogy search comin' along? Just because Tenkiller's brother doesn't want to give a blood sample doesn't mean that there isn't another maternal relative out there," Kel said.

"Easier said than done, boss. Our genealogy consultant got on this as soon as you told her to, but she's drawing blanks," D.S. said. He took a small skip to adjust to Kel's longer stride. Kel's normal walking speed always resembled that of a man about to put his head through a brick wall, but if D.S. hadn't known better, he'd have thought the scientific director was anxious to get to the meeting by the pace he was setting. But he definitely knew better.

"How so?"

"Tenkiller had a brother, younger I think, and that's it. No maternal aunts or uncles, obviously no cousins on that side. No aunts or uncles on either side, for that matter. Both his parents were only children."

"Family tree sort of got sawed off short, huh? Well, tell her to keep lookin'."

"Will do, but these aren't your average records that she's dealing with."

Kel nodded and slowed his pace. "Got a point. Tenkiller's mother was a Cherokee, wasn't she? They aren't one of the Five Civilized Tribes for nothin'. Cherokees keep pretty thorough tribal rolls, from what I understand. Let's give her some more time. You'll see. She'll find someone."

D.S. shook his head. "I dunno—"

"Look, I don't have time to do this myself. There're fifty other cases out on the lab floor. But if I have to start checkin' genealogy records myself, I will."

"Hey, don't bite my head off."

Kel sighed and shook his head. "Sorry." They had reached the commander's door, and Kel paused with his hand lightly cupping the doorknob. They could hear the commander's voice droning on the other side. He shot a quick look at D.S. "Five bucks if you'll sit in this meetin' for me."

"Fifty."

"IOU?"

"Nope."

"C'mon."

"Cash. No checks. You haven't paid for the last time."

Kel closed his eyes and slowly turned the knob.

CHAPTER 27

Fort Campbell, Kentucky
WEDNESDAY, APRIL 16, 2008

The same humorless desk ornament of a major was again guarding the entrance to the general's office. His contempt for Deveroux had grown in direct proportion to the number of hours that Deveroux had spent talking to the general. Deveroux had been around long enough to know that young executive aides, especially those to general officers, often develop proprietary feelings out of all proportion with their responsibilities and duties, and don't share attention readily. This one was no different.

Shuck Deveroux sat quietly in the same chair as yesterday, and the day before, and the day before that. It was standard prison construction; ugly and dysfunctional. It was hard-backed, and what little padding it once had offered had long ago flattened into a vestigial reminder. He had been aware of it before, of how the particleboard pressed painfully against his ass, but now was lost in cavernous thought, picking his way through the thick briar patch of facts that made less and less sense the more he waded into them. He absentmindedly toyed with his wristwatch band.

The unctuous major looked up from his desk, his nostrils flared like an animal's, keen to capture any movement from the general's office; any sound; any change in the circulating air that would signal the general's needs or wants, that would signal opportunity. He had detected a shift in the air currents or the subtle flicker of a shadow. He sniffed.

"The general will see you now," he announced efficiently, no energy wasted where it need not be. "He has a very busy schedule, please limit . . . Warrant Officer Deveroux . . . I said, the general has . . ."

Deveroux stood up slowly at the sounding of his name but made no eye contact with the major. He had stiffened up in the short while he'd been waiting, and his knees reported like distant gunfire at being aroused. It took two steps before he managed to fully straighten up and move without a hitch.

". . . Be mindful of the general's time. Understood, Warrant Officer Deveroux?" Now it was the major's turn to avoid eye contact. He dipped his head and feigned absorption in a memorandum on his desk so as to best dismiss Deveroux as something unimportant to his world.

Deveroux smiled at the major's efforts as he walked into the general's office.

"Let me hazard a guess, Chief Deveroux. You still have nothing to report." General Anderson leaned back in his chair and cradled the back of his head with his hands. His voice was level, even fatherly, and disclosed no sense of its previous impatience or veiled disappointment. That had passed in the first few days of the investigation. Despite his attempt to impart his will to Deveroux, he understood that the case was dead-ended, and he was contemplating making some phone calls to see if someone would pull the plug on the patient.

Deveroux smiled. They had been refining the complex choreography of this dance every afternoon for the last week and a half. At first the general had been impatient for answers, even threatening to demonstrate how a size-twelve jungle boot can be made to fit sideways up a grown man's ass, but lately the tension was absent. Deveroux had no answers, and the general had come to expect none. The question now was how long they would continue these daily meetings. Both men certainly had better things to do with their afternoons, although Deveroux did derive a certain level of satisfaction with the jealousy visibly building within the young major sitting in the outer office. He also was surprised to realize that he enjoyed talking to the general, though he couldn't actually articulate why. Perhaps it was a father complex.

"You should avoid such hazards, General. Actually, I was thinkin' we might just try a change of pace today."

The general continued leaning back in his chair, but his eyes belied any casualness suggested by the lay of his body. "Go on, Chief," he said quietly. "Go on."

"Well, sir, without goin' into more detail than you probably got time to chew on, I got a call yesterday from a buddy with the Central ID Lab. You know, the folks that identify all the MIAs . . ."

"I know who they are. Go on, please."

"Yes, sir. Umm. Seems they're workin' on some old case from the Vietnam War that involves an MIA or a KIA; an American GI who got hisself mixed up with some black market fellas down in Saigon. As I understand it, this American had some high-rankin' ARVN partners . . ."

"And?" The general slowly brought himself upright and rotated his chair a quarter turn so that his left shoulder was to Deveroux and his gaze was focused on a small clump of trees visible through his window. For the first time, Deveroux noticed the black-and-drab octofoil combat patch on the general's left sleeve. Ninth Infantry Division. *Old Reliable.* The office had grown very quiet, and the light through the window made the general's short gray hair look like the thin, prickly, white halo around a peach. Despite the change in posture, he clearly was listening very closely to Deveroux.

"And . . . so this buddy at the CILHI is tryin' to track these ARVN fellas down," Deveroux continued. "He assumes that they're livin' in the United States; that's why he called me. He wants some help in locatin' them so he can talk to them. You know, see if they remember this American, know where he might have last been seen, et cetera."

"I might think you have quite enough on your dance card right now, Chief. Do you need to be taking on extra work?"

"Sir, yes, sir. I do at that—have a lot on my plate, that is. That's certainly true, except for the fact that one of these Vietnamese fellas they're lookin' for appears to be one Mr. Linh Nhu Ngon, late of downtown Louisville, Kentucky, and now minus some hair."

"The body from Fort Knox? You're sure of this?"

"Yes, sir. Fairly. I'm still runnin' it to ground, but, yes, sir, I'm sure. Same name, probably came through Travis Air Force Base out near Oakland."

"And you think there's a connection to this MIA that the Hawaii lab is looking for?" the general said slowly.

"Well now, don't know that I'd hunt that dog just yet, it's probably another dead end, but then I'm not in a position on this case to exclude much of anythin'. Like I said, I just found out about this yesterday afternoon, and I haven't really had a chance to chew on it long enough to tell much. May just be a coincidence, but . . ."

"Probably is just a coincidence." The general still had his shoulder to Deveroux and maintained a steady look out his window. "The American . . . the MIA that they're looking for . . . does he have a name?"

"Yes, sir. He's KIA actually. Name's Tenkiller. Master Sergeant Tenkiller. Indian, I think."

The general remained silent, but his shoulders seemed to stiffen and square. His gaze remained fixed on some soldiers milling about under the clump of trees across the street. Deveroux shifted his weight in his chair, unsure of where to take the briefing. He'd assumed the general would be pleased with any development on the case, but now he wasn't so sure; the body language seemed to suggest otherwise. The general answered his uncertainty.

"As you say, Chief Deveroux, probably a coincidence . . . a dead end . . . but I assume you'll investigate the possibility, nonetheless," the general replied. He swiveled his chair to face his desk and wrote quickly on a small pad of paper, which he then handed to Deveroux. "Perhaps he can help."

Shuck Deveroux looked down at the small cream-colored paper with the embossed red flag bearing the two white stars of a major general. Written in an open, cursive hand was the name *Brig Gen (Ret) Paul Fick.*

CHAPTER 28

"It seems that my good friend thinks I am . . . how did he say it? 'A crazy one,'" General Ngo Van Thu said as he stepped around the door frame into the room. It was dark in the room, and Ngo Van Thu moved with such an oiled grace that he scarcely made a sound.

"So he does," John Bergeron replied. "So he does. Crazy." He was still standing at the shuttered window from which he'd watched Jimmy Lee Tenkiller angrily depart. Short, parallel rectangles of dim light shot past the wooden slats and projected diagonally across his chest like chevrons.

Ngo Van Thu quietly took a seat against the wall and cozied into the comfort of the shadows. Only the small, fiery tip of his cigarette was readily visible. "That is good. I am pleased that I did not shoot my late brother-in-law for no effect." The general exhaled and a thin lens of smoke caught one of the stray shafts of light. It hung, shoulder height, across the room, and undulated slowly in the lazy air.

"I'm sure your late brother-in-law would fully understand, General Ngo. As long as you had a good reason, that is."

"Hmm. Perhaps so. Perhaps not so. He was not an intelligent man, my late brother-in-law, but he made my sister happy. Yes, I am glad for the effect. I am a crazy one, he says. I like that, but tell me, my friend John, perhaps there is too much effect? Your friend may yet find his feet."

"You mean Geronimo there? No, don't you worry about him. He ain't running nowhere; I gonna handle him." Bergeron was still looking out the window, watching the cyclo drivers and motor scooters and the hundreds of people on foot. Everyone in a hurry to arrive at nothing. Saigon in 1970 was like a bottle of soda shaken up. Thousands of bubbles mixed chaotically, waiting to have the pressure released.

"You say no. I am not so sure. He is Indian. A savage race. I would not like such a man to be my enemy."

"He's no enemy, General, and he's no savage. Believe me, he's just running a little nervous. Now's not the time to act like a woman, you."

"Woman? Now I am woman. I am thinking I am . . . what is it? I am a zip-head general, so you said."

"A little theater, General. Nothing but drama. Don't take it to heart."

"Still . . ."

"Still nothing," Bergeron turned to face the shadow. He didn't like the fact that he was in more light than Ngo and subconsciously stepped sideways into deeper shadow. "Like he said, he thinks you're a crazy one, you. That's exactly what we wanted. He's more scared of you than you of him. That's what we want. We're setting in the butter."

"Perhaps. But my friend, John, it is not so good to have a man who is so unpractical."

"Unpredictable."

"Ah, yes. Unpredictable. Perhaps it is wise for me to look elsewhere for a partner."

"Now hold on, General, there's no reason to get your nuts wrung up in a knot. He's harmless. Just a little spooked. He'll be fine. Let's stay the course here. I pay you, you grease the skids, the product gets delivered, I get the information I need, and everyone's happy. Everything's working."

"Provided your Red Indian cooperates. We have much to lose, you and I. Much." Ngo Van Thu lit another cigarette and his face momentarily flashed visible.

"He will, but you and your contacts haven't really made things very easy for him. No. For crying out loud, General, four-deuces? Do you have any idea? Medical supplies are easy . . . a pallet of claymores was hard enough but obviously doable, but a shipment of four-deuce mortars? Four-deuces? That's a logistical nightmare at best. Do you know how much a four-point-two-inch mortar weighs? Over three hundred friggin' pounds without the rounds and the packing. And it's not like they won't be missed either; these aren't like your car keys; you don't just mislay an M-30 mortar. How about something smaller? Sixty-millimeter? Even an eighty-one might be possible. But a four-deuce? What in Christ's name were you thinking?"

"That is what is wanted. It is the price of doing business, my friend, John."

"I hear you. I'm simply saying that it won't be easy."

"It is September, friend John. The planting is finished. Harvest will be soon. You have 120 days as I count. Without the items that my associates have requested, your product will not pass the border. You Americans may control the towns by day, but you do not control the border at any time. My associates will be needed to make this happen. If you wish your product . . ."

"You just make the arrangements; I'll take care of getting your items."

"And Master Sergeant Tenkiller? What of him?"

"What of him?"

"I think he has served his use. He is now unpredictable."

Bergeron tried to focus on the general, but the room had darkened too much and even his shadowy outline was now hard to discern. Bergeron spoke to the glowing tip of the general's cigarette that danced and swerved like an orange firefly. "You saying you want him killed?"

Ngo Van Thu exhaled a lungful of smoke that Bergeron could not see as much as feel and smell. "Perhaps, yes. I think this is perhaps best. I can arrange for this, if you wish not to dirty your hands, John Bergeron."

"No, General," Bergeron replied as he turned and looked again through the shutters at the people outside. "He's my responsibility. I have contacts as well. He'll be taken care of."

CHAPTER 29

Long Binh, Republic of Vietnam
MONDAY, SEPTEMBER 28, 1970

For most of his investigation, Paul Fick found that civilian attire had been the better key to the locked doors he'd been knocking on, but today he'd opted for his khaki uniform. He was going to talk to a career soldier, and for better or worse, career soldiers respected rank and formality.

He'd started with a list of twenty-six; names of men with access to the types of material showing up in the wrong hands, cross-listed by dates in-country. Material had been leaking north for almost two years, which eliminated everyone with a year-and-out ticket, unless the system was so organized that the insider was handing the business off to his replacement, which Fick doubted. At least he hoped there was no revolving door. One turncoat was easier to stomach than institutional treason. Operating from this premise he'd found only twenty-six men in all of the Republic of Vietnam who had access to the types and quantities of materials being traded and who were on the downhill side of two consecutive tours. He'd spent the last three weeks questioning them one by one. Thirteen had subsequently returned stateside and could reasonably be excluded as suspects in the last two transfers of material, one had turned out to be a clerical error caused by a misplaced keystroke in a Social Security number, one had been hit by a car in downtown Saigon six months earlier and was sufficiently dead to eliminate him as a candidate, likewise, another had overdosed on heroin a week after that and could be scratched, one was serving time in the Long Binh Jail for assault when the last two transfers were thought to have taken place, another was in LBJ for rape and couldn't have had a hands-on part of the last transfer, and another six had solid enough alibis that Fick was comfortable eliminating them for the time being. That left two, and Captain Paul Fick, complete with uniform, had made arrangements to meet with one of them today.

Tenkiller, Jimmy L., Master Sergeant, U.S. Army.

The supply depot at Long Binh was billed as the largest supply depot in the world. It probably was. It was often joked that it stocked everything except atomic bombs. It also was sometimes joked that it did. It gave the impression of an anthill that had been poked up with a stick; constant movement in four-dimensional space and time. Twenty-five hours a day, eight days a week.

Captain Paul Fick had met with Master Sergeant Tenkiller's immediate supervisor the day before. A young first lieutenant from St. Joseph, Missouri, whose fair complexion had blistered in the angry sun of South Vietnam to a point where he looked like a stretch of peeling wallpaper. He'd been eager to cooperate, sensing that hard men like Fick were better placated than annoyed, and he'd seen to it that Tenkiller would be available for questioning at the captain's convenience. He'd even arranged for a suitable location, a seldom-used, corrugated half-moon Quonset hut near the motor pool: Building T-13.

Jimmy Lee Tenkiller was already seated at a small wooden table when Fick arrived. The building was not air-conditioned and the unpainted aluminum sheeting clicked and popped as it expanded in the rippling heat. It was obvious why it was seldom used; a single, four-bladed oscillating fan provided the only reason for air movement, and during the dry season the space was close to uninhabitable. Tenkiller shot to attention when he saw Fick enter. His metal folding chair rattled on the plywood floor.

"As you were." Fick patted the air with his left hand. Over the last year he had developed the habit of using his left hand for most things. He told himself that it was the result of habit acquired as the result of the surgery and therapy that his right hand had undergone, though he secretly suspected that some level of subconscious vanity was at the root. It bothered him each time it happened, and he chastised himself, but it kept happening.

Tenkiller collected his chair but remained standing.

"You'd be Master Sergeant Tenkiller? Is that correct?" Fick could see the rank on the sleeve and the nametape on the pocket. It was as much a formality as it was a real question.

"Yes, sir, and you'd be Captain Fick, sir?" Tenkiller could play with the same formality. He'd eased off of attention, but retained a respectful posture as he watched the captain approach the table. He knew little of what this man wanted, though he feared much.

Paul Fick placed his canvas field satchel on the table and took the room in, looking at the ventilation options. He didn't mind for his own sake, he'd been raised to think that discomfort was next to godliness, but he'd long ago learned that the stiffness of a man's tongue was often closely tethered to bodily comfort, and he wanted Tenkiller's tongue to be as limber as possible. He noted the fan; he also noted the closed windows. The constant thrum of two-tons and forklifts outside precluded an open portal of any kind. The fan alone would have to do if they hoped to have any conversation.

"Sit, Master Sergeant, please." Fick made sure to pull back his chair as he spoke. He knew that Tenkiller would wait for him to at least begin sitting down before he'd move. "What have you been told about why I'm here?"

"Very little, sir. The lieutenant said that a captain from Washington wanted to see me. I don't know what this is about, sir."

Fick settled into the metal folding chair opposite Tenkiller and undid the buckle on his satchel, but didn't remove the file folder within. He kept the fingers of his right hand tucked into the canvas bag, his fingertips in contact with the file. He was careful to maintain eye contact. "How long have you been here, Master Sergeant?"

"Vietnam? This is my second tour, sir."

"Consecutive?"

"Yes, sir."

"Volunteered?"

"Yes, sir."

Fick waited for the noise of a forklift passing by the closed window to dissipate before continuing. It provided a ready excuse for sweating Tenkiller. "About due to PCS, aren't you?"

"Yes, sir. I mean, no, sir. I'm due to leave this assignment in a couple of months, but I'm not changing duty stations, I'm getting out."

Fick took the opportunity to extract the file and open it. He kept the folder up so Tenkiller couldn't see how little was actually written on it. "How many you have in, Sergeant?"

Tenkiller's eyes had been looking at the back of the folder and flicked up to catch Fick's before he responded. "Fifteen last June, sir."

"Fifteen." Fick knew the answer but he let a tone of surprise flavor the word. "You made rank fairly quickly. You have some college? That right?"

Now it was Jimmy Lee Tenkiller's turn to wait for the sound of several heavy trucks driving by the building to subside. He needed the time to gather his thoughts. He had no idea where these questions were headed, but something about Fick set him on edge. "A little," he answered. "Oklahoma A&M."

"That right? A&M? It's Oklahoma State now, isn't it?"

"Yes, sir."

Fick leaned his chair back onto the two rear legs and looked down the length of his nose at the man opposite him at the table. "I seem to recall someone named Tenkiller who did some running for A&M. Supposed to be pretty good. Don't remember the event, though. You by chance any relation to that Tenkiller?"

Tenkiller smiled at the thought, not the question. "You could say that."

Fick nodded as if the information meant something. "Going back to school when you get out? That where you're headed? Must take money to do that. 'Course there's always the GI Bill."

"No, sir."

"No, it doesn't take money? Or, no, you've got money? You're not still on scholarship are you?"

"No, sir. I mean I'm not going back to school."

"Why not?"

"Rather not say, sir. Just not, is all."

"But you are going back to Oklahoma when you leave here. Is that correct? Going home?"

"Possibly." Jimmy Lee Tenkiller thought about the bait-and-tackle shop with his brother. This man had no reason to know about it; it was no one's business but Jimmy Lee's. "I haven't completely decided. Right now I'm focused on doing my job. That's what I get paid to do."

Fick nodded again, slowly, as if he were orchestrating each question like a chess move rather than groping. "It's good to get paid, that's a fact. Master Sergeant Tenkiller, let's shift direction. What are your duties here at the depot?"

"I'm a supply NCO."

"You're a master sergeant, I wouldn't be so modest."

"Lots of E-8s here, sir. I just do my job."

"I'm sure you do, but educate me, what job would that be, Sergeant?"

"I handle supplies, sir."

"Good, let's talk about that for a moment." Fick paused and reopened his file folder. "What sort of supplies do you have access to, Master Sergeant Tenkiller?"

"The usual, sir. Socks, watches, beer, soda pop. The stuff that the men doing the fighting need."

"Socks, watches," Fick repeated as if he were reading from the file. "They do need that, Sergeant, they do need that. Been there myself." He looked up at Tenkiller and smiled. "Not to mention the beer and pop. The men do need that too."

"Yes, sir."

"'Course it doesn't hurt to have an M-16 and some ammunition either."

"Yes, sir."

"You handle any of that type of supplies, Sergeant Tenkiller? The killing type?"

Tenkiller hesitated and then realized that he shouldn't have. "Some."

"Some?" Fick asked. "You're a master sergeant at the largest military supply depot in the world, I'd have thought it would be more than just some. How about other supplies? Medical supplies? Morphine? Doxycycline? Primaquine? Anything like that?"

"Sometimes, certainly. Yes, sir."

"How about claymores? Antipersonnel stuff. You ever handle that sort of item?"

"I suppose."

"I suppose you would," Fick said. "I suppose you would. After all, you are a supply NCO, aren't you?"

Tenkiller did not answer, nor did Fick expect him to.

"You married, Master Sergeant Tenkiller?"

"No, sir."

"Girlfriend?"

"No, sir."

"No one at all? You're a handsome man. Athlete. Not even a local girl?"

"No, sir. I do my job. I'm leaving here in a few months; don't need any connections like that."

Fick eyed Tenkiller closely. It was possible. Fick himself had no wife or girlfriend stateside and none in-country either—he'd never gotten *yellow fever* the way so many of the young men did; still, Fick accepted that he was something of an aberration, and while he knew very little of Tenkiller, he doubted that his practiced celibacy was motivated entirely by dedication to duty. He turned his attention back to the few notes he'd scribbled in the file. "I can understand not wanting any . . . entanglements . . . like that. And you do seem to be a hard worker. Fact is, Lieutenant Pruitt says that he almost has to force you to take some time off the job."

"I do my job."

"That's what your lieutenant says. That's what he says. I'm so used to being around infantry Joes, though, that I was skeptical when he said that. Almost two years without a . . . without a 'connection,' as you say, is a long time. I was skeptical until he showed me your leave file. Except for one day every month—just about the same time every month, too—you're here doing your job as a supply NCO."

"Yes, sir."

"That's what's so puzzling, Sergeant Tenkiller."

"Sir?"

"Well, your lieutenant seems to be under the impression that you're meeting your girlfriend when you take leave. Now how'd he get that mistaken impression, I wonder. How about you—does it make you wonder? Why do you suppose he thinks you're sneaking off to meet someone?"

Both men sat staring at each other. Neither spoke for almost a minute.

"Sir, with all due respect, I have duties waiting on me. Does the captain have any more questions?" Tenkiller finally blinked.

Fick took a deep breath and sighed slowly. He'd been groping in the dark, and while something about Jimmy Lee Tenkiller struck him as out of kilter, he really had no idea where to take the questioning. That fact, combined with the swelter and noise of the metal building, made for an easy decision. There was always time to regroup. Fick smiled and placed the file folder back into his canvas satchel. "Not at this time, Sergeant. You're free to go."

Jimmy Lee Tenkiller rose to attention and saluted.

Fick returned the salute, and Tenkiller walked to the door and opened it.

"Master Sergeant Tenkiller," Fick said above the noise of the vehicles outside.

Tenkiller hesitated, partially shutting the door and shutting out the noise. "Sir?"

"Intermediate high hurdles, wasn't it?"

Tenkiller paused, then answered. "Yes, sir. Conference record."

"Do me a favor, Sergeant," Fick said quietly, his back still toward Tenkiller, "don't run anywhere."

CHAPTER 30

Fort Campbell, Kentucky
WEDNESDAY, APRIL 16, 2008

Deveroux stared at the name written on the scrap of paper, crimping his brow in confusion. "Sir?"

The general had already swiveled his chair back to the window and had resumed his gaze out the window. "You've heard of General Fick, I take it?"

"Yes, sir. I suspect just about everyone has. Somethin' of a legend when I was startin' out. Couple tours in Vietnam. Lost three fingers, as I recall. Silver Star. Short tempered; can melt polished brass with his tongue, doesn't suffer fools easily . . ."

"That he doesn't." The general laughed. "For damn sure, he doesn't. I've seen Paul barbecue more than one full bird too. And for the record, you were close; it was three tours and two fingers."

"Yes, sir. You sound like you know him, General."

"Better than some, I guess. He was a year ahead of me at the Academy. A year and a lifetime really. Worked harder than any other two cadets combined. Worked his ass off. That's what was so ironic." He turned to face Deveroux and smiled. "I don't know how much you know about him, but he was raised a Mennonite or a Quaker, or some such shit. Pacifist. But he was dedicated; good God, was he ever dedicated. More like a monk sometimes than a soldier. Hardworking.

Disciplined. Loyal. Rock-solid sense of right and wrong. There is no gray in his world, only stark white and black. Kind of ironic, don't you think?"

"Sir?"

"All that pacifist Mennonite upbringing and he ends up a career warrior." The general smiled. "All those traits, I guess they're good qualities for a soldier."

"Yes, sir. Good traits for anyone, I'd guess."

The general drummed his fingers on the glass sheet covering his desktop as he dropped into silence. To Deveroux it seemed as if he were either trying to plumb his brain for some long-forgotten fact or weighing the propriety of what he was preparing to say.

"Paul Fick spent two tours with the Twenty-fifth ID at Cu Chi. You've heard all the stories about Cu Chi, I assume."

"Yes, sir. That extensive network of tunnels and all."

"Extensive doesn't start to describe it, son. There were miles of tunnels. Mile upon fucking mile. That's where he lost the fingers. Fick's platoon were flushing some of those tunnels when a young kid bobbled a hot grenade; Paul grabbed it and pitched it away just as it went off. Saved more than a couple of lives, they say, but at a cost." General Anderson held up his right hand, bending the third and fourth fingers down so that they didn't show. "Didn't slow him down, although it did end him up stateside. That's when he was sent off to teach AIT at Benning."

Deveroux had heard the story before. His instructor at Advanced Infantry Training School had been an unabashed disciple of Fick's and had often told a similar but more embellished version. "Sir? Did I hear you correctly? Did you say three tours in Vietnam?"

"I did, Chief. The first two were with the Twenty-fifth." He paused. "Back-to-back. Then came the accident. The third . . . I have to admit I don't know much about the third tour. It was early summer of 1970; it was my turn in the shithole. I'd gotten a company command with the Ninth ID out of Dong Tam—Charlie Company, Second of the Sixtieth—getting the ol' ticket punched—I'd been there about three, maybe four months when I had a young kid take a shovel to his squad leader. Times being what they were, Uncle Sam was willing to forget little indiscretions like that provided you hadn't actually killed anybody and you promised to be good and go back on the line and hump a ruck for God and Country, so I ended up having to drive over to Long Binh to sign this Joe Shitbag out of the stockade, and who do I run into?"

"General Fick."

"Affirmative. Well, it was Captain Fick at that time, but, you're right, Chief, none other than Iron Paul."

"Iron Paul? I hadn't heard that one."

"He had lots of names, Iron Paul is simply one of the more favorable. One usable in mixed company." Anderson's tone had lost any reticence and had taken on an air of familiarity bred by easy reminiscence. "I hadn't seen him since his graduation at the Academy, but you hear things, of course. Grapevine. Paul Fick was like the class yardstick; the one that everyone knows is going to do well and who you catch yourself trying to measure up to even if you wouldn't have admitted it. I don't guess anyone ever thought he'd make general, though—too prickly, too . . . too unbending in a Germanic, Teutonic, iconoclastic sort of way. You always sensed that he could hammer roofing nails with his forehead if he'd decided it was the right thing to do. Men like that make too many enemies to gain rank, but damn if you didn't wish you could be like him, even a little. Truth be told, Chief, I guess that's exactly why men like Paul make so many enemies." The general looked up at Deveroux and caught his eyes. He sensed that veiled beneath Deveroux's easy grits-and-sorghum veneer was a vein of similar temper, the innate sense of propriety and clarity, and he realized finally why he had taken a liking to the younger man. A chord had been struck.

"But he made brigadier."

"He did. Sure did. Retired as a BG. Against the odds, really. Goes to show that Big Army sometimes makes the right decisions in spite of itself. Not too often, but enough to give you hope."

Deveroux returned the general's look but remained quiet.

"Anyway, as I was saying, there was Captain Fick, back in the Republic of Vietnam. He remembered me; he was always good at that, and we talked some; I told him I'd heard he'd been injured and was stateside. That sort of thing. He was more tight-lipped than usual, even for him, and the funny thing was that he was in civilian clothes. I can still see him. He was in a white long-sleeved shirt with the sleeves rolled up past his elbows and khaki pants. I didn't think much of it at the time until I ran into him in Saigon a week or so later. He was still in civilian clothes, so I finally asked him about it. Paul was one of those guys who just didn't look right out of uniform. He answered without really answering; the sort of answer that is polite but leaves no room for doubt about whether you should change the subject or not, so I changed the subject. After all, he was Iron Paul."

The general fell quiet, and Deveroux became aware of the fact that the sunlight had faded while they had been talking. Both men sat silently in the darkened room. In the adjoining office Deveroux could hear the major shifting his weight and clearing his throat and germinating enough courage to intrude.

Deveroux broke the silence first. He held the slip of paper up as a reference. "Sir, I guess I don't see what help General Fick might be in my investigation."

General Anderson lifted his head and looked at Deveroux. He seemed almost surprised to find him still sitting amid the shadows, having lost himself in the moist and murk of a decades-old jungle. He blinked, as if to clear the ghosts from his head, and took a deep breath. "I found out later, Chief Deveroux, that Captain Fick was working a special detail, an investigation of some sort; outside normal CID channels. Very outside. He was trying to get a handle on a black market operation that was operating out of the big supply depot at Long Binh." Deveroux sensed that the general was searching his face for a reaction, but in the long-day shadows it was hard to tell for certain. The general paused, then continued. "In particular he was after an American who was funneling material into the hands of the VC. An American. A traitor."

"You think it's the same case? You think there's a connection?"

"I think you should call him, Chief Deveroux."

CHAPTER 31

U.S. Army Central Identification Laboratory, Hawaii
FRIDAY, APRIL 18, 2008

The trade winds had dropped off and what little breeze there was came whiffling out of the southwest. *Kona winds*, they call them. For two days the commercial aircraft that normally flew directly over the CILHI on their final approach to Honolulu International airport were being vectored in from the north. Conversely, the change in the wind also meant that the lab now lay directly under the flight path of massive 747s taking off into the wind bound for Tokyo and Seoul and Beijing. Every few minutes the windows shook and rattled and conversations were momentarily placed on pause.

Davis Smart was looking up at the ceiling as if he could see through the acoustic tiles to the light-blue KAL jet passing low overhead. He waited for the throbbing roar to subside before continuing his questions. "Least it's not F-16s," he commented during the interlude.

Kel looked at his watch and then back at the folder in his lap. "Give 'em time. The Air National Guard should be gettin' wound up soon." He was having a hard time keeping focused and had read and reread the same paragraph without much progress. He'd had a particularly bad run-in with Inspector Botch-It first thing in the morning and had almost tendered his resignation on the spot—his fourth in the last six months. Instead he'd bitten off what remained of the tip of his tongue.

"Have you gotten to it yet? Let me know when you get to it," D.S. impatiently prompted again. He'd brought a folder in for Kel to read and was anxious to discuss it. Kel clearly was taking too much time, and D.S. cleared his throat again, unable to hold back. "Aw, c'mon, Kel, will you skim the damn thing. You read like an old woman; you don't need to read the details, just look at the last two articles."

"Is that how old women read? Payin' attention to details?"

"Why yes, it is. So how about hurrying it up? C'mon, do you see what I see?"

"All right, D.S., calm down. Did these come in this mornin'?" Kel asked as he began shuffling through the pages to the end, forgetting the commander and skimming as requested.

"First thing this morning. FedEx. Your suggestion that the genealogist check newspaper files may be paying off. She still hasn't found a maternal relative for Tenkiller's DNA, but she ran into these and thought we might find them useful."

"Interestin', but I'm not sure how useful," Kel answered. His tone still had an echo of distraction.

"That's why you need to skip to the last two articles. The first ones are sort of background, it's the last couple that are . . ."

"Gettin' there, gettin' there," Kel responded. The file consisted of a dozen or so photocopied eastern Oklahoma newspaper articles dating to the mid-1950s, and all concerned Jimmy Lee Tenkiller and what appeared to be his phenomenal high school track career. Clipping after clipping compared him to a young Jim Thorpe and hinted at a legitimate shot at the 1956 Summer Olympics scheduled for Melbourne. Kel finally worked the last two articles to the top of the stack. "Is this the one you mean, this 'Cowboys and Indian' one?"

"Yeah, that's one of them. Read that—actually, don't read, just skim it and then go to the next one."

Kel glossed the article quickly. Tenkiller had been awarded a full scholarship to Oklahoma A&M in Stillwater; great things were expected of him; chance at being the first A&M Cowboy to win a gold medal in the Olympics, et cetera, et cetera. Kel looked at D.S., still not catching what was supposed to be so obvious.

"Okay," D.S. prompted. He cleared his throat and adjusted his position in his chair. "Bona fide phenomenon. Now, read the last one—especially the final paragraph."

Kel turned to the last article, the one entitled, "Tenkiller Shatters More Than Record: Indian Runner's Olympic Hopes Crumble." Kel read further.

> Stillwater, Oklahoma. The Sooner State's hopes of an Olympic gold medal vanished amid a cloud of dust on the red cinder track of Lewis Field, Monday, when Cowboy running phenomenon Jimmy Lee Tenkiller tumbled in a preliminary heat for the men's intermediate high hurdles, shattering his right outside ankle. Tenkiller, Oklahoma A&M's sophomore track sensation who has been compared to the late Jim Thorpe, was leading the six-man heat in the Green Country Invitational when he caught his trailing leg on the last hurdle and fell to the track in obvious pain.

"What the hell's an 'outside' ankle? Didn't know we had insides and outsides," Kel asked. He kept his focus on the photocopied newspaper clipping.

"Yeah, yeah. Okay, smart-alec, how about reading the last paragraph like I asked? Suppose you could manage that?"

Kel smiled at the obvious sense of frustration building in D.S. "Which one?"

"The last one. Can't you think of something better to do than spin me up? Look, I'm frothing at the mouth. Happy?"

"Yup." Kel quickly held up a supplicating palm. "Okay, okay." He turned his attention back to the paper and read the last paragraph of the article.

> A spokesman for the Oklahoma A&M athletic department told reporters that Tenkiller underwent a two-hour surgical procedure yesterday at the Regional Medical Center in Tulsa,

where two metal screws were required to repair the shattered bone. Doctors say his running career is over, and his academic career may not be any more solid. Following the surgery, Cowboys assistant men's track coach Monty "Red" Coil was quoted as saying that "scholarships are for athletes; you don't run, we don't pay. That's the way it works."

He read the final paragraph again, lingering over each sentence. He was quiet a moment. Finally he closed his eyes and smiled. "Screws," he said looking up.

"Yup," D.S. concurred. "Two of 'em."

CHAPTER 32

Tuesday, General DeWitt Spain Airport, North of Memphis, Tennessee
FRIDAY, APRIL 18, 2008

Brigadier General Paul Fick's voice wasn't anything like Shuck Deveroux had expected it to be. Instead of the napalm and spittle that legend had imbued it with, it was quiet and as cool as river-bottom sand and most efficiently reserved. Deveroux had called him at his small farm near Waynesville, Missouri, the previous evening and introduced himself, saying that he was calling on Major General Anderson's specific recommendation. Fick had been cordial, if noncommittal, and the conversation, while short, had politely wandered somewhat—at least until Deveroux had said he was interested in a thirty-eight-year-old investigation into a black market ring that had operated in Saigon during the war. At that point, Fick's voice had gotten even quieter and cooler; to the point that twice Deveroux had thought the phone connection had been lost. In the end, Fick had simply said that he would be in Memphis on the following morning on business and that they should meet. Later that night Deveroux had received a call from Fick instructing him to be at the DeWitt Spain airport a few miles north of downtown Memphis at nine o'clock in the morning. He could spare him thirty minutes.

Deveroux had been waiting since eight o'clock. Not knowing for sure how long the drive would take, and not wanting to be late for a meeting with the famous Iron Paul Fick, he'd set out from his quarters on Fort Campbell earlier than proved necessary and arrived early. He passed the time drinking strong coffee and watching small, private aircraft take off and land. He hadn't realized it at the time, but the white-and-blue, high-wing Cessna 172 Skyhawk that he'd just watch land was piloted by the man he was waiting on.

Paul Fick was dressed conservatively, light-blue cotton shirt, khaki slacks, brown leather boots, and a blue, lightweight nylon windbreaker. His hair was short and cut in such a way as to square off the top of his head. He carried a thick brown folder tied with a frayed white string under his right arm and made a straight line to where Deveroux was sitting. He pulled back a chair with a squeak. Deveroux started to stand out of an equal mixture of military courtesy and bone-bred southern manners, but the general motioned him down with his left hand. As Fick took his own seat, he dropped the folder onto the seat of the chair to his left and removed his mirrored sunglasses.

"Chief Warrant Officer Deveroux?"

"Yes, sir. Glad to meet you, General Fick. I certainly appreciate you comin' all this way down here to talk with me."

"You can save the appreciation. As I told you, Chief Deveroux, I had business in the area. I was coming here one way or the other. I believe I told you I had thirty minutes. The clock started two minutes ago."

"Yes, sir. Understood. But I still 'ppreciate the opportunity to talk with you."

"Let's get this straight. General Anderson vouched for you. He says you're the type of soldier who puts honor and duty before self-preservation. That you don't have an iota of sense when it comes to your career. That correct?"

Deveroux shrugged in passive acknowledgment.

Fick did nothing to further the conversation. He sat, straight-backed, his mottled gray eyes focused on Deveroux's face, waiting for his lead.

Deveroux shifted his weight and took a quiet sip of coffee. He set the Styrofoam cup down on the white, speckled Formica tabletop and cleared his throat. "Ahh, can I get you somethin' to drink, General? Coffee? It's not much for taste, but it'll clear the head."

"No thank you. My head is quite clear."

"Sure? I mean about not wantin' any coffee."

Fick's expression supplied the answer.

"Yes, sir. Well, ahh . . ." Deveroux took another stalling sip from his cup. "Well, sir, as I mentioned to you on the phone the other day, I mean yesterday, ahh . . . well, I'm 'bout thigh-deep in a double homicide. Two civilians killed within five, six months of one 'nother, one at Fort Campbell, the other over at Knox. Might be coincidental, but I'm sure thinkin' not. The MO was pretty much the same in both cases; one was found dead in his car and the other wasn't, but other than that they were pretty much the same. Both victims were middle-aged Vietnamese businessmen; both former refugees; both were cut up somethin' vicious." He paused his narrative to give Fick an opportunity to respond.

Fick gave a single nod but did no more.

Deveroux tipped his head forward, as if his weight could provide some needed momentum, and continued. "The real kicker, sir, is that one of the men was implicated as a member of a black market ring that was run durin' the Vietnam War. What the connection to the murder is—if there is any—is unknown. But, what I do know, sir, is that I've got two victims hacked up with a machete or an axe or somethin', and on top of that, one of them is tied into the disappearance of an American serviceman during the war."

Deveroux had managed to maintain eye contact with Fick as he spoke, though it was an effort. There was a flint to Fick's eyes that was hard to look at, a depth that bespoke expectation but no courteous compassion. At the mention of the American serviceman, though, Deveroux had detected the smallest of flickers, like a candle flame responding to a whisper.

"Interesting," Fick said evenly as he reached into the side pocket of his jacket and extracted two brown, plastic medicine bottles. He continued looking at Deveroux as he dry-swallowed a handful of colorful pills. "This American have a name?" he said after a pause.

"Sir, you sure I can't get you somethin' to drink? They've got a water fountain if you don't like coffee. I can . . ."

"I'm sure. He have a name?"

"The American? Ahh, why yes, sir, he does. An army master sergeant by the name of Tenkiller. Jimmy Lee Tenkiller. Indian fella, I think."

The two men sat looking at each other.

"What precisely do you think I might be able to help you with, Chief Deveroux?" Fick said after a moment of silence. He tugged up the elastic cuff on his left windbreaker sleeve and looked at his watch.

"Ahhh, well, sir," he glanced down at the table and fingered his coffee cup, slowly turning it around and around. He realized for the first time that he'd unconsciously been carving shapes into the Styrofoam with his thumbnail. Deveroux cleared his throat again, without much effect, for the words were still thick and sticky. "Ahhh, now that's a good question. Fact of the matter, sir, is that I don't know for certain. Not sure you can help. It's just that . . ." He bounced a quick look down at his cup again and then rejoined eye contact. "Truth is, General Fick, I'm absolutely stumped on this one. I'm so dead-ended on this case that Lee Harvey Oswald is startin' to look like a viable suspect to me. That's a fact. So if there's a connection between this Tenkiller and my two dead Vietnamese fellas, I'd sure like to know it."

"As I said, Chief Deveroux, what is it that you want from me?"

Deveroux shook his head. "Help. Answers. My guys have interviewed over three hundred leads so far. Nothin'. We're getting' nowhere real fast. About the only glimmer of light is this fella, Tenkiller, and General Anderson thought . . ."

"Answers?"

"Yes, sir. General Ander . . ." He paused and then raised his eyes to engage Fick's. "Sir, I have a feelin' that you might just know somethin' about this Tenkiller. Somethin' from some investigation you worked on back durin' the war."

"Jim Anderson tell you that?"

"No, sir. General Anderson just suggested I call you. That's all."

Fick's eyes stayed focused on Deveroux's, as if he was waiting for the young man to blink and look away or betray a fiber of weakness. "You know the Bible, Chief Deveroux?"

Deveroux didn't blink, but his voice caught and he had to clear his throat before he could answer. "Umm, no, sir. Not the way I should, I guess, though my mama would skin me if she heard me admit that."

Fick nodded slowly and closed his eyes. His took a breath and his voice assumed an edge, like a brittle shard of glass. "Ecclesiastes 4, verses 2 through 3. 'And I declared that the dead, who had already died, are happier than the living, who are still alive. But better than both is he who has not yet been; who has not yet seen the evil that is done under the sun.'" He sat in silence for a moment and then opened his eyes. He smiled patiently at the confused expression on Deveroux's face. "If you want answers, Chief, maybe you should talk to Master Sergeant Tenkiller."

Now it was Deveroux's turn to smile. He willed himself to maintain eye contact. "I'd like to, sir, but accordin' to the records, Master Sergeant Tenkiller is dead."

"I know," Fick replied quietly. "I killed him."

CHAPTER 33

"Who worked the case?" Kel asked. He rapped the stack of photocopied newspaper clippings on his desk, aligning the edges, before handing them back to D.S.

"Amy."

"She's pretty new," Kel said involuntarily. The words had tumbled out of his mouth like two dice before he knew it. The fact was that the scientific staff got younger each year—the burnout rate of spending six to nine months out of the year in places where the locals eat cats and have never seen a flush toilet took a predictable toll on career longevity. Comparatively, Dr. Amalie August was actually one of the veterans, with five years on the job, but to Kel and D.S. she was still new. Kel paused.

"Ever feel like John Henry?"

"The guy with the big signature?"

"No. That was John Hancock. I said, John Henry."

"Oh." D.S. cast him a look of suspicious confusion, trying to figure if there was a penis joke lurking in the question. Penis jokes play a large, and often unheralded role in science. "Can't say that I do," he said, fully expecting himself to figure in a punch line.

"Technology. You know, 'Before I let that DNA bear me down, I'll die with a caliper in my hand, Lawd, Lawd.' Somethin' like that. Face it, Davis, we're on the road to bein' big ol' lumberin' dinosaurs, and that road leads straight into extinction."

"You're letting Botch-It get to you way too much."

"Don't doubt that, but that's only part of it. I'm talkin' about our piece of the pie. We're on the road, bubba, and that signpost up ahead reads 'extinction.'"

"Hmmm, on the road, maybe, but we're not there yet. What's your point?"

Kel smiled and shook his head slowly. "You're right. We're not there, yet. They say that the day's comin' when you'll just stick a bone in a little box, a little easy-bake ovenlike thing, turn some dials and cranks and watch some colored lights wink on and off, and it'll spit you out an instant DNA readin' like an ATM receipt. No anthropology. No odontology. Won't need real scientists at all, certainly not anthropologists. Just like John Henry and the steel-drivin' machine. The times they are a changin'."

"Okay, I'm a Brontosaurus. I'm still missing the point here."

"Like I said, we're not there yet. We've been chasin' our tail on this DNA stuff when the answer was in the newspaper all along. Did Amy see anythin' on the ankle?"

"Dunno. And she's out taking care of some things; she leaves tomorrow morning for thirty-plus days in Laos and then a follow-on forty-five-day mission to Vietnam. She won't be back here until sometime after the Fourth of July."

"If she's lucky. Are the remains still out on one of the tables?"

"Nope, she's already put her cases away."

Kel pulled a ring of keys from his pocket. He held them up in clear view and gave them a shake as if they were shiny minnows on a string. "How rusty are you, my friend?"

"I creak," D.S. replied as he stood. He paused long enough to toss the stack of newspaper clippings onto Kel's desk, and then joined Kel, already at the double glass doors that opened onto the examination floor. Both men briefly held their identification cards against the small rectangular sensor beside the doorframe, waiting for the beep that indicated the computer had logged both their presence and the time. This was followed by a soft metallic click that signaled the lock disengaging. Kel pulled the right-hand door open and held it for his partner and then followed him onto the exam floor. The door swung shut behind them, and the lock re-engaged.

When not under analysis on one of the lab's twenty examination tables, human remains were kept locked in a secure evidence area. There were only two individuals with keys—the evidence manager and the scientific director. Kel unlocked the sliding door of the evidence area and held his identification card against another magnetic sensor that would disengage a second, electronic lock. The electric motor engaged and the shelving bay slowly slid open to reveal row upon row of rectangular, white, acid-free boxes, each holding the skeletal and dental remains of a human being. Over nine hundred boxes. Over nine hundred American servicemen who never went home.

"What's the case number?" Kel asked as he stepped into the aisle and began scanning the boxes closest to them. The cases were shelved chronologically, and the most recently accessioned ones were near the lab end of the shelf. The labels indicated which country each case had been recovered in, but there were three boxes fresh in from Vietnam.

"One-five-one. Two-thousand-eight-dash-one-five-one."

"One-four-nine, one-five-oh . . . here we go, one-five-one. Last one." He slid the box off the shelf and carried it back onto the lab floor to what was commonly called the sixty-minute table, a large examination table set off from the others and designated for short-term analysis. He grabbed the pistol scanner and logged the case out by scanning the bar codes on the box label and his identification badge while D.S. began pulling the contents and placing them on the foam-covered tabletop. There were several large clear-plastic bags, each sealed with blue evidence tape that would tear if tampered with. The face of each bag had been labeled with the accession number using a black permanent marker.

D.S. sorted the bags by their contents, holding each one close to his face so that he could better see what was sealed inside. He was at a stage in his life where he needed bifocals but could never seem to make them work. Instead he removed his glasses and squinted a lot. Finally, he found the bag he was looking for, the one that contained the bones of the right leg and foot. As Kel joined him, D.S. snapped on a pair of latex gloves and then slit the side of the bag with a pair of scissors, making a three-inch cut, just large enough to remove the bones of the lower leg and foot. He would have to reseal the opening with more evidence tape as soon as they were finished, and that was easier to do if the slit in the bag was kept small. This case hadn't been examined repeatedly and the bag was still relatively free of taped-over cuts. Before it left the lab it would be opened again and again and again—analysis, DNA sampling, peer review, inventory—and sealed again and again and again until it resembled a patchwork quilt of crisscrossing blue tape.

Davis Smart was in his element. He had a natural affinity for bones that wasn't well served by his deskbound managerial duties, and when the opportunity arose to actually handle skeletal material he became almost childlike in his enthusiasm. Holding his glasses in his mouth, he flicked an involuntary look at the ceiling as if to make sure that all the lights were full on and then turned his focus to each of the lower leg bones, the tibia and fibula, holding each up close to his face and squinting. He made small atonal humming noises as he rotated each one several times, before turning to Kel. "There ya go," he said, holding the bones up. "I guess that answers that. Score one for anthropology. You're right. DNA? We don't need no stinkin' DNA."

CHAPTER 34

Doan Minh Tuyen had not aged particularly well. Once tall and thin and manfully constructed of corded sinew and gristle, he had found his later years to be a constant battle against waxing soft corpulence. Being diagnosed with adult-onset diabetes almost ten years earlier had not helped the situation, and at almost sixty-nine he found himself huffing and blowing hard after even the most innocent round of movement, such as hefting himself out of his car and walking to the slatted-steel-and-aluminum bleachers overlooking the baseball diamond at Crane Stadium on the Missouri Central University campus. He'd been inclined to stay seated in the front seat of his 1994 Ford Escort and wait, but lately closed spaces, even the front seat of his own car, had a way of bringing on a gripping claustrophobia that he couldn't explain, let alone deal with satisfactorily. Tonight he favored the crisp, early spring breeze and the smells of new growth that it brought in its wake and the riffling leaves that reminded him of his youth and of change and stability at the same time, to the stale cigarette smell and vertigo inducing odor of canned fruit deodorizer that filled his car. He took a deep breath and held it as long as he could before discharging. A thin fog of condensation formed in the cool air and quickly drifted away toward the street light like his future. He repeated the action, again and again, until he felt an oxygen buzz begin to form in his head.

It was a little past eleven o'clock and by all conventional rights he should be snugged in bed; the one made all too vacant by his third divorce three years ago next Saturday. Instead he sat on the cool aluminum plank of the ballpark bleachers and tapped his foot impatiently—or was it nervously?—and waited for the voice to show itself. The vaporous voice on the phone that seemed to know too much and yet could know nothing at all. The voice from a different time, a different place, a different Doan Minh Tuyen. That Doan Minh Tuyen, the one from thirty-eight years ago, had been young and vital and, despite the chaos of the time, was full of promise; that Doan bore only a faint structural resemblance to the bloated, watery waste that he'd become.

Doan Minh Tuyen had been defrosting a thick slab of frozen pizza and was looking forward to the practiced routine of a mindless stretch of televised sitcoms when the wall phone beside the refrigerator had rung. Reflexively he'd answered, assuming that it was one of his night managers needing some direction. Work calls seemed to be about all he received anymore, and with the quarterly inventory underway at the warehouse he was prepared for a flurry of late-night questions. Instead it was a low, almost muffled voice that began stirring the thick slurry of a life that he'd hoped had long ago settled and stratified.

He wasn't sure why he'd agreed to the meeting. Perhaps it was curiosity, perhaps it was fear, perhaps—had he been able to ever answer the question—it was out of some sort of involuntary obligation, like breathing or digesting. The caller had wanted to meet near a jogging path on Whiteman Air Force Base, but Doan Minh Tuyen had suggested Tompkins baseball field at MCU instead, his pride still stinging from the loss of base privileges. For over twenty years Doan's Show-Me Beverage had maintained a commercial lock on the soft-drink concession on base. It had been a lucrative quarter century, but now Doan Minh Tuyen couldn't even get past the pimple-faced airmen who manned the front gate, who had no idea of what war was really like or where Vietnam was located on the map and who looked at him as if he were an ignorant Mexican gardener come to trim the grass.

Doan tugged at the small bottle in his hand—a cheap, tongue-numbing, generic gin—and held the warm liquid in his mouth momentarily before forcing it down audibly. His ball-busting second wife had got him drinking gin, though certainly not generic brands—she'd just as soon be seen eating cat litter as drinking an off-brand of liquor, let alone cheap generic stuff. *The bitch,* he thought as he closed his eyes and tilted his head backward, feeling the bones in his spine pop and snap with pent-up tension. He slowly swiveled his head round and round, stretching the muscles in his neck as he replaced the screw cap, before setting the bottle beside his feet.

It was dark and there was a creeping moistness that had eased in behind a slow-moving cool front that the weatherman hadn't predicted. In the near distance, somewhere past right field, past the parking lot that abutted Warren Street, a tired bobwhite was working the dim evening. Crickets squeaked and chirped from somewhere unseen, and each yellow-white streetlight illuminated a crawling knot of early spring insects.

Doan Minh Tuyen held his left arm up at eye level and rotated his wrist back and forth until he caught a faint shag of light on the face of his watch. Eleven-fifteen. *Long enough,* he thought as he started to stand, accidentally kicking the gin bottle over and knocking it into the darkness below the bleachers. He heard it hit the ground with a muffled *tink.*

"Shit," Doan said, grabbing at the air. He sighed and slowly stood up, taking a moment to straighten his limbs, and then began to stiffly clunk his way down the aluminum bleacher seats. The gin had taken its effect in the hour or so he'd sat waiting, and now navigating a straight line proved adventurous. He paused in the mud at the bottom, steadying himself with one hand on a fifty-gallon metal drum that served as a trash can, and bent over to better peer under the seats. It was too dark to see and much too dark to go chasing a half-empty bottle of cheap gin. Doan Minh Tuyen might not be as well to do as he once had been, but he also wasn't so hard-put that he had to crawl around under some muddy bleachers, amid the gum and spit and used condoms, to retrieve a few ounces of grain alcohol. But then he saw it—a small glint of light caught by the curve of the bottle. It was within easy reach after all.

It happened as he straightened up. It was painless, at least initially, and quick. He felt his head jerk back, something pressed hard against his mouth, and he heard a soft, rhythmic squirt and splash like someone urinating in the grass. He dropped the bottle.

"My old friend, Major Doan," came the whisper in his ear. It was the voice, the one from the phone. The breath was warm and almost passionate, as a lover's should be. "How have you been all these years?"

Doan Minh Tuyen tried to turn and look at the face behind the words, but his neck wouldn't respond; the muscles wouldn't answer the direction.

It was only then that he realized that his throat had been cut.

CHAPTER 35

U.S. Army Central Identification Laboratory, Hawaii
FRIDAY, APRIL 18, 2008

Kel turned and started walking to the door. He'd gone two steps before pausing and turning back. D.S. was still humming and looking at the tibia in his hand.

"Instead of rebaggin' that stuff immediately, how 'bout we get some x-rays just to make sure. Document it. Can't hurt, can it?" Kel said.

"I was thinking the same thing," D.S. replied. "You want me to do it or assign it out?"

"You're a damn sight better readin' radiographs than me, and almost everyone else is deployed or sick or overworked as it is. Just let me know what you find. I need to go call Thomas Pierce and give him the news."

Kel turned and started back toward the door.

"Hey, Dr. Dinosaur," D.S. called out.

Kel stopped and turned.

D.S. nodded at the door. "Remember when we used to have doorknobs?"

Kel smiled and held his identification card against the small sensor on the doorframe, waiting for the computer to log him off the lab floor. The sensor beeped and the door clicked. He returned to his desk, looked at his watch, and picked up the phone.

Kel knew that it was nearing the end of the normal workday on the East Coast, but Thomas Pierce, director of the Armed Forces DNA Identification Laboratory in Rockville, Maryland, seldom kept normal hours. Kel also knew that as with his own, the most productive part of Pierce's day began in the late afternoon when all the crisis junkies had retired for the day. At nearly fifty, he had closed out a productive military career and was engaged in a new one as the first civilian director of the AFDIL.

"Armed Forces DNA Lab, this is Dr. Pierce."

"Hey, Dr. Pierce, why aren't you at home with your family?" Thomas Pierce was one of Kel's favorite people in the world, and one of the few who he could voluntarily call on the telephone without having to spend thirty minutes working up to it.

"Hey, bubba. What's a family?"

"With all the travelin' that I've been doin', I'm not really sure anymore. I think it's somethin' kinda like Bigfoot; you know, lots of unverified sightings. There's usually a big one with curves and a couple smaller ones that are noisy and sticky."

"That's right." Pierce's Old Dominion drawl flowed through the phone line like thin corn syrup. "Now that you mention it, I remember seein' a story about them in one of those newspapers at the checkout line. What in the world can I do for you, Dr. McKelvey? You must be in big need of somethin' if you're usin' a telephone. That twelve-step program must be payin' off."

"How 'bout that? I even dialed this myself. Actually, it's not what you can do for me, it's more like what I can do for you."

"How so?"

"You remember the Tenkiller case I mentioned to you a few weeks back? Soldier named Jimmy Tenkiller. Vietnam case."

"The deserter?"

"You got it. We sent y'all some bone samples—three, I think it was. Two bone and one from a tooth."

"Sure do. We got sequence data from all three, but we don't have a family reference sample in yet so there's nothin' to compare it to. No livin' relatives is what I hear."

"Except his brother," Kel corrected. He heard a chair spring creak and he envisioned Pierce leaning back and propping his feet up onto his full, but orderly, desktop. By contrast, Kel couldn't even see the top of his desk, let alone find room to prop his feet up. "I've been ridin' the genealogist pretty hard, but she tells me that we shouldn't hold our breaths."

"Right," Pierce said quickly. "And the brother won't give a blood sample for love or money. Do we need to put this one in the inactive category? Lord knows we're shorthanded right now and no one will complain if we back-burner this one for a while."

"Well, that's sorta why I'm callin'. It ain't Tenkiller."

"What ain't Tenkiller?"

"The skeleton we recovered. The one we cut the samples from."

"How'd you figure it out?"

"The old fashioned way, believe it or not. Some old newspaper clippings from 1954. From what they say, Tenkiller was a serious track talent. Even had a fair shot at the Olympics in Melboune."

"Really? Cool."

"Yeah, at least until he broke his foot. They had to reconstruct his ankle with a box of screws and a spool of baling wire . . ."

"Which don't show up in the skeleton you all recovered," Pierce completed the thought. "Good detective work."

"Yeah. Anyhow, we know now that whomever we got, it isn't our man Jimmy Tenkiller."

"Well, that's progress of a sort."

"Maybe."

"So, you're back to the drawin' board?"

"We never got up from it. The problem was that we got so damn fixated on DNA that we forgot the old ways."

"Use them while you can. The old ways. If you listen to my analysts talk, pretty soon, we'll have a little box you can put the bones in and get an instant DNA result."

"Yeah, and I bet that the box won't have a doorknob on it, will it?"

"Ahh . . ."

"Never mind, just my Neanderthal sense of humor."

CHAPTER 36

Stillwater, Oklahoma
FRIDAY, JULY 9, 1954

"Jimmy Lee, you just c'mon in here, son," Red Coil said as he rose from his desk. He swept grandly with his freckled arm to suggest that Jimmy Lee should take a seat. "How's that there leg coming along? Healin' up there okay, is it?"

It had been almost three weeks since the cast had come off, and although Jimmy Lee was still riding a single crutch, it was now used more for balance than support. He took a seat and settled his weight heavily, leaning the crutch up against the front of the desk. "Healing up well, Coach," he responded quickly. He made a show of turning his ankle in shallow rotations, biting back a wince the whole time. "Soon it'll be good as new. You just wait. Soon."

Red Coil moved to the front of his desk and perched on the corner, one leg dangling off the front edge. He fingered the wooden crutch, avoiding prolonged eye contact with Tenkiller. "Good, good; that's real good, son. You seem to be getting around just fine."

"Yes, sir, Coach. I hope to start working out soon. Got some catching up to do," Jimmy Lee said. He liked Coach Coil. The coach had recruited him and helped him fulfill the school's entrance requirements. He'd supported him and had confidence in him—something no one else ever had. Coach Coil thought that Jimmy Lee had a legitimate shot at the upcoming Olympic Games in Australia; that he could be the next Jim Thorpe. The Running Redskin was what the papers had recently taken to calling him. "Got to get ready for next season. I want to be ready for the Olympic trials. You and me, Coach Coil. We're going to Australia."

Coil looked down at his shoe; he'd been bobbing his toe nervously and wished he could stop it. He ran his hands through his thinning gray hair and stood up. He walked over to the window, shoved his hands in his hip pockets, and kept his back to Jimmy Lee as he spoke. "That was about as bad a fracture as I've seen in my thirty-odd years of coaching. Awful bad. The doctors, they aren't as confident as you are, Jimmy Lee. They say you'll never run competitively again."

"Doctors don't know so much, right, Coach? Like you always say, you run with your heart, not your feet. I didn't break my heart. Doctors, they don't understand that."

Red Coil didn't answer.

"Coach?" Jimmy Lee prompted.

"Doctors are smart people, Jimmy Lee. Smart people. They get paid to be smart. Maybe we should listen to them."

"Coach?"

"They're right, Jimmy Lee; you won't run again."

"But Coach Coil, I can run now. I can. I can do it right now, I've just been taking it easy; letting it heal, like you told me, like you said I should do, but I can run right now."

"Look, Jimmy Lee," Red Coil said, turning away from the window to face the young runner for the first time, "I don't doubt that for a minute. I don't doubt that if we went over to Lewis Field right this very goddamn minute, that you could run laps around the rest of the team, but . . ."

"But, Coach, I can run faster than anyone in this conference. You've seen me do it."

"Yes, yes you can, Jimmy Lee. That's a fact. If you hadn't been a freshman, if you'd been on the varsity instead of the JV, it'd be a conference record, that's a fact, but that was . . . Goddamn it, Jimmy Lee, that was before. Don't you get it?"

"But I can still run. You'll see."

"No, Jimmy Lee. No. Try and point your toe. Go on, now." He paused, but when Tenkiller didn't respond, he continued. "You can't. You'll never be able to. Not like before. Them bones is all froze up. Yes, with some work you can probably beat your teammates; hell, you can probably beat most of them right now carrying that crutch. Hell, with some time you might even have gotten competitive in the conference again, but you'll never make the Olympics. It's over, Jimmy Lee. It's all over, son."

"I don't understand. What do you mean, Coach Red?"

"I mean the school's pulling your scholarship; that's what I mean. I mean it's over."

Jimmy Lee sat stunned.

"Hey, you're a bright boy, Jimmy Lee. This isn't the end of the world for you. You'll find a job; something you're good at; something you can do."

Jimmy Lee Tenkiller looked up at Red Coil. His eyes had clouded, and he blinked hard to clear them, but they wouldn't clear. He blinked again, but all he saw were the faces of the old men at the boarding school and the spinsters with their cane switches. "Like what, Coach Coil, like what can I do?"

Red Coil was quiet for a moment, and he looked at the floor before responding. "The Korean conflict has simmered down, Jimmy Lee. It's safe now."

Jimmy Lee Tenkiller looked at the old man in confusion.

"Ever think about joining the army?" the coach asked.

CHAPTER 37

Rolla, Missouri
FRIDAY, APRIL 18, 2008

Michelle Catherine Thu had been born on a sunlit morning, six years and thirty-two days after her parents and two sisters had arrived in the United States—a fact that she had always given great thanks for. As a high-ranking officer of the South Vietnamese Army, her father, General Ngo Van Thu, had been welcomed openly, even if not always warmly, by the Americans, and opportunity had abounded for a man of his energy. He had done well in his adopted country. Very well. But for Michelle, the United States was not adopted, it was home, and while she took pride in her ethnic heritage, she never for a moment thought of herself as anything but an American. Now at age twenty-eight, with a medical degree from the University of Illinois, she was preparing to start her own American family. Tomorrow, in fact, and there were so many last-minute details to get sorted out.

"I'll get it," Michelle yelled as she ran down the stairs and into the den where the nearest phone extension was located. Greg was driving down from St. Louis with his best man, and they were already late. He'd gotten stuck covering a friend's shift at Barnes Hospital where he was completing his residency, and her stomach knotted with the concern that he was going to be delayed even further. She knew how easily that could happen. For the last two months he'd been trading assignments with a half dozen other residents to clear up enough time for a real honeymoon, and the resulting schedule resembled a house of cards waiting for a gust of wind. She grabbed the receiver as she skidded past the end table, her white socks not catching a purchase on the polished wood floor, and looked up to see her two older sisters standing in the kitchen doorway giggling at her. She stuck her tongue out at them before answering. "Greg?"

There was a long silence before a soft voice, which rose and fell in its modulation, responded. "No. Perhaps I have the wrong number; I'm trying to reach Ngo Van Thu. Would this, by any chance, be his residence?"

"Oh, yes," Michelle answered, unable to keep the disappointment out of her voice. "Excuse me, I was expecting someone else. Yes, this is the Thu residence." General Ngo Van Thu had long ago conceded to his adopted neighbors' inability to understand the order of Vietnamese family names and had accepted the inevitability of being called the Thu family. Michelle, in fact, had never known any different.

"Ngo Van Thu? General Ngo Van Thu?"

"Yes."

"And do I have the honor of speaking to Mrs. Ngo?"

Michelle laughed, as much at being mistaken for her mother as at the use of the old family name. "No, not hardly. I'm one of his daughters. Can I help you? Not many people call him general, though. Were you a friend of his during the war?" The reality was that no one called him general. Her father seldom spoke of the war, and Michelle seldom asked. She had been raised in an America that didn't have any interest in discussing Vietnam or the past.

"Why yes, I guess you could say that, but I doubt you can help me out," the voice replied. It rose and fell and was hard to listen to, and Michelle wondered if it was the fault of the person or the connection. "I was simply hoping to pay my respects. Touch the bases, as it were. By any chance is the general home?"

Michelle looked over at her two sisters. They were looking at her with questions in their eyes, since it obviously wasn't Dr. Wonderful on the phone. Ordinarily Michelle would have been excited by the prospect of an old friend of her father's calling out of the blue to reminisce—a diversion like that was what he needed—but right now she couldn't think of anything but the phone's being tied up indefinitely. "Ahh," she hesitated, not wanting to sound impolite, but not wanting to prolong the conversation any longer than necessary, "actually, he's running some errands with my mother. I'm getting married tomorrow, and we're all sort of running around here with our heads cut off."

"You are? Well, my congratulations. I'm sure the general is quite proud. You must be a very lovely young woman."

Michelle laughed self-consciously. "You wouldn't say that if you could see me right this minute. I'm really a mess. I'm sorry my father isn't here. Can I take a message for him?"

"Well now," the voice said, "can't say I've got a message as such; I was passing through the area, and I'd heard tell that the general had settled down here. Sort of thought I should make some contact. Old time's sake and all. No message, but maybe you could have your father call me when he gets a chance?"

"Of course. I'm sure he'll be very excited. He could probably use another man to talk to; I'm afraid all the women in this house are driving him quite crazy. Were you close? You and my father. Were you close friends?"

Now it was the roller coaster voice that hesitated. "You might say that," the voice finally answered. "In fact, well yes, you could say we were almost like brothers."

CHAPTER 38

U.S. Army Central Identification Laboratory, Hawaii
FRIDAY, APRIL 18, 2008

Kel was already late—intentionally—for a meeting with Botch-It when the telephone rang. He'd just hung up with Thomas Pierce, and he grabbed the receiver reflexively without time to work up a typical case of the sweating dreads. He assumed that it was Pierce calling back to say he'd remembered something. It wasn't.

"I'm tryin' to reach Dr. McKelvey," the voice drawled the name out slowly and added a few sleepy syllables that weren't entirely necessary.

"You've got him," Kel answered. He felt his bowels tighten when he realized it wasn't Pierce. *God,* he thought, *I hate telephones.*

"Hey, Kel, it's Shuck Deveroux."

"Shuck." Kel relaxed a little. "I thought it was a guy from the DNA lab callin' me back about somethin'—actually it's that case I called you about a while back. Master Sergeant Tenkiller and the five dwarves. Anyhow, what's up? You at Campbell?"

"Yeah," Deveroux replied. "I am. And as a matter of fact, your Tenkiller's what's up. Got some information to share."

"Really? Great. Can't believe you made the time."

"Wish I could say that I did. More accident than intent on my part. Actually, I was runnin' down another loose end, and I wound up with some information that I thought might interest you."

"Shoot."

"Ever hear of an army general by the name of Fick? One each, Paul Fick. Retired now."

"Sure," Kel said. "Brigadier type. Ahh . . . Vietnam vet, I think. Couple three of the army folks here worked under him way back when. Supposed to be a real ball-buster."

"That's the one. BG retired Paul Fick. He's a friend, or at least an old war buddy, of the commander here at Campbell. I met with him yesterday over near Memphis. Seems he has some interestin' information—if you can pry it out of him—he's not much for talkin', but he did give me a thick folder full of stuff that he'd compiled back in Saigon some thirty-forty years ago."

"On what?"

"Your man Tenkiller, among others."

"I don't understand," Kel replied.

"Not sure I do either. From what I can tell, and I haven't read the whole file yet—must be three inches thick—but from what I can piece together, Fick was sent back to Vietnam in 1970 on a special assignment for the CID. Very special; definitely not the normal channels. In fact, from what I can tell, there's no official record of what he was doin' there. The file he gave me is the only copy. Guess what he was investigatin'?"

"Given that you're callin', I'd have to guess a black market ring operatin' near Saigon."

"Bingo," Deveroux responded. "And more. Fick spent the better part of a year pokin' around and came up empty-handed, at least in terms of what he could prove, but he has a whole lot of speculations. Accordin' to his file, there was a ring of five high-rankin' Vietnamese officers who were referred to as the *Brothers* . . ."

"The *Five* Brothers," Kel added.

"That's right. Tenkiller actually made six—at least from what Fick pieced together. His informant was some French guy, and Fick clearly wasn't all that comfortable with his credibility. Anyhow, there were these five Vietnamese and Tenkiller; total of six. Tenkiller was the inside man at one of the big supply depots in-country, and Fick thinks his involvement was purely monetary; he got paid, he supplied goods—that simple. The Vietnamese, however, well, Fick has them tied into some opium smugglin' business out of the hills of Laos and Burma."

"The Golden Triangle," Kel replied. "That little wedge formed by the borders of Thailand, Burma, and Laos. Lots of heavy-duty opium grown up there. The local governments look the other way, at least until it's time to take their cut. We have to work around the harvest season sometimes when we do recoveries in Laos. Too dangerous for our teams."

"Yeah, that sounds 'bout right. Well, accordin' to Fick, the stuff Tenkiller was supplyin' was tied somehow into smugglin' the opium into South Vietnam. Haven' fully digested all that yet, but he's got some mysterious Cajun fella named Bergeron who may, or may not, have worked for Uncle Sam, involved in the whole thing; actin' like a broker of some kind."

"Interestin'. Shades of Iran Contra?"

"Showin' your age. Now, here's what's really interestin'—and actually the reason I called, the five Vietnamese? Well, it took a while, but I got all their names, and guess what . . . two of them are stiff as kiln-dried boards."

"Yeah?" Kel acknowledged as much as asked.

"Yeah. The homicides that I'm workin'. One at the Louisville ME's office and the other in Nashville. Both of them were part of the Brotherhood. Two of the five. And then of course there's Tenkiller. I still don't see what the connection is, but what are the odds?"

"Well, I'm with you; I don't see the connection between Vietnam in 1970 and now, but at the same time, it's a helluva coincidence."

"Agreed. Thought you'd want to know."

"Thanks. The Tenkiller case has taken a turn on our end, but we'll try and run down some more information for you if it'd help. I owe you."

"I'm glad to hear you say that, 'cause I do need a favor. Look, I'm sure that the medical examiners here and in Louisville are doin' a fine job and all, but I was hopin' to get a second set of eyes on those bodies. You know, there may just be somethin' that the regular docs aren't lookin' for. Some clue of some sort."

"You want an anthropologist to examine the remains?"

"Yeah. Y'all did such a bang-up job on that case at Fort Bliss," Deveroux responded.

"Thanks, but that was a different sort of case. We had a dismembered body in that one; little pieces to reassemble and all."

"So? These guys are almost dismembered; besides, I'm so stumped on this one that I need a jumpstart from somewhere. How about it?"

"So . . . what've we got here? You're talkin' about a temporary duty assignment? Few days? A week? What?"

"Yeah."

"Yeah what?"

"Few days. A week."

"Problem is that we're pretty shorthanded right this minute. I'm not sure who I've got on deck."

"How 'bout you?"

"Me?" Kel asked.

"Why not? You still go TDY don't you?"

"Why not? Good question." He glanced at the Diversity Plan Awareness workbook on the floor beside his couch and thought of the meeting with Botch-It that he was already late for. He'd been taking Les's advice and stalling on the diversity plan as much as possible, but it was getting harder each week. Now Botch-It was requiring weekly progress meetings complete with PowerPoint slides. "No reason, I guess. Tell you the truth, this job is startin' to cause me an itch that I can't seem to scratch. I still love it and all, but lately it's been . . . lately it's been, ahhh, well, startin' to cause me an itch—like I said. Kinda like a bad case of chiggers without the promise of goin' away in a couple of weeks. Office bullshit, you know."

"Which is exactly why you need to come out here on temporary duty for a few days." Deveroux continued to push.

Kel laughed. "Why not? Beats volunteerin' for Iraq again. Tell you what, make the official request. While it's bein' routed, I'll get my orders cut." Kel looked at his watch. "I can be in Nashville by noon Monday if I can catch a tailwind outta this place."

"Ahh . . . well . . . ahhh, to tell you the truth, Kel, I didn't expect such a quick response. That's a little more efficient than I was countin' on. Actually, Monday's not so good for me. My task force—all eight of them—is tied up doin' interviews that are leadin' nowhere but have to be done, and I'm drivin' over to eastern Oklahoma on Sunday and won't be back here till Tuesday late."

"Really? What part of Oklahoma?"

"Little place. I doubt you ever heard of it," Deveroux said.

"Try me. I'm a font of geographical knowledge."

"You asked for it. Place called Onapa."

"Onapa. Sure. Little south of Checotah, right?"

"Dang, that's close. How in the world did you know that? I doubt the people in Onapa have even heard of it."

"Had a high school buddy—his family had a vacation place over on Lake Eufaula near there. Went with him a couple three times. As I recall, Onapa was the closest place that underage kids could get beer. You goin' fishin' or d'you need to buy some three-two beer?"

"Might say that," Deveroux answered. "The fishin' part. Actually I'm goin' to go interview Mr. Ed Tenkiller."

"No shit. Now that's a familiar name. Jimmy Tenkiller's brother, I assume. The one who won't give us a drop of blood for the DNA test?"

"Yup. Goin' to see what he might know about these Five Brothers. Long shot, I know, but I figure maybe brother Jimmy wrote some letters, said somethin', who knows. My wife and kids are up in Sikeston, Missouri, this weekend for her sister's weddin', so I figure I'll spend the day drivin' to Oklahoma."

"You not invited to the weddin'?"

"Oh, yeah. I'm invited. I just can't stand my soon-to-be brother-in-law, and Tenkiller was a ready excuse to miss the festivities."

"I tell you what, partner," Kel proposed, "this is doable, but how about a little quid pro quo here? I'll come look at your bodies if you'll let me tag along with you when you interview Tenkiller. Like you say, he may have some letters or somethin' that'll help me out on my aspect of the case. Promise I'll stay out of your way."

"You got a brother-in-law to avoid too?"

"Naw, but if I stay here I'm likely to do something that'll earn me some jail time. Listen, there's a flight into Tulsa that will get me there before noon on Monday. Can you pick me up?"

"Sure. Why not? Need to warn you, though, I got an old pickup that's long on reliability and very short on comfort."

"I could say the same for my ass. I'm game."

"Okay then. Let me know the flight number and time," Deveroux replied.

"How 'bout I email it to you as soon as I get the reservation?"

"Fine with me."

"Good. Should be fun."

"Yeah. Don't know about fun, but it should at least be interestin'. Who knows, maybe we'll find the link between all these fellas. Lord knows we could use a break in this case."

"Maybe," Kel responded. "I got to admit that it's a hell of a coincidence if there isn't, the Five Brothers and all."

"Yeah, I'm like you. Five guys, six countin' your Tenkiller, all in business together in Vietnam and now a couple of them come up dead. I've got a buddy at INS runnin' the other names down now. I'll be curious to know if they came to this country and whether they still have the tops of their heads attached firmly. Three known dead, maybe three to go . . ."

"Two really. Not sure you can count Tenkiller. The skeleton we've got isn't him. My guess is that he's dead and all, but he likely died thirty-some years ago."

"Hmm. That's not quite what General Fick said."

CHAPTER 39

Rolla, Missouri
SATURDAY, APRIL 19, 2008

Ngo Van Thu was distracted.

Throughout the seemingly endless ceremony he'd watched every movement, his eyes jumping around from face to face, probing each nook and shadow—knowing that it was the shadows that held the greatest attraction, the greatest familiarity and comfort. Saint Patrick's Church was large and filled with good hiding places for a ghost from the past.

There had been lots of faces. As befitting his standing in the community, Ngo Van Thu—with ample help from his wife and daughters—had spared few expenses and had been more than liberal with invitations. And befitting Ngo Van Thu's status in the community, few of the invited had declined to attend and pass up such an opportunity to rub elbows.

There had been lots of faces.

In the end, he had seen nothing, including most of the ceremony. His wife had even had to nudge him when the priest had pronounced the banns. His distraction had followed him to the Hardscrabble Country Club where there were even more faces to scan and more movements to watch. He'd tensed with every unexpected pat on his back and grab of his elbow, turning, expecting to see his forty-year-old nightmare intruding upon his waking present. But as with the ceremony at the church, his vigilance had proven needless. There was no face in the shadow. Now, as the reception began to slow and the band began to stand down on break, he allowed himself to relax and took up a seat at a vacant table near the dance floor. He loosened his tie and poured a full glass of warm champagne that he sipped slowly as he watched his daughter make the last of her predeparture flits. Like a beautiful butterfly touching each flower petal in its path. He closed his eyes and felt the burn and sting of cigarette smoke and strong sunlight and lack of sound sleep. The pain was comforting in an odd sort of way; it reminded him that he was alive. He savored the sting.

"She's very beautiful," the voice behind him said. "Quite beautiful, really. You should be proud, General."

Ngo Van Thu realized he wasn't surprised. Despite the dread and the distraction, despite the ceaseless searching of faces and shadows, when the voice finally spoke he wasn't surprised. He didn't jump, didn't even open his eyes. He savored the sting. "I am," he replied.

"Yes, sir, very beautiful. I wouldn't mind knocking off a piece of that myself. Been a long time since I gon' and had some Viet tail. Especially any of that quality."

"She's my daughter, John Bergeron." Ngo Van Thu set his glass down and turned to look at the man he hadn't seen in over three decades.

John Bergeron had grown corpulent over the years and showed the effects—it always amazed Ngo how Caucasians showed the signs of age—but it was him; Bergeron hadn't changed beyond recognition. Ngo Van Thu had wondered whether he would know him when he finally saw him, whether he could have picked him out of the faces in the church or on the dance floor or in the receiving line, and he smiled at the confirmation.

"They're all someone's daughters, General. Every last one of them is someone's little girl. That little biological fact never seemed to bother you when we were bar-fining tail in Saigon." John Bergeron smiled with the recollection. "Now there's a blast from the sordid past. You still got that—that—what do you call that thing? Swagger stick? Riding crop? You know what I mean. You still got that thing? I bet you do, General, I bet you do. Too many good memories, right? Bet your wife and daughter they don't know about that little museum curiosity, though. Wouldn't understand, would they? Am I right, General?"

"As I said, she's my daughter."

"Come now, you're showing your age. The General Ngo Van Thu that I once knew could peel the skin off some pretty young thing with that riding crop of his and never once worry about her being someone's daughter. The whippin's got your rocks off more than the sex that followed. Don't tell me you're getting soft, General? Not General Ngo Van Thu. Don't you go and become just another lazy American on me."

Ngo Van Thu looked away, his eye catching his daughter's. She waved and smiled so gracefully and easily that he smiled back reflexively.

John Bergeron reached past Thu and grabbed the champagne bottle, which he swirled and held up to the light to better gauge the contents. He emptied the bottle into a glass on the table and hoisted it in the general's direction in mock toast. "No, not much chance of that, is there? Lots of things, maybe, but never lazy." He gestured around the room with his drink. "Doctors, bankers, businessmen. My compliments, General. Talked to a few of these folks while I waited for you to finish shaking hands. Definitely not getting lazy. Very impressive what you've accomplished. Real estate holdings, shares in an investment company, your own construction company. Yes, sir. Now, who was it was telling me? . . . ahhh, there, that man over there, the fat one . . . he was telling me that you've got a lock on all the government contracts at Fort Leonard Wood. Says you've built every new building there for the last fifteen years. Still taking Uncle Sam's checks, I see. What would those contracts add up to? Millions?" He toasted Ngo again. "Yes, sir, here's to old habits' dying hard."

"What do you want, John Bergeron?"

"And now that one over there, the one with the big-titted wife . . . now, he was telling me that there's even a movement afoot to run you for the state legislature this fall. The Right Honorable Ngo Van Thu. It's got a certain ring, but you got to admit, it's going to be a mouthful for the good folks of the Ozarks; don't you think?"

Ngo Van Thu stood up and reached over to an adjacent table, where he checked the contents of two large, dark-green bottles. He selected one and sat down, pouring another glass of champagne.

"So tell me, General, what do you hear from our old friends? You know who I mean, your brothers? You keep in touch with them at all?" Bergeron pushed his glass across the white tablecloth. He nodded in a way that indicated a refill was in order.

Ngo picked the bottle up by the neck and placed it in front of Bergeron, who helped himself. "I am not in contact with them. That is a past that is better left in the past."

"Amen, Brother Thu. I hear ya," Bergeron answered as he filled his glass. "Not the sort of baggage a man planning to take a run at the State House needs to be totin'. Opium deals and gun running are such awkward topics on the golf course. I suspect you've got more than one good reason to want some of those sleeping dogs to keep snoozing, you. Now, as for me, I've got some business goings-on myself—some consulting work, if you understand—and I'd just as soon the past remain in the past as well. That works for me; unfortunately, not everyone seems to feel that way."

Ngo didn't make eye contact but kept watching the guests, now and then nodding at someone across the room.

"So . . . you haven't had contact with any of our former associates? Is that right?" Bergeron continued. "In that case you probably haven't heard the news. Seems as if two of our former buddies have become accident prone." He emptied his glass and smacked loudly. "No offense, General, but with the money I suspect you laid out for this spread, you'd think they could keep the champagne cold. My piss is colder than this. And the music, it could use some pepper too. Maybe some Rosie Ledet or even better, you gon' and get some Clifton Chenier."

Ngo Van Thu didn't respond.

"Yes, sir, but as I was saying, it seems that a couple of the boys have met with accidents lately. Both Colonel Trinh and Major Linh recently fell victim to the lawless streets of America. Nearly decapitated by some violent madman, I hear. Tragic, don't you think? It's shocking the state that this country has gotten itself in. You can't even walk the streets in safety. It's the sort of thing our elected officials need to take a stand against. Maybe I'll write a congressman—what you think, you?"

Ngo made a small gesture with his arm to flag a passing waiter, who stopped and bent slightly at the waist, turning his head to the side to better receive his instructions. Ngo quietly said something to him that Bergeron couldn't hear. As the waiter walked away, Ngo adjusted his posture and returned his gaze to the activity in the room. Bergeron watched him closely, squinting slightly as if he could bring the general into better focus.

"Now that's funny, that really is. You always were a cold fish, General, but I'd have thought that sort of news might warrant a raised eyebrow or something. Two old buddies killed and nothing. I'd have thought that warranted at least an *aw shit*. Why do I suspect you weren't hearing the news for the first time? Why do I suspect that?"

The waiter returned and deposited a cold bottle of champagne on the table. Ngo remained quiet.

"You weren't an easy man to find, General," Bergeron shifted conversational gears. "That shell game you all play with your last names makes it difficult, and you know something else that's funny? As it turns out, all you gentlemen end up living next to active military installations. Now how 'bout that? And you know what else? All of you end up doing business with the U.S. government. You take the cake though, you. But then you always did, didn't you? The others, they were small potatoes; dry-cleaning contract, grocery supplier, petty shit. Nothing like the million-dollar contracts you've pulled off. No sir, you."

"I've been successful."

"That you have, that you have. But success has a price. I guess I don't have to tell you that, though. You've got a lot to lose now, don't you?"

Ngo Van Thu made eye contact, and Bergeron saw the cold blood he'd known so many years earlier.

"We both know this wasn't a coincidence, was it—Messieurs Linh and Trinh. You and I, we both know that. Someone's making sure the past stays in the past, and while I don' disagree with that intent, I'm not necessarily keen on the method—know what I mean? Who's left, General? There's you, me, Major Doan." Bergeron counted off on the fingers of his right hand. "So what you think? You like Major Doan with a wrench in the library? Or maybe it was General Ngo with the candlestick in the observatory? What's your read on the situation?"

"Perhaps you are forgetting one."

Bergeron looked at Ngo, scrunching his eyes into narrow slits as he took stock of his old acquaintance. "Tenkiller? No, General, I'm not forgetting, but I'm surprised you thought of him."

"Why, John Bergeron? Because you were to take care of Master Sergeant Tenkiller and did not? Do you think I did not know? I know everything."

Bergeron smiled. He had often underestimated General Ngo. "You always were fascinated by the Chief, weren't you? Yes, I suspect you're right. It wouldn't do either one of us any good to forget about Big Chief Tenkiller."

"He is a most dangerous man."

"Yeah, but then the world is filled with dangerous men, my friend. Some might even be in this room. What you think?"

"I think you should have taken care of him long ago. He is a most dangerous man, I think. Most violent."

"Maybe I should have, but then who'd have figured he go and run like he done. Kind of upset my timetable when he did. But while we're pointing fingers, General, let me remind you who scared the jumping bejeezus out of that po' boy. I didn't go and drill a drainage hole in Colonel Pham's frontal sinus with my .45."

"Still, John Bergeron, it was your responsibility to take care of Sergeant Tenkiller. We had an agreement."

"We had many agreements, General. Many."

"Yes, many. This one I remember. He is a wild Indian, is he not? A man of much violence. I hope it is not too late. He was your responsibility."

John Bergeron drained his glass of champagne and reached for the bottle. "So he was, General. And so he still is. Just as soon as I find him."

CHAPTER 40

Onapa, Oklahoma
MONDAY, APRIL 21, 2008

Shuck Deveroux turned his white pickup onto the Muskogee Turnpike
and headed east toward Broken Arrow and the Arkansas state line.
Kel's airplane had been delayed out of Denver and had arrived at Tulsa
International airport almost an hour behind schedule. With the afternoon
already on the wane, Deveroux found himself pushing the speed limit,
anxious to get to the small community of Onapa before dinner. When he'd
called and reintroduced himself from the airport, he'd told Ed Tenkiller
that he'd be there by no later than three o'clock. It was already past three
and by dead reckoning they were still at least twenty-five minutes away.
Tenkiller hadn't been too receptive to meeting with Deveroux but had
agreed in the end, and Deveroux didn't want to do anything to spook the
deal. He'd hoped to keep Tenkiller just off balance enough to be loose
tongued without getting so dizzy that his mouth dried up. Now it looked
like the game board was going to be turned, and Deveroux would be the
one off balance and apologizing for being late.

Deveroux looked at Kel and then refocused on the road. He
reached over and turned the tape player down. Vaughn Monroe's
"Ghost Riders in the Sky" was just audible above the roar of the
tires. He thought McKelvey looked worse for the wear of the long
trip. "Glad you're finally here, Doc."

"Thanks. Appreciate you pickin' me up. And don't take offense if I nod off at some point."

"No problem. My only concern is gettin' to Tenkiller's place before it gets any later." He checked his watch. "I'm afraid he won't feel the need to wait on us; he didn't seem just overjoyed to hear we were comin'."

"Hmm, imagine that."

"Yeah. Kinda like pickin' open a scab, don't you think? And an old scab at that."

"Old and painful. More like pickin' open scar tissue. Don't forget, the army carried his brother as a deserter until the mid-eighties sometime. Eighty-four or '85. Somethin' like that. I'm sure this is not Mr. Tenkiller's favorite topic of discussion. I'm bettin' he doesn't break out the family albums for us."

"I suppose not." Deveroux was focused on the road ahead of him again. "General Fick was sayin' that it was the brother that turned all the knobs to get Jimmy Lee Tenkiller declared dead. He said that the army had plenty of doubts but a lack of balls, and in the end they buckled to pressure from some congressmen."

"I hear ya. So Fick thinks Tenkiller really deserted?"

"Who knows?" he shrugged. "I couldn't get him to tell me what he really believes."

"He as tough as they say? Fick. I've always heard stories. Worked with a Special Forces colonel once who claimed he'd actually gotten himself *Ficked*. Described it as a low-yield nuclear blast from outta nowhere; said he melted into slag—and he actually outranked Fick at the time."

Deveroux smiled. "I've heard all those stories, too. I dunno. He was friendly enough to me, but he's definitely a piece of gristle; you can chew on him for hours and still not know quite what you're dealin' with. Plus, he's almost seventy years old now; I suspect the reactor's cooled somewhat from his youth." Deveroux eased the truck into the right lane and approached the exact-change lane of the tollbooth. "I think we get off here," he said. He spoke to Kel over his right shoulder as he handed the toll attendant a dollar and a quarter. "Open up that map, will ya?"

Kel had the map opened on his lap and was tracing one of the thin dark lines with his finger. "Got it." He looked up to verify his bearings, and then put the map on the dashboard. "So, General Fick remembered Tenkiller by name?"

"Sure did, though I suspect he's the sort that can remember the name of every person he's ever met, but in this case, yeah, he remembered Tenkiller quite well."

"How so?

"Well, now, that's what's so interestin'. Seems that their paths crossed twice. First time was in 1970 . . ."

"The year Tenkiller went missin'."

"Right. In fact, he goes missin' a couple of days after Fick first meets him. Like I was tellin' you over the phone, General Fick—'course at that time he was a young captain—he was workin' for CID on some sort of special assignment and had been sent to Vietnam to investigate your black market case. He'd questioned a couple dozen folks or so, and Tenkiller was last on his list. So, in September he finally questions Tenkiller; doesn't get much out of him, but—so he says now—he came away from the meetin' with a real strange feelin' about Master Sergeant Tenkiller." They were approaching Checotah, and Deveroux slowed the truck in anticipation of their next turn. "Here?"

"Yeah. Take a left."

"Roger that. By the way, that thick file of stuff that Fick gave me?" Deveroux continued after completing the turn. "Haven't gone through it all, but some of it is pretty interestin' readin'."

"I'd like to see it. See how it compares to the official file that we have."

"Sure. Anyway, Fick interviews Tenkiller and says he gets a strange feelin' that somethin's not quite right. He plans on lettin' him simmer for a day or two and then rattlin' his birdcage again. Problem is . . ."

"When he goes back, Tenkiller's gone. Right?"

"Right. Story was that he was on leave, at least that's what Tenkiller's CO thinks. Thinks our boy is shacked up in a cheap hotel with a mama-san." They began passing buildings.

"Couple more miles. So, his CO thinks he's out bar-finin' some workin' girls."

"Right. Everyone thinks that he's simply taken a few hard-earned days off for some R and R . . ."

"Except that he doesn't come back," Kel said.

"Except that he doesn't come back."

"And thirty days later, he's dropped from the company roll as a deserter."

"You got it," Deveroux replied. "'Course Fick's always assumed he ran, but the Tenkiller family doesn't see it that way. I say family, actually it's just the one brother, I guess. Anyhow, the brother argued that he didn't fit the profile of a deserter. Career military, approaching early retirement with fifteen-plus in. Ready to redeploy out of Vietnam. No need to run . . ."

"Of course, the idea of spendin' another fifteen in—this time breakin' rocks at Leavenworth—can be a real motivator to stretch your legs."

"That's Fick's position."

"So what was the second time? You said he and Fick had crossed paths twice."

"Yeah, that's the ironic part. By the time the Tenkiller family—the brother, that is—had finally convinced enough congressmen to stir the pot, guess who's sittin' on the review board to examine Sergeant Tenkiller's status."

"No shit."

"Yup," Deveroux answered.

"And Fick voted to amend his status?"

"Nope. He dissented, but the other two on the board voted for it, it only takes a majority. Two to one, and that's how Jimmy Lee Tenkiller became one of your KIAs. Fick likes to say he *killed* Tenkiller, but really all he did was chair the committee that declared him dead." Deveroux again began slowing the truck. "Unless I'm mistaken, this is the place." He turned into a gravel lot and looked at his watch. "And we're only an hour late."

Kel looked out the window at the metal frame building whose parking lot they had just pulled into. The hand-lettered sign on the roof said *The Bait Can.*

■

Eddie John Tenkiller watched them drive up. Business had been slack most of the afternoon, and when they hadn't arrived on time the idea of closing early and leaving began to tickle his imagination. He had no desire to talk to these two strangers any more than he'd wanted to talk to that other white-eye a few months ago, and the urge to shutter the windows and lock the door tugged hard. He watched them stand up and stretch and look up at the sign above his shop.

After all these years, why now? What did they want with him?

Eddie John Tenkiller looked remarkably like his older brother. He was seven years his junior but shared Jimmy Lee's modest proportions, his broad forehead, the sharp cheekbones, the full lips. And yet there was a difference that was not so quickly captured by photographs but would be obvious in the flesh. Eddie John's eyes lacked the glare of a wronged youth; lacked the bottomless clarity of rushed maturity, but then he'd had an easier go of it than had Jimmy Lee. His mother, a small, quiet Cherokee with eyes that lit men's hearts and a smile that could cloud men's thoughts, had died giving birth to her second son, and his father, faced with the prospect of raising two young sons by himself, had sought the answer in the amber contents of a bottle. The foster family that had raised Eddie John, while strict and unbending in many ways, was at least loving and gentle, and stood in stark contrast to the Methodist spinsters and bitter old men at the Indian school who correlated the frequency of canings with the development of Jimmy Lee's God-fearing character.

He watched the two men angle across the empty parking lot. They had parked near the street rather than near the door, as if to give them a moment or two to better evaluate the situation before entering, and they turned this way and that and gazed attentively at the building as if preparing to make an offer on the real estate. Their appearance was military; at least the tall one's, despite the civilian dress. He was cleanly groomed, with broad shoulders that reflected an exercise regimen that was obviously foreign to the smaller of the two, but he walked with a small stutter suggesting stiff knees. The other was slightly older and bearded and conveyed an air of fatigue. They both had on dark glasses that they removed as they opened the door. Just as the other one had.

A two-toned electronic beep signaled the door opening.

Eddie John Tenkiller busied himself with a cardboard display of Rebel fishing lures and purposefully avoided conspicuous eye contact.

The tall one with the bad knees was the first to speak. "Afternoon."

Tenkiller looked up. "Help you?"

"Yes, sir. Hope so. My name is Deveroux, and I'm lookin' for a Mr. Tenkiller."

"Me. I'm Tenkiller."

"Well, sir, I'm Special Agent Deveroux with army CID. We spoke on the phone this mornin'. This here's Dr. Robert McKelvey of the Central ID Lab." He waited for Tenkiller to acknowledge the introductions.

Eddie John nodded once.

"Mr. Tenkiller, first of all, let me apologize for bein' late. We got hung up at the airport in Tulsa, you know how that goes sometimes."

In fact, Eddie John Tenkiller didn't know, he'd never been on an airplane in his life, but he gave another quick nod of acknowledgment in the hope of speeding along the meeting.

"Also, let me thank you for agreein' to meet with us on such short notice." Deveroux was sincere, if a little calculating.

"What can I do for you?" Eddie John directed his question to Deveroux, but his attention was on Kel, who was fingering the display board of fishing lures, seemingly unconnected to what his partner was doing. Eddie John was wondering if this was some of the Good Cop, Bad Cop tactics that he'd read about and heard about.

"Not sure, really, Mr. Tenkiller. Lookin' to ask a few questions is all."

"About what?"

"Your brother."

Eddie John stared in response. It was a hard look.

"Your brother's Jimmy Lee Tenkiller?" Deveroux asked.

"Was. My brother's dead."

"Of course. I didn't mean . . ."

"Can I help you?" Eddie John interrupted. The question was

directed at Kel, who was examining a clear plastic blister package with a colorful lure inside.

Kel looked up in surprise. "What? Ahhh, no, I . . . just lookin'. I worked in a factory that made these one summer when I was growin' up. I used to paint all them dots on the tail there. Kinda caught me by surprise that they're still makin' the same model. Doesn't seem to have changed at all. Dots aren't painted quite as skillfully, maybe. Hard to get good help nowadays."

"It catches plenty of fish," Eddie John responded. "It's a good lure." He was anxious to deflect the conversation onto more stable terrain. The other man, the one who'd come asking about Jimmy Lee last fall, he'd started the same way. He'd just wanted to ask a few questions.

"Ahh, Mr. Tenkiller." When Deveroux had regained Tenkiller's focus, he continued. "Just a few questions. Here's the background. I'm investigatin' a couple of homicides—murders—that happened in Kentucky and Tennessee. Took place on military installations, that's why the army has the lead on the case."

"I've never been to Kentucky or Tennessee."

"No, sir. I never meant to suggest . . . ahh, you aren't a suspect in this case. Don't get that idea."

Eddie John looked at Deveroux but said nothing.

"No, sir. Perhaps there's a, a, umm, is there a place where can sit down and talk?"

"No."

"Okay. Right." Deveroux looked over at Kel, who smiled but now kept his attention focused on a rack of multicolored rubber worms. "Well then . . ."

"I run this place alone. No help. I have to stay here," Eddie John said; he too was watching Kel. "I keep on the lookout for shoplifters."

Deveroux followed Tenkiller's look over to Kel. "Don't blame you at all." He smiled. "Be okay to shoot shoplifters if I had my way." He waited until he'd recaptured Tenkiller's attention. "So . . . yes, okay. A few questions, then. We can do them right here. I guess first, a little more background. These two murder victims that I mentioned were immigrants—former Vietnamese military officers—and we have reason to believe that your brother may have known these two men during the war. In fact, we think that these two, and your brother, were part of a . . . a group of sorts. We also think that there may be three more. By any chance does the expression *Five Brothers* mean anything to you? Ring any bells?"

Eddie John Tenkiller looked down. The eyes had been noncommittal earlier, but when he raised his head they had changed. Now they smoked with undisguised anger. "I had one brother; not five; just one. He died many years ago. Why can't you men let him rest? Why you and that other man not let him be? He asked about Five Brothers too. I have one brother, and he died."

Deveroux looked at Kel, who had abandoned his interest in rubber worms and was staring at Tenkiller.

"Mr. Tenkiller, excuse me for interruptin' Agent Deveroux, but did you say there was another man askin' about your brother? When was this?"

Eddie John returned Kel's stare. "Last October. Another round-eye."

Deveroux again looked over at Kel. "Mr. Ngon, or Mr. Linh—whatever his name is—the first one, at Knox, that was in October." He looked back at Tenkiller. "Round-eye? You mean Caucasian? Did he tell you who he was, or why he was askin'? Say why?"

"Don't remember his name. He said he was a friend of my brother in Vietnam."

"D'you believe him?" Kel asked.

"No."

"Why not?" Deveroux picked up the questioning.

"Jimmy Lee had no friends in Vietnam"

"Any idea who he was?" Kel asked. "From around here?"

"Louisiana."

"Louisiana? Why do you say that? He got an accent, or . . . ?" Deveroux continued.

"No."

"No. Then what makes you say Louisiana?"

"That's what he said."

Deveroux and Kel looked at each other again and then back at Tenkiller. Both men were running the probabilities through their heads. All along, both had been reluctant to believe that the connection between Deveroux's dead Vietnamese and Master Sergeant Tenkiller was anything more than a historical coincidence, but now they were forced to factor in the odds of a stranger asking Eddie John Tenkiller about the Five Brothers, and doing so at the same time as the first murder.

"Mr. Tenkiller, can you give us a better idea of what this man looked like?"

"Like you."

"Me? Us?"

"White."

Deveroux nodded and continued, "Can you narrow that down any? I'm afraid that there's a lot of us white guys around."

Eddie John Tenkiller looked at both men. *There are a lot of white guys around,* he thought. Men like them had beaten his brother. Men like this had robbed him of his future. "I need to close now," he said. "You men should leave."

CHAPTER 41

Onapa, Oklahoma
MONDAY, APRIL 21, 2008

"I'm in serious need of a Slim Jim," Shuck Deveroux said as he pulled his pickup truck off the main road into the parking lot of a small Tote-n-Go convenience store. It rolled to a noisy stop, the muffler rattling against the undercarriage. He turned off the ignition and the motor continued to cough and choke as they walked to the door.

Inside, Deveroux grabbed a couple of Slim Jims from the counter and opened one of the sliding glass doors of a soft drink cooler. He touched several bottles, feeling for the coldest, before pulling two Coca Colas out and handing one to Kel. They were all barely cooler than room temperature. "So, what do you think about all that back there?"

"Thanks," Kel replied, taking the bottle. "Wasn't really Mr. Friendly, was he?"

"No, but then I saw the way you were looking at those lures. Maybe he thought you were goin' to steal one of them."

"I was tempted. He had some nice ones, but I don't think that was his problem."

"Seriously, d'you expect him to be? Friendly, that is. Two strangers come into his bait shop and start askin' personal questions—can't say I'd be too talkative either under those circumstances."

"Probably right. What'd you make of someone else askin' about that Brotherhood business? More than a bit of coincidence, don't you think?"

Deveroux had finally sorted a wad of money into a semblance of order and handed a five-dollar bill to the young woman behind the counter. She had a bright-green smock and an enormous ball of hair the color of a ripe lemon. He smiled at her as he waited on his change. "Thank you, ma'am." He nodded and then turned his attention back to Kel. "Sure. More than a bit, I'd say."

Kel slowly vented the carbonation from his drink, careful to keep it from overflowing. They were turning to leave when the clerk closed her cash register and spoke for the first time. She had a low-pitched, erratic voice that reminded everyone who knew her of two sticks of dry wood being rubbed together. It was as if her throat were about to catch fire. She also had industrial-sized breasts that looked more architectural than biological.

"Bait shop? Y'all talking about Eddie Tenkiller?" she asked.

"Yes, ma'am," Deveroux responded. Both men halted and turned back to face the counter. "You know him?"

"Sure do. Not well, of course; Tenkillers are sort of a private bunch, but I know 'em as good as any around here, I suppose."

"Hard man to get to know?" Kel asked.

"You bet. They come by here for ice sometimes. You know, when they run low. That's mostly during bass or crappie tournaments and all. They'll come by, load up that old truck of theirs with five-pound bags of crushed ice, and be on their way. Won't say but five words the whole dang time."

"*They?*" Kel asked. "Is there a Mrs. Tenkiller?"

"Hardly."

Kel didn't respond but waited for some elaboration.

"Just them two old skinny-assed bachelors. For the longest time, people 'round here used to think they was funny," the woman responded.

"Funny?"

"Yeah. You know. *Funny.*"

"Funny?"

"I think she means gay," Deveroux clarified, stepping into the conversation. He was unsuccessfully gnawing at the plastic wrapper of his Slim Jim trying to initiate a tear.

Kel watched him momentarily before turning back to the woman behind the counter.

"That's right," the woman answered, "'Course that was more in the beginning. Don't nobody think that now. Ain't queer. Just real private folks, is all."

"Is that right?" Kel answered. He was bobbing his head slowly like one of those toy drinking birds. "Ahh, Miss . . ."

"Tawnny Lynn. With two Ns."

"Two Ns?" Deveroux asked.

"Yeah. Two in Tawnny and two in Lynn. That's four Ns, if you add them all up."

"It certainly is."

"Tawnny Lynn," Kel jumped in before Deveroux could say anything else. "Right pretty name. Well, Miss Tawnny Lynn, we only met with Mr. Tenkiller. Ed Tenkiller. Eddie. You keep sayin' *they*; who's the other part of this *they*? If you don't mind us askin'?"

"Tommy."

"With two Ms?" Deveroux asked.

Kel lasered him a look.

"Yup."

"Tommy got hisself a last name?" Kel continued.

"Tenkiller." Her voice conveyed a forced patience that suggested she thought she was covering a matter of common knowledge. She had long ago come to the conclusion that most people from out of town tended to be somewhat slow-witted, and so far these two hadn't unseated that belief.

"Tommy Tenkiller?" Kel clarified.

"Quite a ring to it," Deveroux mumbled. "Two Ts." He'd stopped shaking his head and now had the plastic wrapper of the Slim Jim clamped tightly in his mouth and was pulling on it like a bird tugging on a worm, but his eyes were on Tawnny Lynn.

"That be a relative, I'm guessin'. This Mr. Tommy Tenkiller fella?" Kel ignored Deveroux. His interest was growing.

"Cousin." Tawnny Lynn nodded and pulled her round face into the same tight knot that her ninth-grade geometry teacher had become so familiar with. She couldn't help but wonder if her two customers weren't more than uncommonly thick.

"You from around here, ma'am?" Kel continued.

"Sure am. Whole life. Up to now, that is."

"Looks like a great place to grow up. Great place to raise a family, I'd figure." Kel paused to let the sediment of that comment settle before continuing. "The Tenkiller family, they from around here too?"

"Not originally. From over near Bartlesville, I think. Think they's Osage or Pawnee or some such something. Don't really know for sure. I'm part Cherokee myself—on my daddy's side. See my high cheekbones?"

"Really? Ahh . . . why yes, ahhh—"

"Ever heard of the Trail of Tears. That was my daddy's people."

"That right? Ummm, when they move here? The Tenkillers. Any idea?"

"I dunno, maybe . . . well, now you would have to go and ask me, wouldn't you? Ahh, well, I guess I don't know for sure." Tawnny Lynn cocked her head as if she had a marble in her skull and was trying to get it to roll from one side to the other. It apparently worked, because she soon answered, "Before I was born. Maybe thirty, thirty-five years ago. That'd be my guess. My brothers, they used to buy nightcrawlers off them boys when they first opened their business. That's all t'was at first, big ol' nightcrawlers and lukewarm three-two beer."

"Thirty-five years." Kel bit his lip and worked it around. "What's the cousin like? Tommy?"

Tawnny Lynn shrugged and began straightening a display of herbal energy boosters on the counter. The sign had a jagged lightning bolt and said they were guaranteed to boost vitality and stamina and were endorsed by long-haul truckers. She hummed as she thought through her answer. "Lot like Eddie only more so, I'd say. Quiet. Real quiet. Older. Don't really see Tommy all so much. It's usually Eddie that comes by here, but Tommy's in the truck with him sometimes. He don't usually get out none."

"What's he look like?" Kel pressed. "You know, I mean . . ."

She scrunched her face again. "Y'all sure are interested in the Tenkillers."

Kel smiled but didn't respond.

"What's Tommy look like?" Tawnny Lynn refreshed the question in her own mind. "Well, Indian. You know? He looks like Eddie, only about ten years older. Hair's starting to turn gray. Maybe a bit taller, maybe not. You seldom see him outside the house, and then only in the truck. Little bit of a gimp. Like he's got arthritis or a rock in his shoe."

Kel took a sip of his drink and looked over to Deveroux, who'd been watching the conversation closely. Kel looked back at Tawnny Lynn and smiled. "Well, thank you, ma'am. Appreciate the conversation." He took another sip and turned to Deveroux. "Say, you about ready there, partner?"

"Sure am," he replied, and then he nodded at Tawnny Lynn as well and tapped the brim of his ballcap in an exaggerated manner. "Ma'am."

"Shit," Kel said as soon as they were outside. "Goddamn, Shuck, if we don't look like two monkeys tryin' to fuck a football. What did you make of all that?"

They had parted and flowed around the hood of the vehicle. Deveroux stopped and leaned on the hood, looking over it at Kel as he shoved the rest of the Slim Jim into his mouth. His cheek bulged. "I thought you told me the Tenkiller family tree had pretty much died out. Sure doesn't sound that way." He swallowed and wiped his greasy hands on his thighs before continuing. "Suppose she knows what's she's talkin' about?"

Kel paused by the passenger door and looked back at the convenience store. "You bet."

CHAPTER 42

Lynn Fox had no desire to finish last. He never had, until last year, and he didn't intend to make it a habit. His whole life had involved winning, first at Little League and then as a starting pitcher for the Rice Owls three of his four years. Even when the team sucked, his personal stats were always those of a winner. Even in the two years that he served as an unpaid graduate coaching assistant at Texas while he struggled with his Ph.D., he'd been associated with success on the playing field. Always success. Never failure. At least until last year.

It didn't matter that it was an interdepartmental softball league or that his team was made up of overweight sociologists and a big-haired secretary whose bra size easily eclipsed her IQ by an order of magnitude. It could just as easily have been the World Series as far as he was concerned; he was the coach and manager and starting pitcher and overall driving force. He had always been a winner, never a loser, and that was why they were going to start practice early this year—like it or not. They were not going one-and-thirteen again this year.

Despite the predictable grumbling, Monday mornings from eight-thirty to ten had proven to be a time when almost everyone was free to practice. One professor had class on Mondays from eight-thirty until nine-thirty, and two older graduate students were likewise unavailable, but everyone else professed to being free. Lynn Fox knew better, however, than to expect everyone to show. Most would weasel some lame excuse, and that was acceptable this early in the season, just as long as enough showed up to put together a practice.

He arrived early to get set up and noticed the older, red Ford Escort in the parking lot. He didn't recognize it, but then he also didn't know all of the new players who'd added their names to the sign-up list outside his office, many of them graduate students new to the program. There were even a couple of undergrads who'd changed majors. From what he could tell, no one was in the car, and he saw nobody on the field as he opened his trunk and removed the old army duffel bag that held the department's thirty-some-year-old collection of mismatched bats and balls. It wasn't until he started walking toward the visiting dugout, the duffel bag clunking against the ground as it dragged behind him, that he saw the other person stretched out on one of the lower bleacher seats, either asleep or passed out, he didn't know which. On the seat immediately in front was a paper bag from which the neck of a clear-glass bottle protruded, suggesting that if the person was simply napping, he was doing so with some distilled help.

Lynn Fox shook his head as he set the duffel bag in the dugout and glanced quickly at the sleeping body. He wasn't sure what his duty was. He wasn't a prude, and he'd certainly woken up in someone's lawn covered with dew and vomit more than once in his student career, but that was the point—he wasn't a student anymore. As of two months ago he was a tenured associate professor, and he felt some nagging sense of pedagogical duty to wake the boy up and get him steered in the direction of home, and coffee, and a shower, or at least a proper bed.

"Aw, crap," he muttered to himself, decision made. He tossed his orange Texas Longhorns cap on the concrete bench in the dugout and started over to the bleachers. That's when he realized that something didn't look quite right. The student was lying on his left side, facing away from the field, and wore a dark-blue canvas jacket with the collar turned up high for warmth, or so he'd thought from the dugout. But something was odd; out of proportion.

Lynn Fox was reaching out to shake the boy's ankle when he finally realized what looked so strange.

The boy's head was missing.

CHAPTER 43

Onapa, Oklahoma
MONDAY, APRIL 21, 2008

"Could be a simple explanation." Shuck Deveroux had finished his Slim Jim, but not before wedging a knot of fatty sinew tightly between some porcelain bridgework on his upper right premolars. He'd cracked one of the teeth the previous year when one of his sons had given him some hard candy to chew. Ever since it had been a veritable mousetrap for snagging pieces of food. He worked the area over with his tongue and made intermittent sucking noises in a vain attempt to dislodge the meat. His eyes drifted off the road just long enough to catch Kel's eye. He continued their conversation. "I mean, Tenkiller might have all sorts of cousins that you don't know about. My mama's always sendin' me newspaper weddin' announcements for some far-flung shirttail kin that I've never heard of, and I'm almost forty-seven years old. The way my mama reckons kin, I might even be one of Tenkiller's cousins."

"That's not the case here," Kel answered.

"How you so sure? Maybe y'all's records aren't as complete as you think. No offense, but I work for the federal government, too. Sometimes we're not as efficient—"

"Maybe so," Kel cut him short. "Probably aren't, but it's not just my records that say so."

Deveroux was driving with his left hand and levering his right index finger into his mouth in support of his tongue. The sucking noises grew louder as the remnant Slim Jim proved increasingly intransigent. "Then whose?" Deveroux mumbled.

Deveroux had goosed the truck up to seventy-five, and the road noise made it difficult to hear. Kel was able to anticipate the question even with the mumbled delivery. "Our genealogist's, that's whose," he answered. "You gotta remember, we've been tryin' to find a suitable DNA reference sample for Tenkiller for some time."

There was a short pause while Deveroux continued to work his tooth, then he responded. "So what are you sayin'? Jimmy Tenkiller's dead. KIA, remember?"

"Presumed KIA. Body Not Recovered. *Presumed.* With a big, goddamn capital *P,* and that rhymes with *T,* and that stands for *Trouble.*"

"Still . . ."

"Still nothin'. A presumptive findin' of death is just that, a presumptive findin'. It's *administrative* by definition. Didn't you tell me that even Fick told you he had problems with it?"

"Yeah," Deveroux answered, "but not because he thought Tenkiller was sellin' nightcrawlers in Onapa, Oklahoma. He had problems with it because he thought Tenkiller'd deserted; he wasn't sayin' that he didn't think he was dead."

"Is that what he told you? Did he tell you that he thought Tenkiller was dead?"

Deveroux knotted his face again. "No, but." He reached down and turned the headlights on. Dusk was settling in and the temperature was starting to fall. He looked quickly back at Kel. "You really think so? You think it could be Jimmy Tenkiller?"

"I do. You heard her back there. Eddie Tenkiller's *cousin* looks just like him but older and gimped-up. He'd be what . . . seventy-one, two. And she said he walked like he had a rock in his shoe. Or maybe a screw in his ankle."

Deveroux looked in his rearview mirror and flicked on his turn signal.

Kel looked up to see the off-ramp of an approaching overpass. "Whoa, time-out, partner. Where you headed?"

"Back to Onapa," Deveroux replied. The tone suggested that the answer should have been obvious to even the most casual observer. "I think we need to talk with them Tenkiller boys, don't you?"

"You mean the same Tenkiller who just an hour ago asked us to leave his bait store? That Tenkiller?"

"We can start with him?"

"Oh, can we? Maybe you're right. Maybe it's the small talk that he has trouble with. I suspect if we approach him direct and say, 'Hey, there, Eddie, we want to talk to that no-count, deserter brother of yours who ran a murderous black market business in Vietnam and who's been livin' illegally in the U.S., selling leeches and crawdads for the past thirty-odd years'; we just approach him that way and he'll come out of his shell and just open up to us like a damn ray of sunshine."

"You got a better idea? I was doin' it mostly for you. Until you show me a definite connection to two dead Vietnamese gentlemen, Jimmy Tenkiller's still more your case than mine. What do you want to do?"

Kel looked back out the windshield and thought before answering. "Can't say I know, but I can say that goin' back there right now is a mistake. We need some more information before we try and crack that nut again."

"Like?"

"Like . . . like, I don't know. Like a photo of Jimmy Tenkiller would be nice. Wouldn't you like to have a photo to show around? Maybe see if Miss Tawny Lynn can ID Jimmy Tenkiller as Tommy the Gimp. That would help."

"You got any photos?"

"Maybe," Kel answered. "Not with me, but we might in our files back at the lab. I don't remember offhand; sometimes we do, sometimes not. If he was listed as a deserter, we probably don't have much in the way of photos. The army casualty office in Washington can probably get one if someone asks nicely; the National Personnel Records Center in St. Louis is another option. They take a while, but . . ."

"How about fingerprints?"

"How about them?"

"Just thinkin' that if we found a smooth surface that he'd touched—"

"Nope. We don't have them. If he were a pilot, we might have a footprint card, but unless he's runnin' around barefoot on a sheet of glass, even that wouldn't help. Nope, we don't have any fingerprint cards."

"Maybe the FBI does?" Deveroux suggested.

"Seriously doubt it. They would've at one time, but my understandin' is that they destroyed all the Vietnam-era fingerprints six or seven years after a person was declared dead, and everyone from that war's now classified as dead. Deserters are another matter, but Tenkiller's not a deserter in the eyes of the army anymore. He's dead too. Officially. So . . ."

"So where does that leave us?"

"On the road, that's where. On the interstate headed east. My suggestion is we head back to Nashville. You . . . we can make a few phone calls, and I can get started lookin' at that case you wanted me to. I suspect the medical examiner isn't goin' to want and hold on to that body much longer. I'm surprised the family hasn't demanded it be buried already."

"They have. Rather forcefully, I understand, but ultimately," Deveroux said, "it's a Fed case. The ME's agreed to do some work with it, but he'll get buried when I okay the release—which I haven't. Now, havin' thumped my chest sufficiently to demonstrate that I'm the alpha male, I'll admit that I'd like to cut him loose as soon as I can. No point waitin' for it to get uglier than it already is."

"Well, then, let's head back over to Tennessee and get started. If Jimmy Tenkiller is alive and fishin' in Onapa, Oklahoma, after all these years, I doubt he'll start runnin' again. I mean, where the hell would he go? Can't find a much smaller hole than Onapa. No, we'll have time to come back."

Before Deveroux could answer, the "Chicken Dance" song started playing from his shirt pocket. He sighed.

Kel folded his face into a question.

"You got a couple of young boys, don't you?" Deveroux responded, reaching for the cell phone in his pocket. "Ever tempted to strangle 'em?"

"All the time."

"Me too," Deveroux said as he opened his phone and pressed the talk button. "Yeah, Chief Deveroux speakin'."

CHAPTER 44

Rolla, Missouri
MONDAY, APRIL 21, 2008

Jimmy Lee Tenkiller had been living in his brother's faded-red Ford pickup truck and his own clothes for the last four days. An odd assortment of soft drink cans and paper fast-food wrappers with gray, translucent grease stains lay stratified on the floor of the passenger side, and even with the windows rolled down, both the cab and he had taken on an awkward smell. He'd driven up from Oklahoma late last Thursday afternoon and had spent nearly two hours finding and then verifying the house. After that it was simply a matter of waiting. And watching.

It reminded him of a beaver den he'd seen as a boy, constant activity here and there and an unceasing, rolling bustle. At first he'd thought it might be a funeral, as there seemed to be one florist truck after another, but as he continued to watch, the picture clarified and he realized that it was most likely a wedding. Wedding or funeral, whatever it was, it was a complication.

Too many people.

Too many witnesses.

Jimmy Lee Tenkiller didn't want witnesses. He'd spent the last thirty-eight years of his life avoiding people; avoiding their constant questions and their prying minds and the looks that tried to discern too much.

Thirty-eight years, and now, after all that time he found himself run to ground by a single telephone call. It had come late one Saturday night last October. Jimmy Lee was watching wrestling with his brother when the phone in their den rang. They'd looked at each other for several rings, as neither one of them was accustomed to receiving nighttime calls, or daytime calls for that matter, and there was an unspoken sense of uncertainty about how to respond. In fact, Jimmy Lee had spoken on the phone only twice in the last thirty-eight years; once from a pay phone at a cheap motel outside Travis Air Force Base in 1970 when he'd called Eddie·and asked him to wire some money, and once again twenty-eight years later when his brother had experienced his first heart attack and needed an ambulance. Other than those two instances, Jimmy Lee Tenkiller had avoided any two-way electronic contact with the world, and the world had avoided him. Eddie Tenkiller had cocooned himself almost as well, though the everyday mechanics of life required some interaction with the outside, but together, the two men had intended to coast into old-age anonymity, content with their own company and confidence.

Until the phone rang and everything changed.

Actually, neither Jimmy Lee nor Eddie was surprised by the voice on the other end of the line; both had been living in daily anticipation of its awaited intrusion and had simply pondered what form it would take, what accent, what tone, what words it would begin with, and of course when it would come. When Jimmy Lee heard his brother say into the receiver, *"I'm sorry, sir, you must be mistaken. I have no brother. My brother is dead,"* he knew that it had finally come, and when his brother had added, *"I know nothing of Five Brothers,"* he knew that the past had returned to collect its overdue toll. Oddly, it had settled as much as upset. Like a man who has held his breath to the limit and must finally gasp, Jimmy Lee Tenkiller realized that the phone call was his gasp; the painful relief so long anticipated. The inrush of oxygen made him dizzy.

I know nothing of Five Brothers.

As he sat parked in front of the red-brick colonial house of Ngo Van Thu, he couldn't help but think of a future, both his and Eddie's, that had been not so much deferred as deflected and compromised and destroyed. He looked into the rearview mirror of the truck, at the dark brown eyes so rimmed with black that the irises weren't discernible, and at the deep, concentric creases that sun and sorrow had carved around his eyes, and couldn't help but wonder *why*? Not why the call had come, but why now? What was the trigger after so many years? Was it just time? Was it fate? Was it God?

Jimmy Lee Tenkiller had spent thirty-eight years ducking around corners and living by cash transactions; leaving no trail, no scent. So had his brother. And where had it gotten them? What had it gotten them? Nothing. No family. No friends. No security. Thirty-eight years came crashing down upon him with the ring of a telephone.

He couldn't let that happen. Whatever he'd done in the past—or not done—he'd paid for it; they'd both paid for it, Eddie and he. Men with no pasts have no tomorrows. They have only todays. That was the price he'd paid in a thirty-eight-year installment, and he had no intention of having it all repossessed now. There could be no disclosure now, no matter what it took to ensure that.

No matter what.

Jimmy Lee Tenkiller looked at the shiny blue-black Ruger .22 as he turned it over and back in his right hand. Eddie had bought it years ago to plink at cottonmouths when they were fishing, but it had never been used with any regularity, and it had taken Jimmy Lee quite a while to locate it. Now he held it tightly in his hand and thought back to a small grass hut in a small abandoned village in a country that he couldn't even believe existed anymore. *There's more than one kind of snake,* he caught himself thinking as he pulled on the door handle and swung a leg to the pavement.

Just then a dark-blue Cadillac Seville pulled quickly into Ngo's driveway and stopped. A middle-aged Asian female got out of the driver's side, followed by a younger, quite attractive Asian female from the passenger side. They were laughing and talking animatedly as they walked up the brick sidewalk to the front door. Jimmy Lee had seen them off and on before and had finally assumed them to be Mrs. Ngo and one of her daughters. A family. A family like that he'd never had. A family and a future that General Ngo had enjoyed. He watched them, the young one's long, glossy black hair bouncing with each step, as they opened the front door and went into the house.

Jimmy Lee Tenkiller hesitated and then pulled his leg back into the cab and shut the truck door. He stared at the front door of the house for a minute and then opened the glove box and stowed the pistol before cranking the ignition. His business was with the general, not with his family. There were already too many people who knew, and more witnesses were a problem, not a solution. He checked the rearview mirror as he put the vehicle in gear and pulled away from the curb. The two five-gallon gas cans in the truck bed slid back and banged loudly against the tailgate.

"I've waited thirty-eight years, General, another day or two won't matter now," he said.

CHAPTER 45

Interstate 40, Oklahoma/Arkansas Line
MONDAY, APRIL 21, 2008

"Say again," Shuck Deveroux said into his cell phone. The quick look he caromed off Kel forecast an imminent change in plans. "When did the call come in? They sure? Um-hmm. Hmm. Got it, got it. We are . . . we're on I-Forty 'bout to hit the Arkansas state line. Yeah . . . no . . . far side. The Oklahoma side." He twisted his left wrist on the steering wheel so that he could see the face of his watch in the gathering darkness. "Hold one," he said as he tucked the cell phone into his neck and swiveled his torso to better address his partner. "This is your neck of the woods, isn't it?"

"Sort of," Kel responded. He'd been trying to guess the unheard part of the conversation, without much luck. "Long time ago. Why?"

"You know where Warrensburg, Missouri, is?"

"Sure. Up near Knob Noster. Off of I-Seventy, little ways east and south of Kansas City."

"How far?"

"Hmm, you mean from here? Ahhh . . . don't know . . . maybe . . . maybe six hours, give or take—dependin' on how you drive. They've straightened the road some since I lived here."

Deveroux re-engaged his phone. "Can be there in five hours. Do me a favor. Make a couple of motel reservations, one for me and one for Doc McKelvey. Oh, yeah? Thanks. Good man." He pointed at the glove box, made writing motions in the air, and waggled his fingers to indicate he needed either a pencil or paper or both. "Yeah, yeah . . . slow down. Say again."

Kel provided a pen from his pocket and opened the glove box and rummaged until he found a crumpled old Jiffy Lube receipt. Deveroux grabbed it from him and pinned it to the seat between them with his right hand.

"Okay, gimme that address again," Deveroux said into the phone as he awkwardly wrote on the back of the receipt. "Good, good. I'll give y'all a call when I get there. Yeah. Okay. *Gracias, mi amigo.* Out here." He pressed the off button and returned the phone to his shirt pocket.

"Let me guess, you're supposed to pick up a loaf of bread?" Kel asked.

"Yeah, and a gallon of low-fat milk."

"Thought so."

"And while we're at it, we need to take a look at another body."

"A third?" Kel asked. "Mercy, but they do seem to be pilin' up on you."

Deveroux nodded. "Found up in Warrensburg, Missouri. This one's fresh, so maybe it'll make more sense to start with it rather than the one in Nashville."

"And how fresh is fresh?"

"Catch-of-the-day fresh. This mornin'. Some professor at a college up there . . ."

"Central Missouri State."

"Ahh, I think they call it Missouri Central University, but that's the one. Anyway, this professor finds a body out on a ball field, or somethin'. Thought it was a drunk student passed out. Frat thing."

"Wasn't?"

"Nope. Turned out to be a middle-aged Vietnamese-American gentleman, and he wasn't passed out—at least not from drinkin'. Sound familiar?"

"Interestin', but . . ." Kel commented.

"But . . ."

"It's not on a military base."

"True." Deveroux shrugged. "But there do seem to be some similarities."

"He missin' the top of his head, too?"

"Yup, sort of. Actually his whole head seems to have gotten itself separated from his body. That was Gonzo . . . Sergeant Gonzalez . . . from my office. Seems he got a call from the cops at Whiteman Air Force Base—I guess that's close to Warrensburg?"

"Yeah. Kinda on the outskirts."

"That makes sense. We sent flyers out to some of the military installations in the Midwest concernin' the cases we had at Knox and Campbell. Sort of an if-you-see-anythin'-related-please-let-us-know sort of thing. One of the SPs from Whiteman was at the Warrensburg police station this mornin' on some other sort of business when the call came in. He thought it was mighty coincidental; middle-aged Asian, decapitation, proximity to a military base . . ."

"More like tri-incidental, at this point."

"That's right. If it's connected, it makes three, doesn't it? Anyhow, the locals are willin' to let us take a look at it before they send it over to Kansas City. From what Gonzo said, I guess the local coroner doesn't want to touch it and would be more than happy if someone took it off his hands. Not my jurisdiction, certainly, but maybe now we can lever the FBI into takin' a serious interest in it. Everyone else in my office is tied up, so we're all that's available to run up there. Open that up, will ya?" Deveroux asked, pointing to a thick folder tied with string that rested on the seat between them.

"This?"

"Yup. That's the file folder that General Fick gave me. The results of his investigation all those years ago in Vietnam. There's a list of names on top. Should be in among the first couple of pages, or so." He reached up and flicked on the cab's overhead light.

Kel balanced the folder on his lap and worked through the contents.

He paused and peered at some pages longer than others before finally extracting a single sheet of lined paper, now stained by time, with a series of names written on it with light-blue cartridge pen ink. There were lines connecting several names and stars drawn beside others. "This one?" he asked.

Deveroux took his eyes off the road long enough to verify that the paper was the one he wanted. "Yeah, yeah, that looks like it. See the names? Trinh Han and Linh Nhu Ngon?" His slow pronunciation left a great deal to the imagination.

"So that's how you pronounce them; I always wondered."

"Yeah, yeah. Cut me some slack, Kel; I'm just a dumb, country soldier. I pronounce 'em like I read 'em. You see 'em or not?"

"Roger. Trinh Han. Linh Nhu Ngon . . ." Kel tried to imitate Deveroux, making a point of pronouncing each name slowly and as if he had a head full of thick snot and nowhere to spit.

"Read the other ones."

"Well," Kel set the folder down on the seat between them but held on to the paper. He shifted into a normal voice. "In addition to Trinh and Linh—hmm, I seem to recognize some of these— there's Tenkiller, he seems to have rated two stars in Fick's mind. General Ngo Van Thu got a couple of stars and a whole big mess of arrows—whatever that signifies—a Colonel Pham Van . . . Van-somethin'. It's kinda faded but looks like Pham Van Minh and a couple of arrows and lines but no stars, and a Major Doan Minh Tuyen . . ."

"That's it," Deveroux said excitedly. "That's the one. The last one. I knew it was on there."

"Doan? You mean your third victim?"

"Yup. At least the prelim suggests it. Sergeant Gonzalez said the body had a wallet on him, and they found a car parked nearby that was registered to a Doan Tuyen. They also found a head in a trash can nearby that they think matches his driver's license photo. He was scalped like the other ones so they aren't sure until they run down some dental x-rays, but, yeah, I mean, they're sure."

Kel was looking at the list and shaking his head. "Sure is shit to be you, partner. What're you goin' to do now? Looks like three down, two to go. Probably need to find these other two bubbas as soon as you can."

"Roger that," Deveroux replied. "Assumin' they're still alive, that is. Maybe those other two were really numbers one and two that we just don't know about yet. We may have gotten a late start. They could all be dead by now."

"Maybe, and maybe they didn't survive the war, either."

"Nope. Already checked. At least Ngo survived. INS has no record of that Pham Van Minh character, though." Deveroux scrunched his face and twisted in his seat in a belated attempt to see a road sign that had flashed by in the darkness. He reached up and turned off the cab light. "Were we supposed to turn there?"

Kel also twisted around in his seat so that both men were turned looking out the back window at the quickly receding exit ramp. "Yeah, ahh . . ." He stalled as he turned back to the front. "Ahh, yeah, but it's okay. You can catch Highway Seventy-one up here a little ways. Takes a bit longer. Scenic route—not that we can see much at night. So . . . you say our General Ngo is in this country. I kinda figured he'd be. A lot of the South Vietnamese generals ended up here."

"There's another piece of paper in the file." Deveroux flicked on his turn signal and shifted lanes in preparation for taking the next exit. As soon as he had a hand free, he turned on the dome light again.

"This one?" Kel asked as he extracted a crisp piece of paper from inside the folder.

Deveroux looked over and nodded. "Yeah. That one isn't Fick's. Buddy of mine at the FBI ran those names. Believe it or not, there's a couple dozen or so Ngo Van Thus in the U.S. and at least two more in Canada, one in Vancouver and another in Toronto. Goin' to have to call each one of them and hope we get lucky. We can do that tomorrow after you take a look at the newest body. We're goin' to need some luck, though. That's for sure."

"Hmm," Kel said, studying the list in the dim light. "Maybe.

Maybe not." He found the thought of somehow getting involved in any project that required the prolonged use of a telephone unsettling.

"You got another idea?"

"If it were me," Kel answered, folding the paper so that one of the names about a third of the way down was now at the top of the list. He underscored it with his thumbnail. "I'd start with this one."

CHAPTER 46

Interstate 40, Oklahoma/Arkansas Line
MONDAY, APRIL 21, 2008

It took three tries before the cell phone connected. Kel's cell phone, chronically low on batteries, dropped the signal twice before ringing through.

"Hello," Mary Louise McKelvey answered.

"Hey, hon," Kel replied. He half turned in his seat so that he was facing the passenger window. With the amber dashboard lights inside and the absence of any significant external illumination along the highway, his own reflection stared back at him from the darkened glass. It wasn't so much that he was concerned about Shuck overhearing— there was nothing to be said that was overly private, and besides, the roar of truck's tires on the warm asphalt made eavesdropping anything but a casual exercise. Kel hated using the phone so much that it seemed a gesture of courtesy to not thrust his conversation onto an innocent bystander.

"Well, this is a surprise. Everythin' okay? You're not hurt, are you?" Mary Louise had a soft west Arkansas drawl that was lazy, but not sticky like Deveroux's eastern molasses.

"No, no. Everythin' is all right," Kel answered. The connection was poor and he found himself speaking louder than he wanted. "Just thinkin' about you. Miss you is all."

Mary Louise laughed. "Now, Kel. I don't doubt for a minute you miss me, and for good reason, but I do know that no amount of missin' me could get you to dial a telephone. Someone got a gun to your head?"

"Now that isn't fair, and you know it," Kel protested. It was a formality because he knew full well that his wife had called his bluff. "I was thinkin' about you, and I was missin' you, and—"

"And?"

"Well, and I wanted to tell you that I might be delayed a few days longer, is all."

Mary Louise laughed again. "That's more like it. What's happenin'? Sure you're okay?"

"Yeah, yeah. All's fine. It's just that this case I'm helpin' out on may have taken a twist or two. There's a murder case up in Warrensburg that I'm goin' go take a look at."

"Warrensburg? Missouri?"

"Yeah. Up at the university there."

"Kel."

"Hmm?"

"Kel, you remember Oppie?" Mary Louise was referring to an orange cat that Kel had had all through college and graduate school.

"Oppie the cat? Of course I remember Oppie."

"You remember what Oppie'd do when he was up on the counter and you'd yell at him?"

"Ahhh, Mary Louise, I don't—"

"Kel, what would he do?"

"Hell, I don't know. Apologize?"

"No. He'd begin to lick himself."

"Ah. Right. Are you tellin' me to lick myself?" He checked to see if Shuck was listening. He was, and Kel just smiled and shrugged and turned back to the window.

"Kel."

"'Cause you know, I usually have to pay money for calls like this."

"Kel."

"Ma'am?"

"Just stop talkin'. Just stop."

Kel went silent.

"That's better. No, what he'd do was lick himself rather than look at you. He'd avoid the confrontation. It was a displacement activity."

"That'll teach me to marry a psych major."

"Too late, buster. But seriously, Kel, is that what's goin' on? Chasin' around all over. First Iraq and now, bless your heart, Oklahoma. Are you avoidin' the confrontation? Sooner or later you have to jump down from that counter."

Kel stared at his dim reflection in the side window. He didn't respond.

CHAPTER 47

Warrensburg, Missouri
TUESDAY, APRIL 22, 2008

As was common in rural America, the coroner of Johnson County, Missouri, was a funeral director, and although the coroner's office officially was located amid the other governmental offices in downtown Warrensburg, the refrigerated body of Doan Minh Tuyen was not.

Deveroux and Kel had managed to get lost the previous evening, finding themselves, not once, but twice, on the wrong side of the Kansas-Missouri state line, and it had taken almost nine hours, and a good deal of mutual name calling and eye-rolling, to complete their anticipated five-hour journey. It was well past midnight when they checked into the Slumber-Sack Motel on the outskirts of town, much too late to do much more than tumble into bed and drift off to a quick sleep.

Morning broke in good humor and so did Deveroux, but Kel's goodwill was still jet lagged somewhere over the Pacific and proved slower to respond as he staggered out of his room into the bright sunshine. He groaned and threw an arm up as if warding off an attacker. Deveroux was sitting in the cab of his truck reading a local newspaper and drinking coffee from an enormous, insulated plastic mug with *The Chug-a-Lug Club* silkscreened on it.

"Mornin', Doc," he said as he watched Kel wobble to the hood of the truck, eyes clamped down against the light. "Coffee? It's black; didn't know how you take it." He gestured to another plastic mug balanced on the cracked dashboard.

"I'm blind," Kel groaned, his arms outstretched like Frankenstein's monster's.

Deveroux lowered his newspaper and watched him intently. He leaned over to speak out of the passenger window. "Are you like one of them Mole People? I saw a movie about them when I was a kid. There's this whole race of these Mole People that live underground; can't come out in the daylight except to kidnap voluptuous women in their nightgowns . . ."

"I come from a long and noble line of Mole People." He began groping the air with his outstretched arms.

Deveroux put his coffee mug on the dashboard and began folding his paper as he spoke. "How about seein' if you think you can grope your way over here to the passenger door, so we can get started. Just home in on the sound of my voice. Marco . . ."

"Polo," Kel groaned.

"That's right. Warmer, warmer, there you go," he said as Kel worked his way to the side of the truck and opened the door. "Not a mornin'-type person, huh Kel?"

"Might be if it was truly mornin'. What the hell time is it anyway?"

"Almost seven-thirty."

"Holy sheep shit, Batman," Kel groaned. Three-thirty in the morning. Hawaiian Standard Time.

Deveroux sat with one hand on the steering wheel as he took a sip of coffee and looked at Kel. "Sorry to rush you and all, but I called and arranged a meetin' with the coroner in about," Deveroux paused and looked at his watch, "in about thirty-two minutes from now. Got directions, and the motel clerk says we're only about fifteen minutes away, but I figure after that stellar job of navigatin' that you did last night, we'd better allow for some extra time. I mean, you had the use of your eyes last night, and we still ended up in Kansas."

"Yeah, well the second time wasn't my fault," Kel responded as he groped about for his seatbelt, his eyes still clamped shut. "That was your short-cut. Topeka my ass."

Deveroux laughed and turned the ignition and backed the truck out of its parking space. He pulled onto West Market Street headed east and drove for several minutes in early morning silence. After a while, Deveroux caught Kel out of the corner of his eye and renewed the conversation. "Like I said, made a couple three calls this mornin' while I was waitin' on you to rouse. Scheduled a visit with Mr. Walter Mann, the coroner here in Johnson County. Also called a buddy of mine with the INS for some additional intel." He moved his newspaper on the seat and exposed the list of names they'd discussed the previous night. He tapped one of them. "I think your hunch might be right about this Ngo Van Thu livin' down in Rolla bein' the one we're after. He's the only one in proximity to a military installation, and that seems to be the pattern."

Kel shrugged. "Good a place as any to start—given we're so close anyhow."

"Roger that. Anyhow, I'm not goin' to be of any help at the morgue, so I figured on drivin' on down to Rolla and see if we're right. If so, I'll try and interview this Ngo Van Thu." Deveroux's tongue tripped on itself, and he pronounced the name as if he had a thick glob of peanut butter stuck to the roof of his mouth. "Never know . . . he might just have the key to this whole thing. I should be back this evenin'."

"Don't want any company?" Kel was working hard at getting an eye to stay open.

"Actually I do, but I 'spect you're goin' to be tied up with the body all mornin'. I'm goin' leave my truck with you and rent a car. Figure I can justify the expense on my voucher easier than I can get you reimbursed. I'll try and get one of Mr. Mann's folks to take me to the rental place after I help get you situated. Best I can tell, it's about a four-hour drive down there, so I'd better get started as soon as I can."

"I've seen your drivin'. I'd figure five. Remember to turn around when you see a sign sayin' *Welcome to Louisiana*."

"You're awful funny for a prick. So you figure five?"

"Five-and-a-half, if I were you. Seriously."

"Yeah? That's what General Fick said. I called him too. He lives down near Rolla, and I thought he might like to sit in on the interview. You know, he spent a whole lotta time investigatin' Tenkiller and the Brotherhood way back when. Figure he might still be interested."

"Is he?" Kel asked.

"Says he is."

Deveroux slowed down and blinked for a left turn onto North Warren Street. "Looks like you better get your other eye warmed up there, Doctor. I do believe we're almost there."

Walter Mann's official office in downtown Warrensburg was purely administrative and wholly unsuited to the sometimes pungent reality of the job. When bodies had to be dealt with—outside a hospital setting—they were taken to his family-run funeral home on the eastern edge of town. The Mann and Sons Funeral Home had been a fixture of Warrensburg since 1896 when Adolphus A. Mann had arrived from St. Louis, Missouri, with two toe-pincher cast-iron coffins and a desire to assuage the earthly sorrow of Warrensburg's more well-heeled first families. Over the years, the business had prospered, becoming hereditary in the process, although the most recent generation was showing no interest in continuing the tradition, and Walter Mann was now seriously considering selling the whole operation to a company in Texas.

Mann and Sons Funeral Home was a large two-story building made from mustard-colored bricks and topped with a steep, brown, composite-shingle roof. It was nicely landscaped, but the well-tended yard only served to help accentuate how singularly ugly the building itself was. A wide circular drive centered on the entrance made the place look more like a franchise motel than a funeral home.

Deveroux pulled his truck to a stop under the green canvas portico that extended out from the front door and killed the engine. He looked at his watch and then at Kel. "Not bad," he said as he tossed him the truck keys. "Two minutes early."

The interior entryway was lit by a row of recessed lights in the ceiling that projected a measured, subdued wash of light calculated to comfort rather than illuminate. It was remarkably successful in minimizing the appearance of puffy eyes and reddened noses. Soft, orchestrated Beatles music seeped out from somewhere, and it took Kel a moment to trace the origin to a small, brick-sized speaker hidden behind a large, silk tropical plant beside the door. As they stood, letting their eyes adjust to the inside dimness, a small, energetic woman rounded the corner at a high rate of speed with a face full of purpose.

"Welcome," she said, pulling up short and offering her hand to Kel. "You folks must be Mr. Deveroux and his doctor friend. I'm Margaret Loy. Call me Peg. I'm Mr. Mann's office manager."

"Glad to meet you, Peg. Almost right. I'm Robert McKelvey. Call me Kel. I'm Mr. Deveroux's sidekick . . . and this here's Mr. Deveroux." As he shook her hand, he motioned with a nod of his head to his partner.

"My apologies. Glad to meet you, Kel," she replied. She then took Deveroux's hand. "And you too, Mr. Deveroux. You're right on time."

"Shuck. Call me Shuck. Glad to meet you too, Peg." Deveroux smiled. "You gave good directions."

Margaret Loy was approaching sixty but projected much younger, at least from the standpoint of exuded energy. Her hair was still mostly dark, with considerably more pepper than salt showing, and it was pulled back into a loose knot at the back of her skull that was starting to untangle. She was dressed in old blue jeans and a sleeveless checkered shirt with the tail out. She seemed slightly embarrassed to be seen dressed so informally, and she paused awkwardly and then clapped her hands. "Well, in addition to office manager, I'm also the plumber, part-time janitor, and full-time you-name-it. I was just heading out to plant some marigolds in the bed out front. Did I say I was also the groundskeeper?"

"You sound busy." Deveroux laughed. "Is Mr. Mann around?"

"He surely is. He's waiting for you in the embalming room. Left through the parlor, right past my office—the one with all the pictures of grandbabies taped up—and through the double set of doors. You'll see it easy enough. If you get lost just holler; someone will find you."

She smiled again and waited for them to begin moving before she opened the front door. "Nice to meet y'all," she said behind them as she stepped quickly outside.

As Margaret Loy had told them, it was easy enough to find, left through the parlor, right past her office—the one with all the grandbaby pictures—and through the double set of doors. Even without directions, the rising smell of gardenia and lilac air freshener applied to mask the pungent smell of formalin signaled proximity to the prep room.

Walter Mann was waiting for them. Tall and willow-stick thin, he looked exactly as he should. At seventy-four years old, he was hairless and his taut, smooth, tallow-colored skin was soft and devoid of any signs of age—the occupational side effect of having worked with embalming chemicals for thirty-five years before OSHA complicated things by requiring gloves and respirators. He was dressed in dark-gray, pleated slacks and a light-blue shirt with the sleeves rolled up past his elbows. His conservative blue tie was tucked into his shirt out of the way. He was reading from a brown folder and looked up as the double doors parted.

"You gentlemen must be Mr. Deveroux and Mr. McKelvey," he said. His voice was deeper than it should have been for his spare frame and had a buttery richness to it that, like his complexion, owed much of its character to a lifetime of inhaling formaldehyde fumes.

"Yes, sir, Mr. Mann," Deveroux said, stepping forward and extending his right hand. "I'm Chief Warrant Officer Deveroux, U.S. Army CID. Glad to meet you, sir, and thanks for agreein' to meet with us on such short notice. I know how busy you must be. This here's Dr. McKelvey."

Kel stepped forward and took his turn at shaking hands. "Sir," he said.

Deveroux continued. "Doc McKelvey's the forensic anthropologist I mentioned to you on the phone. He's with the army lab in Hawaii that identifies all the POWs and MIAs and such. He's the director out there, actually."

"Pleasure to meet you, Doctor. You the gentleman who identified the Vietnam Unknown Soldier?"

"Yes, sir," Kel answered. "That was our lab."

"He was a Missouri boy, you know."

"Yes, sir. Just outside St. Louis."

"And now you want to take a look at Warrensburg's Jack-the-Ripper case? Not sure I see the connection to American POWs." Mann's bifocals made his gray watery eyes look like huge pale grapes.

"Ahhh . . ."

Deveroux quickly answered. "No connection, Mr. Mann. That we know of. Doc McKelvey's actually doin' this as a professional favor for me. Kind of a consult. You see, I have reason to believe that our . . . ahh . . . that your victim, here, might be connected to a case that army CID is interested in. Looks that way on the surface, anyway."

"I don't see," Mann said. "But go on."

"Well, actually, Dr. McKelvey and I were headed over to Nashville and then Louisville to look at two possibly related homicide cases when I got the call about this one here in Warrensburg. Similar MOs, and since we were down in Oklahoma when we heard the news, we decided to detour up here first. Just in case."

"Please, Mr. Deveroux, I intend no offense by this, but I am the coroner of Johnson County, you see, and I have to ask this. What jurisdictional interest do you have in this matter?"

Deveroux smiled. "None. That's a fact. The other two happened on military reservations, and so fall square under my umbrella, but this one, this one is in your AO, sir—ahhh, your area of operations. I'm just interested because it looks like it could be connected, and if it is, then a whole lotta folks are goin' get interested and the lid will get unscrewed from this peanut butter jar real fast."

Walter Mann nodded as if he'd already arrived at a similar answer. "I'm not a doctor, you understand. I'm a funeral director by training and a coroner by public election. Cases like this are well beyond my comfort level . . ."

"Cases like this are beyond everyone's comfort level," Kel interjected. When the old man looked over at him, he continued. "Leastways they sure should be."

Mann nodded before responding. "I suspect you're right about that, Doctor. But some people are more comfortable in situations like this than others. In fact, I've arranged for this case to be sent over to Columbia for examination. That's a little east of here. Boone County has a medical examiner, you see. I think he's better suited to this than I am."

"J. D. Cooke?"

"You know him?" Mann asked.

"Yes, sir. Used to at least. Years ago. I did some work in this area. Haven't seen him for quite a while. He's good though. One of the best, I'd say."

Mann nodded again, slowly. Most of his movements were slow and practiced, designed to evoke calm and sympathy, and his slow manner stood in sharp contrast to the percolating energy of his office manager. "Yes, he certainly is. I was planning on transferring the body today—that was before you called." He looked back at Deveroux.

"Yes, sir. Understood," Deveroux re-engaged the conversation. "Doc here doesn't need long—right, Doc? You can be finished up by early afternoon, can't you?"

Kel affirmed with a slight bob of his head.

"So if he can just take a quick look, see what he can tell, make a few notes," Deveroux was nodding at Kel as he spoke. Kel was mimicking the movements. They looked like two bobble-head dogs in the back of a car window. "Then you can get the body over to your ME buddy."

"That was the agreement," Walter Mann said. His tone never changed, and neither Deveroux nor Kel could figure out what he really thought of the agreement. For that matter, they couldn't figure out what he thought of them.

"Good," Deveroux said. He put his hands in his hip pockets and rocked back and forth on his toes in the awkward silence that followed. Finally he spoke again. "So . . . the plan, Mr. Mann, is for Doc here to look at the remains. While he's doin' that, I'm goin' to go and interview someone who may have some information related to this case. So I'm not goin' to be here while y'all are at it."

Mann nodded.

Deveroux nodded.

Kel nodded.

Once again, it was Deveroux who broke the silence. "So . . . ahhh . . . I need Dr. McKelvey here to take me out to the car rental place. I'm goin' be leavin' my truck with him, and I need him to run me out there. Ahhh . . . so as soon as he gets back, if you can have the body ready, he can get started. Right, Doctor?"

"Right, Chief," Kel answered in his best Boy-Friday tone.

As if she'd been listening behind the door for her verbal cue to appear onstage, Margaret Loy plunged through the double doors into the embalming room. The knees of her jeans were muddied, as were her hands, and a few more stray clumps of hair had come loose from their knot and were seriously worrying her face. She made a direct course for the sink.

"No need for that delay, Mr. Deveroux. I'll have my office manager take you, if you don't mind," Mann said.

CHAPTER 48

Walter Mann warmed up to body temperature once Deveroux left the building. His earlier coolness hadn't directly been the result of Deveroux's presence, though like many small-county coroners he hadn't felt completely at ease with a major homicide in his lap and a strange, federal, law enforcement agent asking him questions— regardless of how well the jurisdictional fences were holding up. Ultimately, what had contributed the most to his coolness was the abundance of unfamiliar warm bodies gathered too closely together. After a lifetime in the funeral science business, he'd come to the slow realization that his comfort level lowered in direct proportion to the number of live bodies in the room.

"We can put him on that table over there," Mann said. He was pulling on the thick, heavy stainless-steel refrigerator door with both hands and had to use his chin to point at one of the two porcelain-clad embalming tables. "Light's better over that particular one. Full-spectrum bulbs, you see. True color. It's where we put on the makeup. I keep the other table as a backup." The last part of his sentence was lost as he disappeared into the large walk-in refrigerator. He shortly re-emerged, glasses fogged, pushing a wheeled metal cart. A brown, vinyl body bag lay on top, and immediately moisture began to condense on the cool plastic.

"Not sure what exactly you're interested in looking at, Dr. McKelvey," Mann continued with hardly a break. "Head's separated, you see. They found it in a trash can nearby; so I'm told. I haven't looked at yet. As I said, the formal autopsy's scheduled for Columbia."

Kel grabbed the end of the cart and helped dock it beside the embalming table. "Can't say I really know myself," he answered. "Given that there are two other bodies, one down in Nashville and the other over at Louisville, Agent Deveroux and I were just thinkin' that we should put a set of eyes on these. Maybe they're connected, maybe not, but if they are . . ."

"I hear you, Doctor. If you wouldn't mind . . . take that end, please." Mann had locked the wheels on the cart and had taken hold of the foot end of the bag with both hands. He nodded at the head end for Kel to take. "On three. Ready? One. Two. Three . . ."

Kel gripped the cold, moist plastic, careful to get a firm handhold, and with a heavy thump, the men hefted the bag onto the embalming table. Mann unlocked the wheels with a practiced flick of his toe and pushed the cart aside with his knee. He wiped his moist hands on his pants; Kel did likewise.

"Been a coroner for twelve years, you see. Never had one quite like this. What exactly . . ." Mann hesitated.

"What exactly am I fixin' to do?" Kel shrugged. "That's your call, Mr. Mann. You're the coroner here. You set the parameters. Mainly I just want to get a look-see at this."

Mann bit his lip and seemed to be studying the matter. He held a finger up as if he were testing the wind direction. "I'm thinking that you shouldn't do much. I'm sure you're very skilled at what you do, but just the same. Doctor Cooke probably wants this untouched."

"Agreed. I don't plan on anythin' other than lookin'."

Mann nodded, paused, then reached across the table and grabbed the zipper. As he opened the bag he said, "This is pretty much how the police brought him in. I was planning on sending him straight over to Columbia for a post-mortem." He stepped back from the table, clearing the way.

Kel looked down. A torso was exposed. Snuggled into the bag above the left shoulder was a bloody swaddle; the head wrapped in an ambulance sheet.

"Mind?" Kel asked, pointing at the swaddle.

"Hard to take a look if we don't," Mann answered. He began unwrapping the sheet; as he did so he nodded to a box on the counter. "Gloves there, if you're the type that feels the need."

Kel was and did. He gloved up and patiently waited for Walter Mann to unwrap what appeared to be a bloody head of iceburg lettuce. Mann pulled the sticky fabric back and flattened the folds so that the head looked to be perched on a nest of mottled-red velvet; then he stood back.

Kel bent forward and poked at the head with a gloved finger. It was hard to figure out how it was oriented—it had jagged flaps of raw skin at both ends and was one massive clot of dried blood. Kel moved the lumps and flaps of tissue around until the eyes and nose were recognizable, and then stood back and looked, tilting his head to the side like a portrait artist. Both the coroner and he bobbed and weaved like a couple of pigeons, changing their relative points of perspective without actually handling the head. Trying to get a better look. Everything was bloody; the coarse, black hair—what was left— was matted with rust-colored clumps and hung down like a soiled mop; the face was covered with a thick layer of sticky red dust, and here and there, small tatters and fragments of trash were stuck fast.

Walter Mann tentatively reached out and straightened the hair, lightly brushing it back from the forehead with his fingers, returning it to some semblance of life. In doing so he exposed a circular patch of cream-colored skull, about the size of a playing card, right where the frontal hairline should have started. He stepped back and looked at Kel, as if he expected some sort of explanation. When he got none, he asked, "What do you make of that, Doctor?"

Kel paused, leaned forward, and looked closely at the exposed skull, noting several short, parallel grooves incised into the bone by a sharp metal blade. "Well, sir, if I had to guess, I'd say this fella had been scalped."

CHAPTER 49

Travis Air Force Base, Fairfield, California
THURSDAY, OCTOBER 1, 1970

So far, so good.

He deposited the additional forty-five cents that the operator said was needed and waited for her to complete the connection.

It had proven easier than he'd hoped, though that hadn't kept him from looking over his shoulder for the last twenty-one hours. Expecting a tap on the shoulder. A challenge he couldn't answer. A one-way ride to an eight-by-ten-foot cell, and a future without sun and wind and flat, open ground to run over.

The original plan was to catch a contract flight out of Saigon direct for Honolulu and then San Francisco and from there to simply disappear. That hadn't worked out. When he showed up at the Tri-Service Air Traffic Coordination Office at Tan Son Nhut airbase, he recognized the clerk and realized that there was no way his papers would hold up. Instead he opted for a ticket on the Flying Tiger *Freedom Bird* out of Bien Hoa. Bien Hoa to Alaska and then Braniff to Frisco.

A minor change in plans.

The closest that it had come to unraveling was when an MP at the departure center at Bien Hoa had tossed his duffel bag looking for restricted items. Jimmy Lee Tenkiller had been careful to sanitize his gear, removing everything with a nametape or laundry mark, anything that could betray him, anything that even sniffed of trouble. It was when the MP was helping him stuff everything back into the bag that he picked up Tenkiller's Bible—the one the spinsters in Broken Arrow had given Jimmy Lee so many years ago, the one he'd never read but felt the need to carry with him—and noticed the worn, gold-leaf letters embossed in the upper right-hand corner: *J L Tenkiller.* The MP had looked up at the black, plastic nameplate over Tenkiller's left uniform pocket, his eyes formulating a question.

"A buddy's," Jimmy Lee had said quickly; adding a shrug for emphasis. "Gave it to me for good luck."

"Must have worked," the MP had replied. "You're going home, aren't you . . ." The MP looked again at the name above his pocket. "Master Sergeant Bergeron?"

Tenkiller flinched at the spoken name. It was the first time anyone had said it out loud, and it rang so foreign and sour that it made him swallow hard before he answered. "Yeah, I guess I am."

The rest of the trip had been smooth. His papers were in order. He'd cleared his Company S-1; his PCS orders were signed and countersigned appropriately; he'd scuffed up his newly issued identification card so that it had the career-worn look of an army master sergeant; his khaki Class-B uniform was starched and creased and his shoes glossed with Methodist pride. None of it had proven that difficult to obtain or do—at least for a man with Tenkiller's connections. A man who can get crates of claymores and pallets of four-deuce mortars for the Viet Cong can easily wrangle a new ID card and a new nameplate, and as a senior supply sergeant at the largest supply depot in the world, he had the juice to get small favors done without questions being asked. In the big picture, a set of orders for someone named Master Sergeant James Bergeron had proven to be the least of his problems. Being recognized on the way out was the real concern, for while Jimmy Lee Tenkiller had few friends, he had many acquaintances.

It was close enough to his actual DEROS—Date of Estimated Return from Overseas—that Tenkiller hadn't worried about being seen at the airport. People knew that he was short—a double-digit midget for the last three months—with only a few days left in-country, so if anyone saw him boarding an airplane headed east, they'd just assume his time was up. He could explain being there. The problem would be if they saw his nameplate or his orders or heard the strange name paged—that he couldn't explain—so Jimmy Lee Tenkiller had spent most of the time before boarding hunkered in a bathroom stall, and once on the plane had requested a blanket to cover his chest while he feigned sleep. By the time he changed planes in Alaska, he was relatively sure that none of the other passengers knew him, and he collected his duffel bag quickly at Travis and was on the street before there was an opportunity for a chance encounter.

As he signed the guest ledger at the Thunderbird Motel in Oakland using the name James Bergeron, Jimmy Lee Tenkiller was struck by a profound sadness. The man who once had been cheered by stadiums full of people, who once had been his country's hope for Olympic gold, who had served his country honorably for over fifteen years, had just disappeared. There were no footprints leading out of Vietnam. No fingerprints. No breadcrumbs. Nothing to connect Master Sergeant Jimmy Lee Tenkiller's disappearance to the boarding pass of the nonexistent James Bergeron.

Nothing.

His life was over.

The telephone clicked twice as the operator completed the switching.

"Hello," the voice said. The phone crackled with a poor connection. It hissed and popped like an old phonograph record. "Hello?"

"Eddie? Eddie, it's me," Jimmy Lee Tenkiller said. "Eddie, I need some help."

CHAPTER 50

Rolla, Missouri
WEDNESDAY, APRIL 23, 2008

It had taken Shuck Deveroux almost five-and-a-half hours to make the drive. He hadn't gotten out of Warrensburg until almost ten o'clock, and by the time he'd pulled into the outer skirts of Rolla, Missouri, the sun was pegged square in the clear-blue afternoon sky. As he'd gotten closer to town, and seen that afternoon was waning, he'd called General Ngo Van Thu on his cell phone—completely mushing the man's name into a string of incomprehensible syllables—to say he was running behind schedule. Ngo had responded curtly that he had no more time on the afternoon's calendar, but that he could possibly free up some time to talk with Deveroux in the evening—around eight-thirty—provided it was kept short. Having already invested the better part of the day on the road, Deveroux found himself on the short branch of the decision-making tree and agreed to meet Ngo at his home that evening and forgo returning to Warrensburg until the following morning.

Next had been a courtesy call to the local Rolla PD. He'd spoken to one of the senior homicide detectives to tell him that he was in the area and would be interviewing one of the town's citizens and to make sure he wasn't perceived as stepping onto anyone's turf without permission. The detective—a gruff-sounding man who blew his nose frequently during the conversation and sounded as if he were chewing on something juicy—had been cooperative, though not very inquisitive, and had supplied some useful background information on Ngo Van Thu.

Deveroux had then called General Fick to tell him that the meeting was postponed until later that night, and Fick responded by telling him to take a room at the DeVille Motel in nearby Waynesville and sit tight. It was near Fick's farm, and they could meet at the motel's diner for an early dinner before driving into Rolla for their meeting with Ngo.

Now, sitting at a scuffed, wood-grained Formica table across from Paul Fick, he was taken by the change in the older man's appearance. It was only two weeks since their last meeting—the one at the little airport outside Memphis—but Fick's looks had changed. He was still flint hard, and the eyes still seemed capable of seizing the minute, but now there was a brittle crust of mortality that hadn't been there before.

Deveroux was hungry, having not stopped to eat on the drive down from Warrensburg, and he ordered a jumbo bacon cheeseburger, onion rings, and sweetened iced tea that he'd fortified with three packets of sugar. Fick had ordered only the iced tea, which he drank without any augmentation—a condition that a true, bone-bred southerner like Deveroux found incomprehensible. At first Deveroux had picked politely at his food, almost nibbling, made uncomfortable by having a senior officer—retired or not—sitting at the same table not eating, but in the end his appetite had proven persuasive, and he began taking noisy, enjoyable mouthfuls.

Fick watched him quietly for most of the meal, deflecting any stabs at conversation until the plate of food was well spent. As Deveroux was stirring up the thick slurry of sugar layering the bottom of his tea glass, Fick took a small, preliminary sip from his own glass and opened the conversation.

"You read the file I gave you, Chief Deveroux?"

"Yes, sir, I did. You put a lot of work into that."

"I'm not fishing for compliments, Chief. Don't waste your time. Or mine. I'm wanting to know what you plan to ask General Ngo when we meet with him." Unlike Deveroux's more imaginative handling of the name, Fick's pronunciation betrayed a working familiarity with Vietnamese that was undimmed by almost four decades.

Deveroux took a long swallow of tea, as much to collect his thoughts as to slake his thirst and settle his meal. He carefully placed the glass back on the table's surface, registering it with one of the several water rings, before answering. "Well, sir. I guess I'll start out by askin' him if he's in fact General Ngo."

"And assuming he is?"

"Then I'll ask if he's been in touch with Mr. Doan in Warrensburg, Mr. Trinh—" He took notice of the look on Fick's face. "Forgive how these names are comin' outta my mouth. Ummm, Mr. Trinh, he's the one down in Nashville, or Mr. Linh who got himself killed there at Fort Knox. See if those names ring any bells with him, and if so, when was he last in touch with them. There's obviously a connection between these folks—these five brothers—but the question, I guess, is do they know what it is?"

"Or who?" Fick added.

"You mean who's killin' them?"

Fick nodded.

"Or who, that's right. Is it one of them? One of the brothers. Who's the fifth one? Ahh, Major . . . Colonel . . ." Deveroux picked up the folder that had been resting on the booth seat next to him and began undoing the string.

"Colonel Pham Van Minh," Fick answered. "He was Ngo's brother-in-law."

Deveroux looked up and smiled. "That's it. Good memory, sir. The other four are accounted for, but I haven't figured out where this Colonel Pham Van Minh is yet. A buddy at INS is workin' it, but . . ."

"You won't find him," Fick answered.

Deveroux knotted his forehead and let his face ask the question.

Fick didn't answer immediately. Instead he took a bottle of pills from his pocket and poured out a handful, which he popped into his mouth and swallowed. He took a small sip of tea to work them down, and then he looked at Deveroux, his head slightly inclined to one side. "Colonel Pham Van Minh, Army of the Republic of Vietnam, husband to Ngo Van Thu's youngest sister, Linh, not seen since 12 September 1970—sixteen days before Jimmy Lee Tenkiller sprouted wings." He saw Deveroux begin scanning the file. "Won't find it in there. No proof, but word on the Saigon cocktail circuit at the time was that he got crossways with his brother-in-law, and that no one got crossways with Ngo—even family."

"You sayin' his brother killed him?" Deveroux asked.

"Brother-in-law. Yes, I am."

"The same General Ngo we're goin' to go visit here in a few minutes?" Try as he might to copy Fick, the name still came out sounding as if he had a thick piece of gristle caught in his throat and was about to choke—*EN-go*.

Fick nodded and took another shallow sip of tea.

"You believe it, sir?" Deveroux continued. "From what you know, could Ngo do it? Or was it rumor mongerin'?"

"I do."

Deveroux continued looking at Fick.

"Ngo had a reputation," the general felt the uncharacteristic need to elaborate.

"Reputation?"

Fick nodded. "Word at the time was that he was a sadistic sonofabitch. Used to get his fulfillment by beating young girls almost to death. He had a French . . . not even sure what to call it . . . a swagger stick, a riding crop, baton, some damn thing. Braided leather over a birchwood core. It was said he would almost flay the girls with it."

"Why didn't anyone stop him?" Deveroux asked. "I mean, if everyone knew about it and all; if you knew about it."

Fick closed his eyes and took a long, deep breath. He seemed to have aged and withered just in the time they'd been talking. "Why indeed?" he said quietly. "Someone should have, Chief Deveroux. Maybe I should have, but I was on another mission. I was focused. I wanted that bastard Tenkiller. I wanted the Five Brothers—not just Ngo. The problem was . . . no one else did."

"Sir?"

Paul Fick laughed quietly, without any humor, and continued. "It's hard to understand, Chief, sitting here in Waynesville, Missouri, eight thousand miles away. Thirty, forty years later. Hard even for me, anymore. Vietnam in 1970 was the dark side of the moon, you see. There was no light shining there. Everything was in shadows. We needed it that way; this country needed it that way, you understand. Or maybe you don't. The South Vietnamese were our good allies, poor victims, innocent victims." He paused and the flint returned to his eyes. "You're old enough to remember *Life* magazine. *Look* magazine. The *Post*. Remember the photos? Do you? Especially early on. The South Vietnamese, the poor, poor South Vietnamese held in thrall by the evil North. Remember? It was all bullshit. The North was evil and the South were victims, maybe, but not innocent. They were victims of their own corrupt, spoiled, self-indulgent leaders. Morally bankrupt. But that couldn't be seen—not here in the U.S. of A.; we couldn't let it be seen; not by the folks here in Waynesville, or Cincinnati, or Des Moines. Our boys were dying; our sons and fathers; our brothers and husbands; all the good, young men of a generation getting chewed up in that enormous bloody maw. For what? You see, it had to be something worth dying for; they had to die for something as good and noble and worthy as they themselves were, or it'd all be a waste. So men like Ngo weren't seen. They didn't exist. It wasn't seen. It didn't happen." He paused again. "It wasn't stopped."

Deveroux sat silently watching the sugar settle out at the bottom of his tea glass. It looked like a muddy snow globe. After a moment he cleared his throat and looked up. Fick had his eyes closed. "Sir?"

Fick's eyes flickered under their lids but didn't open.

Deveroux continued. "Sir, the one killed at Campbell, and the one at Knox, now the one they found up near Whiteman Air Force Base, plus the one you mentioned, the one that didn't make it out of Vietnam . . ."

"Colonel Pham."

"Yes, sir, him." Deveroux held up four fingers. "That makes four. I'm assumin' that General Ngo is the last one. The last of the . . ."

"*La Fraternité de Cinq,*" Fick responded, opening his eyes and engaging Deveroux's.

"Yes, sir," Deveroux smiled. "Them."

"It doesn't do to forget Master Sergeant Tenkiller, Chief."

"I'm not, but I'm not sure how he fits in. Is he part of the Five? Like the sixth of the Five Brothers."

"Very much so, Chief Deveroux. Not one of the *Five,* perhaps, but definitely one of them. Very much so, I think."

Deveroux nodded. "I see. Ahh, sir, if four of the . . . the . . . *de Cinq* . . . are accounted for, and the fifth—General Ngo—is here, I mean . . . in Rolla . . . then . . ."

"Yes, Chief. Then he'd better get a bodyguard."

CHAPTER 51

Rolla, Missouri
WEDNESDAY, APRIL 23, 2008

Jimmy Lee Tenkiller was back.

Parked across the tree-lined street from General Ngo's house, as he had been off and on for almost a week, he felt his patience stretched thin and taut, like the translucent skin of a drum. The house had been continuously awash with people—too many people—and he'd been forced to wait and linger.

But no longer.

Tonight was the time—too many people or not. He had a plan.

Tonight was proving to be relatively quiet. Unlike the past few nights, there had been no visitors yet this evening, and as the shadows lengthened, it was increasingly unlikely that there would be any. Jimmy Lee Tenkiller noticed the streetlight in front of Ngo's house start to blink on, and he looked at his watch—seven-ten. *Soon*, he thought, *very soon.*

A middle-aged couple in identical khaki shorts and colorful St. Louis Symphony T-shirts strolled by, passing the truck without a glance, talking animatedly and swinging their arms with angular enthusiasm. Tenkiller watched them pass by, as they had on Monday night and the Saturday night before that. He was struck by how singularly trusting they must be—or how appallingly self-absorbed—to pass by a strange vehicle with out-of-state plates parked on their quiet street night after night and never flicker so much as a look. He closed his eyes and smiled at the thought. He'd never planned for his mission to take this long, and he'd always assumed that someone along the way would take notice of him. He was prepared for that. He'd call Eddie as soon as it was over, and that would be the signal to report the truck as stolen. Keep his brother out of it. After that there was no more plan; just reflex.

With a startle, Jimmy Lee Tenkiller realized that he'd dozed off, though for how long he was uncertain. Living in the truck for a week was taking its toll on him, and he was showing the physical and mental signs of exhaustion. He blinked hard trying to work the sting out of his eyes, and that's when he heard the voices.

Sitting up, suddenly attuned, he looked across the street and in the glow of the blossoming streetlight saw Ngo and his wife walking out to the dark-blue Seville that sat square in the middle of the driveway, its trunk lid standing open like the enormous jaws of an alligator. Ngo was carrying a small overnight bag and walking a step in front of his wife, and a shudder of concern ran through Tenkiller as he realized that Ngo was leaving and his opportunity was about to be lost. Almost frantically Tenkiller opened the glove box, removed the .22 Ruger pistol, and chambered a round. He looked up just as Ngo was slamming the trunk closed.

Jimmy Lee Tenkiller no longer had any plan other than not letting Ngo Van Thu leave. But as he reached for the door handle he heard other voices. Glancing up in the rearview mirror he saw the Symphony strollers returning, having made a giant loop around the block and starting on a second power lap. They still took no notice of Tenkiller, but they also made it impossible to get out of the truck carrying a gun. He watched them close the distance on the truck, and he took a hurried look again across the street. To his surprise, and relief, he saw Mrs. Ngo getting in behind the wheel while the general stood at the open driver's side window, hands on his hips, talking to her. In a moment the car started, the back-up lights came on, and the car pulled out of the driveway. Ngo Van Thu stood illuminated in the middle of the driveway, waving and watching the car stop, turn, and drive away. He paused, then turned, and quickly returned inside the house.

Jimmy Lee Tenkiller smiled. Once again, he had a plan.

CHAPTER 52

Rolla, Missouri
WEDNESDAY, APRIL 23, 2008

They took Deveroux's rental car—a bright-red two-door Chevy Cavalier with Texas plates and a thin white scratch that ran the length of the driver's side—and arrived precisely on time. General Fick had a good working knowledge of Rolla's layout and had navigated the way perfectly, the only miscue coming when they'd driven past the house after missing the number in the dark and had to turn around in a neighbor's driveway and retrace their route. Even so, it was eight-twenty-eight when Deveroux pulled into the driveway of General Ngo's house and killed his engine.

Both men got out of the car and stood, stretching their backs and legs. It had been a relatively short drive, but Deveroux's knees were throbbing and talking to him in a most disagreeable manner, still remembering the six-hour drive earlier in the day and not particularly inclined to forgive him just yet. General Fick seemed to be in some general discomfort but said nothing.

As they walked up the brick sidewalk to the front door, Deveroux took in the street and the surroundings. Ngo's two-story, neocolonial home was, if not the best house on the block, certainly no lower than second or third. The yard was large and professionally cared for, as were the flowerbeds that skirted the front of the house like a colorful necklace. Early season crocuses and tulips had worked their way through a thick mantle of shredded redwood bark and were visible in the dimming light.

Deveroux pressed the lighted doorbell and stepped back, hands on hips military fashion, waiting. Fick stood a few feet farther back, off the front stoop, looking up at the dark second-story windows, surveying the architecture with the same eyes that once had evaluated fields of fire. Across the street they heard a vehicle start up and both turned in time to see a dark-colored pickup truck pull slowly away from under a tree across the street and disappear around the corner.

Suddenly the porch light came on, and Ngo Van Thu answered the door. He was dressed in creased blue jeans and a red-and-blue plaid shirt—the sleeves were turned back two precise rolls—and ribbed, white socks. "Yes," he said.

Shuck Deveroux quickly cleared his throat and answered. "Mr. Ngo? Mr. Ngo Van Thu?"

If Ngo Van Thu found any amusement in Deveroux's molasses-tongued pronunciation of his family name, he didn't convey it. He had heard worse in his thirty years residing in the Ozark plateau. "Yes," he responded again.

"Sir, I'm Agent Deveroux of the army CID. I called you earlier this afternoon about maybe havin' the opportunity to ask you a few questions."

"You have some identification, Agent Deveroux?"

"Yes, sir," Deveroux answered. He hadn't expected to need to flash his tin, since this was an unofficial visit, and it took him a minute to get his badge holder out of his pants pocket. While he was doing so, he noticed that Ngo was watching General Fick closely. Fick was returning the stare. "Here you go, sir," he said as he held his gold CID badge in the light. "And this here's my, ahh, partner . . . ahhh . . . Mr. Fick." At the last minute he'd decided that simply calling him a partner might be easier than explaining why a retired infantry general was tagging along with him.

Ngo never looked at the identification, and without taking his eyes off Fick, stepped back from the door and said, "You may come in, Agent Deveroux. And your partner."

The house was large, even larger than it had appeared to be from the outside, with glossy oak flooring, cream-colored walls, and thick, white crown molding, but it was the décor that proved the most surprising. Everything visible from the entryway—the kitchen straight on, the living room to the right, the formal dining room that opened off to the left, even the spindled stairway and upstairs balcony—was decorated with an *I Love Country* motif. Everywhere. Colorful braided-rag rugs, a painted milk can umbrella stand, cross-stitched homilies framed with driftwood on the walls. It was almost as if an alien from Saturn had tried to replicate the prototype American home—which, Deveroux realized as he was being led into the living room, was probably very close to the truth.

"Sit, please," Ngo said as he motioned the men to a sofa. It was covered in a calico print and matched the cornflower blue puffy drapes. He took a chair near the fireplace, crossed his legs, looked at his watch conspicuously, and then resumed eye contact with Fick.

Deveroux picked up the conversation. "Ahh, sir, I . . . we . . . really do appreciate your time. I hope you and Mrs. Ngo didn't have plans that we're interruptin'."

"My wife is visiting friends in St. Louis, Agent Deveroux. But as to plans, I am a very busy man with many things that must be accomplished." The voice had the coppery taste of one used to giving directions.

"Yes, sir," Deveroux responded. He bounced a quick look at Fick and found him mutually fixated on Ngo. "We won't take long. Just a few questions that you might be able to help us out with."

"Go on."

"Well, for starters, as I mentioned on the phone earlier, I'm with army CID, and I'm lookin' into the deaths of a couple of Vietnamese gentlemen—like yourself—who died, actually they were murdered, on U.S. military installations. Fort Campbell and Fort Knox, over in Kentucky, and then, more recently, just outside Whiteman Air Force Base here in Missouri."

Ngo remained expressionless. He blinked several times slowly but made no other outward sign that he was even listening. He'd been staring at Fick almost without break but now looked at Deveroux. "You must have a very interesting job, Warrant Officer Deveroux. You are a warrant officer, I assume."

"Yes, sir. But I don't know that I'd necessarily call it interestin'."

Ngo looked again at his watch. "Yes. Please, Warrant Officer Deveroux, please tell me what I can do for you."

"Of course. Well, sir, these Vietnamese gentlemen were friends of yours, I think. At least at one time. If not friends, at least acquaintances." He pulled a small green notebook out of his shirt pocket and flipped through several pages. When he found what he was after he folded the top back and cleared his throat. "Forgive the pronunciations, sir. The first one was a Mr. Linh Nhu Ngon from Louisville, then came Mr. Trinh Han, and then two days ago up in Warrensburg, a Mr. Doan Minh Tuyen." He looked up at Ngo. "Am I right about these men bein' acquaintances of yours?"

The Vietnamese general didn't answer immediately but slowly removed a cigarette from a package that lay on an oak pie safe that had been converted into an end table. He lit up, blew the smoke in the direction of the fireplace, and picked at a loose fragment of tobacco on the tip of his tongue before re-engaging Deveroux's eyes. The gesture was intended to convey disdain. "Perhaps these are strange names to you, Warrant Officer, but those are not uncommon names for Vietnamese."

"So you don't know them? Or do?"

Ngo shrugged.

Deveroux could feel a heat rising from Fick and guessed that Ngo's smugness was sandpapering his partner's patience raw. He bunched up his brow in serious thought and then continued. "Ahh, well sir, Mr. Ngo, those may be common names and all, but the INS says that thirty-seven, thirty-eight years ago you entered this country with three Vietnamese nationals with those same, common names. All Vietnamese military officers. Common names or not, I suspect you'll agree that it seems to be more than a coincidence. Are you sure you didn't know them?" He paused and waited for Ngo to respond before preempting him. "And sir, here's the reason I ask, these three Vietnamese men, these . . . possible former acquaintances of yours, they didn't just die by accident. They were murdered, sir, and we don't have any idea of who dunnit or why. And to be quite honest, sir, I mean, I don't pretend to know your business and all, but if I were you, these . . . coincidences . . . well, sir, wouldn't do much for my normal sleep patterns."

"Warrant Officer Deveroux, perhaps these are the same men that I knew, but as you say, that was almost forty years ago. The men that I knew by those names were . . . I am trying to be generous . . . they were weak . . . stupid . . . greedy. Little men. They were, perhaps, the type that men like you and I do not associate with freely." His eyes were on Fick as he spoke.

"So you haven't had any contact with them recently?"

Ngo smiled. "No." He broke eye contact with Fick long enough to arch his neck back and drag on his cigarette. He exhaled toward the ceiling before resuming his stare.

"Any idea of what might be the connectin' link here? Who might have a reason to kill these folks?" Deveroux asked.

"Links? You mean aside from never aspiring to be more than petty businessmen dependent on arrogant GIs to make their living?" Ngo replied, turning to look at Deveroux. "Aside from being zipperheads, you mean? Slant-eyes? Gooks? Yellow bastards? Fish-heads? Cat-eaters? Aside from talkie-funny? Aside from gum-chewing warrant officers' mispronouncing their names and thinking it is acceptable? No, I am not aware of any connecting links—are you?"

Deveroux sat wondering what kind of hornet's nest he'd just whacked. He blinked and shook his head slowly, planning his next sentence carefully. Fick preempted him.

"General Ngo, I don't believe I heard an answer to Chief Deveroux's question. Do you know who might be executing these . . . businessmen?"

Ngo looked directly at Fick, clearly disdaining Deveroux's presence.

"Yes, General Fick, I do. Perhaps someone with a past that cannot be forgotten. Someone with much to lose."

"Who? General Ngo. I still haven't heard who."

Ngo Van Thu smiled, but his grin was that of a carnivore demonstrating his teeth and betrayed no humor. "A most dangerous man, General Fick, a most dangerous man."

CHAPTER 53

"Do me a favor, General, next time remind me to punch that sawed-off little sonofabuck's lights out." Shuck Deveroux had been fuming all the drive back to the DeVille Motel in Waynesville, and like a sore tooth, he kept returning over and over to the same weeping source of irritation.

For his part, Paul Fick had been mostly quiet, absorbed in watching the darkened landscape flow by the speeding window, but now as they approached the interstate off-ramp to the DeVille, he spoke. "There were two kinds of Vietnamese generals during the war. Those who accepted their shortcomings, who knew that they'd bought their ranks with money or marriage or some kind of political coinage, and were awed by any U.S. officer, even butter-bar second lieutenants—or, for that matter, chief warrant officers—and then there were those—no less incompetent—who assumed an air of status and superiority over everyone. Those so connected politically that they were untouchable. Spoiled children, really; dangerous spoiled children. You just met one of those."

"Still," Deveroux countered, "Zipperhead? I don't even know what a Zipperhead is."

"I'm sure Ngo had a sober awakening when he arrived in this

country. His family and rank meant nothing around here. The sting seems to have gone deep."

"I guess. He obviously recognized you, though. He called you *General* Fick—did you catch that? I introduced you as Mister. I never said *General.* Had you met him before?"

"No."

"No? Never?"

"No. About the time I had connected the dots that included him and his associates, the powers in Washington pulled the plug on my investigation. I got close to him a few times, but never talked to him. After Tenkiller disappeared, the problem disappeared."

Deveroux was shaking his head. "Well, I'll tell you what I know. What I know is that that meetin' was about the biggest waste of my time that I've experienced in a long while." He was still shaking his head as he pulled into the parking lot at the DeVille Motel. "The little piece of . . ."

"You can let me off here," Fick quietly interrupted as they drove past a dark-colored Ford Taurus. Whatever color it was, it appeared almost purple in the yellowish glow of the overhead streetlights. "This is my vehicle."

"Yes, sir. You okay to drive home, General? You look kinda beat."

Fick smiled as he opened the car door. "Good night, Chief."

Deveroux waited long enough to ensure that Fick had his keys, but not so long as to tempt the general's patience with his concern, and then continued around the lot to the back side closer to where his room was located. As he pulled into a vacant spot, he recognized his own pickup truck parked nearby. One of the other calls he'd made earlier in the afternoon was to Kel to tell him that there was no way he was going to be able to interview Ngo and get back to Warrensburg before tomorrow morning. They'd agreed that Kel would drive the pickup down to Waynesville as soon as he was finished examining the body and that Deveroux could drop off his rental in Rolla in the morning. He looked at his watch as he climbed out of his car and locked it—almost ten o'clock.

It took a few minutes to hunt Kel down. He was in the small

restaurant attached to the motel, eating a thick, sticky wedge of Karo nut pie and sipping slowly on a perspiring glass of sweetened tea. He looked up as Deveroux walked in and took a seat.

"I see that you made it," Deveroux said as he motioned at the waitress for attention. She grabbed her notepad and started to move.

"Yup," Kel replied in between bites. "You really need to get your speedometer cable greased. Screamed like a sonofabitch the whole way down. I'm half deaf."

"Yeah. Does that sometimes. It'd have stopped eventually if you'd kept goin'." He nodded at the slice of pie. "Any good?"

Kel shrugged and took another mouthful. "Don't know if there's such a thing as a bad nut pie. It'll make your fillings ache, if that's any indication." He shrugged again. "Not as good as my mother-in-law's, but then we ain't at my mother-in-law's."

"I hear ya," Deveroux replied as the waitress reached the table. Close up, Deveroux realized that she was much younger than she'd appeared from across the room. She was no older than nineteen and had the long thin face of a Korean. He'd noticed when he checked in that the motel's owner was a middle-aged Korean, and he wondered if the young waitress was a daughter or a granddaughter. "Evenin', ma'am," Deveroux responded to her smile. "Just a Coke Cola and a wedge of that nut pie, if I could."

The waitress smiled again as she wrote a series of what looked to Deveroux like a mess of squiggles on her notepad. She hadn't said a word, and he wondered whether she spoke any English.

Kel waited until she'd started back toward the kitchen before picking up the first dangling thread of the impending conversation. "How'd it go, boss? Successful?"

"Well, I can tell you one thing. If the rest of the Five Bubbas are anythin' like Mr. Ngo," this time he intentionally dragged out the mispronunciation as *EN-go,* "then it's no wonder they're all endin' up dead. I wanted to kill that little sonofabuck myself. In fact, I've got half a mind to drive back over there right now and pound the livin' snot out of him with a crooked stick."

"That productive, huh?"

"Nothin'. Absolutely nothin'. Hey, you're a man of the world, what's a Zipperhead, anyhow?"

"A what?"

The waitress returned with Deveroux's order and slid it across the table. The plate clinked against the laminate tabletop. She smiled again and hesitated, her expression asking if there was anything else needed, before turning and walking back to the counter, where she busied herself folding napkins for use in the morning.

"Nothin'. Forget it." Deveroux sighed a day's worth of accumulated exhaustion. He shook his head slowly as he took a large bite of pie. "Real piece of work," he mumbled. "He no longer has any stars on his shoulder so he's decided to wear a chip instead. I tell you what, it's like he's ashamed to be Vietnamese or somethin'. I mean, you ought to see this guy's house; I'm not kiddin', it's decorated in like early nineteenth-century Minnie Pearl."

"How 'bout Tenkiller? Mr. Ngo know anythin' about him? D'you get a chance to ask him or were you too preoccupied examinin' his décor?"

"Tenkiller? You kiddin' me? He doesn't even claim to know the other four brothers—they're such common names, in case you didn't know—give me a break—like every Vietnamese male who checks into a cheap motel signs is as Colonel Pham-bam-thank-you-ma'am. And, oh by the way, only four of the five ever made it to the U.S. Fick says that the fifth brother never made it out of Vietnam."

"So there's only four." Kel followed his comment with a sip of tea.

"*Were*. Past tense. Were four."

"Were. Right. And now there's only one. That kinda begs the question, doesn't it? Any chance Ngo's your man? You think he could do it?"

"You mean, is he the killer? Could he be?" Deveroux pursed his lips in what amounted to a shrug. "I didn't give it much thought goin' into it, but after meetin' with him—he's a piece of work, that's for dang sure. Fick says he had quite a reputation durin' the war for roughin' up young women. He may have even rubbed out the fifth partner—his own dang brother-in-law . . . so, yeah, I guess all things considered, he could, but . . ."

"Your gut?"

"My gut says maybe. Not yes, not no, I mean, maybe. But then it's not like I have any other suspects right now either. No, I'd have to say it's not Ngo."

"No pun intended, I'm sure. So, how about Tenkiller?"

"Tenkiller?" Deveroux seemed genuinely caught off balance. "First he's KIA, then he's a deserter, then maybe he's involved in the black market, and now we're talkin' about Tenkiller being the killer? Some résumé."

"It's called multitaskin'."

"Yeah, well . . ."

"Why not? Think about it. We know that he's alive—at least we think we know. He was connected to all of them. He may have a motive."

"Like what?"

Kel smiled and shrugged. "You're the G-man. I'm just an anthropologist. But don't forget that scalpin' business . . ."

"I'm not forgettin' it, but it's kinda obvious, isn't it? No offense there, Doctor, but I suspect that scalpin' is somethin' of a lost art among Indians today. Besides, seems a bit of a stereotype comin' from an anthropologist."

"I didn't say I was a good anthropologist. All right, it's not Ngo, and you also say it's not Tenkiller . . . then who? Takes you back to the drawin' board, doesn't it?"

"That's the question, isn't it? I just wish we knew for sure that all three of these cases were linked."

"What?" Kel's voice betrayed his surprise. "You are shinin' me on, aren't you?" He held out his left hand and ticked off his fingers as he made his points. "Let's see here, Chief Warrant Officer Special Agent Shuck-my-grits Deveroux, count with me here: It's like your monkeys jumpin' on the bed. We start with five Vietnamese gentlemen who form a secret group to engage in illegal activities; next, they all arrive in the Land of Milk and Honey on the same day—at least four of them do, all in the same U.S. government airplane, all end up homesteadin' next

to an active military base—I'm runnin' outta fingers here, Shuck—
they begin showin' up dead within a few months of each other—after
almost forty years of peace and quiet, mind you—and three of them
are now missin' their scalp locks." He held up six fingers, showing
them to Deveroux. "Yeah, you're right. If we could get all these pesky
coincidences out of the way, we might be able to see a pattern."

"Yeah, yeah, yeah. You're real funny, Kel." He put both palms
on the edge of the table and pushed so that his back was tight
against the booth seat. He sighed again. "So, how was your day,
Doctor?"

Kel finished his pie and moved his empty plate aside. He dabbed
at his lips with a red cloth napkin before replying to the change in
subject. "Fair to middlin', I'd say. Ended up drivin' over to Columbia
with the body, and stayed around for the start of the autopsy. I tell
you what, it's pretty interestin' stuff, in a disgustin' sort of way.
It'll be interestin' to see the final report. I'm also anxious to see
the other two—the ones in Louisville and Nashville—see how they
compare."

Shuck Deveroux took another large mouthful of pie before
responding to Kel. "Well, I'm anxious for you to take a look at them,
too. But tell me, what about Mr. What's-his-name?"

Kel knotted up his forehead while he deconstructed the question.
"You mean Mr. Doan Minh Tuyen? The fella in Warrensburg?"

"Yup. I'm not even goin' to try sayin' these names anymore. Gets
me nothin' but grief."

"Well . . . he's seen better days, I 'spect. Dr. Cooke—the ME—
he's pretty damn amazin'. Don't know how many autopsies you've
seen. He started on the head for my benefit. He figured he could do
the full post-mortem after I left. Anyhow, from what he determined,
someone grabbed Mr. Doan from behind and cut him from left ear to
right." He drew his right index finger along his neck. "Your suspect
is probably righthanded."

"Oh, great. That helps. Eliminatin' southpaws and switch-hitters,
and that gets us down to—oh, what d'you think—maybe two hundred
million suspects?"

"Give or take a couple hundred thousand. Not countin' tourists and illegal aliens."

"Yeah, give or take. And to think I was startin' to despair of solvin' this case. Thanks, Doc."

"Just doin' my job, partner. Now, where was I? Cut from here to here," he again mimed the action. "Deep too. Cut clean through both the carotid and jugular. Poor sonofabitch bled out in minutes. Like a stuck pig. Must have looked like a damn PEZ dispenser."

"Deep? Yeah, I guess I'd call cuttin' somebody's head clean off *deep*."

"Yeah, well I guess I'd agree with that, except that his head was cut off later—after his throat was slit. Best Dr. Cooke can figure—at least in the short while I was there—was that the throat was cut first. Slit the throat, drop him to the ground, and then put a foot or knee in the square of his back. There were abrasions on his chest and a muddy impression right between his shoulder blades." Kel stopped and took a sip of tea. "Doc thinks your killer pinned Doan down, foot or knee in the back while he scalped him."

Deveroux leaned forward and lowered his voice. "So he was scalped? I mean, not just an expression. Really scalped? What the cops said was accurate then? Just like the other two. You sure it's not some sort of collateral damage? I mean, somehow incidental to the decapitation."

"Nope. Someone out there's countin' coup."

"What about the head?" Deveroux asked.

"What about it?"

"You said it was cut off afterward? After he was scalped, you mean? How do y'all know that?"

"Well, I don't, but Cooke thinks so." Kel paused and sorted his thoughts. "It's based on where there's blood and where there isn't. That's his area, not mine, but the cuts associated with the actual removal of the head don't show any significant bleedin' in the tissues. Cooke says that the most likely cause is that he'd already bled out by the time those cuts were made—no more blood, no more blood pressure. Also, there's a whole different set of cut marks. The cut

along the throat was deep enough to nick the lower cervical verts—
here and here. Fine, slashing cuts with a sharp blade." Kel pointed
to the base of his neck near his left collarbone. "But the head was
severed higher up—between the third and fourth vertebrae. I tell you
what, you wouldn't know it from all the horror shows on TV, but
heads are actually fastened on pretty damn good and tight. They
don't just come poppin' off like bottle caps the way you see in all the
movies, and unless you know what you're doin', it's a real chore to
get a head loose."

"I'll remember that next time I'm dismemberin' someone."

"Yeah, make sure to budget some extra time, 'cause it's a chore."

"So, you sayin' the killer knew what he was doin'? I mean, like a
doctor?" Deveroux asked.

"Hell, no. You've been watchin' way too many of those movies
I was talkin' about. Fact is, most people don't know how to remove
a head properly, and neither did your boy. Neither do most doctors,
actually. Not much call for it in a normal practice. No, in this case,
the middle cervical verts are chipped all to hell where he got some
thick-bladed knife or somethin' in there and just levered and pried
until he got the damn thing loose."

Deveroux's head was hanging down, shaking slowly from side to
side. "At the risk of chewin' our tobacco twice, how about that?"

"How about what?"

"Takin' the whole head off. You say the three cases are so
similar, but how do you explain the overkill that you see with the
last one?"

"Escalation," Kel answered. "The profiler folks have got some
fancy term for it. Can't recall it right this minute, but these guys
sometimes unravel. They have to escalate the act to get the same
effect. Kinda like eatin' potato chips or dialin' up Internet porn."

"Personal experience talkin'?"

"Yeah. Keep gettin' the computer keyboard all greasy, but, no, it's
true. These guys have to keep uppin' the ante."

Deveroux kept shaking his head. "Yeah, yeah. I went to all those
continuin' education courses as well, but this isn't a sex crime or a
thrill killer. This guy's not unravelin', do you think?"

Kel shrugged as if to admit it was out of his league.

"I just don't understand it, Kel. I mean, what kind of man would do that sort of thing? Until the day I die, I won't understand this sort of thing. What kind of man?"

"One with a lot of hate, Chief. A whole bellyful of pent-up hate."

CHAPTER 54

Rolla, Missouri
THURSDAY, APRIL 24, 2008

Kel rolled over, hoping that the pounding in his head would subside. It didn't. He rolled over again and cracked an eye long enough to read the red, glowing letters of the alarm clock—6:32 A.M.

A born night owl, and still a little jet lagged, he hadn't actually gone to sleep until sometime after four in the morning, and now, less than three hours later, he was awakened by a pounding in his head like someone rapping on the inside of his eyelids. He closed his eye and rolled over a third time. The pounding intruded into his dream.

"Kel. Hey, Kel. Doc. You awake?"

Kel cracked an eye again. It wasn't a pounding in his head. The pounding was at the door.

Bam, bam, bam.

"Hey, Doc. Wake up, bubba."

Kel coaxed the second eye open. He blinked and verified the time on the clock radio.

Six-thirty-three. *Shit.*

"Yeah," he managed to say, though to an outside ear he was sure it sounded more like a death gurgle. He cleared his voice as he rolled out of bed and answered again, only slightly more clearly. "Comin', comin'."

It took a moment to manhandle the chain and deadbolt with his eyes closed, but he managed to work the door open before Deveroux felt the need to knock again. It was painfully bright for so early, and Kel was forced back a stagger. He stood, in his underwear and a faded gray T-shirt that had once read *University of Missouri,* leaning against the television.

Deveroux walked in quickly but held the door open, as if he was in a hurry and didn't intend to stay. "We got to roll, cowboy. I'll fill ya in on the way. Get dressed." He punctuated each statement with a short nod as if he were hammering them in like roofing nails. "Meet you in ten minutes at my truck. You ain't gonna believe this."

"What?" Kel asked. He was still blinking the sleep out of his eyes. "Didn't we establish for the record that I'm not one of your mornin' types?"

"Why, yes. I believe we did. Now, I like standin' around in dark motel rooms lookin' at men in their baggy underwear as much as the next guy, but we really do need to get goin'."

"Where?" Kel blinked hard.

"You just see if you can find your way to my truck. I'll take it from there."

Ten minutes later, Shuck Deveroux put his truck in gear and pulled out of the parking lot at the DeVille Motel and headed northeast toward Rolla.

Kel yawned and shook his head like a wet dog. Sufficiently awake, he restated his question. "Commissioner Gordon flash the ol' symbol again, Batman?"

"Sort of. Ready for another coincidence?" Deveroux shot a quick look at his passenger and then re-engaged the road.

"Sure."

"Got a call this mornin' from a homicide detective in Rolla. Lieutenant Rugelo, Larry Rugelo. I'd called him yesterday as a courtesy, you know, hey, I'm here knockin' around in your sandbox, goin' to be talkin' to one of your fine citizens—you know—just a courtesy thing."

"Sure, I've always said you were the courteous type. So, I'm guessin' he got some information for you?"

Deveroux laughed. "Actually, Kel, he thinks I'm the one with the information. Seems he wants to question me in the death of one Mr. Ngo Van Thu, late of Rolla, Missouri."

"Who?"

"You heard me. Ngo. General Ngo."

Kel blinked hard. "Ngo? Ngo? But . . ."

Deveroux was shaking his head as he replied. "I'm serious as a heart attack, cowboy. Don't have many details. I was sound asleep when Rugelo called, but it seems that Mr. Ngo's house caught fire last night, or early this mornin' some time. I guess they've been fightin' the fire all night and now that it's light, the fire marshal finally got in there to poke around. Found Ngo's body fried up like a pork rind."

Kel joined Deveroux in shaking his head. "I'll be goddamned," he said almost to himself; then he turned to Deveroux. "Any reason to suspect homicide?"

"Hello? Weren't you the one that was tickin' off all the links in these cases? Yeah, I'd say there's every reason in the world to assume the worst, but to answer your question, no, Rugelo didn't give me any reason on the phone, but then I doubt he knows very much just yet. Rolla PD isn't technically involved at this point other than Mr. Ngo seems to have been a fairly influential member of the community so there's the usual interest. Fire marshal called PD as soon as they found the body, but I guess at this point they're still assumin' it was just an accident. Lord knows he was smokin' like a blue-tile chimney while we were there last night, ash trays full and all, maybe he was smokin' in bed. Or maybe he was just so filled up with hate that he went and spontaneously combusted like you read about in them tabloids. We'll find out soon enough, but in the meantime, this cop in Rolla wants to know what I was doin' talkin' to Ngo last night. Can't say I blame him, but it is some kind of ironic."

"How so?" Kel asked.

Deveroux smiled and looked at Kel. "Because, bubba, I sure did feel like kickin' his ass last night. That's a fact."

"Do us both a favor, Shuck, why don't you keep that little tidbit to yourself."

"Plan to."

"Just the same, it doesn't hurt that you have General Fick as an alibi."

The truck's speedometer cable began to whine. Deveroux had to raise his voice to be heard. "You may be jokin', but there may be some truth in that. You'll get a chance to meet him, by the way."

"Who? You mean Fick?" Kel shouted back.

"Yeah. I figured the cops would want to talk to him once they found out he'd been there with me. I know I would. Pays to be proactive sometimes. I gave him a call while I was waitin' on you to get dressed. He said he'd meet us there."

Kel nodded but didn't venture shouting out a response.

The street was filled with people. Most were talking among themselves and pointing dramatically in various directions as they watched ribbons of smoke and steam curl up and off the blackened shell of Ngo Van Thu's house, but others were watching several heavily suited firemen roll up hoses and stow various pieces of equipment on the one fire truck that remained on site. An orange-colored sawhorse sat in the street, shunting vehicular traffic onto long, looping detours around the block. Shuck Deveroux was forced to park on a side street almost two hundred yards away.

As Deveroux and Kel approached the barricade, a large uniformed policeman who'd been standing on the sidewalk talking to a young female jogger saw them and yelled for them to hold up. As he hurried out to meet them, his swollen belly stretched his shirt to the point that it resembled a ripe melon.

Deveroux had his badge ready, and he flashed it in an effort to forgo a confrontation. "It's okay, officer, I'm lookin' for a Detective Rugelo, Lieutenant Larry Rugelo. Supposed to meet him here. He around?"

The officer slackened his hurry but kept approaching, his eyes squinting at the strange-shaped gold badge being held up by a man in blue jeans and dirty Chuck Taylor high-tops. "Ahh, yeah. Lieutenant's over by the fire truck. Blue warmup suit. Bad disposition." He acknowledged the fact that Deveroux and Kel had showed no intention of stopping by waving them on as if he were giving permission. "You two are clear. Be sure to sign in. Proceed."

As they approached the fire truck they saw Detective Rugelo, a short man with graying Brillo-pad hair and thick glasses that resembled wire-framed ice cubes, talking to a middle-aged couple in matching blue Sierra Club T-shirts, khaki shorts, and snow-white Nike walking shoes. They had a small ugly dog that resembled a dirty mop on a leash. Whatever the couple was telling Rugelo, he was interested enough, or compulsively anal enough, to take copious notes. Several yards behind him, on the sidewalk across from the smoldering husk of Ngo's home, hands in the pockets of his blue windbreaker, stood Paul Fick.

Deveroux paused at Rugelo's side long enough to discern the detective's rapt attention before taking hold of Kel's arm and walking over to the sidewalk beside Fick. "Mornin', General," he said as he turned slightly to capture Kel's eye. "Sir, this is Dr. McKelvey of the Central ID Lab in Hawaii—we call him Kel. Kel, this is Brigadier General Paul Fick."

As Kel shook hands, he felt a strange knobbiness and looked down to see the shiny, hard nubs that made up Fick's mangled right hand. He looked up quickly when he realized that he'd been staring. "Pleased to meet you, General Fick."

"Doctor."

"Shuck here says y'all have a mutual interest in Jimmy Tenkiller. Me too. The lab, I mean."

"Is that so?" Fick asked. "What interest does the laboratory in Hawaii have in Tenkiller? As I recall, your unit deals with MIAs. Is that correct?"

"Yes, sir. MIAs and KIAs both. Tenkiller's a KIA-BNR. Killed In Action, Body Not Recovered." Kel answered quickly, almost nervously. He'd misjudged Fick. From a distance, the general's outward appearance suggested a frailty, almost feebleness, but the gray, mottled eyes that now took Kel's measure radiated the crisp intensity of a live circuit.

"Of course." Fick smiled. There was no trace of humor. "I remember. I simply didn't think that the army was spending its resources to look for him."

"We don't pick the cases, General," Kel responded defensively. "He's on the list; he's our responsibility."

Fick nodded. He understood all too well. His eyes lingered on Kel briefly and then shifted back to the remains of the house. He was finished with the conversation. Kel paused, and then he too turned and looked at the smoking rubble. Deveroux did likewise.

"I'm guessing you're Agent Deveroux," a voice behind them said.

Deveroux turned. Detective Rugelo had finished talking to the Sierra Club couple and was standing behind, one hand outstretched, the other holding a small green notebook. His thick glasses made his green eyes look like cat's-eye marbles.

"Yes, sir," Deveroux said, shaking hands. "That's right. You'd be Lieutenant Rugelo. Glad to meet you, sir. Got a real mess here, looks like."

Rugelo nodded, his eyes watching Deveroux closely. "Could say that. Things have changed somewhat from when we spoke earlier."

"How so?" Deveroux responded. Kel had taken notice of the conversation and was now close to Deveroux's shoulder, openly eavesdropping. Deveroux noticed. "Oh, by the way, Lieutenant, this here's Dr. Robert McKelvey, head of the Army Central ID Lab. Kel, this is Detective Lieutenant Rugelo, Rolla PD. He's the one I mentioned earlier."

"Hey." Kel nodded.

Rugelo nodded back and then re-engaged Deveroux. "Wasn't sure before, but now it appears that we're dealing with a probable homicide."

Kel and Deveroux exchanged a look. "What changed to make you think that, Lieutenant?" Deveroux asked.

"Hadn't talked to the fire marshal when I first called you. Now he tells me he doesn't think this was an accident. He's sure it wasn't, in fact." Small nods made it clear that he was referring to the fire, lest there be any misunderstanding.

"Arson?"

"You got it," Rugelo replied. "And if it wasn't an accident, then that means Mr. Thu's death probably wasn't an accident. Appears he was murdered."

Deveroux nodded. "How's he know it was arson?"

"Now, Agent Deveroux, that's the fire marshal's business, not mine. But as I understand it, the pattern of the fire, where it started and how it spread, all that indicates it was intentionally set. He also thinks he found some evidence of an accelerant. He'll run some tests later, but he's relatively sure right now. Coroner's boys are in there with him right now getting the body out. They say it's pretty burned up."

Kel waited for a pause and then spoke. "Probably none of my business, but maybe Ngo—or Mr. Thu—maybe he set the fire. Just 'cause it's arson doesn't make it murder."

"You a cop? Doctor . . ."

"McKelvey. No, sir. Forensic anthropologist."

Rugelo nodded slowly as if suddenly everything had come into focus for him. "I see. Well, Dr. McKelvey, no offense, but I suspect you're right about this not being your business. I'm just a poor small-town cop, but I don't think Mr. Thu is responsible for burning his self up."

"Why not?" Deveroux rejoined the conversation. At some level, he figured it was his business.

Rugelo pointed over to his left at what had once been a garage. "You know what that is, Agent Deveroux? How about you, Dr. McKelvey?"

"Looks like a garage. What's left of one," Deveroux replied.

"Correct," Rugelo said. "That's what we call around here a two-car garage. Now, what else do you see?"

Deveroux and Kel looked at each other and then at the garage. They looked at each other again and then back at Rugelo. Deveroux shrugged.

"Nothing?" Rugelo asked. "If that's your answer, then you're right. Nothing. As in no cars. See, the Thus owned two cars." He paused while he flipped a page in his notebook. "A blue 2006 Cadillac Seville and a white 2007 Lincoln Town Car. Both of which, as you have just observed, are missing."

"Mr. Ngo, I mean Thu, whatever we're callin' him this mornin', told me last night that his wife was visitin' friends up in St. Louis," Deveroux countered.

"One down," Rugelo said. "That leaves one car unaccounted for."

"Maybe it's in the shop," Kel volunteered.

"Maybe," Rugelo answered. He clearly didn't have any patience with Kel. "But you saw that couple I was talking to when you arrived? Nice folks. Live down there," he pointed to the right. "Couple doors up from the intersection. They've gotten interested in fitness recently. Walk around the block three, sometimes four nights a week. Nice folks. So nice in fact that when they saw a strange pickup truck with out-of-state plates on it parked across the street several nights in a row, they didn't think it was their place to report it. They took note of it, but they didn't report it."

"They get the tag number?" Deveroux asked.

"No. Not entirely anyway. The wife, now she remembers it as having an Indian shield with feathers on it. That'd make it an Oklahoma license. She also remembers it beginning E-T-T. Also thinks it might have been red."

"You run the plate?"

"Doing it now, but with only a partial, it'll take a while."

"Interestin'," Shuck Deveroux said with an affected air of finality. "Still doesn't mean it's a homicide. I mean, that still doesn't explain the missin' car."

"Oh, no?" Rugelo's temper began to flame up. "Really? And so just why were you visiting Mr. Thu last night, Agent Deveroux? What was the purpose of your visit? As I recall, you told me you were working on a serial homicide involving several of Mr. Thu's former acquaintances. Cut the bullshit, Deveroux. You're on my turf now, and I happen to have the burned body of a very important resident of this town on my hands, and that isn't doing much for my disposition. I don't give a flying dog fuck who you or Dr. Doolittle here are, but I want more answers and less evasion. You understanding me?"

"Fair enough," Deveroux responded. "I'll make you a deal, Detective Rugelo. I'll sit down with you and answer any questions you got, and in return, you let Doc McKelvey here take a look at Ngo's body." He turned to look at Kel. "That okay by you, cowboy?"

Kel nodded, careful not to rub the detective's patience any more raw than it already was.

"No. Wrong answer," Rugelo replied, "I'm dealing the cards here. Instead, how 'bout you tell me what I want to know because you were the last person to see Mr. Thu alive and because if you don't, I'll park my car sideways up your ass and open the doors? How 'bout that? You do that, and then maybe we can talk deals. And as to letting your doctor buddy here look at the body, that's not my business. In case you hadn't noticed, I'm standing in the street along with you three stooges. Why? Because until the fire marshal gives me a thumbs up, this is his scene, and until the coroner says so, nobody even goes close to the body. That's how it works in Rolla, Missouri, Agent Deveroux. This isn't a military installation; you have no jurisdiction here. And furthermore . . ." Rugelo was interrupted by his cell phone ringing. He took it out of his pocket and checked the number before answering. "Yeah, Lieutenant Rugelo. Yeah. Yeah," he plugged one ear with an index finger and turned away from Deveroux, hunching his shoulders as he spoke. He stepped away. "What? How long ago?"

Deveroux looked over at Kel only to see that he'd bailed out of what was taking on the appearance of an ass-chewing and had joined Fick in watching two heavyset men wearing rubber gloves carry a blue vinyl body bag out of the jagged opening that had once been the front door. The men stepped carefully, treading past smoking embers and chunks of fallen bricks and half-charred wooden beams, and struggled to lift the bag into the back of a white cargo van. Behind him, Deveroux could hear Rugelo saying, "Give me that again," and, "How do you know?"

"Since you've got everythin' here under control, I'm goin' to go see if I can make the acquaintance of the coroner," Kel turned his head and said to Deveroux. He put his hands in his pockets and started walking down what was left of the brick walkway toward a silver-haired man who a minute before had been giving directions to the men with the body bag. "I sure would like to take a look-see at the remains," he said over his shoulder.

"Good idea," Deveroux agreed. "Don't go too far, though. The way it's lookin', the general and I may need you to post bail for us."

He smiled and gave a sideward flip of his head to indicate his reference to Rugelo.

"Well, Agent Deveroux," Lieutenant Rugelo said, snapping his phone closed almost as if cued and walking back to where the men were standing. "Seems like one of us just got very lucky. This is now officially your case."

Kel stopped and turned back.

"My case? How so?" Deveroux asked Rugelo.

"We just found the mystery truck. The one that couple saw parked here."

"Where?"

Rugelo smiled without a trace of humor. "Right smack in the middle of Fort Wood. I believe that puts the ball back in your court."

"Fort Leonard Wood?" Deveroux's eyes met Kel's, and then refocused on Rugelo. "Y'all get a hit on the plate?"

"We did."

Deveroux waited for elaboration. When none came, he sighed. "How about a little help here, Detective? Now that I'm off your suspect list."

Rugelo worked the muscles in his jaw; then he looked again at the notation he'd made in his notebook. "It's registered to a Mr. Eddie Tenkiller of Onapa, Oklahoma."

CHAPTER 55

Fort Leonard Wood, Missouri
THURSDAY, APRIL 24, 2008

The speedometer cable screamed the whole way.

From what he'd been able to pry out of Detective Rugelo and what he'd gathered from talking to the provost marshal on Fort Wood, Deveroux had at least the basics of the situation understood by the time he arrived on the scene. Fick was with him, Kel having opted to accompany the coroner and the body to the morgue in hopes of picking up at least one puzzle piece.

Fort Leonard Wood was locked down tight when they arrived and they were forced to use the shoulder of the road and their horn to get past the almost mile-long line of waiting cars. When they finally reached the gate, Deveroux's CID badge and Fick's ID card, which indicated he was a general officer, proved effective, and the gate had swung open with much saluting and hardly any questions. They were headed for the new multimillion-dollar Army Reserve and National Guard Multipurpose Training Center under construction. The provost marshal had given him directions on the phone, and Fick once again knew his way around post, so they found it quickly. The situation, as it had been explained to Deveroux, was that the construction crew had shown up for work as usual, and found the gate to the chain-link fence surrounding the project site standing wide open. Not a big deal except for the person whose job it was to make sure it was locked down at night, but when the foreman attempted to open the multipurpose building, he found the door barricaded from inside with a thick sheet of plywood. When he finally finished cussing and tried forcing the door, someone inside fired two shots. No one was injured, but the mass confusion that had followed was predictable; every MP and would-be MP for a hundred square miles had descended on the location, all anxious for a piece of the most exciting thing to hit post in fifty years. And there were lots of MPs—Fort Wood being the home of the Military Police Training Center.

Deveroux knew he had found the right location when he saw the cars. Every official vehicle on post—cars, trucks, Humvees, hundreds, it seemed—was arrayed across the landscape with all the organization of a derailed circus train. People were milling about as well, coming and going and spinning in random circular patterns, working in and out between the cars, some being pulled along by big, muscular German shepherds, everyone laden with clanking guns and creaking leather and squawking radios, everyone yelling *Hooah* and *Sir, yes, sir.* All that seemed lacking was the cotton-candy hawkers. Deveroux pulled his truck over the curb and braked to a stop on a grassy field a hundred yards away from the outer ring of vehicles. He didn't wait for Fick but went sprinting toward the thickest clot of people.

"Halt," a young sergeant, replete in flak vest, Kevlar helmet, and M-16 rifle intercepted him with a challenge. Deveroux had been so focused that he hadn't seen where the soldier had come from. "This area is controlled access. You will turn your vehicle around and wait back there." He made a chopping motion with his right hand, fingers held out straight like a knife blade, toward the field where Deveroux had just parked.

In his blue jeans and old, white cotton shirt, Shuck Deveroux realized that the young guard probably assumed he was either one of the construction workers or a gawker. He slackened his stride slightly and held his badge up where the soldier could see it clearly. "Agent Deveroux. CID," he said. "I've got this scene."

"*Hooah.* Good to go, Chief," the soldier responded. He adjusted his rifle sling and made another chopping motion to indicate his approval to proceed.

Deveroux looked over his shoulder at the sergeant as he went past. "That man, the one that's comin' up behind me, that's General Fick. He's with me. Understand?"

"Roger that," the soldier replied.

Deveroux turned and ran backward a few steps. He had another question. "Who's got tactical command of this situation, son?"

"That'd be Captain Walters, Chief."

"Thanks," Deveroux responded as he turned. It took a couple of steps before the words caught up with him. He turned back to the young soldier. "Say again, Sergeant? Who?"

"Captain Walters."

"Aw, Jesus H. Christ," Deveroux muttered. He shook his head. "Jeeesus Holy Christ."

He was challenged two more times before he reached the nerve center of confusion. Both times he'd simply held his badge aloft and didn't even verbally respond. As he feared, Captain Walters, the former Lieutenant Walters, was in the thick of the knot of people, bawling out orders that even Deveroux, fresh on the scene, could tell were contradictory and wholly confusing. He slowed as he drew near, as much to regain his breath as to ease off the pressure on his knees, and tried to summon up as much military decorum as he could muster. *Jesus Christ,* he thought.

"Mornin', Captain Walters," he said politely as he shouldered through a ring of stand-arounds. "Looks like we got us a situation here."

Walters recognized the voice. As he turned, Deveroux saw him clearly for the first time. It had only been a month since they'd had their run-in at Fort Campbell, and in that time Walters had grown even fatter—if that was possible. He looked more like an overweight Boy Scout leader than a professional soldier, and Deveroux couldn't help but wonder what kind of connections he must have to not only stay in the army, but continue to get promoted in it. Surely it had absolutely no correlation to intelligence or talent.

"Warrant Officer Deveroux. Sightseeing?" Walters responded.

"If you don't mind, I have—as you so astutely observed—a situation here. Notice that I said *I* not *We*. I'm large and in charge, and this requires my attention. So, if you don't mind, please remove yourself from this AO—now." He started to turn his back and launch another round of misguided instructional missiles.

"Captain Walters—sir—with respect, sir, I'm afraid I do mind. I'm assumin' tactical control here—now. Effective immediately. This is my area of operations, and there's really no time to dick-dance today."

"I don't think so." Walters started toward Deveroux until his brain registered the mismatch in their physical sizes. Even with the protective mantle of his rank, Walters stopped and took a small step backward. "I shouldn't have to instruct you in—"

"Sir," Deveroux quickly interrupted, sensing that his patience was about to play out and that he might do something that both men would regret. "I can assure you that I need no instructions in anythin' from you. Now, sir, we can do this one of two ways. You can either step aside and perhaps learn somethin', or I can get on the phone to the provost marshal or the post commander and have you step aside. One way or the other . . ."

"One way or nothing," Walters responded angrily. "Here're the two options as I see them. You either get your hick ass off my crime scene, or I'll have you handcuffed to my bumper as a trophy. I've had about all—"

"Captain, I wouldn't advise either course of action," Paul Fick said as he pushed his way through the crowd of wide-eyed spectators.

"And who the hell are you?" Walters challenged. All he saw was a frail old man in civilian clothes.

"I'm Brigadier General Fick. Paul Fick. And if Chief Deveroux can't do it, I assure you that I certainly can make your life miserable."

Walters swallowed audibly and stood, eyes bouncing back and forth from Deveroux to Fick. He was preparing to make an ill-advised response when he was interrupted.

"Captain," a female soldier in full battle dress stepped forward. She rattled and clacked from all the belts and gear she had strapped on. She was holding a cell phone. "Sir, someone wishes to speak with you."

"Not now, Staff Sergeant," Walters responded. He eyes kept shifting from Deveroux to Fick.

"But sir . . . it's *him,* sir."

"Him?" Walters turned to challenge the young woman. Whether he was up to taking on a BG and his sidekick warrant officer, he hadn't decided, but Captain Walters was clearly up to the task of chewing up a female staff sergeant. "You have a hearing problem, Staff Sergeant? I'm busy. Who is it?"

"*Him,* sir. The suspect. In the building," she replied.

Walters's eyes narrowed. He looked at the building and then back at the staff sergeant. "He's not a suspect. We know he's in there, we don't suspect he's in there. Whoever *he* is, *he's* a perpetrator."

"Yes, sir," the young staff sergeant patiently acknowledged the semantic lesson. "Well, sir, the *perpetrator* wants to talk to whoever's in charge."

Walters started to reach for the phone but Deveroux grabbed it first. "Goddammit Walters, we don't have time for this," Deveroux snapped. Even amid the adrenaline buzz of the moment, he realized that he'd cussed for the first time that he could remember in his adult life. Despite the shock, it felt good. "And remember to spell insubordination correctly in your report." He kept eye contact with Walters as he held the phone up to his ear and paused, trying to modulate his voice, trying to resurrect a veneer of calm. "This is Agent Deveroux, army CID, to whom am I speakin'?"

"Army CID?" said the voice. "Well, I guess I should feel honored. The Pros from Dover. From what I was watching, I assumed that it was a little more unorganized. Looks like an anthill out there; all the little ants crawling around. Are you a worker ant, or the queen, or maybe just a drone, Agent . . . what was it again?"

"Deveroux."

"Agent Deveroux. You a Cajun boy, Agent Deveroux?"

"I'm whatever you need me to be, Mr. . . . ." Deveroux's inflection asked a question.

"What I need, Agent Deveroux, is for you to answer my question. What kind of ant am I speaking to? You a worker? A queen? Or are you just a drone? Or is that only with bees?"

"I'm the queen," Deveroux responded. "At least for the day. We can talk. Now, sir, I believe I've answered two of your questions, how 'bout you answerin' one of mine? Who are you?"

"How about not."

"Your choice. You're the one that called. Why'd you call if you don't want to talk? How'd you know where to call?"

"More questions, Agent Deveroux? All right, I'll answer these. I do want to talk, and as to knowing where, I simply called the post operator and asked to be patched through to the fat-assed officer laying siege to the Alamo. They seemed to know who I was referring to right away, although I'm guessing that you're not him. He didn't seem like CID from what I could see of him. More like a chubby park ranger. Not sure what the army's coming to these days. Are you?"

Deveroux looked around at the reference to Walters, trying to spot him among the green suits, but the fat little MP had disappeared to lick his embarrassment in private. "Despite our agreement on that evaluation, you still haven't told me why you called, or what you want."

"But I did tell you," the voice replied. "I want to talk."

"That's fine. You got somethin' to talk about?"

The voice chuckled. "Maybe I'm just lonely. My friend in here isn't talking much, and it looks like a county fair out there; thought I'd get in on some of the fun."

"You have someone with you?" Deveroux looked around for Walters, wanting confirmation that there might be a second suspect or, even worse, a hostage.

"So, are we going to talk?"

Deveroux craned his body to look over the vehicles and people at the barricaded front door of the multipurpose building. He thought of his conversation with Kel. He took a chance. "Let's cut to the chase, shall we? At the risk of soundin' like a bad movie, we've got the place surrounded . . . you can't get out . . . Jimmy."

There was a silence on the other end of the phone, and Deveroux worried that the voice had hung up. Finally he heard a reply. "And just what did you call me, Agent Deveroux?"

"Jimmy," Deveroux answered. He scanned the front of the building looking for any sign of movement at the windows. "That's your name, isn't it? You are Jimmy Tenkiller, aren't you?"

There was another long silence.

"You best come in," the voice said quietly. "I do believe we need to talk."

CHAPTER 56

Rolla, Missouri
THURSDAY, APRIL 24, 2008

Kel was standing in the front yard of Ngo Van Thu's house, talking to the Phelps County coroner, when Deveroux and General Fick went screaming down the quiet tree-lined road headed for Fort Wood, a Rolla PD cruiser, its lights on, leading the way.

"Somebody's in a mighty big hurry," Gary Hoey said. His smile was hidden by a brushy white mustache that matched his equally brushy and equally white head of hair. He was wearing a light-blue sport coat and a red-and-blue-striped tie and seemed tidy and proper in a manner wholly out of place amid the burned-out tumble and rubble that had been Ngo's home.

"Yes, sir," Kel answered. "Sure seems to be. I guess they got a lead on who's responsible for all this." He stopped and used a nod to indicate the shell behind them. "Hope it pans out."

"You and me both, Dr. McKelvey. This is Phelps County, Missouri; we don't get too many homicides like this—if that's what it turns out to be. Mr. Thu, I think you called him Ngo, is that right? Mr. Thu was a prominent citizen around this town. Involved in lots of things. His construction company employs a whole slew of people. He's got a couple of multimillion-dollar jobs going on right now, in fact. Just finished a big FEMA contract to build some trailer parks down in

New Orleans; got another big contract down at Fort Leonard Wood; another for the university over in Rolla; even has some bids for work in Iraq. Yes, sir, I'll be tickled to no end if we can wrap this one up quickly and quietly. I know old Lieutenant Rugelo, over there; he'll be just as glad."

"I can imagine," Kel replied. "Speakin' of which, when do you think you'll do the autopsy on this case? Any chance you'll do it today?"

Gary Hoey blinked several times in thought. He was a small man, and he had to look up at Kel when he responded. "Mind me asking why you care?"

Kel shrugged.

Hoey seemed to accept that response. "Ordinarily we'd do it tomorrow morning. I'm a coroner, not a medical examiner; I don't do the autopsies, you see. Sign 'em, but don't do 'em. We have a pathologist from the hospital who comes over and does them on contract to the county. He likes to work in the mornings, but in this case . . . well, I just know that we'll be under a lot of pressure on this one given who's dead and all. Especially once the fire marshal releases his findings. I'm thinking we'll try and do it this evening, if I can get hold of the doctor."

Kel nodded. He kicked at a couple of blackened brick cobbles and tried to sound nonchalant. "I know this is a touchy case for y'all, but, ummm, you suppose there's any chance we might take a look at the remains before then—you and me?"

Hoey shook his head. "I don't know . . ."

Kel responded quickly. "All noninvasive, you understand? No cuttin'. Nothin' that will interfere with your pathologist. Just a look-see, is all."

Hoey blinked again, in a manner that seemed to indicate that he was processing some information. "Perhaps if you could explain your interest. I'm still not clear on how you think this case relates to what you and your friends are interested in."

"Not sure that it does, Mr. Hoey," Kel replied, "but I tell you what, if it does end up bein' connected, your headache meter is going to peg slam out. That's a fact, and the way I look at it, the sooner we know if there's a connection, the sooner we'll know if we need to take some aspirin."

"I still don't understand, Dr. McKelvey, I don't. How are you going to know if this is connected to your case?"

Kel paused. "Let's just say that the other cases had a common thread. A rather distinctive common thread."

Hoey shook his head and smiled. He looked up at Kel. "Can't say that explains much, but one thing I do understand is that aspirin upset my stomach. Why don't we go to my office."

CHAPTER 57

Rolla, Missouri
THURSDAY, APRIL 24, 2008

The Phelps County coroner, like the one in Johnson County, operated the more stomach-churning aspects of the business out of a private funeral home.

Hoey's staff, understanding as well as their boss the outside interest that the death of Mr. Ngo Van Thu would inevitably generate in the community, had efficiently logged the case in, anxious to make sure there were no slip-ups or reasons to point fingers. By the time Hoey and Kel arrived at the Elysian Gate Funeral Home, Case PC08-0042 was already tagged, rebagged, and collecting a beaded film of condensation in the reefer.

Gary Hoey was slow and pragmatic, a licensed funeral director wise in the practiced arts of comforting anguished survivors; he did nothing quickly or without proper deliberation. For Kel, practiced in the arts of chaos management and anxious to see the charred remains of Ngo, it seemed as if the transit from the front door to the embalming room was taking longer than had the drive from the murder scene. Hoey had stopped to talk to his office manager, stopped to check his mail, stopped to adjust the thermostat in the hallway, stopped to rearrange a vase of flowers in the entryway, stopped and ensured that Kel had met and shaken hands with everyone in the building, before leading the way to the white-tiled embalming room.

Two of Hoey's employees were lifting the body bag containing Ngo's remains onto a stainless-steel embalming table when they walked in. After proper introductions and additional handshaking, one of the employees unzipped the bag and exposed the greasy, blackened remains. The smell of cooked meat and swollen viscera filled the room. No one flinched, all of them having seen, and smelled, much worse.

Kel recognized the pattern immediately. Tongue swollen and protruding grotesquely as if mocking the living, arms drawn up in supplication or readiness for a fight—the result of the large muscles in the arms contracting in the heat, the brain case cracked and oozing soft, yellowish brain and cooked fat. Kel hadn't dealt with many arson cases, but he'd seen enough victims of aircraft crashes to know the pattern of death by fire.

"Remember now, Doctor, I can't let you alter anything before the autopsy. Just look, please." Hoey was walking around the table, bent over, hands behind his back, closely looking at the remains as he spoke.

"Right, that's all I'm fixin' to do," Kel answered. He too was circling the table, bent at the waist, looking closely at the remains. "Y'all got some gloves I could borrow?"

"Prep or exam?" one of Hoey's employees asked. They were both standing off to the side, hands in pockets, watching their boss and his visitor circling the body bag on the table like two wary wrestlers.

"Exam will work. But whatever you got."

The man produced a box that looked as if it should hold tissues but instead was crammed full of purple nitrile rubber gloves.

Kel rolled his sleeves back another full turn and snapped out two gloves from the box and wiggled them on. He looked over and saw that Hoey was picking away at charred tissue with his bare hands. Kel smiled as he bent over the head, gently wedging the tips of his fingers between the engorged tongue and the upper front teeth. "Shovel-shaped incisors," he said, to anyone who was interested, referring to the cupping he could feel on the tongue side of the two central

front teeth. "Typical mongoloid trait. Skull's nice and round, too."
He stood up and looked at the head from arm's length. "Malars—the
cheek bones—are very prominent. Nose is wide. Everythin' consistent
with an adult mongoloid male. Don't see any obvious trauma, though,
but given all this charred tissue and the way the skull's cracked open
from the heat, that may not be sayin' much. I'll be interested in what
your pathologist says." He waited until Hoey looked up and made
eye contact. "If you could, you might have him look real close at
the frontal bone, couple, three centimeters anterior to bregma, right
around here," he said, using a finger to make a circular movement at
the crest of the forehead. "Looks like a small-caliber gunshot wound.
Can't really tell without gettin' some of this charred tissue out of the
way and gluin' the fragments back together."

Hoey nodded and blinked but didn't feel compelled to ask any
questions.

Kel began working his way down the body. He looked closely at
the throat, but saw nothing amid the charred and weeping tissue.
Likewise the chest wall. He was preparing to examine the abdomen,
which had ruptured in the intense heat and spilled out the soft, colorful
viscera, but Hoey was bent over it closely, blinking rapidly, probably
calculating the best way to handle the embalming. Instead of crowding
in, Kel moved to the foot end, stripped off his gloves, and crossed
his arms while he thought. He looked at the broad cheekbones now
blackened and burned to the consistency of greasy charcoal and the
arms and legs, constricted by the shrinking muscle to the point where
the bones had snapped. *Guy was well muscled,* he thought. And that's
when it hit him. Quickly Kel reached out and grabbed the feet.

Hoey straightened up. "Now, wait there, Mr. McKelvey. You were
just going to look—"

Kel ignored him. He looked around for the box of gloves, but
seeing none dove into the burned tissue with his bare hands. The body
had been wearing athletic shoes and the synthetic material had melted
and globbed and stuck to the bone and tissue. Kel tapped a blob of
melted plastic on the right foot, listening to the hard sound it made.
"Shit, shit, shit."

"Mr. McKelvey, I don't think—"

Kel tapped the shoe again, harder, and the blob of plastic fell away taking a mass of charred muscle with it, exposing the clean, buttery yellow bone underneath.

Kel stared at what he saw.

Hoey noticed the change in Kel's body language and looked down at the source of interest. "Why, I'll be," he said as he moved closer. "Will you look at that? That should make the identification part of this case all the easier. Don't know that I've ever seen one quite like that. How about you, Doctor? You ever seen anything quite like that before?"

Kel stared.

"Doctor?" Hoey repeated.

"You have a car?" Kel asked.

"What?" Hoey responded. "Yes, of course. Why? Is that something important?"

"Yeah," Kel answered. "Very."

CHAPTER 58

Fort Leonard Wood, Missouri
THURSDAY, APRIL 24, 2008

"This is the last thing I need to be doin'. Last thing. I've got a wife and kids and a big old stupid dog—they all need me—at least the dog does," Shuck Deveroux muttered, almost to himself. As he handed his cell phone over to Fick for safekeeping, he said, "You're a general, why don't you order me to not do this?"

Paul Fick had been standing by watching, quietly; now he responded. "I'm retired, remember, Chief? Besides, you wouldn't listen to me if I did anyhow."

"Try me, General."

Fick smiled. "In that case, stand down, Chief Deveroux. I'm ordering you to stay here."

Now it was Deveroux's turn to smile. He shot a quick look at the barricaded door of the multipurpose building and then back at Fick. "No offense, sir, but you're retired." He took a couple of deep breaths and then said, "General, do me a favor." He waited for a slight nod of agreement and then dropped the volume of his voice. "Keep these boys here from doin' somethin' stupid while I'm in there. Especially that chucklehead Captain Walters. Don't know where he slithered off to, but if he comes back here, distract him somehow. Ask him to recite the multiplication table or somethin'—especially the times twelves . . ."

Deveroux's cell phone interrupted by playing the "Chicken Dance" song. Fick looked at it oddly and handed it back to Deveroux, who hesitated, unsure whether to take it. He didn't recognize the number showing on the screen.

"Agent Deveroux," he finally answered. "Make it quick."

"Shuck, it's me, Kel. Listen, partner . . ."

"Not now, Doc. Not now. This is really, really a bad time. I'll call you back in a bit—I hope."

"No, Shuck, wait. I'm on my way there. Listen, it's *Tenkiller.* You hear me, bubba? It's Tenkiller."

"I know," Deveroux replied. "He's got himself boarded up in an empty buildin' here at Fort Wood. Maybe has a hostage. I'm gettin' fixed to go in to try and talk to him. I'll call you—"

"No," Kel almost screamed into the phone. "I mean it's Tenkiller. Here. The body from the house, the one that's all burned up. It's him. Tenkiller."

"What? What're you sayin'? Tenkiller? How do you know?" Deveroux looked again at the building and then back at Fick. The old general's face suggested he could overhear Kel's part of the conversation leaking past Deveroux's ear.

"Screws. His ankle, it looks like a goddamn hardware store. He's got screws in his ankle."

"But . . ."

"But nothin'," Kel said. "I've seen Tenkiller's file. It's him."

"You sure?"

"Positive."

"Then who's boarded up here?" Deveroux asked.

"Got me, Shuck, but it sure ain't Tenkiller."

Fick, seeing the question in Deveroux's face, shrugged a response.

"Thanks, Kel." Deveroux paused and took a deep breath. "Guess there's only one good way to find out."

"No. Wait," Kel shouted into the phone. "Don't do anythin' till I get there."

Shuck Deveroux wasn't listening. He had his eyes on the boarded-up door. "I'll call you as soon as I can. Deveroux out," he said, almost absentmindedly, as he snapped the phone shut and handed it back to Fick. He swallowed hard.

Fick shook his head slowly, indicating that it was okay for Shuck to not go.

"Remember, General," Deveroux said, "nobody, and I mean nobody, does nothin' stupid."

"Roger, Chief, nothing stupid."

Shuck Deveroux patted himself down again as if he were getting ready to walk through an airport metal detector. It provided an excuse to stall a moment longer. "Did I say my old dog needs me?"

"You did," Fick responded. "You don't have to do this, Chief."

Deveroux smiled wanly. "Maybe not, but . . . this guy's killed at least four people. And he may have a hostage in there right now. Maybe Ngo. There isn't a trained negotiator within two hours of here." He paused and smiled again. "Remember now . . ."

"Nothing stupid," Fick finished the thought.

CHAPTER 59

Fort Leonard Wood, Missouri
THURSDAY, APRIL 24, 2008

Deveroux walked out from behind the Humvee that they'd been using as a shield and slowly made his way across the open asphalt to the front door of the multipurpose building. It was a long walk, at least seemingly so, and he kept his hands slightly raised to his sides, not assuming the posture of a prisoner, but clearing advertising the fact that he was unarmed and nonhostile. He had to assume he was being watched.

The sheet of half-inch plywood that had barricaded the door earlier in the morning was now partly ajar, fastened to the inside of the doorframe only on one side with a couple of sixteen-penny nails. Deveroux paused and examined the wood, noting the splintered margins of two bullet holes about shoulder height. As he poked his head around the edge of the plywood sheet, he called out, "It's Warrant Officer Deveroux. I'm alone. Unarmed. Hello?" He waited and listened. Nothing. "I'm comin' on in. Just me. Alone. Unarmed. We talked. Unarmed."

He pushed on into the building. It was dark. It smelled of pooled rainwater and drying latex paint. He was in an open, three-story atrium with plenty of windows, but most were either boarded over or covered with protective sheets of foggy, thick plastic film, and stepping in from the bright sunlight, Deveroux's eyes shut down. Signs of construction were everywhere, spools of cable, metal scaffolding, paint cans, crushed soft drink cans, and crumpled sandwich wrappers.

Deveroux stood in the middle of the atrium, rotating in a slow circle, hands still outstretched. "It's Warrant Officer Deveroux. The one you talked to. I'm here. You said we should talk. I'm here. Unarmed. To talk. I'm here."

"So you are, Agent Deveroux," said a voice from somewhere off to the side.

Deveroux looked but could see only bands of shadow and tangles of wire near an elaborate tubular scaffold that rose thirty feet to the glass skylight. "Yes, sir. Here I am, and here you are. You wanted to talk."

"I did, didn't I?"

"Yes, sir, you did."

"What would you like to talk about, Agent Deveroux?"

"Your call. Anythin' you want. We can start by you tellin' me who you are." He squinted, trying to pattern the form from the shadow. His sight was slow to return, and he turned his head slightly to the side to enhance his vision in the dimness.

"I'm Jimmy Tenkiller, remember?"

Deveroux hesitated while he tried to work out the next several moves. Finally he spoke. "No, sir. I don't think you are."

"Now that's interesting. If you don't mind my asking, what happened in the last ten minutes that changed your mind?"

"Maybe the fact that we've just identified the body from Mr. Ngo's house as that of Tenkiller."

"Interesting. That's really very interesting. In that case, me being Jimmy Tenkiller would be a bit problematic, right, Agent Deveroux?"

"Yes, sir. That's the way I see it. Very problematic."

The shadow laughed. "Po' Jimmy. Po' Master Sergeant Tenkiller. He was quite a runner in his day, did you know that Agent Deveroux? Quite a runner. The Running Redskin, they called him. That was back when you could say that sort of thing and nobody got upset. Political Correctness, and all. The Running Redskin."

Deveroux had turned and was facing the shadow square on. His vision was slowly returning. He dropped his hands to his sides. "You wanted to talk, so why don't we shift topics. You know who I am, now how 'bout tellin' me who I'm talkin' with? Only fair."

"No, Agent Deveroux," the shadow replied. "We can start with you telling me what your interest in Tenkiller is. Or should I say, was? I'm curious how much you know, or at least think you know."

Deveroux took a step toward the shadow.

A gun cocked. "I'd stay put if I were you, Agent Deveroux," the voice said.

CHAPTER 60

Fort Leonard Wood, Missouri
THURSDAY, APRIL 24, 2008

Kel was forced to leave Mr. Hoey's car several blocks away, behind a barricade. In the distance, less than two hundred yards away, he could see a mill of people around several Humvees and military police cars. Lights were flashing and there was constant movement of men in full battle array. He took off running, flashing his CILHI badge and shouting officiously at any of the guards who challenged him, careful not to stop or even slacken his stride. As he neared the crowd, he scanned the faces for Deveroux but saw General Fick instead and made a path to him.

"Thank God, General. Where's Chief Deveroux?" he asked Fick as he muscled into the knot of people. Many had taken up positions behind vehicles, their weapons pointed at the opening of a building directly ahead; others were talking into radios and cell phones and pointing in different directions. Several young soldiers took notice of him but no one made a move to stop him.

Fick nodded to the building, his eyes focused on the boarded-up doorway.

"Shit," Kel said. "Crazy bastard. I told him to stay put until I got here. Please tell me he's not alone."

Fick didn't answer.

"Shit. Who's in charge here?" Kel scanned the faces around him. "General?"

"Chief Deveroux," Fick replied quietly.

"Shit. Who's second? There's got to be a second."

"I was asked to make sure no one did anything stupid."

"No offense, but then you should have stopped Deveroux. We need to talk, General. That was Tenkiller back there in Rolla. And he wasn't just burnt to a crisp—someone killed him before they set the place on fire. Shot the sonofabitch right here." He tapped the middle of his forehead. "And my guess is that that someone is in there with Deveroux right now. And that someone's got absolutely nothin' to lose."

"My guess, Dr. McKelvey, is that you're correct," Fick said.

"Yes, sir. So what are we goin' to do?"

"I have no real authority here, Dr. McKelvey." Fick kept his eyes on the front of the building.

"This is no time to be modest, General. You're Paul Fick. Even civilians have heard about you. You could order the sun to stand still. What are we goin' to do? We gotta do somethin'."

"You have a weapon, Doctor?"

"A wea—? Of course not. I'm a goddamn anthropologist."

Fick looked directly into Kel's eyes. "Then the question is what am I going to do about it?"

CHAPTER 61

Fort Leonard Wood, Missouri
THURSDAY, APRIL 24, 2008

"Who are you?" Deveroux asked.

The man stepped out of the shadows; he was smiling. "You never know, I just might be a dangerous man, but in any case, I asked you a question: What's your interest in our boy, Jimmy Tenkiller?"

"Tenkiller's wanted."

"Is he, now? By whom?"

"The army," Shuck responded. He'd taken some control of his knees, but the shake had moved into his hands.

The man laughed. "Now that's interesting, considering that Mr. Tenkiller's dead."

"So I hear. You kill him?"

"Me? No, sir. Now as I understand it, he was KIA in Vietnam. Isn't that the army's position, Agent Deveroux? K-I-A."

"Who are you?" Deveroux asked again.

"His name is John Bergeron, and he lives in the shadows," Paul Fick said.

Deveroux stiffened at the sound of Fick's voice. Out of the corner of his eye, he saw the old general standing just inside the doorway, squinting into the shadows, legs bent and spread, his left hand steadying the butt of a nickel-plated pistol. It looked to be a .45

semiautomatic service piece. He'd had no idea that Fick had snuck in, or when, or that he was armed, but he was glad for the arrival of the cavalry, even if it took the form of a civilian whose only authority was what was seated in his right hand.

He looked back at the shadowy form Fick had called John Bergeron, his eyes drawn magnetically to the black Glock nine-millimeter that had been pointed in his direction but was now aimed at Fick.

"Well, well. If I'm not mistaken, that would be Captain Fick of the Royal Canadian Mounted Police. Always get your man, right, Mountie Fick?" Bergeron's voice suggested he was enjoying the whole situation much more than could be considered prudent under the circumstances. He was either very much in control or very much not. "You're not looking so good, ol' boy. The years they haven't been kind to you."

"Y'all know each other, General?" Deveroux was still scared witless, but the idea that Fick hadn't been completely forthcoming with him was raising his pissed-off quotient to record levels. Had he not been the only one in the room unarmed, he'd have made his point more forcefully.

"General?" Bergeron's voice carried genuine surprise. "Congratulations, Fick. Really. My heartfelt congratulations. I don' remember getting an invitation to any promotion parties; I guess that'll teach me to leave a better forwarding address." Bergeron shifted his eyes but not his body or the gun. He looked at Deveroux. "Now, in answer to your question, Agent Deveroux, no, I can't say that the captain—the *general*—pardon me—and I have ever formally met. But when a man spends a couple of months sniffing on your trail the way Mountie Fick did some forty years ago, you get to where you feel like you're family. Isn't that right, Captain?" He shifted his full attention back to Fick. "We're almost family—you, me, Tenkiller . . . almost like . . . what would you call us? Brothers? I like that—we're almost a Brotherhood, you might say."

"In case you haven't checked the scorecard recently, Bergeron, your family seems to be on the verge of extinction," Fick replied. "First Colonel Pham, then Major Doan, Colonel Trinh, Major Linh—now Tenkiller. Being a member of your fraternity seems to come at quite an admission price."

"You forgetting someone, Captain? Seems like there's someone missing from your roll call."

Fick tightened his grip on his pistol. Bergeron did likewise.

"Now calm down there, cowboy," Deveroux responded quickly, trying to dilute the tension. He managed to put more calm into his voice than he really felt. "Mr. Bergeron, where's General Ngo? Is he here with you? Is he here?"

Bergeron smiled at Deveroux's contorted pronunciation, but he kept his eyes and gun on Fick. "General *En-go* is inspecting the building. The burden of management—having to check up on your workers all the time. I guess it's worth it, though, they tell me he's raking in millions off this construction contract. He always did like working for Uncle Sam."

Deveroux looked toward an open doorway on his right and then back at Bergeron. The heavyset man's eyes betrayed affirmation.

"Now let's just stay calm," Deveroux repeated as he slowly sidestepped to the open doorway. He kept his eyes on Bergeron until his right shoulder touched the doorjamb. "Holy Christ," he said as he peered around the wall into the adjoining room. There, amid the coils of electrical wire and empty, white-plastic buckets of latex paint was the curled body of General Ngo Van Thu. Even in the dim light and from ten feet away, Deveroux could see that he was dead; there was a gunshot entry wound to the left temple and a large creeping Rorschach blot of blood on the concrete.

Deveroux closed his eyes and sighed, letting his head rest on the doorframe momentarily, knowing that the prospect of negotiating a marketable solution to the problem at hand had just gotten harder.

He filled his lungs with air and turned back to see a smiling John Bergeron. A flick of his eyes to the side established that General Fick was still coiled tightly.

"Why, Mr. Bergeron? Why'd you do it?" Deveroux asked.

"Do it?"

"Yes, sir. Why? Why'd you kill them. Tenkiller, Ngo, all them others. You killed them all, didn't you? Why?"

Bergeron narrowed his eyes and seemed to be seriously considering the question. "Now, you just might be jumping to the wrong conclusion there. Doesn't pay for a special agent to jump to conclusions. No, sir. Didn't they teach you that in special agent school? Ask General Fick here. He was a special agent once. Most special. No, if you want to know who killed Master Sergeant Tenkiller, you'll have to go ask the man sleeping in there."

"Ngo?"

"None other."

"But . . ."

"But why?" Bergeron asked. He shook his head as he spoke but he kept the gun on Fick. "Who can figure those inscrutible yellow bastards, right? You know, I always liked Jimmy. I recruited him. You know that? Not for the army, of course, he got himself into that, but I signed him up for a little operation that I had going on the side. Good kid. Not very bright, but likable in an odd way. The Running Redskin. Ngo on the other hand, now he's a—guess I should say *was,* given his recent induction into the past tense society—that man, he was a real shitbag. Smart, but a real shitbag."

Bergeron took a deep breath, as if he were preparing to tell a long story. "Truth is, Tenkiller went and got spooked. After all these years, he went and got himself spooked." Bergeron smiled. "Maybe I had something to do with that. I paid his brother a visit a while back, up there in Oklahoma. You know what's so ironic? I actually wanted to warn Jimmy—I did. I always liked him, like I said. I wanted to warn him that someone seemed intent upon settling up some old scores. I wasn't positive who, but I had my suspicions, and me, I figured there was a real good chance that Jimmy was on Ngo's dancecard. Me too, for that matter. Jimmy now, he wasn't the smartest redstick in the tipi, no, but he could add two plus two, and when he did, he got five. He came to the same conclusion I did—the Fifth Brother—General Ngo Van Thu." He paused to assess the situation in the room.

Fick seemed intent upon listening to Bergeron talk.

"So, our boy Jimmy gets himself spooked, and when Jimmy got spooked, he did what he always did—he ran. The Running Redskin. But in this case, he ran straight to the home of the big ol' Billy Goat Gruff. I don't think he intended to hurt Ngo, maybe thought he could just scare him off. Don't know. What I do know is that Jimmy was no match for Ngo one on one; few men were. That sonofabitch was some serious bad news. Always was. So it's not surprising that when Jimmy shows up last night at Ngo's with a damn can-plinker .22 and starts to wave it around, that he's the one who ends up dead."

"You're saying Ngo did it," Fick entered the conversation.

"Why yes, General Fick, I am. Don't tell me you're surprised, you? You of all people shouldn't be."

"Then how'd you get involved?" Fick asked.

"Another good question. I'd been watching Ngo's house. I didn't trust him any more than Jimmy did. Or you did, General, for that matter." Bergeron smiled as he shrugged. "So there I was, sitting and watching, and who to my wondering eyes should appear but Chief Tenkiller. I followed him into the house. Watched the whole thing unfold."

"Then why didn't you stop Ngo?" Deveroux asked. "You said you liked Tenkiller. You try to stop him?"

Bergeron smiled. "Hmmm. Well, for one thing, it happened too fast, and for another thing—well, let's just say that while I liked Tenkiller, I really did, I liked him, but let's just say that he also had the potential to be a major embarrassment. And, after all, who was going to miss him? He was already dead—isn't that right, General Fick? KIA. In fact, if I'm not mistaken, I think you signed the death certificate, didn't you?'

There was a thin squeak as Fick tightened his grip on his pistol. His interest in what Bergeron had to say was about exhausted.

"If that's the case, why'd Ngo burn up his own house? And why'd he come here with you?" Deveroux asked quickly in an effort to regain control of the situation. He wanted to keep Bergeron talking and distracted.

"Who said he did?" Bergeron smiled again. He too had tightened his grip. His skin, too, squeaked against the pistol's handle. "I get to claim credit for the housewarming. When I showed up—properly armed, I might add," he wiggled the Glock slightly to illustrate his point, "Ngo saw the logic of entering into a one-time limited partnership, you might say. He was always a shrewd businessman, I must give him that. Neither one of us particularly wanted some of our youthful indiscretions coming to light, you see, and Tenkiller's death—while presenting a slight logistical problem—was probably for the best. The problem was that we had a body to get rid of, and with the two of you having just been poking around Ngo's house, it seemed best if the body was not found anywhere close by. Ngo thought of this building. They're set to pour a cement slab out to the side later this morning, and he proposed that the two of us bury poor Jimmy in the sand foundation. If everything had gone as planned, by this afternoon there wouldn't have been a trace."

"Of either one of them," Deveroux added. "You intended to get rid of Ngo as well."

Bergeron actually laughed. "You ought to be a CID agent, you."

"Thanks. I'll talk to the army recruiter at school. But what about the house? Why'd you torch it?"

"Think about it." Bergeron looked intensely at Deveroux. "Think it through, special agent. Tenkiller's fingerprints, my fingerprints. I have to thank Jimmy for the idea really. He'd brought a couple of gas cans with him. Like I said, I don't know if he really intended to hurt Ngo, but he sure as hell intended to take away his nice house, his fancy belongings, his clothes—all the things that Jimmy had had to forgo in his life as a hermit. So Jimmy gets a point and a half for the idea, but I'm the one who put it in motion. That was always my specialty. I'm an operations-type guy."

"But why'd Ngo agree to it? You said this was a partnership. Why would he agree to let you burn his house up?" Deveroux kept up the conversation.

"He didn't," Bergeron replied. He seemed surprised, and disappointed, that Deveroux's comprehension was lagging so far behind. "I convinced Ngo to come on in here ahead of me and start digging the requisite hole in the sand; I couldn't get in here without attracting attention, but the big boss man could. I had him bring Jimmy's truck. I said I'd clean up the mess at the house and bring the body in as soon as he had the hole dug. With Ngo's car and its military window sticker, I could get past the guard easier. Plus, by him coming on ahead, we weren't sitting around on a military post with a dead body in the trunk for any longer than we had to. He agreed."

"And as soon as he drove off . . ."

Bergeron laughed again. "You got it. I torched the house. This is Rolla, Missouri, Agent Deveroux. I figured there was a real good chance that they'd misidentify Jimmy boy as Ngo, and once I buried the real Ngo—here in the cement—the case would be closed. On the other hand, if they got lucky and did identify po' ol' Jimmy, then they'd start a manhunt for Ngo, who, mysteriously enough, would have disappeared. Either way, no one would be looking for me, and there'd be no more loose lips sinking anybody's ships." He paused and drew his mouth into a humorless smile. "But now things have gotten very complicated—haven't they, General?" Bergeron's almost giddy enjoyment at relating the events of the last twelve hours suddenly ebbed, and his whole demeanor became tense. With a jerk he readjusted the aim of his pistol at Fick's head.

"Whoa, cowboy," Deveroux said quickly. "Whoa, whoa, whoa. There is no reason in God's green earth for this thing to spiral out of control." He had both hands up, palms forward, fingers spread as if he could will a sense of calm. "This just is gettin' way too serious to be doin' anyone any good."

"Perhaps you should tell him," Bergeron said, a quick nod in Fick's direction.

Deveroux bounced a quick look over his shoulder at Fick and then returned his attention to the man in front of him. "This has got bad time stenciled all over it. Ain't nothin' good goin' come out of y'all wavin' all these guns about." He put a wide smile on his face and bent his knees, putting himself into a semicrouch. "Ain't nothin' good at all."

"I doubt much good is going to come out of this no matter what," Bergeron said. His head motioned to the adjoining room and the curled-up body of Ngo Van Thu.

"You may be right, but I tell you what, good is a relative thing. There's good, and then there's good; and this here ain't good. There's two of us and only one of you."

"True, but at the risk of stating the obvious, Deputy Fife, you seem to be somewhat empty-handed at the moment. While I, on the other hand . . ."

Deveroux smiled. It was obvious, and it wasn't a fact that he needed reminding of. "Well, that's right, that's right, but as I see this, this is goin' to play out one of two ways. Now, you shoot me, and the general here drills a good-size hole in your head. And believe me, he'll do it. He's not much on foolishness, and right about now I suspect he thinks both of us are pretty danged foolish. That's one option, and it ain't so good for either you or me." Bergeron seemed to be listening. "But, on the other hand, I'm a mite bigger than you. That's a fact. You shoot the general, and I'll be all over you before your brass even hits the floor. Good for me, but not so good for either you or the general." He arched both eyebrows.

"Decisions, decisions." Bergeron smiled. "This is like the fox, the duck, and the bushel of grain. Quite a puzzle here."

"Maybe, but the way I figure it, either way ends up bein' a bad end to your day."

"So you say. I guess I really have to pick the lesser of my two devils, then. Yes, you might be bigger than me, that seems to be true, but then, no offense, I watched you walk across the parking lot, you. You limp like my old grandmother. I'm banking on your old knees slowing you down long enough to at least make it interesting." Bergeron raised his arms slightly, locking his elbows. He sighted down the barrel at Fick, but his eyes kept flicking in Deveroux's direction.

"Whoa, whoa, time-out there." Deveroux took a quick step forward while using one hand to dampen Fick's response. "Let's think this one through some more. There's another option here."

"Do tell, Agent Deveroux."

"We can all calm down and put all these dang guns down; that's what we can do. I hate them things."

"I'd probably feel the same way if I was standing in your shoes, empty-handed, but right now I get a certain sense of satisfaction from the feel of this one."

"I hear ya, Mr. Bergeron, believe me, I hear you. Loud and clear. But let's everybody just sit tight and work out some sort of solution we can all live with. Okay?"

"How about him?" Bergeron asked. "I'm looking at his eyes,

you're not. I suspect General Fick wants to dampen my afternoon, regardless of what you want. Don't you, General?"

Deveroux could tell that the general's left hand was tightening around the butt of the pistol grip, he could hear it, and he realized that Fick had trouble holding the gun steady with only the three fingers of his right hand. He looked back at Bergeron.

"Aw, shucks. You know how generals are. Their eyes always look that a'way. Comes with the stars. But General Fick, here, he'll put his gun down if you do—right, General?" He turned his head in Fick's direction but kept his eyes on Bergeron. "He'll do it. Right, sir? You'll put your gun down. Right?"

"Correct," Paul Fick answered. The tone was even and efficient—as always.

"There you go, Mr. Bergeron. See? You set down, and the general sets his down, and then we all just hunker down here and work this out. Simple. No muss, no fuss, no one gets hurt, no one here redecorates the Sheetrock. Easy."

"Easy for you, Deputy Fife. You won' be leaving here in handcuffs."

"You got that right, cowboy, but then none of us will have to leave here in a body bag either. Besides, you know our dang legal system. We can't convict anybody in this country even when they confess on TV. You'll be makin' money on the talk-show circuit and signin' fancy book deals before you know it." He took another step toward Bergeron, trying to close the distance should he have to react.

Bergeron caught the movement and flicked his gun at Deveroux. Behind him, Deveroux could feel Fick's body tense.

Deveroux took a half step back and raised both hands palms outward. "Ho, now. Calm down, bubba. Let's put the gun down. You know it's the right thing to do."

"Him first." Bergeron had recentered Fick in his sights.

"No, sir. That dog won't hunt, and you know it. It's got to be you first. Gotta be. That's just the way it is."

Bergeron's eyes shot back and forth. He seemed on the verge of movement. "We all put the guns away. That right? We talk. Work something out."

"You got it. That's the smart play. Everyone's a winner. Now go on . . ."

Bergeron hesitated, and then he slowly began to bend at the waist and knees, keeping his arms parallel to the floor and the barrel pointed at Fick. When the gun was a few feet from the ground he broke his elbows and slowly placed the weapon on the floor with his right hand, his left held upward in supplication. He shifted his attention from Fick to Deveroux and back.

"That's right. Now that's the right decision. Now, take a step back, and the general here will set his down as well."

Bergeron slowly stepped back a half step while straightening up. His eyes were back on Fick, waiting for him to follow the lead.

"Now, General, if you'd be a mind to set your weapon down." Deveroux watched Bergeron carefully, trusting Fick to cooperate.

Fick didn't move.

Bergeron's eyes began rapidly shifting between the two men. His body was tense and Deveroux sensed that he was about to get spooked.

"Calm down, Mr. Bergeron." Deveroux's hands began patting the air again as if he were stroking a cat. "Calm down. General Fick's goin' to set his piece down now. Don't worry. You got my word on that." He looked over at Fick. "Ain't that right, Paul? He's got my word."

Fick didn't move.

"Paul? General Fick?" Deveroux looked at Fick's hands. He saw the awkward grip of the right hand. He saw him take up tension on the trigger. "General Fick?"

Behind him he heard a shuffle as Bergeron moved.

The explosion of Fick's .45-caliber semiautomatic in the small room was stunning. Deveroux felt himself pushed backward a step by the concussion, his ears ringing so loudly that he couldn't hear the sound of Bergeron's body hitting the floor. The big, copper-jacketed slug had caught him square in the forehead and had removed the back of his skull.

CHAPTER 62

Fort Leonard Wood, Missouri
THURSDAY, APRIL 24, 2008

Kel sat in the front seat of a Humvee, his legs swung out to the side; Shuck Deveroux sat in the backseat, elbows on his knees, face buried in his hands. His whole body shook. It was slight but noticeable.

"How'd that happen? Can you tell me?" Deveroux asked. He'd been repeating the same question for the last five minutes. "It's like we got dumber and dumber as the case went on. Least I did. How'd that happen?"

Kel had been sitting quietly, not responding, assuming that no response was warranted. He was content at first to let Deveroux vent, but as the questions were repeated over and over, he finally weighed in. "Goddamn, Shuck, you're bein' way too hard on yourself. You've been watchin' too many cop shows on TV. This is how it is in real life. You do get dumber and dumber. That's how these cases work." He shifted in his seat so that he could look at Deveroux more easily. "It's like pilots gettin' fixated on the target. We've identified a lot of pilots—good pilots—that got so focused on the target they couldn't pull out of the bomb run in time. Flew right into the ground. Called target fixation. That's what happens to us. All the damn time. You get so focused on some aspect of the case that you can't pull out when you need to. Target fixation. Doesn't make us bad investigators.

That's just how it works sometimes. And when the shit finally breaks, guess what, you feel absolutely pinheaded for not being able to see it sooner."

"But I should have seen this comin'.'"

"Yeah, maybe so, but you didn't. Beatin' yourself up isn't goin' to change that. Not today and not tomorrow either."

"A man's dead."

"Yeah, you're right. A bad man is dead, and you'd better be damn glad that he is. Could have been you."

"Easy for you to say. You've never had someone's brains splattered over you."

Kel sighed. "You might be surprised," he said quietly.

Deveroux looked up and caught Kel's eye. He saw something that he didn't understand but respected, nonetheless. "Sorry."

"Look, my read on this is that only one of you was comin' out of that buildin' alive. My money's usually on the one with the gun. If Fick hadn't charged in there when he did . . ."

"I know. I know," Deveroux replied. "It's just . . . it's just that I didn't see this comin' until it was right on top of me."

"Cut the crap, Shuck. What do you mean? You went in there knowing what could happen."

"Did I? I went in there because I wasn't thinkin' it through. Because I thought he might have a hostage. Because I was so sure this case was dead-ended that I never figured anythin' like this would happen. I feel pretty worthless."

"Look, Shuck, you know what bein' good is? Bein' good is not havin' all the answers—hell, you may not have any of the answers. Leave that for the cheap novels. Bein' good is about positionin' yourself to catch the pieces when the roof finally falls in. You were there, partner. You caught the pieces. And your skin is intact. That's all that counts."

"And how many men died?"

"Some of those men died a long time ago."

Neither man spoke for several minutes.

"So what are you goin' to do?" Deveroux finally asked.

"Me?" Kel arched his back and took a deep breath. "Well, my

guess is that there's a coroner in Rolla that could use some help. I assume you'll want some reports to close out your files. I'll tie up some loose ends here, and then," he paused, "and then, I've got a beautiful wife whom I need to spend some time with. And two sons who are growin' up way too fast. And a lab to run. People to take care of. Hell, son, I even have a Diversity Awareness Plan that's six months overdue."

"Sounds like you've got it all figured out."

Kel laughed. "Hardly. For all my big talk, I'm the one who's been gettin' dumber and dumber as time's gone by. I've been fixated on the wrong target the last few months. My way of dealin' with my problems has been to run and hide." He opened his hands as if to indicate the present surroundings. "I think it's time for me to get on home and try to catch some of those pieces when they fall."

The silence returned.

Kel broke it. "How about you? What are you goin' to do?"

Deveroux slowly nodded and then stood. The shaking had stopped. "I guess I have to go arrest Paul Fick."

CHAPTER 63

Fort Campbell, Kentucky
SATURDAY, OCTOBER 18, 2008

Chief Warrant Officer Shuck Deveroux had just removed his plastic bankcard from the credit union ATM when his cell phone began playing "Play That Funky Music, White Boy." He looked over at his two boys wrestling like bear cubs in the cab of his truck, and smiled.

For months he'd been promising them that as soon as things returned to normal—which they knew to be a relative term—that he'd make some time, to do something with them, but in the aftermath of Bergeron's death, and Tenkiller's, and Ngo's, and the others', he'd been so completely ensnared in a tailless ball of red tape and debriefings that it simply hadn't worked out. They'd come close a couple of times, but at the last minute someone had lit some sort of administrative fire that required stomping out, and Shuck Deveroux always seemed to have the biggest set of fireman's boots.

But not today. Today he was taking time off—it had been cleared for weeks—and nothing was going to derail his plan. Fast breakfast of powdered doughnuts and twenty-ounce Coca Colas, hour drive to Memphis, and a long, pleasant autumn afternoon with his boys watching the Mississippi State Bulldogs whup-up on the Memphis Tigers at Liberty Bowl Memorial Stadium. The boys were in the truck, waiting patiently, if not quietly. A quick stop at the ATM and then on into the city for some serious college football.

And then the phone rang.

He started to not answer it. The tiny LCD screen showed it was the office number. Almost against his will, his thumb moved and hit the *Talk* button. He sighed. "This better be good."

"Shuck, my man. Hey, buddy, sure hate to bother you on your day off and all," Mark Abbott was again covering the office. "Know you had this all planned out, and I really hate to do this . . ."

"Then don't, Mark. Just don't. As I recollect, the last time we waltzed this dance, it ended up with four or five folks dead. I got other plans today." He looked again at his sons.

"Sorry, brother. Really am, but the boss called."

"I assume you mean my wife?"

"You wish. No it's the old man. Anderson. Correction; make that the weasely little prick major who guards the inner sanctum for him. He says the general wants you over at his office P-D . . ."

"I know, I know, P-D-friggin'-Q," Deveroux clipped him short. "C'mon on, what's it all about? This is a Saturday mornin' last time I checked, and you've got the desk this mornin', last time I checked."

"Beats the living shit out of me, bro. All I know is that Major Limpstick says your presence is strongly requested."

"I'm sure he used the word *requested*."

"I'm sure he did."

Shuck Deveroux looked at his watch. "Can I take my kids, or is this another you-better-take-'em-home deals?"

"Like I said, you got me. I'm just the designated messenger boy, so don't shoot."

"Roger that," Deveroux sighed. "On my way."

The drive was short. In fact, had Deveroux's knees not been barking at him so early in the morning, it would have been faster to walk over to the general's office than to drive and park. But his knees were barking, and it was going to be a long day. Deveroux just hoped it wouldn't be longer than he'd planned. He left his kids wrestling in the truck as he went inside.

"The general's waiting, Warrant Officer. Please go on in," the aide said as soon as Deveroux entered the outer office. He obviously wasn't happy about being called into work on a Saturday and seemed to hold Deveroux accountable. "Please be sensitive of the general's time—this is his day off."

"Yes, sir, Major," Deveroux said. "Always." He smiled at the aide and then turned and rapped on the door to General Anderson's office.

"Shuck," the general boomed in response as if they were old fishing buddies. "Come on in here, son. Thanks for coming on such short notice."

Deveroux entered and noticed a thin, attractive brunette occupying a chair in front of Anderson's desk. She rose as Deveroux entered. So did Anderson.

"Chief Deveroux, let me introduce Ms. Feldman. Ms. Feldman, this is Chief Warrant Officer Deveroux."

"Ma'am," Deveroux responded, taking her hand. It was cool and felt small.

"Warrant Officer."

"Ms. Feldman here is an attorney, Shuck," the general continued. He walked around to the front of his desk and took up another one of the padded chairs similar to the one the young woman had been seated on. "Sit down, sit down, please."

Deveroux waited for both the general and Feldman to sit down again before taking a seat on a small couch opposite the general's desk.

"Once again, thanks for coming in, Shuck," General Anderson continued. "I understand you had the day off. Spending some time with your children. Boys, I think. More than well deserved. This shouldn't take too long, should it, Ms. Feldman?"

The young woman smiled efficiently. "I wouldn't expect so."

The three of them sat quietly for a moment, no one initiating the conversation.

"Ma'am," Deveroux finally started. He cleared his throat. "The general said you're a lawyer. If you don't mind me askin', what's this all about?"

"Of course not, Mr. Deveroux—is *Mister* appropriate? I'm afraid I don't deal very much with the military."

"Yes, ma'am. That'll work fine. So will Shuck."

"Well then, Mr. Deveroux, as General Anderson has already said, I'm an attorney with Kaiser and Waggoner out of St. Louis. To be exact, I'm the attorney for Paul Fick. General Paul Fick."

Deveroux caromed a quick look off Anderson. "Yes, ma'am, but I thought that the charges against the general had been dropped. Is there a new problem? I'm afraid I've been a little out of the loop." In the aftermath of the shooting death of John Bergeron, the army had initially brought charges against Paul Fick, but later dropped them. No convincing reason was ever given, but since everyone was quick to pin the tail for all the deaths on Bergeron's donkey, and no one seemed interested in blaming a respected retired general for ridding the world of a sadistic multiple murderer, it wasn't too much of a surprise. Deveroux harbored mixed feelings about the course of events; he was happy that Fick wasn't facing a trial, but he also suspected that political connections and considerations were more responsible for the decision than was the quality of the evidence. It surprised him, though, that Fick had a civilian attorney rather than a JAG. Fick was by-the-book enough that Deveroux had just assumed he'd use an army lawyer should the need arise, but apparently he hadn't.

The lawyer's face took on a mask of confusion, and she looked at General Anderson. Deveroux followed the confused look.

"Chief . . . ahh . . . well, I just assumed you'd heard," Anderson said.

"Sir?"

It was the woman who answered. Clipped and efficient. "Mr. Deveroux, I think both General Anderson and I jumped to the conclusion that you'd heard. I'm sorry. Let me back up a bit. You see, Paul Fick is dead; he passed away last month."

Deveroux again sought out Anderson's face.

"Pancreatic cancer, Shuck," Anderson said softly in response to Deveroux's look. "Diagnosed about a year ago, I understand. Pretty vicious stuff, so they tell me. By the time it's diagnosed, well—"

Deveroux thought back to how Fick's appearance had declined in the short period of time he'd known him. "I guess I should have figured somethin' was wrong. Now that I think about it, he didn't look good the last time I saw him."

Anderson nodded slowly. "Nothing much they could do for him, but even the little they could, Paul refused. Took some painkillers, I guess . . . to help take the edge off . . . so that he could function. But it was a matter of time."

The silence returned, until the woman, having weekend plans herself that did not include spending time at Fort Campbell, decided to move the purpose along. "Mr. Deveroux, I didn't know General Fick well, didn't know him personally at all. Fact is, I only met him three times. He first contacted me almost twelve months ago when he was first diagnosed; asked me to draft a will and attend to some trust matters. Which I did." She waited to let the words seep through the thickened silence. "Relatively easy from my standpoint. Paul Fick requested that his entire estate be liquidated—his ranch, some cattle, he had a small airplane, some miscellaneous real estate and investment holdings. Totaled almost one-point-six million and change when we got everything sold."

Deveroux continued looking at the woman.

She continued. "As I said, easy from my standpoint. Paul Fick left everything to two people; he had no relatives, you see, and . . . from what I understand . . . few friends." She paused, waiting for the words to register. When they didn't seem to, she continued. "One of those two individuals is you."

"I don't quite understand, Ms. Feldman. I hardly knew the general," Deveroux responded.

"I don't understand either, Mr. Deveroux, but then that's the beauty of law, I don't have to." She paused again and looked at Anderson and then back at Deveroux, then she bent forward and lifted a paper Famous Barr shopping bag off the floor and onto her lap. She paused and then held it out for Deveroux to take. "Given the . . . nature . . . of the bequest, it was easier to deliver it in person. Please excuse the bag, not very formal, I'm afraid, but it was the only thing I had that was big enough."

Deveroux took the bag and looked again at Anderson. He found no answer in his eyes. He turned back to the woman. "Yes, ma'am, uh . . . thank you," he said. "Ahh . . ."

"There's an envelope with it." The lawyer nodded at the bag. "I can only assume that it explains everything. Any questions, Mr. Deveroux?"

Shuck Deveroux was looking down into the paper bag at the strange contents. He didn't know what to say. "Ahh, no, ma'am. I mean, yes, ma'am, I suspect I've got lots of questions, but none that I guess you can answer."

The woman smiled professionally. "Well, if you should think of any, my card is in the sack as well. Give me a call." She smoothed her skirt and stood up, offering her hand to the general. "And so, General Anderson . . ."

Both Anderson and Deveroux rose to their feet. Deveroux was still painfully confused and it showed.

"Ms. Feldman," General Anderson replied as he shook her hand.

"General," she responded. She then offered her hand to Deveroux. "And Mr. Deveroux. A pleasure. Give me a call if you think of anything. Now, if we're finished here, I'll—"

"Ma'am?" Deveroux interrupted.

"Yes."

"Ahh, yes, ma'am, I do have a question, if you don't mind. You said General Fick didn't have any family."

"That's correct."

"But he left everythin' to me and one other person. Do you mind if I ask who that was? The other person?"

"Not at all, Mr. Deveroux." She smiled again. "Her name is Penny Kegin."

CHAPTER 64

Vietnam War Memorial, *The Wall*, Washington, D.C.
SATURDAY, NOVEMBER 1, 2008

It was a sunny day, cool and sharp, but bright and full of unsuspecting promise. Soon the late-season gray would arrive, and it would all change.

It was a good day for his purpose. He was glad he hadn't waited any longer.

Shuck Deveroux sat on a bench, *The Wall* back over his left shoulder, the bronze statue of the Vietnam soldiers off to his right. His family—Susan Elaine and the boys—had gone on ahead and were slowly working their way along the panels, one by one, reading the names. They'd been here once before, several years ago when he'd had to attend a week-long meeting at Fort Belvoir, but the boys, especially Thomas, the youngest, remembered very little.

He'd brought the box with him, still in the white Famous Barr shopping bag that the lawyer, Ms. Feldman, had put it in. He'd brought the envelope with him as well, the one with his name written on it in Fick's small, precise hand. He'd already opened it and read the letter from Fick. He'd read it several times, but now it was time to act, to follow the instructions. His first inclination had been to wait until Veterans' Day; it was only a couple more weeks away and certainly more symbolic, but then he'd reread the letter. Fick was a simple, pragmatic soldier, a simple, pragmatic man who hadn't needed symbolism or gold braid or rows of color on his chest for self-validation, and he'd wanted it done sooner rather than later—that's what he'd written. Veterans' Day would be busy, full of more eyes than necessary, and the task before Deveroux seemed best accomplished with quiet and reserve.

He opened the letter and read it one last time:

30 August 2008

Chief Deveroux,

I will not insult you with some hackneyed, melodramatic phrase. I will leave the—"If you are reading this I am already dead" language to the movies and shoddy novels. But as I write this, my cancer has entered into a terminal stage that requires attending to some final administrative matters. If I were a poetic man I might allude to the cancer that has been eating at my soul for forty years—but I am not a poetic man—I am simply a dying man.

I will not insult you by saying that I sensed a bond between us, some sort of kindred spirit. In fact, I hardly know you. I have no family. I have few friends who are still alive. I have few acquaintances whom I fully trust for this purpose. I chose you because I have few other options and even less time.

Accompanying this note is a box. If you've ever been to Vietnam you'll recognize it as a common tourist souvenir— a simple black, lacquered box with some mother-of-pearl inlay. I purchased it in Saigon thirty-seven years ago when I was young and thought that buying a souvenir was the thing to do. It has no symbolism or meaning other than that— the impulsive act of a very young man very far from home. Inside the box, however, are some items that do have some symbolism and meaning to me, for me. If I were a poetic man I might say that the contents were my attempt at self-medication, but then I am not a poetic man, I am simply a dying man, and I will not glorify my actions nor imbue them with nobility and worth. I did what I did because I had to. No other reason. I did what I did because I thought that it would help in some way. Because I thought that it would somehow balance the scale. Because sixteen young men have kept me awake for thirty-seven years, and I am so very tired. Because the time left to me is so fleeting.

Chief Deveroux, I am asking for a favor. I realize that you have no obligation to grant this, but my health will no longer allow me to accomplish this task myself—an admitted miscalculation on my part—and I must rely on your goodwill. Goodwill and what I perceive as your sense of honor and duty.

My request is simple. I would like the box to be placed at the base of panel W4 at The Wall—*the Vietnam Memorial in Washington, D.C. I will leave the time in which this is to be accomplished to your judgment, though the sooner the better. The box is sealed, and I would prefer it to remain so. Of course, I have no way to ensure this request will be fulfilled, and once again, must rely solely on the strength and quality of your character.*

I have always believed that being a soldier is an honorable and worthy profession. I have found that it is a profession often followed by those with no honor and little worth, by those unworthy of the title.

I consider you a soldier.

Paul Fick

Shuck Deveroux folded the letter and put it in his shirt pocket. He tugged up the zipper on his jacket and sat quietly for a moment. He was thinking of General Fick when he overheard a man standing over at the statue. He was loudly telling two or three young boys—high-school-aged by the looks of them—some improbable war story of how he was decorated twice for taking up an M-16 and single-handedly beating back a VC attack on his motorpool. He choked and caught his throat in a practiced manner as he told how he was haunted by all the men he had killed. He was overweight and had a long, graying ponytail. His wrists clanked with silver and turquoise bracelets, and he was wearing a sleeveless black leather biker jacket over a long-sleeve POW/MIA T-shirt. Deveroux stood, his knees popping loudly, and he thought of men like Paul Fick, who suffered his demons quietly, and he thought of loud, overweight men and women who invented demons to compensate for their deficient lives.

I consider you a soldier, Paul Fick had written. Now it was time to act like one and do his duty.

It was a short stroll over the grassy hillock and down the cobbled walkway to the center of the wall. He saw Susan Elaine and the boys at the far end of the memorial, pointing at names and talking among themselves. He knew that the west panels would be to the left of the center of the vee, toward the Lincoln Memorial; his eyes scanned the black granite panels as he walked. He stopped when he got to the panel with the small number W4 etched into the lower righthand corner. The names on the panel meant nothing to him. Name after name, indistinguishable from those on the panels to the right or the left. Indistinguishable from the other 138 black panels. Names.

The crowd was light, despite the clear skies and seasonally warm afternoon weather, but it obviously had been heavier before noon. The detritus of grief lay scattered along the base of the panels. An odd assortment of offerings. Single-stem red roses, combat medals, an unopened can of JAX beer, dog tags, photographs of soldiers or children or souped-up vintage cars, assorted military patches, envelopes, a Bible, stuffed animals. Lots of little American flags on wooden sticks.

Shuck Deveroux stood in front of W4, awkwardly holding the paper bag, unsure how to proceed. It didn't seem right, somehow, to just leave the box on the ground.

I consider you a soldier.

Reaching into the sack, he pulled out the lacquered wooden box. The contents shifted as he held it in his left hand and folded the paper bag in two. He looked around; there were no trash cans in sight so he folded the bag again and stuffed it into the front pocket of his jacket.

I consider you a soldier.

Deveroux bent formally at the waist, as much out of respect as out of deference to his stiff and complaining knees, and placed the box at the base of panel W4. He adjusted the angle twice before standing upright. Something wasn't right. The situation called for more formality, for more ceremony, for some sense of finality for the final act of General Fick's life.

Without realizing at first that he was doing it, Chief Warrant Officer Thomas Edward Lafayette Deveroux took a precise half step back, locked his heels softly, and saluted crisply. "You were a soldier, sir," he said.

"Who's a soldier, Dad?" It was his youngest son, Thomas, who'd seen his father acting strangely and felt the need to investigate. He grabbed his father's left forearm near the elbow.

Deveroux looked down and smiled. "Just someone I met once. Someone I hardly knew."

Thomas seemed to take this nonanswer in easy stride. After a moment he changed directions. "Mom says that these are all the people who died in the war." He reached out and touched one of the names cut into the rock, following the curves of the letters with his fingertip. "In Vietnam? They all died there?"

It took Deveroux a moment to answer. "No, son. Not all of them. Just some of them." He looked up and saw that his wife and other son were working their way along the wall toward him. He looked back at his youngest and finished his answer. "There are others. Others not on the wall. Some died during the war; some folks took years to die."

"What are y'all talkin' about? Who took years to die?" Susan Elaine said as she walked up and took her husband's other arm. She put her chin on his shoulder.

"Someone Dad used to know," Thomas replied as if he was the target of the question. "A soldier. Just like Dad."

Susan Elaine smiled in that way that still made Deveroux's breath catch in his throat and reminded him of how wonderful his life really was. "That's your father, all right," she said. "Always a soldier."

Before he could respond, the phone on his belt began to play the theme from *Mighty Mouse*. He reached for it out of reflex, and then stopped and looked again at Susan Elaine, and that smile. Instead of answering it, he hit the button on the side of the phone, muting the ring. He smiled back at his wife and grabbed both of his sons by their hair, shaking their heads playfully. He remembered what Kel had said.

Time to start picking up the pieces, he thought.

EPILOGUE

Gene Marino was starting the second week of his year-long internship at the National Park Service, Museum and Resource Center, in Landover, Maryland. He was still learning the ropes and was glad for the help that Chris Pulliam was always quick to offer.

"Hey, what do I do with something like this?" Marino asked. He'd been cataloging artifacts that had been left at the Vietnam Memorial—flags, identification tags, letters, the usual offerings—but he hadn't dealt with anything like this before. Not in his two weeks on the job.

"Like what?" Pulliam called out from over the wall of his cubicle.

"I don't know. It's like a . . . a box."

"Like a box? How's it like a box?"

"Well, I guess it *is* a box," Marino replied. "Not too big, 'bout the size of a shoebox. Little smaller. Black. Real shiny wood. Pearl design. It's a picture of a woman in one of those funny cone-shaped hats bending over doing something. Pulling up weeds or something."

"Is she naked?" Pulliam's voice indicated his preference in the matter.

"Nope. But she's got one of those long dresses with a slit."

"What's in it?" Pulliam asked as he walked around the corner to join Marino.

"The box? Dunno. It's locked or something."

"Best get it x-rayed." Pulliam sighed at the hassle. "It may be a bomb or a pound of that Agent Orange stuff, or something. Anthrax maybe. We can't curate an unopened box. Too many nutzoids out there."

"I hate nutzoids, don't you?" Marino nodded.

"Don't you know it."

"I haven't had anything x-rayed before. How do I do it?"

"Well, you gotta call . . . ahhh . . . never mind. That'll take too long." Pulliam looked around to see who else was within earshot. "Look, it's not a bomb. We know that, right? I mean, really. Probably some love letters or dirty pictures; something like that. Just go ahead and open it. Is there a lock or anything?"

"Don't see one."

"Hmm, well then, in that case," Pulliam looked around again, "there's two ways to skin that cat. We can call the conservators, they'll come over here all snooty and yell at you for not wearing cotton gloves or some other war crime, or—this is my personal favorite—we take a screwdriver to the sonofabitch and pop it open. Just do me a favor and wait until I'm back in my cubicle so I can deny I even know you when you get your ass handed to you in a Dixie cup."

It took longer to find a flathead screwdriver than to force the lid on the box. It separated with a cracking sound when the thin bead of glue around the top gave way.

"Cool beans," Gene Marino said as his eyes caught the contents.

"What is it?" Pulliam again responded over the wall of his cubicle. "I didn't hear an explosion."

"Nope. No explosion."

"Any anthrax? Cloud of spores?"

"Nope. Come see. Lots of neat shit. There's a cool knife."

"Knife?" Pulliam replied as he rejoined Marino and saw what he was holding. "That's no knife, bro. That's a real Vietnam-era bayonet."

"Yeah? Even cooler. And look, it's got something scratched into the back of the handle. K-E-N-D . . . looks like a name, doesn't it? Kendrick? I wonder if his name's on *The Wall*."

"Maybe. We can check that later. What else is there? What's that?"

"Some medals. These are Purple Hearts, aren't they? And are these Silver Stars?"

Pulliam took the items from Marino. "These two are Purple Hearts, this one's a Silver Star—you're right about that—but these two other stars aren't medals. These are rank insignia. They look like they're from a general's uniform—probably a brigadier. You know, like a one-star general?"

"Way cool," Marino replied. "Suppose this Kendrick guy was a general?"

Pulliam shrugged. "What's that? Dog tags?"

"Yeah." Marino removed a chain from the box and was counting the dog tags strung onto it. "Bunch of them. Two, four, six . . . there's sixteen here, and look, one of them's for our buddy, Kendrick." He held the tag at an angle to better illuminate the embossing. "Kendrick-comma-Patrick-R-period."

"Let me see," Pulliam said.

As Chris Pulliam was reading the names on the tags, and counting them a second time, Gene Marino removed a small OD-green cloth bag from the bottom of the box and undid the drawstring. "Gross," he spurted out, dropping the bag onto the tabletop.

"What is it?' Pulliam asked as he put the dog tags aside and reached for the bag.

"Dunno. Looks like a bunch of dead mice or something."

"Mice?" Pulliam repeated skeptically. He poured the contents of the bag out and gingerly fingered the three items. He was silent for a moment as he thought. "It ain't dead mice."

"Yeah? What d'you think it is, then?" Marino asked. "Looks like mice."

"Not sure, but . . ."

"But?"

"I got a buddy who's an anthropologist at the Smithsonian,"

Pulliam replied. "He lives out this way. I'll see if he can stop by on the way home and take a look at this."

"Why? What do you think they are?"

Pulliam shook his head slowly and flipped one of the items over with the tip of a pencil. "Not my field, but they sure look like . . ." he paused.

"Like what?" Marino asked.

"Human scalps."

ACKNOWLEDGMENTS

So here we are again, at the end of a story that took the efforts and work of a great many people. There's the usual cast of characters. David Rosenthal, publisher at Simon & Schuster, should be near the front of the receiving line, followed very, very closely by Marysue Rucci, a great editor and a delightful lunch companion. Leigh Feldman is a super agent and an equally nice person. Then, of course, there are the folks who actually turn the pig's ear into a silk purse. They include Ginny Smith and Al Madocs of Simon & Schuster and Ros Perrotta of Darhansoff, Verrill, and Feldman. I can only hope they get a year-end bonus for their patience.

My wife, Mary, was there from the beginning, of course—as she always is and always will be. She read, reread, and then, read again the manuscript and resisted blessing my heart as much as she could. This is noteworthy, because to a southern woman, people who need their hearts blessed include congenital half-wits, mass murderers (whose mothers certainly didn't raise them that way), and individuals so hopelessly headed down the wrong path that there's no reasonable expectation of redemption. I suspect she saw me in at least one of those categories. I hope that one day we encounter the devil at a backyard party just so that I can watch Mary bless his heart.

As I've pointed out before, the U.S. Army CILHI is no more, having evolved into the larger Department of Defense Joint POW/MIA

Accounting Command. The CILHI's legacy is carved into the marble headstones of literally tens of thousands of American servicemen who have been recovered, identified, and returned home. The mission continues under new management. It is an awesome job.

This is a novel, which I think, if I remember tenth-grade literature class correctly (though I must admit to blanking out on most of my adolescent years—something to do with a lack of blood getting to my brain), means that it is a fictional story. Bits and pieces of it resemble cases and situations that I have been involved in over my career, and while those cases and situations served as some sort of launching point, it is, in the end, a fictional flight. This means that the characters are made up and that any resemblance to persons living or dead is entirely coincidental—so don't try to read too much into it. And don't blame the U.S. Army or the U.S. government, either.

Finally, research for this book, to a very large degree, involved driving dust-strewn rural back roads, looking out the windows, and sucking in what it meant to grow up and mature in Arkansas. My companion on many of these road trips was my brother, Jim. We have taken our last journey together and though the ache throbs undiminished, it was a wonderful life.